The Conspiracy of Pontiac Volume I and Volume II

FRANCIS PARKMAN

Published in 1870

TABLE OF CONTENTS

DEDICATION
PREFACE TO THE SIXTH EDITION
PREFACE TO THE FIRST EDITION
VOLUME I. THE CONSPIRACY OF PONTIAC
INTRODUCTORY
FRANCE AND ENGLAND IN AMERICA
THE FRENCH, THE ENGLISH, AND THE INDIANS
COLLISION OF THE RIVAL COLONIES
THE WILDERNESS
THE ENGLISH TAKE POSSESSION OF THE WESTERN POSTS
ANGER OF THE INDIANS
INDIAN PREPARATION
THE COUNCIL AT THE RIVER ECORCES
DETROIT
TREACHERY OF PONTIAC
PONTIAC AT THE SIEGE OF DETROIT
ROUT OF CUYLER'S DETACHMENT
THE INDIANS CONTINUE TO BLOCKADE DETROIT
THE FIGHT OF BLOODY BRIDGE
MICHILLIMACKINAC
THE MASSACRE
VOLUME II. CONSPIRACY OF PONTIAC
FRONTIER FORTS AND SETTLEMENTS
THE WAR ON THE BORDERS
THE BATTLE OF BUSHY RUN
THE IROQUOIS
DESOLATION OF THE FRONTIERS
THE INDIANS RAISE THE SIEGE OF DETROIT
THE PAXTON MEN
THE RIOTERS MARCH ON PHILADELPHIA

BRADSTREET'S ARMY ON THE LAKES
BOUQUET FORCES THE DELAWARES
THE ILLINOIS
PONTIAC RALLIES THE WESTERN TRIBES
RUIN OF THE INDIAN CAUSE
DEATH OF PONTIAC
APPENDIX A
APPENDIX C
APPENDIX D
APPENDIX E
APPENDIX F

DEDICATION

TO JARED SPARKS, LL.D., PRESIDENT OF HARVARD UNIVERSITY, THESE VOLUMES ARE DEDICATED AS A TESTIMONIAL OF HIGH PERSONAL REGARD, AND A TRIBUTE OF RESPECT FOR HIS DISTINGUISHED SERVICES TO AMERICAN HISTORY.

PREFACE TO THE SIXTH EDITION

I chose the subject of this book as affording better opportunities than any other portion of American history for portraying forest life and the Indian character; and I have never seen reason to change this opinion. In the nineteen years that have passed since the first edition was published, a considerable amount of additional material has come to light. This has been carefully collected, and is incorporated in the present edition. The most interesting portion of this new material has been supplied by the Bouquet and Haldimand Papers, added some years ago to the manuscript collections of the British Museum. Among them are several hundred letters from officers engaged in the Pontiac war, some official, others personal and familiar, affording very curious illustrations of the events of the day and of the characters of those engaged in them. Among the facts which they bring to light, some are sufficiently startling; as, for example, the proposal of the Commander-in-Chief to infect the hostile tribes with the small-pox, and that of a distinguished subordinate officer to take revenge on the Indians by permitting an unrestricted sale of rum.

The two volumes of the present edition have been made uniform with those of the series "France and England in North America." I hope to continue that series to the period of the extinction of French power on this continent. "The Conspiracy of Pontiac" will then form a sequel; and its introductory chapters will be, in a certain sense, a summary of what has preceded. This will involve some repetition in the beginning of the book, but I have nevertheless thought it best to let it remain as originally written.
Boston, 16 September, 1870.

PREFACE TO THE FIRST EDITION

The conquest of Canada was an event of momentous consequence in American history. It changed the political aspect of the continent, prepared a way for the independence of the British colonies, rescued the vast tracts of the interior from the rule of military despotism, and gave them, eventually, to the keeping of an ordered democracy. Yet to the red natives of the soil its results were wholly disastrous. Could the French have maintained their ground, the ruin of the Indian tribes might long have been postponed; but the victory of Quebec was the signal of their swift decline. Thenceforth they were destined to melt and vanish before the advancing waves of Anglo-American power, which now rolled westward unchecked and unopposed. They saw the danger, and, led by a great and daring champion, struggled fiercely to avert it. The history of that epoch, crowded as it is with scenes of tragic interest, with marvels of suffering and vicissitude, of heroism and endurance, has been, as yet, unwritten, buried in the archives of governments, or among the obscurer records of private adventure. To rescue it from oblivion is the object of the following work. It aims to portray the American forest and the American Indian at the period when both received their final doom.

It is evident that other study than that of the closet is indispensable to success in such an attempt. Habits of early reading had greatly aided to prepare me for the task; but necessary knowledge of a more practical kind has been supplied by the indulgence of a strong natural taste, which, at various intervals, led me to the wild regions of the north and west. Here, by the camp-fire, or in the canoe, I gained familiar acquaintance with the men and scenery of the wilderness. In 1846, I visited various primitive tribes of the Rocky Mountains, and was, for a time, domesticated in a village of the western Dahcotah, on the high plains between Mount Laramie and the range of the Medicine Bow.

The most troublesome part of the task was the collection of4 the necessary documents. These consisted of letters, journals, reports, and despatches, scattered among numerous public offices, and private families, in Europe and America. When brought together, they amounted to about three thousand four hundred manuscript pages. Contemporary newspapers, magazines, and pamphlets have also been examined, and careful search made for every book which, directly or indirectly, might throw light upon the subject. I have visited the sites of all the principal events recorded in the narrative, and gathered such local traditions as seemed worthy of confidence.

I am indebted to the liberality of Hon. Lewis Cass for a curious collection of papers relating to the siege of Detroit by the Indians. Other important contributions have been obtained from the state paper offices of London and Paris, from the archives of New York, Pennsylvania, and other states, and from the manuscript collections of several historical societies. The late William L. Stone, Esq., commenced an elaborate biography of Sir William Johnson, which it is much to be lamented he did not live to complete. By the kindness of Mrs. Stone, I was permitted to copy from his extensive collection of documents such portions as would serve the purposes of the following History.

To President Sparks of Harvard University, General Whiting, U. S. A., Brantz Mayer, Esq., of Baltimore, Francis J. Fisher, Esq., of Philadelphia, and Rev. George E. Ellis, of Charlestown, I beg to return a warm acknowledgment for counsel and assistance. Mr. Benjamin Perley Poore and Mr. Henry Stevens procured copies of valuable documents from the archives of Paris and London. Henry R. Schoolcraft, Esq., Dr. Elwyn, of Philadelphia, Dr. O'Callaghan, of Albany, George H. Moore, Esq., of New York, Lyman C. Draper, Esq., of Philadelphia, Judge Law, of Vincennes, and many others, have kindly contributed materials to the work. Nor can I withhold an expression of thanks to the aid so freely rendered in the dull task of proof-reading and correction.

The crude and promiscuous mass of materials presented an aspect by no means inviting. The field of the history was uncultured and unreclaimed, and the labor that awaited me was like that of the border settler, who, before he builds his rugged dwelling, must fell the forest-trees, burn the undergrowth,5 clear the ground, and hew the fallen trunks to due proportion.

Several obstacles have retarded the progress of the work. Of these, one of the most considerable was the condition of my sight. For about three years, the light of day was insupportable, and every attempt at reading or writing completely debarred. Under these circumstances, the task of sifting the materials and composing the work was begun and finished. The papers were repeatedly read aloud by an amanuensis, copious notes and extracts were made, and the narrative written down from my dictation. This process, though extremely slow and laborious, was not without its advantages; and I am well convinced that the authorities have been even more minutely examined, more scrupulously collated, and more thoroughly digested, than they would have been under ordinary circumstances.

In order to escape the tedious circumlocution, which, from the nature of the subject, could not otherwise have been avoided, the name English is applied, throughout the volume, to the British American colonists, as well as to the people of the mother country. The necessity is somewhat to be regretted, since, even at an early period, clear distinctions were visible between the offshoot and the parent stock.

Boston, August 1, 1851.

VOLUME I. THE CONSPIRACY OF PONTIAC

INTRODUCTORY

Indian Tribes East Of The Mississippi.

The Indian is a true child of the forest and the desert. The wastes and solitudes of nature are his congenial home. His haughty mind is imbued with the spirit of the wilderness, and the light of civilization falls on him with a blighting power. His unruly pride and untamed freedom are in harmony with the lonely mountains, cataracts, and rivers among which he dwells; and primitive America, with her savage scenery and savage men, opens to the imagination a boundless world, unmatched in wild sublimity.

The Indians east of the Mississippi may be divided into several great families, each distinguished by a radical peculiarity of language. In their moral and intellectual, their social and political state, these various families exhibit strong shades of distinction; but, before pointing them out, I shall indicate a few prominent characteristics, which, faintly or distinctly, mark the whole in common.

All are alike a race of hunters, sustaining life wholly, or in part, by the fruits of the chase. Each family is split into tribes; and these tribes, by the exigencies of the hunter life, are again divided into sub-tribes, bands, or villages, often scattered far asunder, over a wide extent of wilderness. Unhappily for the strength and harmony of the Indian race, each tribe is prone to regard itself, not as the member of a great whole, but as a sovereign and independent nation, often arrogating to itself an importance superior to all the rest of mankind; and the warrior whose petty horde might muster a few scores of half-starved fighting men, strikes his hand upon his heart, and exclaims, in all the pride of patriotism, "I am a Menomone."

In an Indian community, each man is his own master. He abhors restraint, and owns no other authority than his own16 capricious will; and yet this wild notion of liberty is not inconsistent with certain gradations of rank and influence. Each tribe has its sachem, or civil chief, whose office is in a manner hereditary, and, among many, though by no means among all tribes, descends in the female line; so that the brother of the incumbent, or the son of his sister, and not his own son, is the rightful successor to his dignities. If, however, in the opinion of the old men and subordinate chiefs, the heir should be disqualified for the exercise of the office by cowardice, incapacity, or any defect of character, they do not scruple to discard him, and elect another in his place, usually fixing their choice on one of his relatives. The office of the sachem is no enviable one. He has neither laws to administer nor power to enforce his commands. His counsellors are the inferior chiefs and principal men of the tribe; and he never sets himself in opposition to the popular will, which is the sovereign power of these savage democracies. His province is to advise, and not to dictate; but, should he be a man of energy, talent, and address, and especially should he be supported by numerous relatives and friends, he may often acquire no small easure of respect and power. A clear distinction is drawn between the civil and military authority, though both are often united in the same person. The functions of war-chief may, for the most part, be exercised by any one whose prowess and reputation are sufficient to induce the young men to follow him to battle; and he may, whenever he thinks proper, raise a band of volunteers, and go out against the common enemy.

We might imagine that a society so loosely framed would soon resolve itself into anarchy; yet this is not the case, and an Indian village is singularly free from wranglings and petty strife. Several causes conspire to this result. The necessities of the hunter life, preventing the accumulation of large communities, make more stringent organization needless; while a species of self-control, inculcated from childhood upon every individual, enforced by a sentiment of dignity and manhood, and greatly aided by the peculiar temperament of the race, tends strongly to the promotion of harmony. Though he owns no law, the Indian is inflexible in his adherence to ancient usages and customs; and the principle of hero-worship, which belongs to his nature, inspires him with deep respect for the sages and captains of his tribe. The very rudeness of his condition, and the absence of the passions which wealth, luxury, and the other incidents of civilization engender, are favorable to internal harmony; and to the same cause must likewise be ascribed too many of his virtues, which would quickly vanish, were he elevated from his savage state.

A peculiar social institution exists among the Indians, very curious in its character; and though I am not prepared to say that it may be traced through all the tribes east of the Mississippi, yet its prevalence is so general, and its influence on political relations so important, as to claim especial attention. Indian communities, independently of their local distribution into tribes, bands, and villages, are composed of several distinct clans. Each clan has its emblem, consisting of the figure of some bird, beast, or reptile; and each is distinguished by the name of the animal which it thus bears as its device; as, for example, the clan of the Wolf, the Deer, the Otter, or the Hawk. In the language of the Algonquins, these emblems are known by the name of Totems. The members of the same clan, being connected, or supposed to be so, by ties of kindred, more or less remote, are prohibited from intermarriage. Thus Wolf cannot marry Wolf; but he may, if he chooses, take a wife from the clan of Hawks, or any other clan but his own. It follows that when this prohibition is rigidly observed, no single clan can live apart from the rest; but the whole must be mingled together, and in every family the husband and wife must be of different clans.

To different totems attach different degrees of rank and dignity; and those of the Bear, the Tortoise, and the Wolf are among the first in honor. Each man is proud of his badge, jealously asserting its claims to respect; and the members of the same clan, though they may, perhaps, speak different dialects, and dwell far asunder, are yet bound together by the closest ties of fraternity. If a man is killed, every member of the clan feels called upon to avenge him; and the wayfarer, the hunter, or the warrior is sure of a cordial welcome in the distant lodge of the clansman whose face perhaps he has never seen. It may be added that certain privileges, highly prized as hereditary rights, sometimes reside in particular clans; such as that of furnishing a sachem to the tribe, or of performing certain religious ceremonies or magic rites.

The Indians east of the Mississippi may be divided into three great families: the Iroquois, the Algonquin, and the Mobilian, each speaking a language of its own, varied by numerous dialectic forms. To these families must be added a few stragglers from the great western race of the Dahcotah, besides several distinct tribes of the south, each of which has been regarded as speaking a tongue peculiar to itself. The Mobilian group embraces the motley confederacy of the Creeks, the crafty Choctaws, and the stanch and warlike Chickasaws. Of these, and of the distinct tribes dwelling in their vicinity, or within their limits, I shall only observe that they offer, with many modifications, and under different aspects, the same essential features which mark the Iroquois and the Algonquins, the two great families of the north. The latter, who were the conspicuous actors in the events of the ensuing narrative, demand a closer attention.

THE IROQUOIS FAMILY.

Foremost in war, foremost in eloquence, foremost in their savage arts of policy, stood the fierce people called by themselves the Hodenosaunee, and by the French the Iroquois, a name which has since been applied to the entire family of which they formed the dominant member. They extended their conquests and their depredations from Quebec to the Carolinas, and from the western prairies to the forests of Maine. On the south, they forced tribute from the subjugated Delawares, and pierced the mountain fastnesses of the Cherokees with incessant forays. On the north, they uprooted the ancient settlements of the Wyandots; on the west they exterminated the Eries and the Andastes, and spread havoc and dismay among the tribes of the Illinois; and on the east, the Indians of New England fled at the first peal of the Mohawk war-cry. Nor was it the Indian race alone who quailed before their ferocious valor. All Canada shook with the fury of their onset; the people fled to the forts for refuge; the blood-besmeared conquerors roamed like wolves among the burning settlements, and the colony trembled on the brink of ruin.

The Iroquois in some measure owed their triumphs to the position of their country; for they dwelt within the present limits of the State of New York, whence several great rivers and the inland oceans of the northern lakes opened ready thoroughfares to their roving warriors through all the adjacent wilderness. But the true fountain of their success is to be sought in their own inherent energies, wrought to the most effective action under a political fabric well suited to the Indian life; in their mental and moral organization; in their insatiable ambition and restless ferocity.

In their scheme of government, as in their social customs and religious observances, the Iroquois displayed, in full symmetry and matured strength, the same characteristics which in other tribes are found distorted, withered, decayed to the root, or, perhaps, faintly visible in an imperfect germ. They consisted of five tribes or nations—the Mohawks, the Oneidas, the Onondagas, the Cayugas, and the Senecas, to whom a sixth, the Tuscaroras, was afterwards added. To each of these tribes belonged an organization of its own. Each had several sachems, who, with the subordinate chiefs and principal men, regulated all its internal affairs; but, when foreign powers were to be treated with, or matters involving the whole confederacy required deliberation, all the sachems of the several tribes convened in general assembly at the great council-house, in the Valley of Onondaga. Here ambassadors were received, alliances were adjusted, and all subjects of general interest discussed with exemplary harmony. The order of debate was prescribed by time-honored customs; and, in the fiercest heat of controversy, the assembly maintained its self-control.

But the main stay of Iroquois polity was the system of totemship. It was this which gave the structure its elastic strength; and but for this, a mere confederacy of jealous and warlike tribes must soon have been rent asunder by shocks from without or discord from within. At some early period, the Iroquois probably formed an individual nation; for the whole people, irrespective of their separation into tribes, consisted of eight totemic clans; and the members of each clan, to what nation soever they belonged, were mutually bound to one another by those close ties of fraternity which mark this singular institution. Thus the five nations of the confederacy were laced together by an eight-fold band; and to this hour their slender remnants cling to one another with invincible tenacity.

It was no small security to the liberties of the Iroquois—liberties which they valued beyond any other possession—that by the Indian custom of descent in the female line, which among them was more rigidly adhered to than elsewhere, the office of the sachem must pass, not to his son, but to his brother, his sister's son, or some yet remoter kinsman. His power was constantly deflected into the collateral branches of his family; and thus one of the strongest temptations of ambition was cut off. The Iroquois had no laws; but they had ancient customs which took the place of laws. Each man, or rather, each clan, was the avenger of its own wrongs; but the manner of the retaliation was fixed by established usage. The tribal sachems, and even the great council at Onondaga, had no power to compel the execution of their decrees; yet they were looked up to with a respect which the soldier's bayonet or the sheriff's staff would never have commanded; and it is highly to the honor of the Indian character that they could exert so great an authority where there was nothing to enforce it but the weight of moral power.

The origin of the Iroquois is lost in hopeless obscurity. That they came from the west; that they came from the north; that they sprang from the soil of New York, are the testimonies of three conflicting traditions, all equally worthless as aids to historic inquiry. It is at the era of their confederacy—the event to which the five tribes owed all their greatness and power, and to which we need assign no remoter date than that of a century before the first arrival of the Dutch in New York—that faint rays of light begin to pierce the gloom, and the chaotic traditions of the earlier epoch mould themselves into forms more palpable and distinct.

Taounyawatha, the God of the Waters—such is the belief of the Iroquois—descended to the earth to instruct his favorite people in the arts of savage life; and when he saw how they were tormented by giants, monsters, and evil spirits, he urged the divided tribes, for the common defence, to band themselves together in an everlasting league. While the injunction was as yet unfulfilled, the sacred messenger was recalled to the Great Spirit; but, before his departure, he promised that another should appear, empowered to instruct the people in all that pertained to their confederation. And accordingly, as a band of Mohawk warriors was threading the funereal labyrinth of an ancient pine forest, they heard, amid its blackest depths, a hoarse voice chanting in measured cadence; and, following the sound, they saw, seated among the trees, a monster so hideous, that they stood benumbed with terror. His features were wild and frightful. He was encompassed by hissing rattlesnakes, which, Medusa-like, hung writhing from his head; and on the ground around him were strewn implements of incantation, and magic vessels formed of human skulls. Recovering from their amazement, the warriors could perceive that in the mystic words of the chant, which he still poured forth, were couched the laws and principles of the destined confederacy. The tradition further declares that the monster, being surrounded and captured, was presently transformed to human shape, that he became a chief of transcendent wisdom and prowess, and to the day of his death ruled the councils of the now united tribes. To this hour the presiding sachem of the council at Onondaga inherits from him the honored name of Atotarho.

The traditional epoch which preceded the auspicious event of the confederacy, though wrapped in clouds and darkness, and defying historic scrutiny, has yet a character and meaning of its own. The gloom is peopled thick with phantoms; with monsters and prodigies, shapes of wild enormity, yet offering, in the Teutonic strength of their conception, the evidence of a robustness of mind unparalleled among tribes of a different lineage. In these evil days, the scattered and divided Iroquois were beset with every form of peril and disaster. Giants, cased in armor of stone, descended on them from the mountains of the north. Huge beasts trampled down their forests like fields of grass. Human heads, with streaming hair and glaring eyeballs, shot through the air like meteors, shedding pestilence and death throughout the land. A great horned serpent rose from Lake Ontario; and only the thunder-bolts of the skies could stay his ravages, and drive him back to his native deeps. The skeletons of men, victims of some monster of the forest, were seen swimming in the Lake of Teungktoo; and around the Seneca village on the Hill of Genundewah, a two-headed serpent coiled himself, of size so monstrous that the wretched people were unable to ascend his scaly sides, and perished in multitudes by his pestilential breath. Mortally wounded at length by the magic arrow of a child, he rolled down the steep, sweeping away the forest with his writhings, and plunging into the lake below, where he lashed the black waters till they boiled with blood and foam, and at length, exhausted with his agony, sank, and perished at the bottom. Under the Falls of Niagara dwelt the Spirit of the Thunder, with his brood of giant sons; and the Iroquois trembled in their villages when, amid the blackening shadows of the storm, they heard his deep shout roll along the firmament.

The energy of fancy, whence these barbarous creations drew their birth, displayed itself, at a later period, in that peculiar eloquence which the wild democracy of the Iroquois tended to call forth, and to which the mountain and the forest, the torrent and the storm, lent their stores of noble imagery. That to this imaginative vigor was joined mental power of a different stamp, is witnessed by the caustic irony of Garangula and Sagoyewatha, and no less by the subtle policy, sagacious as it was treacherous, which marked the dealings of the Iroquois with surrounding tribes.

With all this mental superiority, the arts of life among them had not emerged from their primitive rudeness; and their coarse pottery, their spear and arrow heads of stone, were in no way superior to those of many other tribes. Their agriculture deserves a higher praise. In 1696, the invading army of Count Frontenac found the maize fields extending a league and a half or two leagues from their villages; and, in 1779, the troops of General Sullivan were filled with amazement at their abundant stores of corn, beans, and squashes, and at the old apple orchards which grew around their settlements.

Their dwellings and works of defence were far from contemptible, either in their dimensions or in their structure; and though by the several attacks of the French, and especially by the invasion of De Nonville, in 1687, and of Frontenac, nine years later, their fortified towns were levelled to the earth, never again to reappear; yet, in the works of Champlain and other early writers we find abundant evidence of their pristine condition. Along the banks of the Mohawk, among the hills and hollows of Onondaga, in the forests of Oneida and Cayuga, on the romantic shores of Seneca Lake and the rich borders of the Genesee, surrounded by waving maize fields, and encircled from afar by the green margin of the forest, stood the ancient strongholds of the confederacy. The clustering dwellings were encompassed by palisades, in single, double, or triple rows, pierced with loopholes, furnished with platforms within, for the convenience of the defenders, with magazines of stones to hurl upon the heads of the enemy, and with water conductors to extinguish any fire which might be kindled from without.

The area which these defences enclosed was often several acres in extent, and the dwellings, ranged in order within, were sometimes more than a hundred feet in length. Posts, firmly driven into the ground, with an intervening framework of poles, formed the basis of the structure; and its sides and arched roof were closely covered with layers of elm bark. Each of the larger dwellings contained several distinct families, whose separate fires were built along the central space, while compartments on each side, like the stalls of a stable, afforded some degree of privacy. Here, rude couches were prepared, and bear and deer skins spread; while above, the ripened ears of maize, suspended in rows, formed a golden tapestry.

In the long evenings of midwinter, when in the wilderness without the trees cracked with biting cold, and the forest paths were clogged with snow, then, around the lodge-fires of the Iroquois, warriors, squaws, and restless naked children were clustered in social groups, each dark face brightening in the fickle fire-light, while, with jest and laugh, the pipe passed round from hand to hand. Perhaps some shrivelled old warrior, the story-teller of the tribe, recounted to attentive ears the deeds of ancient heroism, legends of spirits and monsters, or tales of witches and vampires—superstitions not less rife among this all-believing race, than among the nations of the transatlantic world.

The life of the Iroquois, though void of those multiplying phases which vary the routine of civilized existence, was one of sharp excitement and sudden contrast. The chase, the warpath, the dance, the festival, the game of hazard, the race of political ambition, all had their votaries. When the assembled sachems had resolved on war against some foreign tribe, and when, from their great council-house of bark, in the Valley of Onondaga, their messengers had gone forth to invite the warriors to arms, then from east to west, through the farthest bounds of the confederacy, a thousand warlike hearts caught up the summons. With fasting and praying, and consulting dreams and omens, with invoking the war-god, and dancing the war-dance, the warriors sought to insure the triumph of their arms, and then, their rites concluded, they began their stealthy progress through the devious pathways of the forest. For days and weeks, in anxious expectation, the villagers awaited the result. And now, as evening closed, a shrill, wild cry, pealing from afar, over the darkening forest, proclaimed the return of the victorious warriors. The village was alive with sudden commotion, and snatching sticks and stones, knives and hatchets, men, women, and children, yelling like fiends let loose, swarmed out of the narrow portal, to visit upon the captives a foretaste of the deadlier torments in store for them. The black arches of the forest glowed with the fires of death, and with brandished torch and firebrand the frenzied multitude closed around their victim. The pen shrinks to write, the heart sickens to conceive, the fierceness of his agony, yet still, amid the din of his tormentors, rose his clear voice of scorn and defiance. The work was done, the blackened trunk was flung to the dogs, and, with clamorous shouts and hootings, the murderers sought to drive away the spirit of their victim.

The Iroquois reckoned these barbarities among their most exquisite enjoyments, and yet they had other sources of pleasure, which made up in frequency and in innocence what they lacked in intensity. Each passing season had its feasts and dances, often mingling religion with social pastime. The young had their frolics and merry-makings, and the old had their no less frequent councils, where conversation and laughter alternated with grave deliberations for the public weal. There were also stated periods marked by the recurrence of momentous ceremonies, in which the whole community took part—the mystic sacrifice of the dogs, the orgies of the dream feast, and the loathsome festival of the exhumation of the dead. Yet in the intervals of war and hunting, these resources would often fail; and, while the women were toiling in the cornfields, the lazy warriors beguiled the hours with smoking or sleeping, with gambling or gallantry.

If we seek for a single trait preëminently characteristic of the Iroquois, we shall find it in that boundless pride which impelled them to style themselves, not inaptly as regards their own race, "the men surpassing all others." "Must I," exclaimed one of their great warriors, as he fell wounded among a crowd of Algonquins,—"must I, who have made the whole earth tremble, now die by the hands of children?" Their power kept pace with their pride. Their war-parties roamed over half America, and their name was a terror from the Atlantic to the Mississippi; but, when we ask the numerical strength of the dreaded confederacy, when we discover that, in the days of their greatest triumphs, their united cantons could not have mustered four thousand warriors, we stand amazed at the folly and dissension which left so vast a region the prey of a handful of bold marauders. Of the cities and villages now so thickly scattered over the lost domain of the Iroquois, a single one might boast a more numerous population than all the five united tribes.

From this remarkable people, who with all the ferocity of their race blended heroic virtues and marked endowments of intellect, I pass to other members of the same great family, whose different fortunes may perhaps be ascribed rather to the force of circumstance, than to any intrinsic inferiority. The peninsula between the Lakes Huron, Erie, and Ontario was occupied by two distinct peoples, speaking dialects of the Iroquois tongue. The Hurons or Wyandots, including the tribe called by the French the Dionondadies, or Tobacco Nation, dwelt among the forests which bordered the eastern shores of the fresh-water sea, to which they have left their name; while the Neutral Nation, so called from their neutrality in the war between the Hurons and the Five Nations, inhabited the northern shores of Lake Erie, and even extended their eastern flank across the strait of Niagara.

The population of the Hurons has been variously stated at from ten thousand to thirty thousand souls, but probably did not exceed the former estimate. The Franciscans and the Jesuits were early among them, and from their descriptions it is apparent that, in legends and superstitions, manners and habits, religious observances and social customs, they were closely assimilated to their brethren of the Five Nations. Their capacious dwellings of bark, and their palisaded forts, seemed copied after the same model. Like the Five Nations, they were divided into tribes, and cross-divided into totemic clans; and, as with them, the office of sachem descended in the female line. The same crude materials of a political fabric were to be found in both; but, unlike the Iroquois, the Wyandots had not as yet wrought them into a system, and woven them into a harmonious whole.

Like the Five Nations, the Wyandots were in some measure an agricultural people; they bartered the surplus products of their maize fields to surrounding tribes, usually receiving fish in exchange; and this traffic was so considerable, that the Jesuits styled their country the Granary of the Algonquins.

Their prosperity was rudely broken by the hostilities of the Five Nations; for though the conflicting parties were not ill matched in point of numbers, yet the united counsels and ferocious energies of the confederacy swept all before them. In the year 1649, in the depth of winter, their warriors invaded the country of the Wyandots, stormed their largest villages, and involved all within in indiscriminate slaughter. The survivors fled in panic terror, and the whole nation was broken and dispersed.

Some found refuge among the French of Canada, where, at the village of Lorette, near Quebec, their descendants still remain; others were incorporated with their conquerors; while others again fled northward, beyond Lake Superior, and sought an asylum among the wastes which bordered on the north-eastern bands of the Dahcotah. Driven back by those fierce bison-hunters, they next established themselves about the outlet of Lake Superior, and the shores and islands in the northern parts of Lake Huron. Thence, about the year 1680, they descended to Detroit, where they formed a permanent settlement, and where, by their superior valor, capacity, and address, they soon acquired an ascendency over the surrounding Algonquins.

The ruin of the Neutral Nation followed close on that of the Wyandots, to whom, according to Jesuit authority, they bore an exact resemblance in character and manners. The Senecas soon found means to pick a quarrel with them; they were assailed by all the strength of the insatiable confederacy, and within a few years their destruction as a nation was complete.

South of Lake Erie dwelt two members of the Iroquois family. The Andastes built their fortified villages along the valley of the Lower Susquehanna; while the Erigas, or Eries, occupied the borders of the lake which still retains their name. Of these two nations little is known, for the Jesuits had no missions among them, and few traces of them survive beyond their names and the record of their destruction. The war with the Wyandots was scarcely over, when the Five Nations turned their arms against their Erie brethren.

In the year 1655, using their canoes as scaling ladders, they stormed the Erie stronghold, leaped down like tigers among the defenders, and butchered them without mercy. The greater part of the nation was involved in the massacre, and the remnant was incorporated with the conquerors, or with other tribes, to which they fled for refuge. The ruin of the Andastes came next in turn; but this brave people fought for twenty years against their inexorable assailants, and their destruction was not consummated until the year 1672, when they shared the fate of the rest.

Thus, within less than a quarter of a century, four nations, the most brave and powerful of the North American savages, sank before the arms of the confederates. Nor did their triumphs end here. Within the same short space they subdued their southern neighbors the Lenape, the leading members of the Algonquin family, and expelled the Ottawas, a numerous people of the same lineage, from the borders of the river which bears their name. In the north, the west, and the south, their conquests embraced every adjacent tribe; and meanwhile their war parties were harassing the French of Canada with reiterated inroads, and yelling the war-whoop under the walls of Quebec.

They were the worst of conquerors. Inordinate pride, the lust of blood and dominion, were the mainsprings of their warfare; and their victories were strained with every excess of savage passion. That their triumphs must have cost them dear; that, in spite of their cautious tactics, these multiplied conflicts must have greatly abridged their strength, would appear inevitable. Their losses were, in fact, considerable; but every breach was repaired by means of a practice to which they, in common with other tribes, constantly adhered. When their vengeance was glutted by the sacrifice of a sufficient number of captives, they spared the lives of the remainder, and adopted them as members of their confederated tribes, separating wives from husbands, and children from parents, and distributing them among different villages, in order that old ties and associations might be more completely broken up. This policy is said to have been designated among them by a name which signifies "flesh cut into pieces and scattered among the tribes."

In the years 1714-15, the confederacy received a great accession of strength. Southwards, about the headwaters of the rivers Neuse and Tar, and separated from their kindred tribes by intervening Algonquin communities, dwelt the Tuscaroras, a warlike people belonging to the generic stock of the Iroquois. The wrongs inflicted by white settlers, and their own undistinguishing vengeance, involved them in a war with the colonists, which resulted in their defeat and expulsion. They emigrated to the Five Nations, whose allies they had been in former wars with southern tribes, and who now gladly received them, admitting them as a sixth nation, into their confederacy.

It is a remark of Gallatin, that, in their career of conquest, the Five Nations encountered more stubborn resistance from the tribes of their own family, than from those of a different lineage. In truth, all the scions of this warlike stock seem endued with singular vitality and force, and among them we must seek for the best type of the Indian character. Few tribes could match them in prowess, constancy, moral energy, or intellectual vigor. The Jesuits remarked that they were more intelligent, yet less tractable, than other savages; and Charlevoix observes that, though the Algonquins were readily converted, they made but fickle proselytes; while the Hurons, though not easily won over to the church, were far more faithful in their adherence. Of this tribe, the Hurons or Wyandots, a candid and experienced observer declares, that of all the Indians with whom he was conversant, they alone held it disgraceful to turn from the face of an enemy when the fortunes of the fight were adverse.

Besides these inherent qualities, the tribes of the Iroquois race derived great advantages from their superior social organization. They were all, more or less, tillers of the soil, and were thus enabled to concentrate a more numerous population than the scattered tribes who live by the chase alone. In their well-peopled and well-constructed villages, they dwelt together the greater part of the year; and thence the religious rites and social and political usages, which elsewhere existed only in the germ, attained among them a full development. Yet these advantages were not without alloy, and the Jesuits were not slow to remark that the stationary and thriving Iroquois were more loose in their observance of social ties, than the wandering and starving savages of the north.

THE ALGONQUIN FAMILY.

Except the detached nation of the Tuscaroras, and a few smaller tribes adhering to them, the Iroquois family was confined to the region south of the Lakes Erie and Ontario, and the peninsula east of Lake Huron. They formed, as it were, an island in the vast expanse of Algonquin population, extending from Hudson's Bay on the north to the Carolinas on the south; from the Atlantic on the east to the Mississippi and Lake Winnipeg on the west. They were Algonquins who greeted Jacques Cartier, as his ships ascended the St. Lawrence. The first British colonists found savages of the same race hunting and fishing along the coasts and inlets of Virginia; and it was the daughter of an Algonquin chief who interceded with her father for the life of the adventurous Englishman. They were Algonquins who, under Sassacus the Pequot, and Philip of Mount Hope, waged war against the Puritans of New England; who dwelt at Penacook, under the rule of the great magician, Passaconaway, and trembled before the evil spirits of the White Hills; and who sang aves and told their beads in the forest chapel of Father Rasles, by the banks of the Kennebec. They were Algonquins who, under the great tree at Kensington, made the covenant of peace with William Penn; and when French Jesuits and fur-traders explored the Wabash and the Ohio, they found their valleys tenanted by the same far-extended race. At the present day, the traveller, perchance, may find them pitching their bark lodges along the beach at Mackinaw, spearing fish among the rapids of St. Mary's, or skimming the waves of Lake Superior in their birch canoes.

Of all the members of the Algonquin family, those called by the English the

Delawares, by the French the Loups, and by themselves Lenni Lenape, or Original Men, hold the first claim to attention; for their traditions declare them to be the parent stem whence other Algonquin tribes have sprung. The latter recognized the claim, and, at all solemn councils, accorded to the ancestral tribe the title of Grandfather.

The first European colonists found the conical lodges of the Lenape clustered in frequent groups about the waters of the Delaware and its tributary streams, within the present limits of New Jersey, and Eastern Pennsylvania. The nation was separated into three divisions, and three sachems formed a triumvirate, who, with the council of old men, regulated all its affairs. They were, in some small measure, an agricultural people; but fishing and the chase were their chief dependence, and through a great part of the year they were scattered abroad, among forests and streams, in search of sustenance.

When William Penn held his far-famed council with the sachems of the Lenape, he extended the hand of brotherhood to a people as unwarlike in their habits as his own pacific followers. This is by no means to be ascribed to any inborn love of peace. The Lenape were then in a state of degrading vassalage to the Five Nations, who, that they might drain to the dregs the cup of humiliation, had forced them to assume the name of Women, and forego the use of arms. Dwelling under the shadow of the tyrannical confederacy, they were long unable to wipe out the blot; but at length, pushed from their ancient seats by the encroachments of white men, and removed westward, partially beyond the reach of their conquerors, their native spirit began to revive, and they assumed a tone of defiance. During the Old French War they resumed the use of arms, and while the Five Nations fought for the English, they espoused the cause of France. At the opening of the Revolution, they boldly asserted their freedom from the yoke of their conquerors; and a few years after, the Five Nations confessed, at a public council, that the Lenape were no longer women, but men. Ever since that period, they have stood in high repute for bravery, generosity, and all the savage virtues; and the settlers of the frontier have often found, to their cost, that the women of the Iroquois have been transformed into a race of formidable warriors. At the present day, the small remnant settled beyond the Mississippi are among the bravest marauders of the west. Their war-parties pierce the farthest wilds of the Rocky Mountains; and the prairie traveller may sometimes meet the Delaware warrior returning from a successful foray, a gaudy handkerchief bound about his brows, his snake locks fluttering in the wind, and his rifle resting across his saddle-bow, while the tarnished and begrimed equipments of his half-wild horse bear witness that the rider has waylaid and plundered some Mexican cavalier.

Adjacent to the Lenape, and associated with them in some of the most notable passages of their history, dwelt the Shawanoes, the Chaouanons of the French, a tribe of bold, roving, and adventurous spirit. Their eccentric wanderings, their sudden appearances and disappearances, perplex the antiquary, and defy research; but from various scattered notices, we may gather that at an early period they occupied the valley of the Ohio; that, becoming embroiled with the Five Nations, they shared the defeat of the Andastes, and about the year 1672 fled to escape destruction. Some found an asylum in the country of the Lenape, where they lived tenants at will of the Five Nations; others sought refuge in the Carolinas and Florida, where, true to their native instincts, they soon came to blows with the owners of the soil. Again, turning northwards, they formed new settlements in the valley of the Ohio, where they were now suffered to dwell in peace, and where, at a later period, they were joined by such of their brethren as had found refuge among the Lenape.

Of the tribes which, single and detached, or cohering in loose confederacies, dwelt within the limits of Lower Canada, Acadia, and New England, it is needless to speak; for they offered no distinctive traits demanding notice. Passing the country of the Lenape and the Shawanoes, and descending the Ohio, the traveller would have found its valley chiefly occupied by two nations, the Miamis or Twightwees, on the Wabash and its branches, and the Illinois, who dwelt in the neighborhood of the river to which they have given their name, while portions of them extended beyond the Mississippi. Though never subjugated, as were the Lenape, both the Miamis and the Illinois were reduced to the last extremity by the repeated attacks of the Five Nations; and the Illinois, in particular, suffered so much by these and other wars, that the population of ten or twelve thousand, ascribed to them by the early French writers, had dwindled, during the first quarter of the eighteenth century, to a few small villages. According to Marest, they were a people sunk in sloth and licentiousness; but that priestly father had suffered much at their hands, and viewed them with a jaundiced eye. Their agriculture was not contemptible; they had permanent dwellings as well as portable lodges; and though wandering through many months of the year among their broad prairies and forests, there were seasons when their whole population was gathered, with feastings and merry-making, within the limits of their villages.

Turning his course northward, traversing Lakes Michigan and Superior, and skirting the western margin of Lake Huron, the voyager would have found the solitudes of the wild waste around him broken by scattered lodges of the Ojibwas, Pottawattamies, and Ottawas. About the bays and rivers west of Lake Michigan, he would have seen the Sacs, the Foxes, and the Menomonies; and penetrating the frozen wilderness of the north, he would have been welcomed by the rude hospitality of the wandering Crees or Knisteneaux.

The Ojibwas, with their kindred, the Pottawattamies, and their friends the

Ottawas,—the latter of whom were fugitives from the eastward, whence they had fled from the wrath of the Iroquois,—were banded into a sort of confederacy. They were closely allied in blood, language, manners and character. The Ojibwas, by far the most numerous of the three, occupied the basin of Lake Superior, and extensive adjacent regions. In their boundaries, the career of Iroquois conquest found at length a check. The fugitive Wyandots sought refuge in the Ojibwa hunting-grounds; and tradition relates that, at the outlet of Lake Superior, an Iroquois war-party once encountered a disastrous repulse.

In their mode of life, they were far more rude than the Iroquois, or even the southern Algonquin tribes. The totemic system is found among them in its most imperfect state. The original clans have become broken into fragments, and indefinitely multiplied; and many of the ancient customs of the institution are but loosely regarded. Agriculture is little known, and, through summer and winter, they range the wilderness with restless wandering, now gorged to repletion, and now perishing with want. In the calm days of summer, the Ojibwa fisherman pushes out his birch canoe upon the great inland ocean of the north; and, as he gazes down into the pellucid depths, he seems like one balanced between earth and sky. The watchful fish-hawk circles above his head; and below, farther than his line will reach, he sees the trout glide shadowy and silent over the glimmering pebbles. The little islands on the verge of the horizon seem now starting into spires, now melting from the sight, now shaping themselves into a thousand fantastic forms, with the strange mirage of the waters; and he fancies that the evil spirits of the lake lie basking their serpent forms on those unhallowed shores. Again, he explores the watery labyrinths where the stream sweeps among pine-tufted islands, or runs, black and deep, beneath the shadows of moss-bearded firs; or he drags his canoe upon the sandy beach, and, while his camp-fire crackles on the grass-plat, reclines beneath the trees, and smokes and laughs away the sultry hours, in a lazy luxury of enjoyment.

But when winter descends upon the north, sealing up the fountains, fettering the streams, and turning the green-robed forests to shivering nakedness, then, bearing their frail dwellings on their backs, the Ojibwa family wander forth into the wilderness, cheered only on their dreary track by the whistling of the north wind, and the hungry howl of wolves. By the banks of some frozen stream, women and children, men and dogs, lie crouched together around the fire. They spread their benumbed fingers over the embers, while the wind shrieks through the fir-trees like the gale through the rigging of a frigate, and the narrow concave of the wigwam sparkles with the frost-work of their congealed breath. In vain they beat the magic drum, and call upon their guardian manitoes;—the wary moose keeps aloof, the bear lies close in his hollow tree, and famine stares them in the face. And now the hunter can fight no more against the nipping cold and blinding sleet. Stiff and stark, with haggard cheek and shrivelled lip, he lies among the snow-drifts; till, with tooth and claw, the famished wildcat strives in vain to pierce the frigid marble of his limbs. Such harsh schooling is thrown away on the incorrigible mind of the northern Algonquin. He lives in misery, as his fathers lived before him. Still, in the brief hour of plenty he forgets the season of want; and still the sleet and the snow descend upon his houseless head.

I have thus passed in brief review the more prominent of the Algonquin tribes; those whose struggles and sufferings form the theme of the ensuing History. In speaking of the Iroquois, some of the distinctive peculiarities of the Algonquins have already been hinted at. It must be admitted that, in moral stability and intellectual vigor, they are inferior to the former; though some of the most conspicuous offspring of the wilderness, Metacom, Tecumseh, and Pontiac himself, owned their blood and language.

The fireside stories of every primitive people are faithful reflections of the form and coloring of the national mind; and it is no proof of sound philosophy to turn with contempt from the study of a fairy tale. The legendary lore of the Iroquois, black as the midnight forests, awful in its gloomy strength, is but another manifestation of that spirit of mastery which uprooted whole tribes from the earth, and deluged the wilderness with blood. The traditional tales of the Algonquins wear a different aspect. The credulous circle around an Ojibwa lodge-fire listened to wild recitals of necromancy and witchcraft—men transformed to beasts, and beasts transformed to men, animated trees, and birds who spoke with human tongue. They heard of malignant sorcerers dwelling among the lonely islands of spell-bound lakes; of grisly weendigoes, and bloodless geebi; of evil manitoes lurking in the dens and fastnesses of the woods; of pygmy champions, diminutive in stature but mighty in soul, who, by the potency of charm and talisman, subdued the direst monsters of the waste; and of heroes, who, not by downright force and open onset, but by subtle strategy, tricks, or magic art, achieved marvellous triumphs over the brute force of their assailants. Sometimes the tale will breathe a different spirit, and tell of orphan children abandoned in the heart of a hideous wilderness, beset with fiends and cannibals. Some enamored maiden, scornful of earthly suitors, plights her troth to the graceful manito of the grove; or bright aerial beings, dwellers of the sky, descend to tantalize the gaze of mortals with evanescent forms of loveliness.

The mighty giant, the God of the Thunder, who made his home among the caverns, beneath the cataract of Niagara, was a characteristic conception of Iroquois imagination. The Algonquins held a simpler faith, and maintained that the thunder was a bird who built his nest on the pinnacle of towering mountains. Two daring boys once scaled the height, and thrust sticks into the eyes of the portentous nestlings; which hereupon flashed forth such wrathful scintillations, that the sticks were shivered to atoms.

The religious belief of the Algonquins—and the remark holds good, not of the Algonquins only, but of all the hunting tribes of America—is a cloudy bewilderment, where we seek in vain for system or coherency. Among a primitive and savage people, there were no poets to vivify its images, and no priests to give distinctness and harmony to its rites and symbols. To the Indian mind, all nature was instinct with deity. A spirit was embodied in every mountain, lake, and cataract; every bird, beast, or reptile, every tree, shrub, or grass-blade, was endued with mystic influence; yet this untutored pantheism did not exclude the conception of certain divinities, of incongruous and ever shifting attributes. The sun, too, was a god, and the moon was a goddess. Conflicting powers of good and evil divided the universe: but if, before the arrival of Europeans, the Indian recognized the existence of one, almighty, self-existent Being, the Great Spirit, the Lord of Heaven and Earth, the belief was so vague and dubious as scarcely to deserve the name. His perceptions of moral good and evil were perplexed and shadowy; and the belief in a state of future reward and punishment was by no means universal.

Of the Indian character, much has been written foolishly, and credulously believed. By the rhapsodies of poets, the cant of sentimentalists, and the extravagance of some who should have known better, a counterfeit image has been tricked out, which might seek in vain for its likeness through every corner of the habitable earth; an image bearing no more resemblance to its original, than the monarch of the tragedy and the hero of the epic poem bear to their living prototypes in the palace and the camp. The shadows of his wilderness home, and the darker mantle of his own inscrutable reserve, have made the Indian warrior a wonder and a mystery. Yet to the eye of rational observation there is nothing unintelligible in him. He is full, it is true, of contradiction. He deems himself the centre of greatness and renown; his pride is proof against the fiercest torments of fire and steel; and yet the same man would beg for a dram of whiskey, or pick up a crust of bread thrown to him like a dog, from the tent door of the traveller. At one moment, he is wary and cautious to the verge of cowardice; at the next, he abandons himself to a very insanity of recklessness; and the habitual self-restraint which throws an impenetrable veil over emotion is joined to the unbridled passions of a madman or a beast.

Such inconsistencies, strange as they seem in our eyes, when viewed under a novel aspect, are but the ordinary incidents of humanity. The qualities of the mind are not uniform in their action through all the relations of life. With different men, and different races of men, pride, valor, prudence, have different forms of manifestation, and where in one instance they lie dormant, in another they are keenly awake. The conjunction of greatness and littleness, meanness and pride, is older than the days of the patriarchs; and such antiquated phenomena, displayed under a new form in the unreflecting, undisciplined mind of a savage, call for no special wonder, but should rather be classed with the other enigmas of the fathomless human heart. The dissecting knife of a Rochefoucault might lay bare matters of no less curious observation in the breast of every man.

Nature has stamped the Indian with a hard and stern physiognomy. Ambition, revenge, envy, jealousy, are his ruling passions; and his cold temperament is little exposed to those effeminate vices which are the bane of milder races. With him revenge is an overpowering instinct; nay, more, it is a point of honor and a duty. His pride sets all language at defiance. He loathes the thought of coercion; and few of his race have ever stooped to discharge a menial office. A wild love of liberty, an utter intolerance of control, lie at the basis of his character, and fire his whole existence. Yet, in spite of this haughty independence, he is a devout hero-worshipper; and high achievement in war or policy touches a chord to which his nature never fails to respond. He looks up with admiring reverence to the sages and heroes of his tribe; and it is this principle, joined to the respect for age springing from the patriarchal element in his social system, which, beyond all others, contributes union and harmony to the erratic members of an Indian community. With him the love of glory kindles into a burning passion; and to allay its cravings, he will dare cold and famine, fire, tempest, torture, and death itself.

These generous traits are overcast by much that is dark, cold, and sinister, by sleepless distrust, and rankling jealousy. Treacherous himself, he is always suspicious of treachery in others. Brave as he is,—and few of mankind are braver,—he will vent his passion by a secret stab rather than an open blow. His warfare is full of ambuscade and stratagem; and he never rushes into battle with that joyous self-abandonment, with which the warriors of the Gothic races flung themselves into the ranks of their enemies. In his feasts and his drinking bouts we find none of that robust and full-toned mirth, which reigned at the rude carousals of our barbaric ancestry. He is never jovial in his cups, and maudlin sorrow or maniacal rage is the sole result of his potations.

Over all emotion he throws the veil of an iron self-control, originating in a peculiar form of pride, and fostered by rigorous discipline from childhood upward. He is trained to conceal passion, and not to subdue it. The inscrutable warrior is aptly imaged by the hackneyed figure of a volcano covered with snow; and no man can say when or where the wildfire will burst forth. This shallow self-mastery serves to give dignity to public deliberation, and harmony to social life. Wrangling and quarrel are strangers to an Indian dwelling; and while an assembly of the ancient Gauls was garrulous as a convocation of magpies, a Roman senate might have taken a lesson from the grave solemnity of an Indian council. In the midst of his family and friends, he hides affections, by nature none of the most tender, under a mask of icy coldness; and in the torturing fires of his enemy, the haughty sufferer maintains to the last his look of grim defiance.

His intellect is as peculiar as his moral organization. Among all savages, the powers of perception preponderate over those of reason and analysis; but this is more especially the case with the Indian. An acute judge of character, at least of such parts of it as his experience enables him to comprehend; keen to a proverb in all exercises of war and the chase, he seldom traces effects to their causes, or follows out actions to their remote results. Though a close observer of external nature, he no sooner attempts to account for her phenomena than he involves himself in the most ridiculous absurdities; and quite content with these puerilities, he has not the least desire to push his inquiries further. His curiosity, abundantly active within its own narrow circle, is dead to all things else; and to attempt rousing it from its torpor is but a bootless task. He seldom takes cognizance of general or abstract ideas; and his language has scarcely the power to express them, except through the medium of figures drawn from the external world, and often highly picturesque and forcible. The absence of reflection makes him grossly improvident, and unfits him for pursuing any complicated scheme of war or policy.

Some races of men seem moulded in wax, soft and melting, at once plastic and feeble. Some races, like some metals, combine the greatest flexibility with the greatest strength. But the Indian is hewn out of a rock. You can rarely change the form without destruction of the substance. Races of inferior energy have possessed a power of expansion and assimilation to which he is a stranger; and it is this fixed and rigid quality which has proved his ruin. He will not learn the arts of civilization, and he and his forest must perish together. The stern, unchanging features of his mind excite our admiration from their very immutability; and we look with deep interest on the fate of this irreclaimable son of the wilderness, the child who will not be weaned from the breast of his rugged mother. And our interest increases when we discern in the unhappy wanderer the germs of heroic virtues mingled among his vices,—a hand bountiful to bestow as it is rapacious to seize, and even in extremest famine, imparting its last morsel to a fellow-sufferer; a heart which, strong in friendship as in hate, thinks it not too much to lay down life for its chosen comrade; a soul true to its own idea of honor, and burning with an unquenchable thirst for greatness and renown.

The imprisoned lion in the showman's cage differs not more widely from the lord of the desert, than the beggarly frequenter of frontier garrisons and dramshops differs from the proud denizen of the woods. It is in his native wilds alone that the Indian must be seen and studied. Thus to depict him is the aim of the ensuing History; and if, from the shades of rock and forest, the savage features should look too grimly forth, it is because the clouds of a tempestuous war have cast upon the picture their murky shadows and lurid fires.

FRANCE AND ENGLAND IN AMERICA

1608 to 1763

The American colonies of France and England grew up to maturity under widely different auspices. Canada, the offspring of Church and State, nursed from infancy in the lap of power, its puny strength fed with artificial stimulants, its movements guided by rule and discipline, its limbs trained to martial exercise, languished, in spite of all, from the lack of vital sap and energy. The colonies of England, outcast and neglected, but strong in native vigor and self-confiding courage, grew yet more strong with conflict and with striving, and developed the rugged proportions and unwieldy strength of a youthful giant.
In the valley of the St. Lawrence, and along the coasts of the Atlantic, adverse principles contended for the mastery. Feudalism stood arrayed against Democracy; Popery against Protestantism; the sword against the ploughshare. The priest, the soldier, and the noble, ruled in Canada. The ignorant, light-hearted Canadian peasant knew nothing and cared nothing about popular rights and civil liberties. Born to obey, he lived in contented submission, without the wish or the capacity for self-rule. Power, centered in the heart of the system, left the masses inert. The settlements along the margin of the St. Lawrence were like a camp, where an army lay at rest, ready for the march or the battle, and where war and adventure, not trade and tillage, seemed the chief aims of life. The lords of the soil were petty nobles, for the most part soldiers, or the sons of soldiers, proud and ostentatious, thriftless and poor; and the people were their vassals. Over every cluster of small white houses glittered the sacred emblem of the cross. The church, the convent, and the roadside shrine were seen at every turn; and in the towns and villages, one met each moment the black robe of the

Jesuit, the gray garb of the Recollet, and the formal habit of the Ursuline nun. The names of saints, St. Joseph, St. Ignatius, St. Francis, were perpetuated in the capes, rivers, and islands, the forts and villages of the land; and with every day, crowds of simple worshippers knelt in adoration before the countless altars of the Roman faith.

If we search the world for the sharpest contrast to the spiritual and temporal vassalage of Canada, we shall find it among her immediate neighbors, the Puritans of New England, where the spirit of non-conformity was sublimed to a fiery essence, and where the love of liberty and the hatred of power burned with sevenfold heat. The English colonist, with thoughtful brow and limbs hardened with toil; calling no man master, yet bowing reverently to the law which he himself had made; patient and laborious, and seeking for the solid comforts rather than the ornaments of life; no lover of war, yet, if need were, fighting with a stubborn, indomitable courage, and then bending once more with steadfast energy to his farm, or his merchandise,—such a man might well be deemed the very pith and marrow of a commonwealth.

In every quality of efficiency and strength, the Canadian fell miserably below his rival; but in all that pleases the eye and interests the imagination, he far surpassed him. Buoyant and gay, like his ancestry of France, he made the frozen wilderness ring with merriment, answered the surly howling of the pine forest with peals of laughter, and warmed with revelry the groaning ice of the St. Lawrence. Careless and thoughtless, he lived happy in the midst of poverty, content if he could but gain the means to fill his tobacco-pouch, and decorate the cap of his mistress with a ribbon. The example of a beggared nobility, who, proud and penniless, could only assert their rank by idleness and ostentation, was not lost upon him. A rightful heir to French bravery and French restlessness, he had an eager love of wandering and adventure; and this propensity found ample scope in the service of the fur-trade, the engrossing occupation and chief source of income to the colony. When the priest of St. Ann's had shrived him of his sins; when, after the parting carousal, he embarked with his comrades in the deep-laden canoe; when their oars kept time to the measured cadence of their song, and the blue, sunny bosom of the Ottawa opened before them; when their frail bark quivered among the milky foam and black rocks of the rapid; and when, around their camp-fire, they wasted half the night with jests and laughter,— then the Canadian was in his element. His footsteps explored the farthest hiding-places of the wilderness. In the evening dance, his red cap mingled with the scalp-locks and feathers of the Indian braves; or, stretched on a bear-skin by the side of his dusky mistress, he watched the gambols of his hybrid offspring, in happy oblivion of the partner whom he left unnumbered leagues behind.

The fur-trade engendered a peculiar class of restless bush-rangers, more akin to Indians than to white men. Those who had once felt the fascinations of the forest were unfitted ever after for a life of quiet labor; and with this spirit the whole colony was infected. From this cause, no less than from occasional wars with the English, and repeated attacks of the Iroquois, the agriculture of the country was sunk to a low ebb; while feudal exactions, a ruinous system of monopoly, and the intermeddlings of arbitrary power, cramped every branch of industry. Yet, by the zeal of priests and the daring enterprise of soldiers and explorers, Canada, though sapless and infirm, spread forts and missions through all the western wilderness. Feebly rooted in the soil, she thrust out branches which overshadowed half America; a magnificent object to the eye, but one which the first whirlwind would prostrate in the dust.

Such excursive enterprise was alien to the genius of the British colonies. Daring activity was rife among them, but it did not aim at the founding of military outposts and forest missions. By the force of energetic industry, their population swelled with an unheard-of rapidity, their wealth increased in a yet greater ratio, and their promise of future greatness opened with every advancing year. But it was a greatness rather of peace than of war. The free institutions, the independence of authority, which were the source of their increase, were adverse to that unity of counsel and promptitude of action which are the soul of war. It was far otherwise with their military rival. France had her Canadian forces well in hand. They had but one will, and that was the will of a mistress. Now here, now there, in sharp and rapid onset, they could assail the cumbrous masses and unwieldy strength of their antagonists, as the king-bird attacks the eagle, or the sword-fish the whale. Between two such combatants the strife must needs be a long one.

Canada was a true child of the Church, baptized in infancy and faithful to the last. Champlain, the founder of Quebec, a man of noble spirit, a statesman and a soldier, was deeply imbued with fervid piety. "The saving of a soul," he would often say, "is worth more than the conquest of an empire;" and to forward the work of conversion, he brought with him four Franciscan monks from France. At a later period, the task of colonization would have been abandoned, but for the hope of casting the pure light of the faith over the gloomy wastes of heathendom. All France was filled with the zeal of proselytism. Men and women of exalted rank lent their countenance to the holy work. From many an altar daily petitions were offered for the well-being of the mission; and in the Holy House of Mont-Martre, a nun lay prostrate day and night before the shrine, praying for the conversion of Canada. In one convent, thirty nuns offered themselves for the labors of the wilderness; and priests flocked in crowds to the colony. The powers of darkness took alarm; and when a ship, freighted with the apostles of the faith, was tempest-tost upon her voyage, the storm was ascribed to the malice of demons, trembling for the safety of their ancient empire.

The general enthusiasm was not without its fruits. The Church could pay back with usury all that she received of aid and encouragement from the temporal power; and the ambition of Richelieu could not have devised a more efficient enginery for the accomplishment of its schemes, than that supplied by the zeal of the devoted propagandists. The priest and the soldier went hand in hand; and the cross and the fleur de lis were planted side by side.

Foremost among the envoys of the faith were the members of that mighty order, who, in another hemisphere, had already done so much to turn back the advancing tide of religious freedom, and strengthen the arm of Rome. To the Jesuits was assigned, for many years, the entire charge of the Canadian missions, to the exclusion of the Franciscans, early laborers in the same barren field. Inspired with a self-devoting zeal to snatch souls from perdition, and win new empires to the cross; casting from them every hope of earthly pleasure or earthly aggrandizement, the Jesuit fathers buried themselves in deserts, facing death with the courage of heroes, and enduring torments with the constancy of martyrs. Their story is replete with marvels—miracles of patient suffering and daring enterprise. They were the pioneers of Northern America. We see them among the frozen forests of Acadia, struggling on snowshoes, with some wandering Algonquin horde, or crouching in the crowded hunting-lodge, half stifled in the smoky den, and battling with troops of famished dogs for the last morsel of sustenance. Again we see the black-robed priest wading among the white rapids of the Ottawa, toiling with his savage comrades to drag the canoe against the headlong water. Again, radiant in the vestments of his priestly office, he administers the sacramental bread to kneeling crowds of plumed and painted proselytes in the forests of the Hurons; or, bearing his life in his hand, carries his sacred mission into the strongholds of the Iroquois, like one who invades unarmed a den of angry tigers. Jesuit explorers traced the St. Lawrence to its source, and said masses among the solitudes of Lake Superior, where the boldest fur-trader scarcely dared to follow. They planted missions at St. Mary's and at Michillimackinac; and one of their fraternity, the illustrious Marquette, discovered the Mississippi, and opened a new theatre to the boundless ambition of France.

The path of the missionary was a thorny and a bloody one; and a life of weary apostleship was often crowned with a frightful martyrdom. Jean de Brebeuf and Gabriel Lallemant preached the faith among the villages of the Hurons, when their terror-stricken flock were overwhelmed by an irruption of the Iroquois. The missionaries might have fled; but, true to their sacred function, they remained behind to aid the wounded and baptize the dying. Both were made captive, and both were doomed to the fiery torture. Brebeuf, a veteran soldier of the cross, met his fate with an undaunted composure, which amazed his murderers. With unflinching constancy he endured torments too horrible to be recorded, and died calmly as a martyr of the early church, or a war-chief of the Mohawks.

The slender frame of Lallemant, a man younger in years and gentle in spirit, was enveloped in blazing savin-bark. Again and again the fire was extinguished; again and again it was kindled afresh; and with such fiendish ingenuity were his torments protracted, that he lingered for seventeen hours before death came to his relief.

Isaac Jogues, taken captive by the Iroquois, was led from canton to canton, and village to village, enduring fresh torments and indignities at every stage of his progress. Men, women, and children vied with each other in ingenious malignity. Redeemed, at length, by the humane exertions of a Dutch officer, he repaired to France, where his disfigured person and mutilated hands told the story of his sufferings. But the promptings of a sleepless conscience urged him to return and complete the work he had begun; to illumine the moral darkness upon which, during the months of his disastrous captivity, he fondly hoped that he had thrown some rays of light. Once more he bent his footsteps towards the scene of his living martyrdom, saddened with a deep presentiment that he was advancing to his death. Nor were his forebodings untrue. In a village of the Mohawks, the blow of a tomahawk closed his mission and his life.

Such intrepid self-devotion may well call forth our highest admiration; but when we seek for the results of these toils and sacrifices, we shall seek in vain. Patience and zeal were thrown away upon lethargic minds and stubborn hearts. The reports of the Jesuits, it is true, display a copious list of conversions; but the zealous fathers reckoned the number of conversions by the number of baptisms; and, as Le Clercq observes, with no less truth than candor, an Indian would be baptized ten times a day for a pint of brandy or a pound of tobacco. Neither can more flattering conclusions be drawn from the alacrity which they showed to adorn their persons with crucifixes and medals. The glitter of the trinkets pleased the fancy of the warrior; and, with the emblem of man's salvation pendent from his neck, he was often at heart as thorough a heathen as when he wore in its place a necklace made of the dried forefingers of his enemies. At the present day, with the exception of a few insignificant bands of converted Indians in Lower Canada, not a vestige of early Jesuit influence can be found among the tribes. The seed was sown upon a rock.

While the church was reaping but a scanty harvest, the labors of the missionaries were fruitful of profit to the monarch of France. The Jesuit led the van of French colonization; and at Detroit, Michillimackinac, St. Mary's, Green Bay, and other outposts of the west, the establishment of a mission was the precursor of military occupancy. In other respects no less, the labors of the wandering missionaries advanced the welfare of the colony.

Sagacious and keen of sight, with faculties stimulated by zeal and sharpened by peril, they made faithful report of the temper and movements of the distant tribes among whom they were distributed. The influence which they often gained was exerted in behalf of the government under whose auspices their missions were carried on; and they strenuously labored to win over the tribes to the French alliance, and alienate them from the heretic English. In all things they approved themselves the stanch and steadfast auxiliaries of the imperial power; and the Marquis du Quesne observed of the missionary Picquet, that in his single person he was worth ten regiments.

Among the English colonies, the pioneers of civilization were for the most part rude, yet vigorous men, impelled to enterprise by native restlessness, or lured by the hope of gain. Their range was limited, and seldom extended far beyond the outskirts of the settlements. With Canada it was far otherwise. There was no energy in the bulk of her people. The court and the army supplied the mainsprings of her vital action, and the hands which planted the lilies of France in the heart of the wilderness had never guided the ploughshare or wielded the spade. The love of adventure, the ambition of new discovery, the hope of military advancement, urged men of place and culture to embark on bold and comprehensive enterprise. Many a gallant gentleman, many a nobleman of France, trod the black mould and oozy mosses of the forest with feet that had pressed the carpets of Versailles. They whose youth had passed in camps and courts grew gray among the wigwams of savages; and the lives of Castine, Joncaire, and Priber are invested with all the interest of romance.

Conspicuous in the annals of Canada stands the memorable name of Robert Cavelier de La Salle, the man who, beyond all his compeers, contributed to expand the boundary of French empire in the west. La Salle commanded at Fort Frontenac, erected near the outlet of Lake Ontario, on its northern shore, and then forming the most advanced military outpost of the colony. Here he dwelt among Indians, and half-breeds, traders, voyageurs, bush-rangers, and Franciscan monks, ruling his little empire with absolute sway, enforcing respect by his energy, but offending many by his rigor. Here he brooded upon the grand design which had long engaged his thoughts. He had resolved to complete the achievement of Father Marquette, to trace the unknown Mississippi to its mouth, to plant the standard of his king in the newly-discovered regions, and found colonies which should make good the sovereignty of France from the Frozen Ocean to Mexico. Ten years of his early life had passed, it is said, in connection with the Jesuits, and his strong mind had hardened to iron under the discipline of that relentless school. To a sound judgment, and a penetrating sagacity, he joined a boundless enterprise and an adamantine constancy of purpose. But his nature was stern and austere; he was prone to rule by fear rather than by love; he took counsel of no man, and chilled all who approached him by his cold reserve.

At the close of the year 1678, his preparations were complete, and he despatched his attendants to the banks of the river Niagara, whither he soon followed in person. Here he began a little fort of palisades, and was the first military tenant of a spot destined to momentous consequence in future wars. Two leagues above the cataract, on the eastern bank of the river, he built the first vessel which ever explored the waters of the upper lakes. Her name was the Griffin, and her burden was forty-five tons. On the seventh of August, 1679, she began her adventurous voyage amid the speechless wonder of the Indians, who stood amazed, alike at the unwonted size of the wooden canoe, at the flash and roar of the cannon from her decks, and at the carved figure of a griffin, which sat crouched upon her prow. She bore on her course along the virgin waters of Lake Erie, through the beautiful windings of the Detroit, and among the restless billows of Lake Huron, where a furious tempest had well nigh ingulphed her. La Salle pursued his voyage along Lake Michigan in birch canoes, and after protracted suffering from famine and exposure reached its southern extremity on the eighteenth of October.

He led his followers to the banks of the river now called the St. Joseph. Here, again, he built a fort; and here, in after years, the Jesuits placed a mission and the government a garrison. Thence he pushed on into the unknown region of the Illinois; and now dangers and difficulties began to thicken about him. Indians threatened hostility; his men lost heart, clamored, grew mutinous, and repeatedly deserted; and worse than all, nothing was heard of the vessel which had been sent back to Canada for necessary supplies. Weeks wore on, and doubt ripened into certainty. She had foundered among the storms of these wilderness oceans; and her loss seemed to involve the ruin of the enterprise, since it was vain to proceed farther without the expected supplies. In this disastrous crisis, La Salle embraced a resolution characteristic of his intrepid temper. Leaving his men in charge of a subordinate at a fort which he had built on the river Illinois, he turned his face again towards Canada. He traversed on foot more than a thousand miles of frozen forest, crossing rivers, toiling through snow-drifts, wading ice-encumbered swamps, sustaining life by the fruits of the chase, and threatened day and night by lurking enemies. He gained his destination, but it was only to encounter a fresh storm of calamities. His enemies had been busy in his absence; a malicious report had gone abroad that he was dead; his creditors had seized his property; and the stores on which he most relied had been wrecked at sea, or lost among the rapids of the St. Lawrence. Still he battled against adversity with his wonted vigor, and in Count Frontenac, the governor of the province,—a spirit kindred to his own,—he found a firm friend. Every difficulty gave way before him; and with fresh supplies of men, stores, and ammunition, he again embarked for the Illinois. Rounding the vast circuit of the lakes, he reached the mouth of the St. Joseph, and hastened with anxious speed to the fort where he had left his followers. The place was empty. Not a man remained. Terrified, despondent, mutinous, and embroiled in Indian wars, they had fled to seek peace and safety, he knew not whither.

Once more the dauntless discoverer turned back towards Canada. Once more he stood before Count Frontenac, and once more bent all his resources and all his credit to gain means for the prosecution of his enterprise. He succeeded. With his little flotilla of canoes, he left his fort, at the outlet of Lake Ontario, and slowly retraced those interminable waters, and lines of forest-bounded shore, which had grown drearily familiar to his eyes. Fate at length seemed tired of the conflict with so stubborn an adversary. All went prosperously with the voyagers. They passed the lakes in safety, crossed the rough portage to the waters of the Illinois, followed its winding channel, and descended the turbid eddies of the Mississippi, received with various welcome by the scattered tribes who dwelt along its banks. Now the waters grew bitter to the taste; now the trampling of the surf was heard; and now the broad ocean opened upon their sight, and their goal was won. On the ninth of April, 1682, with his followers under arms, amid the firing of musketry, the chanting of the Te Deum, and shouts of "Vive le roi," La Salle took formal possession of the vast valley of the Mississippi, in the name of Louis the Great, King of France and Navarre.

The first stage of his enterprise was accomplished, but labors no less arduous remained behind. Repairing to the court of France, he was welcomed with richly merited favor, and soon set sail for the mouth of the Mississippi, with a squadron of vessels freighted with men and material for the projected colony. But the folly and obstinacy of a jealous naval commander blighted his fairest hopes. The squadron missed the mouth of the river; and the wreck of one of the vessels, and the desertion of the commander, completed the ruin of the expedition. La Salle landed with a band of half-famished followers on the coast of Texas; and, while he was toiling with untired energy for their relief, a few vindictive miscreants conspired against him, and a shot from a traitor's musket closed the career of the iron-hearted discoverer.

It was left with another to complete the enterprise on which he had staked his life; and, in the year 1699, Lemoine d'Iberville planted the germ whence sprang the colony of Louisiana.

Years passed on. In spite of a vicious plan of government, in spite of the bursting of the memorable Mississippi bubble, the new colony grew in wealth and strength. And now it remained for France to unite the two extremities of her broad American domain, to extend forts and settlements across the fertile solitudes between the valley of the St. Lawrence and the mouth of the Mississippi, and intrench herself among the forests which lie west of the Alleghanies, before the swelling tide of British colonization could overflow those mountain barriers. At the middle of the eighteenth century, her great project was fast advancing towards completion. The lakes and streams, the thoroughfares of the wilderness, were seized and guarded by a series of posts distributed with admirable skill. A fort on the strait of Niagara commanded the great entrance to the whole interior country. Another at Detroit controlled the passage from Lake Erie to the north. Another at St. Mary's debarred all hostile access to Lake Superior. Another at Michillimackinac secured the mouth of Lake Michigan. A post at Green Bay, and one at St. Joseph, guarded the two routes to the Mississippi, by way of the rivers Wisconsin and Illinois; while two posts on the Wabash, and one on the Maumee, made France the mistress of the great trading highway from Lake Erie to the Ohio. At Kaskaskia, Cahokia, and elsewhere in the Illinois, little French settlements had sprung up; and as the canoe of the voyager descended the Mississippi, he saw, at rare intervals, along its swampy margin, a few small stockade forts, half buried amid the redundancy of forest vegetation, until, as he approached Natchez, the dwellings of the habitans of Louisiana began to appear.

The forest posts of France were not exclusively of a military character. Adjacent to most of them, one would have found a little cluster of Canadian dwellings, whose tenants lived under the protection of the garrison, and obeyed the arbitrary will of the commandant; an authority which, however, was seldom exerted in a despotic spirit. In these detached settlements, there was no principle of increase. The character of the people, and of the government which ruled them, were alike unfavorable to it. Agriculture was neglected for the more congenial pursuits of the fur-trade, and the restless, roving Canadians, scattered abroad on their wild vocation, allied themselves to Indian women, and filled the woods with a mongrel race of bush-rangers.

Thus far secure in the west, France next essayed to gain foothold upon the sources of the Ohio; and about the year 1748, the sagacious Count Galissonnière proposed to bring over ten thousand peasants from France, and plant them in the valley of that beautiful river, and on the borders of the lakes. But while at Quebec, in the Castle of St. Louis, soldiers and statesmen were revolving schemes like this, the slowly-moving power of England bore on with silent progress from the east. Already the British settlements were creeping along the valley of the Mohawk, and ascending the eastern slopes of the Alleghanies. Forests crashing to the axe, dark spires of smoke ascending from autumnal fires, were heralds of the advancing host; and while, on one side of the mountains, Celeron de Bienville was burying plates of lead, engraved with the arms of France, the ploughs and axes of Virginian woodsmen were enforcing a surer title on the other. The adverse powers were drawing near. The hour of collision was at hand.

THE FRENCH, THE ENGLISH, AND THE INDIANS

1608 to 1763

The French colonists of Canada held, from the beginning, a peculiar intimacy of relation with the Indian tribes. With the English colonists it was far otherwise; and the difference sprang from several causes. The fur-trade was the life of Canada; agriculture and commerce were the chief sources of wealth to the British provinces. The Romish zealots of Canada burned for the conversion of the heathen; their heretic rivals were fired with no such ardor. And finally while the ambition of France grasped at empire over the farthest deserts of the west, the steady industry of the English colonists was contented to cultivate and improve a narrow strip of seaboard. Thus it happened that the farmer of Massachusetts and the Virginian planter were conversant with only a few bordering tribes, while the priests and emissaries of France were roaming the prairies with the buffalo-hunting Pawnees, or lodging in the winter cabins of the Dahcotah; and swarms of savages, whose uncouth names were strange to English ears, descended yearly from the north, to bring their beaver and otter skins to the market of Montreal.

The position of Canada invited intercourse with the interior, and eminently favored her schemes of commerce and policy. The river St. Lawrence, and the chain of the great lakes, opened a vast extent of inland navigation; while their tributary streams, interlocking with the branches of the Mississippi, afforded ready access to that mighty river, and gave the restless voyager free range over half the continent. But these advantages were well nigh neutralized. Nature opened the way, but a watchful and terrible enemy guarded the portal. The forests south of Lake Ontario gave harborage to the five tribes of the Iroquois, implacable foes of Canada. They waylaid her trading parties, routed her soldiers, murdered her missionaries, and spread havoc and woe through all her settlements.

It was an evil hour for Canada, when, on the twenty-eighth of May, 1609, Samuel de Champlain, impelled by his own adventurous spirit, departed from the hamlet of Quebec to follow a war-party of Algonquins against their hated enemy, the Iroquois. Ascending the Sorel, and passing the rapids at Chambly, he embarked on the lake which bears his name, and with two French attendants, steered southward, with his savage associates, toward the rocky promontory of Ticonderoga. They moved with all the precaution of Indian warfare, when, at length, as night was closing in, they descried a band of the Iroquois in their large canoes of elm bark approaching through the gloom. Wild yells from either side announced the mutual discovery. The Iroquois hastened to the shore, and all night long the forest resounded with their discordant war-songs and fierce whoops of defiance. Day dawned, and the fight began. Bounding from tree to tree, the Iroquois pressed forward to the attack, but when Champlain advanced from among the Algonquins, and stood full in sight before them, with his strange attire, his shining breastplate, and features unlike their own,—when they saw the flash of his arquebuse, and beheld two of their chiefs fall dead,—they could not contain their terror, but fled for shelter into the depths of the wood. The Algonquins pursued, slaying many in the flight, and the victory was complete.

Such was the first collision between the white men and the Iroquois, and Champlain flattered himself that the latter had learned for the future to respect the arms of France. He was fatally deceived. The Iroquois recovered from their terrors, but they never forgave the injury, and yet it would be unjust to charge upon Champlain the origin of the desolating wars which were soon to scourge the colony. The Indians of Canada, friends and neighbors of the French, had long been harassed by inroads of the fierce confederates, and under any circumstances the French must soon have become parties to the quarrel.

Whatever may have been its origin, the war was fruitful of misery to the youthful colony. The passes were beset by ambushed war-parties. The routes between Quebec and Montreal were watched with tiger-like vigilance. Bloodthirsty warriors prowled about the outskirts of the settlements. Again and again the miserable people, driven within the palisades of their forts, looked forth upon wasted harvests and blazing roofs. The Island of Montreal was swept with fire and steel. The fur-trade was interrupted, since for months together all communication was cut off with the friendly tribes of the west. Agriculture was checked; the fields lay fallow, and frequent famine was the necessary result. The name of the Iroquois became a by-word of horror through the colony, and to the suffering Canadians they seemed troops of incarnate fiends. Revolting rites and monstrous superstitions were imputed to them; and, among the rest, it was currently believed that they cherished the custom of immolating young children, burning them, and drinking the ashes mixed with water to increase their bravery. Yet the wildest imaginations could scarcely exceed the truth. At the attack of Montreal, they placed infants over the embers, and forced the wretched mothers to turn the spit; and those who fell within their clutches endured torments too hideous for description. Their ferocity was equalled only by their courage and address.

At intervals, the afflicted colony found respite from its sufferings; and, through the efforts of the Jesuits, fair hopes began to rise of propitiating the terrible foe. At one time, the influence of the priests availed so far, that under their auspices a French colony was formed in the very heart of the Iroquois country; but the settlers were soon forced to a precipitate flight, and the war broke out afresh. The French, on their part, were not idle; they faced their assailants with characteristic gallantry. Courcelles, Tracy, De la Barre, and De Nonville invaded by turns, with various success, the forest haunts of the confederates; and at length, in the year 1696, the veteran Count Frontenac marched upon their cantons with all the force of Canada. Stemming the surges of La Chine, gliding through the romantic channels of the Thousand Islands, and over the glimmering surface of Lake Ontario, and trailing in long array up the current of the Oswego, they disembarked on the margin of the Lake of Onondaga; and, startling the woodland echoes with the clangor of their trumpets, urged their march through the mazes of the forest. Never had those solitudes beheld so strange a pageantry. The Indian allies, naked to the waist and horribly painted, adorned with streaming scalp-locks and fluttering plumes, stole crouching among the thickets, or peered with lynx-eyed vision through the labyrinths of foliage. Scouts and forest-rangers scoured the woods in front and flank of the marching columns—men trained among the hardships of the fur-trade, thin, sinewy, and strong, arrayed in wild costume of beaded moccason, scarlet leggin, and frock of buck-skin, fantastically garnished with many-colored embroidery of porcupine. Then came the levies of the colony, in gray capotes and gaudy sashes, and the trained battalions from old France in cuirass and head-piece, veterans of European wars. Plumed cavaliers were there, who had followed the standards of Condé or Turenne, and who, even in the depths of a wilderness, scorned to lay aside the martial foppery which bedecked the camp and court of Louis the Magnificent. The stern commander was borne along upon a litter in the midst, his locks bleached with years, but his eye kindling with the quenchless fire which, like a furnace, burned hottest when its fuel was almost spent. Thus, beneath the sepulchral arches of the forest, through tangled thickets, and over prostrate trunks, the aged nobleman advanced to wreak his vengeance upon empty wigwams and deserted maize-fields.

Even the fierce courage of the Iroquois began to quail before these repeated attacks, while the gradual growth of the colony, and the arrival of troops from France, at length convinced them that they could not destroy Canada. With the opening of the eighteenth century, their rancor showed signs of abating; and in the year 1726, by dint of skilful intrigue, the French succeeded in establishing a permanent military post at the important pass of Niagara, within the limits of the confederacy. Meanwhile, in spite of every obstacle, the power of France had rapidly extended its boundaries in the west. French influence diffused itself through a thousand channels, among distant tribes, hostile, for the most part, to the domineering Iroquois. Forts, mission-houses, and armed trading stations secured the principal passes. Traders, and coureurs de bois pushed their adventurous traffic into the wildest deserts; and French guns and hatchets, French beads and cloth, French tobacco and brandy, were known from where the stunted Esquimaux burrowed in their snow caves, to where the Camanches scoured the plains of the south with their banditti cavalry. Still this far-extended commerce continued to advance westward. In 1738, La Verandrye essayed to reach those mysterious mountains which, as the Indians alleged, lay beyond the arid deserts of the Missouri and the Saskatchawan. Indian hostility defeated his enterprise, but not before he had struck far out into these unknown wilds, and formed a line of trading posts, one of which, Fort de la Reine, was planted on the Assinniboin, a hundred leagues beyond Lake Winnipeg. At that early period, France left her footsteps upon the dreary wastes which even now have no other tenants than the Indian buffalo-hunter or the roving trapper.

The fur-trade of the English colonists opposed but feeble rivalry to that of their hereditary foes. At an early period, favored by the friendship of the Iroquois, they attempted to open a traffic with the Algonquin tribes of the great lakes; and in the year 1687, Major McGregory ascended with a boat-load of goods to Lake Huron, where his appearance excited great commotion, and where he was seized and imprisoned by the French. From this time forward, the English fur-trade languished, until the year 1725, when Governor Burnet, of New York, established a post on Lake Ontario, at the mouth of the river Oswego; whither, lured by the cheapness and excellence of the English goods, crowds of savages soon congregated from every side, to the unspeakable annoyance of the French. Meanwhile, a considerable commerce was springing up with the Cherokees and other tribes of the south; and during the first half of the century, the people of Pennsylvania began to cross the Alleghanies, and carry on a lucrative traffic with the tribes of the Ohio. In 1749, La Jonquière, the Governor of Canada, learned, to his great indignation, that several English traders had reached Sandusky, and were exerting a bad influence upon the Indians of that quarter; and two years later, he caused four of the intruders to be seized near the Ohio, and sent prisoners to Canada.

These early efforts of the English, considerable as they were, can ill bear comparison with the vast extent of the French interior commerce. In respect also to missionary enterprise, and the political influence resulting from it, the French had every advantage over rivals whose zeal for conversion was neither kindled by fanaticism nor fostered by an ambitious government. Eliot labored within call of Boston, while the heroic Brebeuf faced the ghastly perils of the western wilderness; and the wanderings of Brainerd sink into insignificance compared with those of the devoted Rasles. Yet, in judging the relative merits of the Romish and Protestant missionaries, it must not be forgotten that while the former contented themselves with sprinkling a few drops of water on the forehead of the proselyte, the latter sought to wean him from his barbarism and penetrate his savage heart with the truths of Christianity.

In respect, also, to direct political influence, the advantage was wholly on the side of France. The English colonies, broken into separate governments, were incapable of exercising a vigorous and consistent Indian policy; and the measures of one government often clashed with those of another. Even in the separate provinces, the popular nature of the constitution and the quarrels of governors and assemblies were unfavorable to efficient action; and this was more especially the case in the province of New York, where the vicinity of the Iroquois rendered strenuous yet prudent measures of the utmost importance. The powerful confederates, hating the French with bitter enmity, naturally inclined to the English alliance; and a proper treatment would have secured their firm and lasting friendship. But, at the early periods of her history, the assembly of New York was made up in great measure of narrow-minded men, more eager to consult their own petty interests than to pursue any far-sighted scheme of public welfare. Other causes conspired to injure the British interest in this quarter. The annual present sent from England to the Iroquois was often embezzled by corrupt governors or their favorites. The proud chiefs were disgusted by the cold and haughty bearing of the English officials, and a pernicious custom prevailed of conducting Indian negotiations through the medium of the fur-traders, a class of men held in contempt by the Iroquois, and known among them by the significant title of "rum carriers." In short, through all the counsels of the province Indian affairs were grossly and madly neglected.

With more or less emphasis, the same remark holds true of all the other English colonies. With those of France, it was far otherwise; and this difference between the rival powers was naturally incident to their different forms of government, and different conditions of development. France labored with eager diligence to conciliate the Indians and win them to espouse her cause. Her agents were busy in every village, studying the language of the inmates, complying with their usages, flattering their prejudices, caressing them, cajoling them, and whispering friendly warnings in their ears against the wicked designs of the English. When a party of Indian chiefs visited a French fort, they were greeted with the firing of cannon and rolling of drums; they were regaled at the tables of the officers, and bribed with medals and decorations, scarlet uniforms and French flags. Far wiser than their rivals, the French never ruffled the self-complacent dignity of their guests, never insulted their religious notions, nor ridiculed their ancient customs. They met the savage half way, and showed an abundant readiness to mould their own features after his likeness. Count Frontenac himself, plumed and painted like an Indian chief, danced the war-dance and yelled the war-song at the camp-fires of his delighted allies. It would have been well had the French been less exact in their imitations, for at times they copied their model with infamous fidelity, and fell into excesses scarcely credible but for the concurrent testimony of their own writers. Frontenac caused an Iroquois prisoner to be burnt alive to strike terror into his countrymen; and Louvigny, French commandant at Michillimackinac, in 1695, tortured an Iroquois ambassador to death, that he might break off a negotiation between that people and the Wyandots. Nor are these the only well-attested instances of such execrable inhumanity. But if the French were guilty of these cruelties against their Indian enemies, they were no less guilty of unworthy compliance with the demands of their Indian friends, in cases where Christianity and civilization would have dictated a prompt refusal. Even Montcalm stained his bright name by abandoning the hapless defenders of Oswego and William Henry to the tender mercies of an Indian mob.

In general, however, the Indian policy of the French cannot be charged with obsequiousness. Complaisance was tempered with dignity. At an early period, they discerned the peculiarities of the native character, and clearly saw that while on the one hand it was necessary to avoid giving offence, it was not less necessary on the other to assume a bold demeanor and a show of power; to caress with one hand, and grasp a drawn sword with the other. Every crime against a Frenchman was promptly chastised by the sharp agency of military law; while among the English, the offender could only be reached through the medium of the civil courts, whose delays, uncertainties and evasions excited the wonder and provoked the contempt of the Indians.

It was by observance of the course indicated above, that the French were enabled to maintain themselves in small detached posts, far aloof from the parent colony, and environed by barbarous tribes where an English garrison would have been cut off in a twelvemonth. They professed to hold these posts, not in their own right, but purely through the grace and condescension of the surrounding savages; and by this conciliating assurance they sought to make good their position, until, with their growing strength, conciliation should no more be needed.

In its efforts to win the friendship and alliance of the Indian tribes, the French government found every advantage in the peculiar character of its subjects—that pliant and plastic temper which forms so marked a contrast to the stubborn spirit of the Englishman. From the beginning, the French showed a tendency to amalgamate with the forest tribes. "The manners of the savages," writes the Baron La Hontan, "are perfectly agreeable to my palate;" and many a restless adventurer of high or low degree might have echoed the words of the erratic soldier. At first, great hopes were entertained that, by the mingling of French and Indians, the latter would be won over to civilization and the church; but the effect was precisely the reverse; for, as Charlevoix observes, the savages did not become French, but the French became savages. Hundreds betook themselves to the forest, never more to return. These outflowings of French civilization were merged in the waste of barbarism, as a river is lost in the sands of the desert. The wandering Frenchman chose a wife or a concubine among his Indian friends; and, in a few generations, scarcely a tribe of the west was free from an infusion of Celtic blood. The French empire in America could exhibit among its subjects every shade of color from white to red, every gradation of culture from the highest civilization of Paris to the rudest barbarism of the wigwam.

The fur-trade engendered a peculiar class of men, known by the appropriate name of bush-rangers, or coureurs de bois, half-civilized vagrants, whose chief vocation was conducting the canoes of the traders along the lakes and rivers of the interior; many of them, however, shaking loose every tie of blood and kindred, identified themselves with the Indians, and sank into utter barbarism. In many a squalid camp among the plains and forests of the west, the traveller would have encountered men owning the blood and speaking the language of France, yet, in their swarthy visages and barbarous costume, seeming more akin to those with whom they had cast their lot. The renegade of civilization caught the habits and imbibed the prejudices of his chosen associates. He loved to decorate his long hair with eagle feathers, to make his face hideous with vermilion, ochre, and soot, and to adorn his greasy hunting-frock with horse-hair fringes. His dwelling, if he had one, was a wigwam. He lounged on a bear-skin while his squaw boiled his venison and lighted his pipe. In hunting, in dancing, in singing, in taking a scalp, he rivalled the genuine Indian. His mind was tinctured with the superstitions of the forest. He had faith in the magic drum of the conjuror; he was not sure that a thunder cloud could not be frightened away by whistling at it through the wing bone of an eagle; he carried the tail of a rattlesnake in his bullet pouch by way of amulet; and he placed implicit trust in his dreams. This class of men is not yet extinct. In the cheerless wilds beyond the northern lakes, or among the mountain solitudes of the distant west, they may still be found, unchanged in life and character since the day when Louis the Great claimed sovereignty over this desert empire.

The borders of the English colonies displayed no such phenomena of mingling races; for here a thorny and impracticable barrier divided the white man from the red. The English fur-traders, and the rude men in their employ, showed it is true an ample alacrity to fling off the restraints of civilization; but though they became barbarians, they did not become Indians; and scorn on the one side and hatred on the other still marked the intercourse of the hostile races. With the settlers of the frontier it was much the same. Rude, fierce and contemptuous, they daily encroached upon the hunting-grounds of the Indians, and then paid them for the injury with curses and threats. Thus the native population shrank back from before the English, as from before an advancing pestilence; while, on the other hand, in the very heart of Canada, Indian communities sprang up, cherished by the government, and favored by the easy-tempered people. At Lorette, at Caughnawaga, at St. Francis, and elsewhere within the province, large bands were gathered together, consisting in part of fugitives from the borders of the hated English, and aiding in time of war to swell the forces of the French in repeated forays against the settlements of New York and New England.

There was one of the English provinces marked out from among the rest by the peculiar character of its founders, and by the course of conduct which was there pursued towards the Indian tribes. William Penn, his mind warmed with a broad philanthropy, and enlightened by liberal views of human government and human rights, planted on the banks of the Delaware the colony which, vivified by the principles it embodied, grew into the great commonwealth of Pennsylvania. Penn's treatment of the Indians was equally prudent and humane, and its results were of high advantage to the colony; but these results have been exaggerated, and the treatment which produced them made the theme of inordinate praise. It required no great benevolence to urge the Quakers to deal kindly with their savage neighbors. They were bound in common sense to propitiate them; since, by incurring their resentment, they would involve themselves in the dilemma of submitting their necks to the tomahawk, or wielding the carnal weapon, in glaring defiance of their pacific principles. In paying the Indians for the lands which his colonists occupied,—a piece of justice which has been greeted with a general clamor of applause,—Penn, as he himself confesses, acted on the prudent counsel of Compton, Bishop of London. Nor is there any truth in the representations of Raynal and other eulogists of the Quaker legislator, who hold him up to the world as the only European who ever acquired Indian lands by purchase, instead of seizing them by fraud or violence. The example of purchase had been set fifty years before by the Puritans of New England; and several of the other colonies had more recently pursued the same just and prudent course.

With regard to the alleged results of the pacific conduct of the Quakers, our admiration will diminish on closely viewing the circumstances of the case. The position of the colony was a most fortunate one. Had the Quakers planted their colony on the banks of the St. Lawrence, or among the warlike tribes of New England, their shaking of hands and assurances of tender regard would not long have availed to save them from the visitations of the scalping-knife. But the Delawares, the people on whose territory they had settled, were like themselves debarred the use of arms. The Iroquois had conquered them, disarmed them, and forced them to adopt the opprobrious name of women. The humble Delawares were but too happy to receive the hand extended to them, and dwell in friendship with their pacific neighbors; since to have lifted the hatchet would have brought upon their heads the vengeance of their conquerors, whose good will Penn had taken pains to secure.

The sons of Penn, his successors in the proprietorship of the province, did not evince the same kindly feeling towards the Indians which had distinguished their father. Earnest to acquire new lands, they commenced through their agents a series of unjust measures, which gradually alienated the Indians, and, after a peace of seventy years, produced a disastrous rupture. The Quaker population of the colony sympathized in the kindness which its founder had cherished towards the benighted race. This feeling was strengthened by years of friendly intercourse; and except where private interest was concerned, the Quakers made good their reiterated professions of attachment. Kindness to the Indian was the glory of their sect. As years wore on, this feeling was wonderfully reënforced by the influence of party spirit. The time arrived when, alienated by English encroachment on the one hand and French seduction on the other, the Indians began to assume a threatening attitude towards the province; and many voices urged the necessity of a resort to arms. This measure, repugnant alike to their pacific principles and to their love of the Indians, was strenuously opposed by the Quakers. Their affection for the injured race was now inflamed into a sort of benevolent fanaticism. The more rabid of the sect would scarcely confess that an Indian could ever do wrong. In their view, he was always sinned against, always the innocent victim of injury and abuse; and in the days of the final rupture, when the woods were full of furious war-parties, and the German and Irish settlers on the frontier were butchered by hundreds; when the western sky was darkened with the smoke of burning settlements, and the wretched fugitives were flying in crowds across the Susquehanna, a large party among the Quaker, secure by their Philadelphia firesides, could not see the necessity of waging even a defensive war against their favorite people.

The encroachments on the part of the proprietors, which have been alluded to above, and which many of the Quakers viewed with disapproval, consisted in the fraudulent interpretation of Indian deeds of conveyance, and in the granting out of lands without any conveyance at all. The most notorious of these transactions, and the one most lamentable in its results, was commenced in the year 1737, and was known by the name of the walking purchase. An old, forgotten deed was raked out of the dust of the previous century; a deed which was in itself of doubtful validity, and which had been virtually cancelled by a subsequent agreement. On this rotten title the proprietors laid claim to a valuable tract of land on the right bank of the Delaware. Its western boundary was to be defined by a line drawn from a certain point on Neshaminey Creek, in a north-westerly direction, as far as a man could walk in a day and a half. From the end of the walk, a line drawn eastward to the river Delaware was to form the northern limit of the purchase. The proprietors sought out the most active men who could be heard of, and put them in training for the walk; at the same time laying out a smooth road along the intended course, that no obstructions might mar their speed. By this means an incredible distance was accomplished within the limited time. And now it only remained to adjust the northern boundary. Instead of running the line directly to the Delaware, according to the evident meaning of the deed, the proprietors inclined it so far to the north as to form an acute angle with the river, and enclose many hundred thousand acres of valuable land, which would otherwise have remained in the hands of the Indians. The land thus obtained lay in the Forks of the Delaware, above Easton, and was then occupied by a powerful branch of the Delawares, who, to their amazement, now heard the summons to quit for ever their populous village and fields of half-grown maize. In rage and distress they refused to obey, and the proprietors were in a perplexing dilemma. Force was necessary; but a Quaker legislature would never consent to fight, and especially to fight against Indians. An expedient was hit upon, at once safe and effectual. The Iroquois were sent for. A deputation of their chiefs appeared at Philadelphia, and having been well bribed, and deceived by false accounts of the transaction, they consented to remove the refractory Delawares. The delinquents were summoned before their conquerors, and the Iroquois orator, Canassatego, a man of tall stature and imposing presence, looking with a grim countenance on his cowering auditors, addressed them in the following words:—

"You ought to be taken by the hair of the head and shaken soundly till you recover your senses. You don't know what you are doing. Our brother Onas's cause is very just. On the other hand, your cause is bad, and you are bent to break the chain of friendship. How came you to take upon you to sell land at all? We conquered you; we made women of you; you know you are women, and can no more sell land than women. This land you claim is gone down your throats; you have been furnished with clothes, meat, and drink, by the goods paid you for it, and now you want it again, like children as you are. What makes you sell land in the dark? Did you ever tell us you had sold this land? Did we ever receive any part, even the value of a pipe-shank, from you for it? We charge you to remove instantly; we don't give you the liberty to think about it. You are women. Take the advice of a wise man and remove immediately. You may return to the other side of Delaware, where you came from; but we do not know whether, considering how you have demeaned yourselves, you will be permitted to live there; or whether you have not swallowed that land down your throats as well as the land on this side. We therefore assign you two places to go, either to Wyoming or Shamokin. We shall then have you more under our eye, and shall see how you behave. Don't deliberate, but take this belt of wampum, and go at once."

The unhappy Delawares dared not disobey. They left their ancient homes, and removed, as they had been ordered, to the Susquehanna, where some settled at Shamokin, and some at Wyoming. From an early period, the Indians had been annoyed by the unlicensed intrusion of settlers upon their lands, and, in 1728, they had bitterly complained of the wrong. The evil continued to increase. Many families, chiefly German and Irish, began to cross the Susquehanna and build their cabins along the valleys of the Juniata and its tributary waters. The Delawares sent frequent remonstrances from their new abodes, and the Iroquois themselves made angry complaints, declaring that the lands of the Juniata were theirs by right of conquest, and that they had given them to their cousins, the Delawares, for hunting-grounds. Some efforts at redress were made; but the remedy proved ineffectual, and the discontent of the Indians increased with every year. The Shawanoes, with many of the Delawares, removed westward, where for a time they would be safe from intrusion; and by the middle of the century, the Delaware tribe was separated into two divisions, one of which remained upon the Susquehanna, while the other, in conjunction with the Shawanoes, dwelt on the waters of the Alleghany and the Muskingum.

But now the French began to push their advanced posts into the valley of the Ohio. Unhappily for the English interest, they found the irritated minds of the Indians in a state which favored their efforts at seduction, and held forth a flattering promise that tribes so long faithful to the English might soon be won over to the cause of France.

While the English interests wore so inauspicious an aspect in this quarter, their prospects were not much better among the Iroquois. Since the peace of Utrecht, in 1713, these powerful tribes had so far forgotten their old malevolence against the French, that the latter were enabled to bring all their machinery of conciliation to bear upon them. They turned the opportunity to such good account, as not only to smooth away the asperity of the ancient grudge, but also to rouse in the minds of their former foes a growing jealousy against the English. Several accidental circumstances did much to aggravate this feeling. The Iroquois were in the habit of sending out frequent war-parties against their enemies, the Cherokees and Catawbas, who dwelt near the borders of Carolina and Virginia; and in these forays the invaders often became so seriously embroiled with the white settlers, that sharp frays took place, and an open war seemed likely to ensue.

It was with great difficulty that the irritation caused by these untoward accidents was allayed; and even then enough remained in the neglect of governments, the insults of traders, and the haughty bearing of officials, to disgust the proud confederates with their English allies. In the war of 1745, they yielded but cold and doubtful aid; and fears were entertained of their final estrangement. This result became still more imminent, when, in the year 1749, the French priest Picquet established his mission of La Présentation on the St. Lawrence, at the site of Ogdensburg. This pious father, like the martial churchmen of an earlier day, deemed it no scandal to gird on earthly armor against the enemies of the faith. He built a fort and founded a settlement; he mustered the Indians about him from far and near, organized their governments, and marshalled their war-parties. From the crenelled walls of his mission-house the warlike apostle could look forth upon a military colony of his own creating, upon farms and clearings, white Canadian cabins, and the bark lodges of Indian hordes which he had gathered under his protecting wing. A chief object of the settlement was to form a barrier against the English; but the purpose dearest to the missionary's heart was to gain over the Iroquois to the side of France; and in this he succeeded so well, that, as a writer of good authority declares, the number of their warriors within the circle of his influence surpassed the whole remaining force of the confederacy.

Thoughtful men in the English colonies saw with anxiety the growing defection of the Iroquois, and dreaded lest, in the event of a war with France, her ancient foes might now be found her friends. But in this ominous conjuncture, one strong influence was at work to bind the confederates to their old alliance; and this influence was wielded by a man so remarkable in his character, and so conspicuous an actor in the scenes of the ensuing history, as to demand at least some passing notice.

About the year 1734, in consequence it is said of the hapless issue of a love affair, William Johnson, a young Irishman, came over to America at the age of nineteen, where he assumed the charge of an extensive tract of wild land in the province of New York, belonging to his uncle, Admiral Sir Peter Warren. Settling in the valley of the Mohawk, he carried on a prosperous traffic with the Indians; and while he rapidly rose to wealth, he gained, at the same time, an extraordinary influence over the neighboring Iroquois. As his resources increased, he built two mansions in the valley, known respectively by the names of Johnson Castle and Johnson Hall, the latter of which, a well-constructed building of wood and stone, is still standing in the village of Johnstown. Johnson Castle was situated at some distance higher up the river. Both were fortified against attack, and the latter was surrounded with cabins built for the reception of the Indians, who often came in crowds to visit the proprietor, invading his dwelling at all unseasonable hours, loitering in the doorways, spreading their blankets in the passages, and infecting the air with the fumes of stale tobacco.

Johnson supplied the place of his former love by a young Dutch damsel, who bore him several children; and, in justice to them, he married her upon her death-bed. Soon afterwards he found another favorite in the person of Molly Brant, sister of the celebrated Mohawk war-chief, whose black eyes and laughing face caught his fancy, as, fluttering with ribbons, she galloped past him at a muster of the Tryon county militia.

Johnson's importance became so conspicuous, that when the French war broke out in 1755, he was made a major-general; and, soon after, the colonial troops under his command gained the battle of Lake George against the French forces of Baron Dieskau. For this success, for which however he was entitled to little credit, he was raised to the rank of baronet, and rewarded with a gift of five thousand pounds from the king. About this time, he was appointed superintendent of Indian affairs for the northern tribes, a station in which he did signal service to the country. In 1759, when General Prideaux was killed by the bursting of a cohorn in the trenches before Niagara, Johnson succeeded to his command, routed the French in another pitched battle, and soon raised the red cross of England on the ramparts of the fort. After the peace of 1763, he lived for many years at Johnson Hall, constantly enriched by the increasing value of his vast estate, and surrounded by a hardy Highland tenantry, devoted to his interests; but when the tempest which had long been brewing seemed at length about to break, and signs of a speedy rupture with the mother country thickened with every day, he stood wavering in an agony of indecision, divided between his loyalty to the sovereign who was the source of all his honors, and his reluctance to become the agent of a murderous Indian warfare against his countrymen and friends. His final resolution was never taken. In the summer of 1774, he was attacked with a sudden illness, and died within a few hours, in the sixtieth year of his age, hurried to his grave by mental distress, or, as many believed, by the act of his own hand.

Nature had well fitted him for the position in which his propitious stars had cast his lot. His person was tall, erect, and strong; his features grave and manly. His direct and upright dealings, his courage, eloquence, and address, were sure passports to favor in Indian eyes. He had a singular facility of adaptation. In the camp, or at the council-board, in spite of his defective education, he bore himself as became his station; but at home he was seen drinking flip and smoking tobacco with the Dutch boors, his neighbors, and talking of improvements or the price of beaver-skins; while in the Indian villages he would feast on dog's flesh, dance with the warriors, and harangue his attentive auditors with all the dignity of an Iroquois sachem. His temper was genial; he encouraged rustic sports, and was respected and beloved alike by whites and Indians.

His good qualities, however, were alloyed with serious defects. His mind was as coarse as it was vigorous; he was vain of his rank and influence, and being quite free from any scruple of delicacy, he lost no opportunity of proclaiming them. His nature was eager and ambitious; and in pushing his own way, he was never distinguished by an anxious solicitude for the rights of others.

At the time of which we speak, his fortunes had not reached their zenith; yet his influence was great; and during the war of 1745, when he held the chief control of Indian affairs in New York, it was exercised in a manner most beneficial to the province. After the peace of Aix la Chapelle, in 1748, finding his measures ill supported, he threw up his office in disgust. Still his mere personal influence sufficed to embarrass the intrigues of the busy priest at La Présentation; and a few years later, when the public exigency demanded his utmost efforts, he resumed, under better auspices, the official management of Indian affairs.

And now, when the blindest could see that between the rival claimants to the soil of America nothing was left but the arbitration of the sword, no man friendly to the cause of England could observe without alarm how France had strengthened herself in Indian alliances. The Iroquois, it is true, had not quite gone over to her side; nor had the Delawares wholly forgotten their ancient league with William Penn. The Miamis, too, in the valley of the Ohio, had lately taken umbrage at the conduct of the French, and betrayed a leaning to the side of England, while several tribes of the south showed a similar disposition. But, with few and slight exceptions, the numerous tribes of the great lakes and the Mississippi, besides a host of domiciliated savages in Canada itself, stood ready at the bidding of France to grind their tomahawks and turn loose their ravenous war-parties; while the British colonists had too much reason to fear that even those tribes which seemed most friendly to their cause, and which formed the sole barrier of their unprotected borders, might, at the first sound of the war-whoop, be found in arms against them.

COLLISION OF THE RIVAL COLONIES

1700 to 1755

The people of the northern English colonies had learned to regard their Canadian neighbors with the bitterest enmity. With them, the very name of Canada called up horrible recollections and ghastly images: the midnight massacre of Schenectady, and the desolation of many a New England hamlet; blazing dwellings and reeking scalps; and children snatched from their mothers' arms, to be immured in convents and trained up in the abominations of Popery. To the sons of the Puritans, their enemy was doubly odious. They hated him as a Frenchman, and they hated him as a Papist. Hitherto he had waged his murderous warfare from a distance, wasting their settlements with rapid onsets, fierce and transient as a summer storm; but now, with enterprising audacity, he was intrenching himself on their very borders. The English hunter, in the lonely wilderness of Vermont, as by the warm glow of sunset he piled the spruce boughs for his woodland bed, started as a deep, low sound struck faintly on his ear, the evening gun of Fort Frederic, booming over lake and forest. The erection of this fort, better known among the English as Crown Point, was a piece of daring encroachment which justly kindled resentment in the northern colonies. But it was not here that the immediate occasion of a final rupture was to arise. By an article of the treaty of Utrecht, confirmed by that of Aix la Chapelle, Acadia had been ceded to England; but scarcely was the latter treaty signed, when debates sprang up touching the limits of the ceded province. Commissioners were named on either side to adjust the disputed boundary; but the claims of the rival powers proved utterly irreconcilable, and all negotiation was fruitless. Meantime, the French and English forces in Acadia began to assume a belligerent attitude, and indulge their ill blood in mutual aggression and reprisal. But while this game was played on the coasts of the Atlantic, interests of far greater moment were at stake in the west.

The people of the middle colonies, placed by their local position beyond reach of the French, had heard with great composure of the sufferings of their New England brethren, and felt little concern at a danger so doubtful and remote. There were those among them, however, who with greater foresight had been quick to perceive the ambitious projects of the rival nation; and, as early as 1716, Spotswood, governor of Virginia, had urged the expediency of securing the valley of the Ohio by a series of forts and settlements. His proposal was coldly received, and his plan fell to the ground. The time at length was come when the danger was approaching too near to be slighted longer. In 1748, an association, called the Ohio Company, was formed with the view of making settlements in the region beyond the Alleghanies; and two years later, Gist, the company's surveyor, to the great disgust of the Indians, carried chain and compass down the Ohio as far as the falls at Louisville. But so dilatory were the English, that before any effectual steps were taken, their agile enemies appeared upon the scene.

In the spring of 1753, the middle provinces were startled at the tidings that French troops had crossed Lake Erie, fortified themselves at the point of Presqu' Isle, and pushed forward to the northern branches of the Ohio. Upon this, Governor Dinwiddie, of Virginia, resolved to despatch a message requiring their removal from territories which he claimed as belonging to the British crown; and looking about him for the person best qualified to act as messenger, he made choice of George Washington, a young man twenty-one years of age, adjutant general of the Virginian militia.

Washington departed on his mission, crossed the mountains, descended to the bleak and leafless valley of the Ohio, and thence continued his journey up the banks of the Alleghany until the fourth of December. On that day he reached Venango, an Indian town on the Alleghany, at the mouth of French Creek. Here was the advanced post of the French; and here, among the Indian log cabins and huts of bark, he saw their flag flying above the house of an English trader, whom the military intruders had unceremoniously ejected. They gave the young envoy a hospitable reception, and referred him to the commanding officer, whose headquarters were at Le Bœuf, a fort which they had just built on French Creek, some distance above Venango. Thither Washington repaired, and on his arrival was received with stately courtesy by the officer, Legardeur de St. Pierre, whom he describes as an elderly gentleman of very soldier-like appearance. To the message of Dinwiddie, St. Pierre replied that he would forward it to the governor general of Canada; but that, in the mean time, his orders were to hold possession of the country, and this he should do to the best of his ability. With this answer Washington, through all the rigors of the midwinter forest, retraced his steps, with one attendant, to the English borders.

With the first opening of spring, a newly raised company of Virginian backwoodsmen, under Captain Trent, hastened across the mountains, and began to build a fort at the confluence of the Monongahela and Alleghany, where Pittsburg now stands; when suddenly they found themselves invested by a host of French and Indians, who, with sixty bateaux and three hundred canoes, had descended from Le Bœuf and Venango. The English were ordered to evacuate the spot; and, being quite unable to resist, they obeyed the summons, and withdrew in great discomfiture towards Virginia. Meanwhile Washington, with another party of backwoodsmen, was advancing from the borders; and, hearing of Trent's disaster, he resolved to fortify himself on the Monongahela, and hold his ground, if possible, until fresh troops could arrive to support him. The French sent out a scouting party under M. Jumonville, with the design, probably, of watching his movements; but, on a dark and stormy night, Washington surprised them, as they lay lurking in a rocky glen not far from his camp, killed the officer, and captured the whole detachment. Learning that the French, enraged by this reverse, were about to attack him in great force, he thought it prudent to fall back, and retired accordingly to a spot called the Great Meadows, where he had before thrown up a slight intrenchment. Here he found himself assailed by nine hundred French and Indians, commanded by a brother of the slain Jumonville. From eleven in the morning till eight at night, the backwoodsmen, who were half famished from the failure of their stores, maintained a stubborn defence, some fighting within the intrenchment, and some on the plain without. In the evening, the French sounded a parley, and offered terms. They were accepted, and on the following day Washington and his men retired across the mountains, leaving the disputed territory in the hands of the French.

While the rival nations were beginning to quarrel for a prize which belonged to neither of them, the unhappy Indians saw, with alarm and amazement, their lands becoming a bone of contention between rapacious strangers. The first appearance of the French on the Ohio excited the wildest fears in the tribes of that quarter, among whom were those who, disgusted by the encroachments of the Pennsylvanians, had fled to these remote retreats to escape the intrusions of the white men. Scarcely was their fancied asylum gained, when they saw themselves invaded by a host of armed men from Canada. Thus placed between two fires, they knew not which way to turn. There was no union in their counsels, and they seemed like a mob of bewildered children. Their native jealousy was roused to its utmost pitch. Many of them thought that the two white nations had conspired to destroy them, and then divide their lands. "You and the French," said one of them, a few years afterwards, to an English emissary, "are like the two edges of a pair of shears, and we are the cloth which is cut to pieces between them."

The French labored hard to conciliate them, plying them with gifts and flatteries, and proclaiming themselves their champions against the English. At first, these arts seemed in vain, but their effect soon began to declare itself; and this effect was greatly increased by a singular piece of infatuation on the part of the proprietors of Pennsylvania. During the summer of 1754, delegates of the several provinces met at Albany, to concert measures of defence in the war which now seemed inevitable. It was at this meeting that the memorable plan of a union of the colonies was brought forward; a plan, the fate of which was curious and significant, for the crown rejected it as giving too much power to the people, and the people as giving too much power to the crown. A council was also held with the Iroquois, and though they were found but lukewarm in their attachment to the English, a treaty of friendship and alliance was concluded with their deputies. It would have been well if the matter had ended here; but, with ill-timed rapacity, the proprietary agents of Pennsylvania took advantage of this great assemblage of sachems to procure from them the grant of extensive tracts, including the lands inhabited by the very tribes whom the French were at that moment striving to seduce. When they heard that, without their consent, their conquerors and tyrants, the Iroquois, had sold the soil from beneath their feet, their indignation was extreme; and, convinced that there was no limit to English encroachment, many of them from that hour became fast allies of the French.

The courts of London and Versailles still maintained a diplomatic intercourse, both protesting their earnest wish that their conflicting claims might be adjusted by friendly negotiation; but while each disclaimed the intention of hostility, both were hastening to prepare for war. Early in 1755, an English fleet sailed from Cork, having on board two regiments destined for Virginia, and commanded by General Braddock; and soon after, a French fleet put to sea from the port of Brest, freighted with munitions of war and a strong body of troops under Baron Dieskau, an officer who had distinguished himself in the campaigns of Marshal Saxe. The English fleet gained its destination, and landed its troops in safety. The French were less fortunate. Two of their ships, the Lys and the Alcide, became involved in the fogs of the banks of Newfoundland; and when the weather cleared, they found themselves under the guns of a superior British force, belonging to the squadron of Admiral Boscawen, sent out for the express purpose of intercepting them. "Are we at peace or war?" demanded the French commander. A broadside from the Englishman soon solved his doubts, and after a stout resistance the French struck their colors. News of the capture caused great excitement in England, but the conduct of the aggressors was generally approved; and under pretence that the French had begun the war by their alleged encroachments in America, orders were issued for a general attack upon their marine. So successful were the British cruisers, that, before the end of the year, three hundred French vessels and nearly eight thousand sailors were captured and brought into port. The French, unable to retort in kind, raised an outcry of indignation, and Mirepoix their ambassador withdrew from the court of London.

Thus began that memorable war which, kindling among the forests of America, scattered its fires over the kingdoms of Europe, and the sultry empire of the Great Mogul; the war made glorious by the heroic death of Wolfe, the victories of Frederic, and the exploits of Clive; the war which controlled the destinies of America, and was first in the chain of events which led on to her Revolution with all its vast and undeveloped consequences. On the old battle-ground of Europe, the contest bore the same familiar features of violence and horror which had marked the strife of former generations—fields ploughed by the cannon ball, and walls shattered by the exploding mine, sacked towns and blazing suburbs, the lamentations of women, and the license of a maddened soldiery. But in America, war assumed a new and striking aspect. A wilderness was its sublime arena. Army met army under the shadows of primeval woods; their cannon resounded over wastes unknown to civilized man. And before the hostile powers could join in battle, endless forests must be traversed, and morasses passed, and everywhere the axe of the pioneer must hew a path for the bayonet of the soldier.

Before the declaration of war, and before the breaking off of negotiations between the courts of France and England, the English ministry formed the plan of assailing the French in America on all sides at once, and repelling them, by one bold push, from all their encroachments. A provincial army was to advance upon Acadia, a second was to attack Crown Point, and a third Niagara; while the two regiments which had lately arrived in Virginia under General Braddock, aided by a strong body of provincials, were to dislodge the French from their newly-built fort of Du Quesne. To Braddock was assigned the chief command of all the British forces in America; and a person worse fitted for the office could scarcely have been found. His experience had been ample, and none could doubt his courage; but he was profligate, arrogant, perverse, and a bigot to military rules. On his first arrival in Virginia, he called together the governors of the several provinces, in order to explain his instructions and adjust the details of the projected operations. These arrangements complete, Braddock advanced to the borders of Virginia, and formed his camp at Fort Cumberland, where he spent several weeks in training the raw backwoodsmen, who joined him, into such discipline as they seemed capable of; in collecting horses and wagons, which could only be had with the utmost difficulty; in railing at the contractors, who scandalously cheated him; and in venting his spleen by copious abuse of the country and the people. All at length was ready, and early in June, 1755, the army left civilization behind, and struck into the broad wilderness as a squadron puts out to sea.

It was no easy task to force their way over that rugged ground, covered with an unbroken growth of forest; and the difficulty was increased by the needless load of baggage which encumbered their march. The crash of falling trees resounded in the front, where a hundred axemen labored with ceaseless toil to hew a passage for the army. The horses strained their utmost strength to drag the ponderous wagons over roots and stumps, through gullies and quagmires; and the regular troops were daunted by the depth and gloom of the forest which hedged them in on either hand, and closed its leafy arches above their heads. So tedious was their progress, that, by the advice of Washington, twelve hundred chosen men moved on in advance with the lighter baggage and artillery, leaving the rest of the army to follow, by slower stages, with the heavy wagons. On the eighth of July, the advanced body reached the Monongahela, at a point not far distant from Fort du Quesne. The rocky and impracticable ground on the eastern side debarred their passage, and the general resolved to cross the river in search of a smoother path, and recross it a few miles lower down, in order to gain the fort. The first passage was easily made, and the troops moved, in glittering array, down the western margin of the water, rejoicing that their goal was well nigh reached, and the hour of their expected triumph close at hand.

Scouts and Indian runners had brought the tidings of Braddock's approach to the French at Fort du Quesne. Their dismay was great, and Contrecœur, the commander, thought only of retreat; when Beaujeu, a captain in the garrison, made the bold proposal of leading out a party of French and Indians to waylay the English in the woods, and harass or interrupt their march. The offer was accepted, and Beaujeu hastened to the Indian camps.

Around the fort and beneath the adjacent forest were the bark lodges of savage hordes, whom the French had mustered from far and near; Ojibwas and Ottawas, Hurons and Caughnawagas, Abenakis and Delawares. Beaujeu called the warriors together, flung a hatchet on the ground before them, and invited them to follow him out to battle; but the boldest stood aghast at the peril, and none would accept the challenge. A second interview took place with no better success; but the Frenchman was resolved to carry his point. "I am determined to go," he exclaimed. "What, will you suffer your father to go alone?" His daring proved contagious. The warriors hesitated no longer; and when, on the morning of the ninth of July, a scout ran in with the news that the English army was but a few miles distant, the Indian camps were at once astir with the turmoil of preparation. Chiefs harangued their yelling followers, braves bedaubed themselves with war-paint, smeared themselves with grease, hung feathers in their scalp-locks, and whooped and stamped till they had wrought themselves into a delirium of valor.

That morning, James Smith, an English prisoner recently captured on the frontier of Pennsylvania, stood on the rampart, and saw the half-frenzied multitude thronging about the gateway, where kegs of bullets and gunpowder were broken open, that each might help himself at will. Then band after band hastened away towards the forest, followed and supported by nearly two hundred and fifty French and Canadians, commanded by Beaujeu. There were the Ottawas, led on, it is said, by the remarkable man whose name stands on the title-page of this history; there were the Hurons of Lorette under their chief, whom the French called Athanase, and many more, all keen as hounds on the scent of blood. At about nine miles from the fort, they reached a spot where the narrow road descended to the river through deep and gloomy woods, and where two ravines, concealed by trees and bushes, seemed formed by nature for an ambuscade. Beaujeu well knew the ground; and it was here that he had resolved to fight; but he and his followers were well nigh too late; for as they neared the ravines, the woods were resounding with the roll of the British drums.

It was past noon of a day brightened with the clear sunlight of an American midsummer, when the forces of Braddock began, for a second time, to cross the Monongahela, at the fording-place, which to this day bears the name of their ill-fated leader. The scarlet columns of the British regulars, complete in martial appointment, the rude backwoodsmen with shouldered rifles, the trains of artillery and the white-topped wagons, moved on in long procession through the shallow current, and slowly mounted the opposing bank. Men were there whose names have become historic: Gage, who, twenty years later, saw his routed battalions recoil in disorder from before the breastwork on Bunker Hill; Gates, the future conqueror of Burgoyne; and one destined to a higher fame,—George Washington, a boy in years, a man in calm thought and self-ruling wisdom.

With steady and well ordered march, the troops advanced into the great labyrinth of woods which shadowed the eastern borders of the river. Rank after rank vanished from sight. The forest swallowed them up, and the silence of the wilderness sank down once more on the shores and waters of the Monongahela.

Several engineers and guides and six light horsemen led the way; a body of grenadiers under Gage was close behind, and the army followed in such order as the rough ground would permit, along a narrow road, twelve feet wide, tunnelled through the dense and matted foliage. There were flanking parties on either side, but no scouts to scour the woods in front, and with an insane confidence Braddock pressed on to meet his fate. The van had passed the low grounds that bordered the river, and were now ascending a gently rising ground, where, on either hand, hidden by thick trees, by tangled undergrowth and rank grasses, lay the two fatal ravines. Suddenly, Gordon, an engineer in advance, saw the French and Indians bounding forward through the forest and along the narrow track, Beaujeu leading them on, dressed in a fringed hunting-shirt, and wearing a silver gorget on his breast. He stopped, turned, and waved his hat, and his French followers, crowding across the road, opened a murderous fire upon the head of the British column, while, screeching their war-cries, the Indians thronged into the ravines, or crouched behind rocks and trees on both flanks of the advancing troops. The astonished grenadiers returned the fire, and returned it with good effect; for a random shot struck down the brave Beaujeu, and the courage of the assailants was staggered by his fall. Dumas, second in command, rallied them to the attack; and while he, with the French and Canadians, made good the pass in front, the Indians from their lurking places opened a deadly fire on the right and left. In a few moments, all was confusion. The advance guard fell back on the main body, and every trace of subordination vanished. The fire soon extended along the whole length of the army, from front to rear. Scarce an enemy could be seen, though the forest resounded with their yells; though every bush and tree was alive with incessant flashes; though the lead flew like a hailstorm, and the men went down by scores. The regular troops seemed bereft of their senses. They huddled together in the road like flocks of sheep; and happy did he think himself who could wedge his way into the midst of the crowd, and place a barrier of human flesh between his life and the shot of the ambushed marksmen. Many were seen eagerly loading their muskets, and then firing them into the air, or shooting their own comrades in the insanity of their terror. The officers, for the most part, displayed a conspicuous gallantry; but threats and commands were wasted alike on the panic-stricken multitude. It is said that at the outset Braddock showed signs of fear; but he soon recovered his wonted intrepidity. Five horses were shot under him, and five times he mounted afresh. He stormed and shouted, and, while the Virginians were fighting to good purpose, each man behind a tree, like the Indians themselves, he ordered them with furious menace to form in platoons, where the fire of the enemy mowed them down like grass. At length, a mortal shot silenced him, and two provincials bore him off the field. Washington rode through the tumult calm and undaunted. Two horses were killed under him, and four bullets pierced his clothes; but his hour was not come, and he escaped without a wound. Gates was shot through the body, and Gage also was severely wounded. Of eighty-six officers, only twenty-three remained unhurt; and of twelve hundred soldiers who crossed the Monongahela, more than seven hundred were killed and wounded. None suffered more severely than the Virginians, who had displayed throughout a degree of courage and steadiness which put the cowardice of the regulars to shame. The havoc among them was terrible, for of their whole number scarcely one-fifth left the field alive.

The slaughter lasted three hours; when, at length, the survivors, as if impelled by a general impulse, rushed tumultuously from the place of carnage, and with dastardly precipitation fled across the Monongahela. The enemy did not pursue beyond the river, flocking back to the field to collect the plunder, and gather a rich harvest of scalps. The routed troops pursued their flight until they met the rear division of the army, under Colonel Dunbar; and even then their senseless terrors did not abate. Dunbar's soldiers caught the infection. Cannon, baggage, provisions and wagons were destroyed, and all fled together, eager to escape from the shadows of those awful woods, whose horrors haunted their imagination. They passed the defenceless settlements of the border, and hurried on to Philadelphia, leaving the unhappy people to defend themselves as they might against the tomahawk and scalping-knife.

The calamities of this disgraceful rout did not cease with the loss of a few hundred soldiers on the field of battle; for it brought upon the provinces all the miseries of an Indian war. Those among the tribes who had thus far stood neutral, wavering between the French and English, now hesitated no longer. Many of them had been disgusted by the contemptuous behavior of Braddock. All had learned to despise the courage of the English, and to regard their own prowess with unbounded complacency. It is not in Indian nature to stand quiet in the midst of war; and the defeat of Braddock was a signal for the western savages to snatch their tomahawks and assail the English settlements with one accord, murdering and pillaging with ruthless fury, and turning the frontier of Pennsylvania and Virginia into one wide scene of havoc and desolation.

The three remaining expeditions which the British ministry had planned for that year's campaign were attended with various results. Acadia was quickly reduced by the forces of Colonel Monkton; but the glories of this easy victory were tarnished by an act of cruelty. Seven thousand of the unfortunate people, refusing to take the prescribed oath of allegiance, were seized by the conquerors, torn from their homes, placed on shipboard like cargoes of negro slaves, and transported to the British provinces. The expedition against Niagara was a total failure, for the troops did not even reach their destination. The movement against Crown Point met with no better success, as regards the main object of the enterprise. Owing to the lateness of the season, and other causes, the troops proceeded no farther than Lake George; but the attempt was marked by a feat of arms, which, in that day of failures, was greeted, both in England and America, as a signal victory.

General Johnson, afterwards Sir William Johnson, had been charged with the conduct of the Crown Point expedition; and his little army, a rude assemblage of hunters and farmers from New York and New England, officers and men alike ignorant of war, lay encamped at the southern extremity of Lake George. Here, while they languidly pursued their preparations, their active enemy anticipated them. Baron Dieskau, who, with a body of troops, had reached Quebec in the squadron which sailed from Brest in the spring, had intended to take forcible possession of the English fort of Oswego, erected upon ground claimed by the French as a part of Canada. Learning Johnson's movements, he changed his plan, crossed Lake Champlain, made a circuit by way of Wood Creek, and gained the rear of the English army, with a force of about two thousand French and Indians. At midnight, on the seventh of September, the tidings reached Johnson that the army of the French baron was but a few miles distant from his camp. A council of war was called, and the resolution formed of detaching a thousand men to reconnoitre. "If they are to be killed," said Hendrick, the Mohawk chief, "they are too many; if they are to fight, they are too few." His remonstrance was unheeded; and the brave old savage, unable from age and corpulence to fight on foot, mounted his horse, and joined the English detachment with two hundred of his warriors. At sunrise, the party defiled from the camp, and entering the forest disappeared from the eyes of their comrades.

Those who remained behind labored with all the energy of alarm to fortify their unprotected camp. An hour elapsed, when from the distance was heard a sudden explosion of musketry. The excited soldiers suspended their work to listen. A rattling fire succeeded, deadened among the woods, but growing louder and nearer, till none could doubt that their comrades had met the French, and were defeated.

This was indeed the case. Marching through thick woods, by the narrow and newly-cut road which led along the valley southward from Lake George, Williams, the English commander, had led his men full into an ambuscade, where all Dieskau's army lay in wait to receive them. From the woods on both sides rose an appalling shout, followed by a storm of bullets. Williams was soon shot down; Hendrick shared his fate; many officers fell, and the road was strewn with dead and wounded soldiers. The English gave way at once. Had they been regular troops, the result would have been worse; but every man was a woodsman and a hunter. Some retired in bodies along the road; while the greater part spread themselves through the forest, opposing a wide front to the enemy, fighting stubbornly as they retreated, and shooting back at the French from behind every tree or bush that could afford a cover. The Canadians and Indians pressed them closely, darting, with shrill cries, from tree to tree, while Dieskau's regulars, with steadier advance, bore all before them. Far and wide through the forest rang shout and shriek and Indian whoop, mingled with the deadly rattle of guns. Retreating and pursuing, the combatants passed northward towards the English camp, leaving the ground behind them strewn with dead and dying.

A fresh detachment from the camp came in aid of the English, and the pursuit was checked. Yet the retreating men were not the less rejoiced when they could discern, between the brown columns of the woods, the mountains and waters of Lake George, with the white tents of their encampments on its shore. The French followed no farther. The blast of their trumpets was heard recalling their scattered men for a final attack.

During the absence of Williams's detachment, the main body of the army had covered the front of their camp with a breastwork,—if that name can be applied to a row of logs,—behind which the marksmen lay flat on their faces. This preparation was not yet complete, when the defeated troops appeared issuing from the woods. Breathless and perturbed, they entered the camp, and lay down with the rest; and the army waited the attack in a frame of mind which boded ill for the result. Soon, at the edge of the woods which bordered the open space in front, painted Indians were seen, and bayonets glittered among the foliage, shining, in the homely comparison of a New-England soldier, like a row of icicles on a January morning. The French regulars marched in column to the edge of the clearing, and formed in line, confronting the English at the distance of a hundred and fifty yards. Their complete order, their white uniforms and bristling bayonets, were a new and startling sight to the eyes of Johnson's rustic soldiers, who raised but a feeble cheer in answer to the shouts of their enemies. Happily, Dieskau made no assault. The regulars opened a distant fire of musketry, throwing volley after volley against the English, while the Canadians and Indians, dispersing through the morasses on each flank of the camp, fired sharply, under cover of the trees and bushes. In the rear, the English were protected by the lake; but on the three remaining sides, they were hedged in by the flash and smoke of musketry.

The fire of the French had little effect. The English recovered from their first surprise, and every moment their confidence rose higher and their shouts grew louder. Levelling their long hunting guns with cool precision, they returned a fire which thinned the ranks of the French, and galled them beyond endurance. Two cannon were soon brought to bear upon the morasses which sheltered the Canadians and Indians; and though the pieces were served with little skill, the assailants were so terrified by the crashing of the balls among the trunks and branches, that they gave way at once. Dieskau still persisted in the attack. From noon until past four o'clock, the firing was scarcely abated, when at length the French, who had suffered extremely, showed signs of wavering. At this, with a general shout, the English broke from their camp, and rushed upon their enemies, striking them down with the buts of their guns, and driving them through the woods like deer. Dieskau was taken prisoner, dangerously wounded, and leaning for support against the stump of a tree. The slaughter would have been great, had not the English general recalled the pursuers, and suffered the French to continue their flight unmolested. Fresh disasters still awaited the fugitives; for, as they approached the scene of that morning's ambuscade, they were greeted by a volley of musketry. Two companies of New York and New Hampshire rangers, who had come out from Fort Edward as a scouting party, had lain in wait to receive them. Favored by the darkness of the woods,—for night was now approaching,—they made so sudden and vigorous an attack, that the French, though far superior in number, were totally routed and dispersed.

This memorable conflict has cast its dark associations over one of the most beautiful spots in America. Near the scene of the evening fight, a pool, half overgrown by weeds and water lilies, and darkened by the surrounding forest, is pointed out to the tourist, and he is told that beneath its stagnant waters lie the bones of three hundred Frenchmen, deep buried in mud and slime.

The war thus begun was prosecuted for five succeeding years with the full energy of both nations. The period was one of suffering and anxiety to the colonists, who, knowing the full extent of their danger, spared no exertion to avert it. In the year 1758, Lord Abercrombie, who then commanded in America, had at his disposal a force amounting to fifty thousand men, of whom the greater part were provincials. The operations of the war embraced a wide extent of country, from Cape Breton and Nova Scotia to the sources of the Ohio; but nowhere was the contest so actively carried on as in the neighborhood of Lake George, the waters of which, joined with those of Lake Champlain, formed the main avenue of communication between Canada and the British provinces. Lake George is more than thirty miles long, but of width so slight that it seems like some broad and placid river, enclosed between ranges of lofty mountains; now contracting into narrows, dotted with islands and shadowed by cliffs and crags, now spreading into a clear and open expanse. It had long been known to the French. The Jesuit Isaac Jogues, bound on a fatal mission to the ferocious Mohawks, had reached its banks on the eve of Corpus Christi Day, and named it Lac St. Sacrement. Its solitude was now rudely invaded. Armies passed and repassed upon its tranquil bosom. At its northern point the French planted their stronghold of Ticonderoga; at its southern stood the English fort William Henry, while the mountains and waters between were a scene of ceaseless ambuscades, surprises, and forest skirmishing. Through summer and winter, the crack of rifles and the cries of men gave no rest to their echoes; and at this day, on the field of many a forgotten fight, are dug up rusty tomahawks, corroded bullets, and human bones, to attest the struggles of the past.

The earlier years of the war were unpropitious to the English, whose commanders displayed no great degree of vigor or ability. In the summer of 1756, the French general Montcalm advanced upon Oswego, took it, and levelled it to the ground. In August of the following year, he struck a heavier blow. Passing Lake George with a force of eight thousand men, including about two thousand Indians, gathered from the farthest parts of Canada, he laid siege to Fort William Henry, close to the spot where Dieskau had been defeated two years before. Planting his batteries against it, he beat down its ramparts and dismounted its guns, until the garrison, after a brave defence, were forced to capitulate. They marched out with the honors of war; but scarcely had they done so, when Montcalm's Indians assailed them, cutting down and scalping them without mercy. Those who escaped came in to Fort Edward with exaggerated accounts of the horrors from which they had fled, and a general terror was spread through the country. The inhabitants were mustered from all parts to repel the advance of Montcalm; but the French general, satisfied with what he had done, repassed Lake George, and retired behind the walls of Ticonderoga.

In the year 1758, the war began to assume a different aspect, for Pitt was at the head of the government. Sir Jeffrey Amherst laid siege to the strong fortress of Louisburg, and at length reduced it; while in the south, General Forbes marched against Fort du Quesne, and, more fortunate than his predecessor, Braddock, drove the French from that important point. Another successful stroke was the destruction of Fort Frontenac, which was taken by a provincial army under Colonel Bradstreet. These achievements were counterbalanced by a great disaster. Lord Abercrombie, with an army of sixteen thousand men, advanced to the head of Lake George, the place made memorable by Dieskau's defeat and the loss of Fort William Henry. On a brilliant July morning, he embarked his whole force for an attack on Ticonderoga. Many of those present have recorded with admiration the beauty of the spectacle, the lines of boats filled with troops stretching far down the lake, the flashing of oars, the glitter of weapons, and the music ringing back from crags and rocks, or dying in mellowed strains among the distant mountains. At night, the army landed, and, driving in the French outposts, marched through the woods towards Ticonderoga. One of their columns, losing its way in the forest, fell in with a body of the retreating French; and in the conflict that ensued, Lord Howe, the favorite of the army, was shot dead. On the eighth of July, they prepared to storm the lines which Montcalm had drawn across the peninsula in front of the fortress. Advancing to the attack, they saw before them a breastwork of uncommon height and thickness. The French army were drawn up behind it, their heads alone visible, as they levelled their muskets against the assailants, while, for a hundred yards in front of the work, the ground was covered with felled trees, with sharpened branches pointing outward. The signal of assault was given. In vain the Highlanders, screaming with rage, hewed with their broadswords among the branches, struggling to get at the enemy. In vain the English, with their deep-toned shout, rushed on in heavy columns. A tempest of musket-balls met them, and Montcalm's cannon swept the whole ground with terrible carnage. A few officers and men forced their way through the branches, passed the ditch, climbed the breastwork, and, leaping among the enemy, were instantly bayonetted. The English fought four hours with determined valor, but the position of the French was impregnable; and at length, having lost two thousand of their number, the army drew off, leaving many of their dead scattered upon the field. A sudden panic seized the defeated troops. They rushed in haste to their boats, and, though no pursuit was attempted, they did not regain their composure until Lake George was between them and the enemy. The fatal lines of Ticonderoga were not soon forgotten in the provinces; and marbles in Westminster Abbey preserve the memory of those who fell on that disastrous day.

This repulse, far from depressing the energies of the British commanders, seemed to stimulate them to new exertion; and the campaign of the next year, 1759, had for its object the immediate and total reduction of Canada. This unhappy country was full of misery and disorder. Peculation and every kind of corruption prevailed among its civil and military chiefs, a reckless licentiousness was increasing among the people, and a general famine seemed impending, for the population had of late years been drained away for military service, and the fields were left untilled. In spite of their sufferings, the Canadians, strong in rooted antipathy to the English, and highly excited by their priests, resolved on fighting to the last. Prayers were offered up in the churches, masses said, and penances enjoined, to avert the wrath of God from the colony, while every thing was done for its defence which the energies of a great and patriotic leader could effect.

By the plan of this summer's campaign, Canada was to be assailed on three sides at once. Upon the west, General Prideaux was to attack Niagara; upon the south, General Amherst was to advance upon Ticonderoga and Crown Point; while upon the east, General Wolfe was to besiege Quebec; and each of these armies, having accomplished its particular object, was directed to push forward, if possible, until all three had united in the heart of Canada. In pursuance of the plan, General Prideaux moved up Lake Ontario and invested Niagara. This post was one of the greatest importance. Its capture would cut off the French from the whole interior country, and they therefore made every effort to raise the siege. An army of seventeen hundred French and Indians, collected at the distant garrisons of Detroit, Presqu' Isle, Le Bœuf, and Venango, suddenly appeared before Niagara. Sir William Johnson was now in command of the English, Prideaux having been killed by the bursting of a cohorn. Advancing in order of battle, he met the French, charged, routed, and pursued them for five miles through the woods. This success was soon followed by the surrender of the fort.

In the mean time, Sir Jeffrey Amherst had crossed Lake George, and appeared before Ticonderoga; upon which the French blew up their works, and retired down Lake Champlain to Crown Point. Retreating from this position also, on the approach of the English army, they collected all their forces, amounting to little more than three thousand men, at Isle Aux Noix, where they intrenched themselves, and prepared to resist the farther progress of the invaders. The lateness of the season prevented Amherst from carrying out the plan of advancing into Canada, and compelled him to go into winter-quarters at Crown Point. The same cause had withheld Prideaux's army from descending the St. Lawrence.

While the outposts of Canada were thus successfully attacked, a blow was struck at a more vital part. Early in June, General Wolfe sailed up the St. Lawrence with a force of eight thousand men, and formed his camp immediately below Quebec, on the Island of Orleans. From thence he could discern, at a single glance, how arduous was the task before him. Piles of lofty cliffs rose with sheer ascent on the northern border of the river; and from their summits the boasted citadel of Canada looked down in proud security, with its churches and convents of stone, its ramparts, bastions, and batteries; while over them all, from the brink of the precipice, towered the massive walls of the Castle of St. Louis. Above, for many a league, the bank was guarded by an unbroken range of steep acclivities. Below, the River St. Charles, flowing into the St. Lawrence, washed the base of the rocky promontory on which the city stood. Lower yet lay an army of fourteen thousand men, under an able and renowned commander, the Marquis of Montcalm. His front was covered by intrenchments and batteries, which lined the bank of the St. Lawrence; his right wing rested on the city and the St. Charles; his left, on the cascade and deep gulf of Montmorenci; and thick forests extended along his rear. Opposite Quebec rose the high promontory of Point Levi; and the St. Lawrence, contracted to less than a mile in width, flowed between, with deep and powerful current. To a chief of less resolute temper, it might well have seemed that art and nature were in league to thwart his enterprise; but a mind like that of Wolfe could only have seen in this majestic combination of forest and cataract, mountain and river, a fitting theatre for the great drama about to be enacted there.

Yet nature did not seem to have formed the young English general for the conduct of a doubtful and almost desperate enterprise. His person was slight, and his features by no means of a martial cast. His feeble constitution had been undermined by years of protracted and painful disease. His kind and genial disposition seemed better fitted for the quiet of domestic life than for the stern duties of military command; but to these gentler traits he joined a high enthusiasm, and an unconquerable spirit of daring and endurance, which made him the idol of his soldiers, and bore his slender frame through every hardship and exposure.

The work before him demanded all his courage. How to invest the city, or even bring the army of Montcalm to action, was a problem which might have perplexed a Hannibal. A French fleet lay in the river above, and the precipices along the northern bank were guarded at every accessible point by sentinels and outposts. Wolfe would have crossed the Montmorenci by its upper ford, and attacked the French army on its left and rear; but the plan was thwarted by the nature of the ground and the vigilance of his adversaries. Thus baffled at every other point, he formed the bold design of storming Montcalm's position in front; and on the afternoon of the thirty-first of July, a strong body of troops was embarked in boats, and, covered by a furious cannonade from the English ships and batteries, landed on the beach just above the mouth of the Montmorenci. The grenadiers and Royal Americans were the first on shore, and their ill-timed impetuosity proved the ruin of the plan. Without waiting to receive their orders or form their ranks, they ran, pell-mell, across the level ground, and with loud shouts began, each man for himself, to scale the heights which rose in front, crested with intrenchments and bristling with hostile arms. The French at the top threw volley after volley among the hot-headed assailants. The slopes were soon covered with the fallen; and at that instant a storm, which had long been threatening, burst with sudden fury, drenched the combatants on both sides with a deluge of rain, extinguished for a moment the fire of the French, and at the same time made the steeps so slippery that the grenadiers fell repeatedly in their vain attempts to climb. Night was coming on with double darkness. The retreat was sounded, and, as the English re-embarked, troops of Indians came whooping down the heights, and hovered about their rear, to murder the stragglers and the wounded; while exulting cries of Vive le roi, from the crowded summits, proclaimed the triumph of the enemy.

With bitter agony of mind, Wolfe beheld the headlong folly of his men, and saw more than four hundred of the flower of his army fall a useless sacrifice. The anxieties of the siege had told severely upon his slender constitution; and not long after this disaster, he felt the first symptoms of a fever, which soon confined him to his couch. Still his mind never wavered from its purpose; and it was while lying helpless in the chamber of a Canadian house, where he had fixed his headquarters, that he embraced the plan of the enterprise which robbed him of life, and gave him immortal fame.

This plan had been first proposed during the height of Wolfe's illness, at a council of his subordinate generals, Monkton, Townshend, and Murray. It was resolved to divide the little army; and, while one portion remained before Quebec to alarm the enemy by false attacks, and distract their attention from the scene of actual operation, the other was to pass above the town, land under cover of darkness on the northern shore, climb the guarded heights, gain the plains above, and force Montcalm to quit his vantage-ground, and perhaps to offer battle. The scheme was daring even to rashness; but its audacity was the secret of its success.

Early in September, a crowd of ships and transports, under Admiral Holmes, passed the city under the hot fire of its batteries; while the troops designed for the expedition, amounting to scarcely five thousand, marched upward along the southern bank, beyond reach of the cannonade. All were then embarked; and on the evening of the twelfth, Holmes's fleet, with the troops on board, lay safe at anchor in the river, several leagues above the town. These operations had not failed to awaken the suspicions of Montcalm; and he had detached M. Bougainville to watch the movements of the English, and prevent their landing on the northern shore.

The eventful night of the twelfth was clear and calm, with no light but that of the stars. Within two hours before daybreak, thirty boats, crowded with sixteen hundred soldiers, cast off from the vessels, and floated downward, in perfect order, with the current of the ebb tide. To the boundless joy of the army, Wolfe's malady had abated, and he was able to command in person. His ruined health, the gloomy prospects of the siege, and the disaster at Montmorenci, had oppressed him with the deepest melancholy, but never impaired for a moment the promptness of his decisions, or the impetuous energy of his action. He sat in the stern of one of the boats, pale and weak, but borne up to a calm height of resolution. Every order had been given, every arrangement made, and it only remained to face the issue. The ebbing tide sufficed to bear the boats along, and nothing broke the silence of the night but the gurgling of the river, and the low voice of Wolfe, as he repeated to the officers about him the stanzas of Gray's "Elegy in a Country Churchyard," which had recently appeared and which he had just received from England. Perhaps, as he uttered those strangely appropriate words,—

"The paths of glory lead but to the grave,"

the shadows of his own approaching fate stole with mournful prophecy across his mind. "Gentlemen," he said, as he closed his recital, "I would rather have written those lines than take Quebec tomorrow."

As they approached the landing-place, the boats edged closer in towards the northern shore, and the woody precipices rose high on their left, like a wall of undistinguished blackness.

"Qui vive?" shouted a French sentinel, from out the impervious gloom.

"La France!" answered a captain of Fraser's Highlanders, from the foremost boat.

"A quel régiment?" demanded the soldier.

"De la Reine!" promptly replied the Highland captain, who chanced to know that the regiment so designated formed part of Bougainville's command. As boats were frequently passing down the river with supplies for the garrison, and as a convoy from Bougainville was expected that very night, the sentinel was deceived, and allowed the English to proceed.

A few moments after, they were challenged again, and this time they could discern the soldier running close down to the water's edge, as if all his suspicions were aroused; but the skilful replies of the Highlander once more saved the party from discovery.

They reached the landing-place in safety,—an indentation in the shore, about a league above the city, and now bearing the name of Wolfe's Cove. Here a narrow path led up the face of the heights, and a French guard was posted at the top to defend the pass. By the force of the current, the foremost boats, including that which carried Wolfe himself, were borne a little below the spot. The general was one of the first on shore. He looked upward at the rugged heights which towered above him in the gloom. "You can try it," he coolly observed to an officer near him; "but I don't think you'll get up."

At the point where the Highlanders landed, one of their captains, Donald Macdonald, apparently the same whose presence of mind had just saved the enterprise from ruin, was climbing in advance of his men, when he was challenged by a sentinel. He replied in French, by declaring that he had been sent to relieve the guard, and ordering the soldier to withdraw. Before the latter was undeceived, a crowd of Highlanders were close at hand, while the steeps below were thronged with eager climbers, dragging themselves up by trees, roots, and bushes. The guard turned out, and made a brief though brave resistance. In a moment, they were cut to pieces, dispersed, or made prisoners; while men after men came swarming up the height, and quickly formed upon the plains above. Meanwhile, the vessels had dropped downward with the current, and anchored opposite the landing-place. The remaining troops were disembarked, and, with the dawn of day, the whole were brought in safety to the shore.

The sun rose, and, from the ramparts of Quebec, the astonished people saw the Plains of Abraham glittering with arms, and the dark-red lines of the English forming in array of battle. Breathless messengers had borne the evil tidings to Montcalm, and far and near his wide-extended camp resounded with the rolling of alarm drums and the din of startled preparation. He, too, had had his struggles and his sorrows. The civil power had thwarted him; famine, discontent, and disaffection were rife among his soldiers; and no small portion of the Canadian militia had dispersed from sheer starvation. In spite of all, he had trusted to hold out till the winter frosts should drive the invaders from before the town; when, on that disastrous morning, the news of their successful temerity fell like a cannon shot upon his ear. Still he assumed a tone of confidence. "They have got to the weak side of us at last," he is reported to have said, "and we must crush them with our numbers." With headlong haste, his troops were pouring over the bridge of the St. Charles, and gathering in heavy masses under the western ramparts of the town. Could numbers give assurance of success, their triumph would have been secure; for five French battalions and the armed colonial peasantry amounted in all to more than seven thousand five hundred men. Full in sight before them stretched the long, thin lines of the British forces,—the half-wild Highlanders, the steady soldiery of England, and the hardy levies of the provinces,—less than five thousand in number, but all inured to battle, and strong in the full assurance of success. Yet, could the chiefs of that gallant army have pierced the secrets of the future, could they have foreseen that the victory which they burned to achieve would have robbed England of her proudest boast, that the conquest of Canada would pave the way for the independence of America, their swords would have dropped from their hands, and the heroic fire have gone out within their hearts.

It was nine o'clock, and the adverse armies stood motionless, each gazing on the other. The clouds hung low, and, at intervals, warm light showers descended, besprinkling both alike. The coppice and cornfields in front of the British troops were filled with French sharpshooters, who kept up a distant, spattering fire. Here and there a soldier fell in the ranks, and the gap was filled in silence.

At a little before ten, the British could see that Montcalm was preparing to advance, and, in a few moments, all his troops appeared in rapid motion. They came on in three divisions, shouting after the manner of their nation, and firing heavily as soon as they came within range. In the British ranks, not a trigger was pulled, not a soldier stirred; and their ominous composure seemed to damp the spirits of the assailants. It was not till the French were within forty yards that the fatal word was given, and the British muskets blazed forth at once in one crashing explosion. Like a ship at full career, arrested with sudden ruin on a sunken rock, the ranks of Montcalm staggered, shivered, and broke before that wasting storm of lead. The smoke, rolling along the field, for a moment shut out the view; but when the white wreaths were scattered on the wind, a wretched spectacle was disclosed; men and officers tumbled in heaps, battalions resolved into a mob, order and obedience gone; and when the British muskets were levelled for a second volley, the masses of the militia were seen to cower and shrink with uncontrollable panic. For a few minutes, the French regulars stood their ground, returning a sharp and not ineffectual fire. But now, echoing cheer on cheer, redoubling volley on volley, trampling the dying and the dead, and driving the fugitives in crowds, the British troops advanced and swept the field before them. The ardor of the men burst all restraint. They broke into a run, and with unsparing slaughter chased the flying multitude to the gates of Quebec. Foremost of all, the light-footed Highlanders dashed along in furious pursuit, hewing down the Frenchmen with their broadswords, and slaying many in the very ditch of the fortifications. Never was victory more quick or more decisive.

In the short action and pursuit, the French lost fifteen hundred men, killed, wounded, and taken. Of the remainder, some escaped within the city, and others fled across the St. Charles to rejoin their comrades who had been left to guard the camp. The pursuers were recalled by sound of trumpet; the broken ranks were formed afresh, and the English troops withdrawn beyond reach of the cannon of Quebec. Bougainville, with his corps, arrived from the upper country, and, hovering about their rear, threatened an attack; but when he saw what greeting was prepared for him, he abandoned his purpose and withdrew. Townshend and Murray, the only general officers who remained unhurt, passed to the head of every regiment in turn, and thanked the soldiers for the bravery they had shown; yet the triumph of the victors was mingled with sadness, as the tidings went from rank to rank that Wolfe had fallen.

In the heat of the action, as he advanced at the head of the grenadiers of Louisburg, a bullet shattered his wrist; but he wrapped his handkerchief about the wound, and showed no sign of pain. A moment more, and a ball pierced his side. Still he pressed forward, waving his sword and cheering his soldiers to the attack, when a third shot lodged deep within his breast. He paused, reeled, and, staggering to one side, fell to the earth. Brown, a lieutenant of the grenadiers, Henderson, a volunteer, an officer of artillery, and a private soldier, raised him together in their arms, and, bearing him to the rear, laid him softly on the grass. They asked if he would have a surgeon; but he shook his head, and answered that all was over with him. His eyes closed with the torpor of approaching death, and those around sustained his fainting form. Yet they could not withhold their gaze from the wild turmoil before them, and the charging ranks of their companions rushing through fire and smoke. "See how they run," one of the officers exclaimed, as the French fled in confusion before the levelled bayonets. "Who run?" demanded Wolfe, opening his eyes like a man aroused from sleep. "The enemy, sir," was the reply; "they give way everywhere." "Then," said the dying general, "tell Colonel Burton to march Webb's regiment down to Charles River, to cut off their retreat from the bridge. Now, God be praised, I will die in peace," he murmured; and, turning on his side, he calmly breathed his last.

Almost at the same moment fell his great adversary, Montcalm, as he strove, with vain bravery, to rally his shattered ranks. Struck down with a mortal wound, he was placed upon a litter and borne to the General Hospital on the banks of the St. Charles. The surgeons told him that he could not recover. "I am glad of it," was his calm reply. He then asked how long he might survive, and was told that he had not many hours remaining. "So much the better," he said; "I am happy that I shall not live to see the surrender of Quebec." Officers from the garrison came to his bedside to ask his orders and instructions. "I will give no more orders," replied the defeated soldier; "I have much business that must be attended to, of greater moment than your ruined garrison and this wretched country. My time is very short; therefore, pray leave me." The officers withdrew, and none remained in the chamber but his confessor and the Bishop of Quebec. To the last, he expressed his contempt for his own mutinous and half-famished troops, and his admiration for the disciplined valor of his opponents. He died before midnight, and was buried at his own desire in a cavity of the earth formed by the bursting of a bombshell.

The victorious army encamped before Quebec, and pushed their preparations for the siege with zealous energy; but before a single gun was brought to bear, the white flag was hung out, and the garrison surrendered. On the eighteenth of September, 1759, the rock-built citadel of Canada passed forever from the hands of its ancient masters.

The victory on the Plains of Abraham and the downfall of Quebec filled all England with pride and exultation. From north to south, the land blazed with illuminations, and resounded with the ringing of bells, the firing of guns, and the shouts of the multitude. In one village alone all was dark and silent amid the general joy; for here dwelt the widowed mother of Wolfe. The populace, with unwonted delicacy, respected her lonely sorrow, and forbore to obtrude the sound of their rejoicings upon her grief for one who had been through life her pride and solace, and repaid her love with a tender and constant devotion.

Canada, crippled and dismembered by the disasters of this year's campaign, lay waiting, as it were, the final stroke which was to extinguish her last remains of life, and close the eventful story of French dominion in America. Her limbs and her head were lopped away, but life still fluttered at her heart. Quebec, Niagara, Frontenac, and Crown Point had fallen; but Montreal and the adjacent country still held out, and thither, with the opening season of 1760, the British commanders turned all their energies. Three armies were to enter Canada at three several points, and, conquering as they advanced, converge towards Montreal as a common centre. In accordance with this plan, Sir Jeffrey Amherst embarked at Oswego, crossed Lake Ontario, and descended the St. Lawrence with ten thousand men; while Colonel Haviland advanced by way of Lake Champlain and the River Sorel, and General Murray ascended from Quebec, with a body of the veterans who had fought on the Plains of Abraham.

By a singular concurrence of fortune and skill, the three armies reached the neighborhood of Montreal on the same day. The feeble and disheartened garrison could offer no resistance, and on the eighth of September, 1760, the Marquis de Vaudreuil surrendered Canada, with all its dependencies, to the British crown.

THE WILDERNESS

1755 to 1763

And Its Tenants At The Close Of The French War.

We have already seen how, after the defeat of Braddock, the western tribes rose with one accord against the English. Then, for the first time, Pennsylvania felt the scourge of Indian war; and her neighbors, Maryland and Virginia, shared her misery. Through the autumn of 1755, the storm raged with devastating fury; but the following year brought some abatement of its violence. This may be ascribed partly to the interference of the Iroquois, who, at the instances of Sir William Johnson, urged the Delawares to lay down the hatchet, and partly to the persuasions of several prominent men among the Quakers, who, by kind and friendly treatment, had gained the confidence of the Indians. By these means, that portion of the Delawares and their kindred tribes who dwelt upon the Susquehanna, were induced to send a deputation of chiefs to Easton, in the summer of 1757, to meet the provincial delegates; and here, after much delay and difficulty, a treaty of peace was concluded.

This treaty, however, did not embrace the Indians of the Ohio, who comprised the most formidable part of the Delawares and Shawanoes, and who still continued their murderous attacks. It was not till the summer of 1758, when General Forbes, with a considerable army, was advancing against Fort du Quesne, that these exasperated savages could be brought to reason. Well knowing that, should Forbes prove successful, they might expect a summary chastisement for their misdeeds, they began to waver in their attachment to the French; and the latter, in the hour of peril, found themselves threatened with desertion by allies who had shown an ample alacrity in the season of prosperity. This new tendency of the Ohio Indians was fostered by a wise step on the part of the English. A man was found bold and hardy enough to venture into the midst of their villages, bearing the news of the treaty at Easton, and the approach of Forbes, coupled with proposals of peace from the governor of Pennsylvania.

This stout-hearted emissary was Christian Frederic Post, a Moravian missionary, who had long lived with the Indians, had twice married among them, and, by his upright dealings and plain good sense, had gained their confidence and esteem. His devout and conscientious spirit, his fidelity to what he deemed his duty, his imperturbable courage, his prudence and his address, well fitted him for the critical mission. His journals, written in a style of quaint simplicity, are full of lively details, and afford a curious picture of forest life and character. He left Philadelphia in July, attended by a party of friendly Indians, on whom he relied for protection. Reaching the Ohio, he found himself beset with perils from the jealousy and malevolence of the savage warriors, and the machinations of the French, who would gladly have destroyed him. Yet he found friends wherever he went, and finally succeeded in convincing the Indians that their true interest lay in a strict neutrality. When, therefore, Forbes appeared before Fort du Quesne, the French found themselves abandoned to their own resources; and, unable to hold their ground, they retreated down the Ohio, leaving the fort an easy conquest to the invaders. During the autumn, the Ohio Indians sent their deputies to Easton, where a great council was held, and a formal peace concluded with the provinces.

While the friendship of these tribes was thus lost and regained, their ancient tyrants, the Iroquois, remained in a state of very doubtful attachment. At the outbreak of the war, they had shown, it is true, many signs of friendship; but the disasters of the first campaign had given them a contemptible idea of British prowess. This impression was deepened, when, in the following year, they saw Oswego taken by the French, and the British general, Webb, retreat with dastardly haste from an enemy who did not dream of pursuing him. At this time, some of the confederates actually took up the hatchet on the side of France, and there was danger that the rest might follow their example. But now a new element was infused into the British counsels. The fortunes of the conflict began to change. Du Quesne and Louisburg were taken, and the Iroquois conceived a better opinion of the British arms. Their friendship was no longer a matter of doubt; and in 1760, when Amherst was preparing to advance on Montreal, the warriors flocked to his camp like vultures to the carcass. Yet there is little doubt, that, had their sachems and orators followed the dictates of their cooler judgment, they would not have aided in destroying Canada; for they could see that in the colonies of France lay the only barrier against the growing power and ambition of the English provinces.

The Hurons of Lorette, the Abenakis, and other domiciliated tribes of Canada, ranged themselves on the side of France throughout the war; and at its conclusion, they, in common with the Canadians, may be regarded in the light of a conquered people.

The numerous tribes of the remote west had, with few exceptions, played the part of active allies of the French; and warriors might be found on the farthest shores of Lake Superior who garnished their war-dress with the scalp-locks of murdered Englishmen. With the conquest of Canada, these tribes subsided into a state of inaction, which was not long to continue.

And now, before launching into the story of the sanguinary war which forms our proper and immediate theme, it will be well to survey the grand arena of the strife, the goodly heritage which the wretched tribes of the forest struggled to retrieve from the hands of the spoiler.

One vast, continuous forest shadowed the fertile soil, covering the land as the grass covers a garden lawn, sweeping over hill and hollow in endless undulation, burying mountains in verdure, and mantling brooks and rivers from the light of day. Green intervals dotted with browsing deer, and broad plains alive with buffalo, broke the sameness of the woodland scenery. Unnumbered rivers seamed the forest with their devious windings. Vast lakes washed its boundaries, where the Indian voyager, in his birch canoe, could descry no land beyond the world of waters. Yet this prolific wilderness, teeming with waste fertility, was but a hunting-ground and a battle-field to a few fierce hordes of savages. Here and there, in some rich meadow opened to the sun, the Indian squaws turned the black mould with their rude implements of bone or iron, and sowed their scanty stores of maize and beans. Human labor drew no other tribute from that exhaustless soil.

So thin and scattered was the native population, that, even in those parts which were thought well peopled, one might sometimes journey for days together through the twilight forest, and meet no human form. Broad tracts were left in solitude. All Kentucky was a vacant waste, a mere skirmishing ground for the hostile war-parties of the north and south. A great part of Upper Canada, of Michigan, and of Illinois, besides other portions of the west, were tenanted by wild beasts alone. To form a close estimate of the numbers of the erratic bands who roamed this wilderness would be impossible; but it may be affirmed that, between the Mississippi on the west and the ocean on the east, between the Ohio on the south and Lake Superior on the north, the whole Indian population, at the close of the French war, did not greatly exceed ten thousand fighting men. Of these, following the statement of Sir William Johnson, in 1763, the Iroquois had nineteen hundred and fifty, the Delawares about six hundred, the Shawanoes about three hundred, the Wyandots about four hundred and fifty, and the Miami tribes, with their neighbors the Kickapoos, eight hundred; while the Ottawas, the Ojibwas, and other wandering tribes of the north, defy all efforts at enumeration.

A close survey of the condition of the tribes at this period will detect some signs of improvement, but many more of degeneracy and decay. To commence with the Iroquois, for to them with justice the priority belongs: Onondaga, the ancient capital of their confederacy, where their council-fire had burned from immemorial time, was now no longer what it had been in the days of its greatness, when Count Frontenac had mustered all Canada to assail it. The thickly clustered dwellings, with their triple rows of palisades, had vanished. A little stream, twisting along the valley, choked up with logs and driftwood, and half hidden by woods and thickets, some forty houses of bark, scattered along its banks, amid rank grass, neglected clumps of bushes, and ragged patches of corn and peas,—such was Onondaga when Bartram saw it, and such, no doubt, it remained at the time of which I write. Conspicuous among the other structures, and distinguished only by its superior size, stood the great council-house, whose bark walls had often sheltered the congregated wisdom of the confederacy, and heard the highest efforts of forest eloquence. The other villages of the Iroquois resembled Onondaga; for though several were of larger size, yet none retained those defensive stockades which had once protected them. From their European neighbors the Iroquois had borrowed many appliances of comfort and subsistence. Horses, swine, and in some instances cattle, were to be found among them. Guns and gunpowder aided them in the chase. Knives, hatchets, kettles, and hoes of iron, had supplanted their rude household utensils and implements of tillage; but with all this, English whiskey had more than cancelled every benefit which English civilization had conferred.

High up the Susquehanna were seated the Nanticokes, Conoys, and Mohicans, with a portion of the Delawares. Detached bands of the western Iroquois dwelt upon the head waters of the Alleghany, mingled with their neighbors, the Delawares, who had several villages upon this stream. The great body of the latter nation, however, lived upon the Beaver Creeks and the Muskingum, in numerous scattered towns and hamlets, whose barbarous names it is useless to record. Squalid log cabins and conical wigwams of bark were clustered at random, or ranged to form rude streets and squares. Starveling horses grazed on the neighboring meadows; girls and children bathed and laughed in the adjacent river; warriors smoked their pipes in haughty indolence; squaws labored in the cornfields, or brought fagots from the forest, and shrivelled hags screamed from lodge to lodge. In each village one large building stood prominent among the rest, devoted to purposes of public meeting, dances, festivals, and the entertainment of strangers. Thither the traveller would be conducted, seated on a bear-skin, and plentifully regaled with hominy and venison.

The Shawanoes had sixteen small villages upon the Scioto and its branches.

Farther towards the west, on the waters of the Wabash and the Maumee, dwelt the Miamis, who, less exposed, from their position, to the poison of the whiskey-keg, and the example of debauched traders, retained their ancient character and customs in greater purity than their eastern neighbors. This cannot be said of the Illinois, who dwelt near the borders of the Mississippi, and who, having lived for more than half a century in close contact with the French, had become a corrupt and degenerate race. The Wyandots of Sandusky and Detroit far surpassed the surrounding tribes in energy of character and in social progress. Their log dwellings were strong and commodious, their agriculture was very considerable, their name stood high in war and policy, and they were regarded with deference by all the adjacent Indians. It is needless to pursue farther this catalogue of tribes, since the position of each will appear hereafter as they advance in turn upon the stage of action.

The English settlements lay like a narrow strip between the wilderness and the sea, and, as the sea had its ports, so also the forest had its places of rendezvous and outfit. Of these, by far the most important in the northern provinces was the frontier city of Albany. From thence it was that traders and soldiers, bound to the country of the Iroquois, or the more distant wilds of the interior, set out upon their arduous journey. Embarking in a bateau or a canoe, rowed by the hardy men who earned their livelihood in this service, the traveller would ascend the Mohawk, passing the old Dutch town of Schenectady, the two seats of Sir William Johnson, Fort Hunter at the mouth of the Scoharie, and Fort Herkimer at the German Flats, until he reached Fort Stanwix at the head of the river navigation. Then crossing over land to Wood Creek, he would follow its tortuous course, overshadowed by the dense forest on its banks, until he arrived at the little fortification called the Royal Blockhouse, and the waters of the Oneida Lake spread before him. Crossing to its western extremity, and passing under the wooden ramparts of Fort Brewerton, he would descend the River Oswego to Oswego, on the banks of Lake Ontario. Here the vast navigation of the Great Lakes would be open before him, interrupted only by the difficult portage at the Cataract of Niagara.

The chief thoroughfare from the middle colonies to the Indian country was from Philadelphia westward, across the Alleghanies, to the valley of the Ohio. Peace was no sooner concluded with the hostile tribes, than the adventurous fur-traders, careless of risk to life and property, hastened over the mountains, each eager to be foremost in the wilderness market. Their merchandise was sometimes carried in wagons as far as the site of Fort du Quesne, which the English rebuilt after its capture, changing its name to Fort Pitt. From this point the goods were packed on the backs of horses, and thus distributed among the various Indian villages. More commonly, however, the whole journey was performed by means of trains, or, as they were called, brigades of pack-horses, which, leaving the frontier settlements, climbed the shadowy heights of the Alleghanies, and threaded the forests of the Ohio, diving through thickets, and wading over streams. The men employed in this perilous calling were a rough, bold, and intractable class, often as fierce and truculent as the Indians themselves. A blanket coat, or a frock of smoked deer-skin, a rifle on the shoulder, and a knife and tomahawk in the belt, formed their ordinary equipment. The principal trader, the owner of the merchandise, would fix his headquarters at some large Indian town, whence he would despatch his subordinates to the surrounding villages, with a suitable supply of blankets and red cloth, guns and hatchets, liquor, tobacco, paint, beads, and hawks' bells. This wild traffic was liable to every species of disorder; and it is not to be wondered at that, in a region where law was unknown, the jealousies of rival traders should become a fruitful source of broils, robberies, and murders.

In the backwoods, all land travelling was on foot, or on horseback. It was no easy matter for a novice, embarrassed with his cumbrous gun, to urge his horse through the thick trunks and undergrowth, or even to ride at speed along the narrow Indian trails, where at every yard the impending branches switched him across the face. At night, the camp would be formed by the side of some rivulet or spring; and, if the traveller was skilful in the use of his rifle, a haunch of venison would often form his evening meal. If it rained, a shed of elm or basswood bark was the ready work of an hour, a pile of evergreen boughs formed a bed, and the saddle or the knapsack a pillow. A party of Indian wayfarers would often be met journeying through the forest, a chief, or a warrior, perhaps, with his squaws and family. The Indians would usually make their camp in the neighborhood of the white men; and at meal-time the warrior would seldom fail to seat himself by the traveller's fire, and gaze with solemn gravity at the viands before him. If, when the repast was over, a fragment of bread or a cup of coffee should be handed to him, he would receive these highly prized rarities with an ejaculation of gratitude; for nothing is more remarkable in the character of this people than the union of inordinate pride and a generous love of glory with the mendicity of a beggar or a child.

He who wished to visit the remoter tribes of the Mississippi valley—an attempt, however, which, until several years after the conquest of Canada, no Englishman could have made without great risk of losing his scalp—would find no easier course than to descend the Ohio in a canoe or bateau. He might float for more than eleven hundred miles down this liquid highway of the wilderness, and, except the deserted cabins of Logstown, a little below Fort Pitt, the remnant of a Shawanoe village at the mouth of the Scioto, and an occasional hamlet or solitary wigwam along the deeply wooded banks, he would discern no trace of human habitation through all this vast extent. The body of the Indian population lay to the northward, about the waters of the tributary streams. It behooved the voyager to observe a sleepless caution and a hawk-eyed vigilance. Sometimes his anxious scrutiny would detect a faint blue smoke stealing upward above the green bosom of the forest, and betraying the encamping place of some lurking war-party. Then the canoe would be drawn in haste beneath the overhanging bushes which skirted the shore; nor would the voyage be resumed until darkness closed, when the little vessel would drift swiftly and safely by the point of danger.

Within the nominal limits of the Illinois Indians, and towards the southern extremity of the present state of Illinois, were those isolated Canadian settlements, which had subsisted here since the latter part of the preceding century. Kaskaskia, Cahokia, and Vincennes were the centres of this scattered population. From Vincennes one might paddle his canoe northward up the Wabash, until he reached the little wooden fort of Ouatanon. Thence a path through the woods led to the banks of the Maumee. Two or three Canadians, or half-breeds, of whom there were numbers about the fort, would carry the canoe on their shoulders, or, for a bottle of whiskey, a few Miami Indians might be bribed to undertake the task. On the Maumee, at the end of the path, stood Fort Miami, near the spot where Fort Wayne was afterwards built. From this point one might descend the Maumee to Lake Erie, and visit the neighboring fort of Sandusky, or, if he chose, steer through the Strait of Detroit, and explore the watery wastes of the northern lakes, finding occasional harborage at the little military posts which commanded their important points. Most of these western posts were transferred to the English, during the autumn of 1760; but the settlements of the Illinois remained several years longer under French control.

Eastward, on the waters of Lake Erie, and the Alleghany, stood three small forts, Presqu' Isle, Le Bœuf, and Venango, which had passed into the hands of the English soon after the capture of Fort du Quesne. The feeble garrisons of all these western posts, exiled from civilization, lived in the solitude of military hermits. Through the long, hot days of summer, and the protracted cold of winter, time hung heavy on their hands. Their resources of employment and recreation were few and meagre. They found partners in their loneliness among the young beauties of the Indian camps. They hunted and fished, shot at targets, and played at games of chance; and when, by good fortune, a traveller found his way among them, he was greeted with a hearty and open-handed welcome, and plied with eager questions touching the great world from which they were banished men. Yet, tedious as it was, their secluded life was seasoned with stirring danger. The surrounding forests were peopled with a race dark and subtle as their own sunless mazes. At any hour, those jealous tribes might raise the war-cry. No human foresight could predict the sallies of their fierce caprice, and in ceaseless watching lay the only safety.

When the European and the savage are brought in contact, both are gainers, and both are losers. The former loses the refinements of civilization, but he gains, in the rough schooling of the wilderness, a rugged independence, a self-sustaining energy, and powers of action and perception before unthought of. The savage gains new means of comfort and support, cloth, iron, and gunpowder; yet these apparent benefits have often proved but instruments of ruin. They soon become necessities, and the unhappy hunter, forgetting the weapons of his fathers, must thenceforth depend on the white man for ease, happiness, and life itself.

Those rude and hardy men, hunters and traders, scouts and guides, who ranged the woods beyond the English borders, and formed a connecting link between barbarism and civilization, have been touched upon already. They were a distinct, peculiar class, marked with striking contrasts of good and evil. Many, though by no means all, were coarse, audacious, and unscrupulous; yet, even in the worst, one might often have found a vigorous growth of warlike virtues, an iron endurance, an undespairing courage, a wondrous sagacity, and singular fertility of resource. In them was renewed, with all its ancient energy, that wild and daring spirit, that force and hardihood of mind, which marked our barbarous ancestors of Germany and Norway. These sons of the wilderness still survive. We may find them to this day, not in the valley of the Ohio, nor on the shores of the lakes, but far westward on the desert range of the buffalo, and among the solitudes of Oregon. Even now, while I write, some lonely trapper is climbing the perilous defiles of the Rocky Mountains, his strong frame cased in time-worn buck-skin, his rifle griped in his sinewy hand. Keenly he peers from side to side, lest Blackfoot or Arapahoe should ambuscade his path. The rough earth is his bed, a morsel of dried meat and a draught of water are his food and drink, and death and danger his companions. No anchorite could fare worse, no hero could dare more; yet his wild, hard life has resistless charms; and, while he can wield a rifle, he will never leave it. Go with him to the rendezvous, and he is a stoic no more. Here, rioting among his comrades, his native appetites break loose in mad excess, in deep carouse, and desperate gaming. Then follow close the quarrel, the challenge, the fight,—two rusty rifles and fifty yards of prairie.

The nursling of civilization, placed in the midst of the forest, and abandoned to his own resources, is helpless as an infant. There is no clew to the labyrinth. Bewildered and amazed, he circles round and round in hopeless wanderings. Despair and famine make him their prey, and unless the birds of heaven minister to his wants, he dies in misery. Not so the practised woodsman. To him, the forest is a home. It yields him food, shelter, and raiment, and he threads its trackless depths with undeviating foot. To lure the game, to circumvent the lurking foe, to guide his course by the stars, the wind, the streams, or the trees,—such are the arts which the white man has learned from the red. Often, indeed, the pupil has outstripped his master. He can hunt as well; he can fight better; and yet there are niceties of the woodsman's craft in which the white man must yield the palm to his savage rival. Seldom can he boast, in equal measure, that subtlety of sense, more akin to the instinct of brutes than to human reason, which reads the signs of the forest as the scholar reads the printed page, to which the whistle of a bird can speak clearly as the tongue of man, and the rustle of a leaf give knowledge of life or death. With us the name of the savage is a byword of reproach. The Indian would look with equal scorn on those who, buried in useless lore, are blind and deaf to the great world of nature.

THE ENGLISH TAKE POSSESSION OF THE WESTERN POSTS

1760

The war was over. The plains around Montreal were dotted with the white tents of three victorious armies, and the work of conquest was complete. Canada, with all her dependencies, had yielded to the British crown; but it still remained to carry into full effect the terms of the surrender, and take possession of those western outposts, where the lilies of France had not as yet descended from the flagstaff. The execution of this task, neither an easy nor a safe one, was assigned to a provincial officer, Major Robert Rogers.

Rogers was a native of New Hampshire. He commanded a body of provincial rangers, and stood in high repute as a partisan officer. Putnam and Stark were his associates; and it was in this woodland warfare that the former achieved many of those startling adventures and hair-breadth escapes which have made his name familiar at every New-England fireside. Rogers's Rangers, half hunters, half woodsmen, trained in a discipline of their own, and armed, like Indians, with hatchet, knife, and gun, were employed in a service of peculiar hardship. Their chief theatre of action was the mountainous region of Lake George, the debatable ground between the hostile forts of Ticonderoga and William Henry. The deepest recesses of these romantic solitudes had heard the French and Indian yell, and the answering shout of the hardy New-England men. In summer, they passed down the lake in whale boats or canoes, or threaded the pathways of the woods in single file, like the savages themselves. In winter, they journeyed through the swamps on snowshoes, skated along the frozen surface of the lake, and bivouacked at night among the snow-drifts. They intercepted

French messengers, encountered French scouting parties, and carried off prisoners from under the very walls of Ticonderoga. Their hardships and adventures, their marches and countermarches, their frequent skirmishes and midwinter battles, had made them famous throughout America; and though it was the fashion of the day to sneer at the efforts of provincial troops, the name of Rogers's Rangers was never mentioned but with honor. Their commander was a man tall and strong in person, and rough in feature. He was versed in all the arts of woodcraft, sagacious, prompt, and resolute, yet so cautious withal that he sometimes incurred the unjust charge of cowardice. His mind, naturally active, was by no means uncultivated; and his books and unpublished letters bear witness that his style as a writer was not contemptible. But his vain, restless, and grasping spirit, and more than doubtful honesty, proved the ruin of an enviable reputation. Six years after the expedition of which I am about to speak, he was tried by a court-martial for a meditated act of treason, the surrender of Fort Michillimackinac into the hands of the Spaniards, who were at that time masters of Upper Louisiana. Not long after, if we may trust his own account, he passed over to the Barbary States, entered the service of the Dey of Algiers, and fought two battles under his banners. At the opening of the war of independence, he returned to his native country, where he made professions of patriotism, but was strongly suspected by many, including Washington himself, of acting the part of a spy. In fact, he soon openly espoused the British cause, and received a colonel's commission from the crown. His services, however, proved of little consequence. In 1778, he was proscribed and banished, under the act of New Hampshire, and the remainder of his life was passed in such obscurity that it is difficult to determine when and where he died.

On the twelfth of September, 1760, Rogers, then at the height of his reputation, received orders from Sir Jeffrey Amherst to ascend the lakes with a detachment of rangers, and take possession, in the name of his Britannic Majesty, of Detroit, Michillimackinac, and other western posts included in the late capitulation. He left Montreal, on the following day, with two hundred rangers, in fifteen whale boats. Stemming the surges of La Chine and the Cedars, they left behind them the straggling hamlet which bore the latter name, and formed at that day the western limit of Canadian settlement. They gained Lake Ontario, skirted its northern shore, amid rough and boisterous weather, and crossing at its western extremity, reached Fort Niagara on the first of October. Carrying their boats over the portage, they launched them once more above the cataract, and slowly pursued their voyage; while Rogers, with a few attendants, hastened on in advance to Fort Pitt, to deliver despatches, with which he was charged, to General Monkton. This errand accomplished, he rejoined his command at Presqu' Isle, about the end of the month, and the whole proceeded together along the southern margin of Lake Erie. The season was far advanced. The wind was chill, the lake was stormy, and the woods on shore were tinged with the fading hues of autumn. On the seventh of November, they reached the mouth of a river called by Rogers the Chogage. No body of troops under the British flag had ever before penetrated so far. The day was dull and rainy, and, resolving to rest until the weather should improve, Rogers ordered his men to prepare their encampment in the neighboring forest.

Soon after the arrival of the rangers, a party of Indian chiefs and warriors entered the camp. They proclaimed themselves an embassy from Pontiac, ruler of all that country, and directed, in his name, that the English should advance no farther until they had had an interview with the great chief, who was already close at hand. In truth, before the day closed, Pontiac himself appeared; and it is here, for the first time, that this remarkable man stands forth distinctly on the page of history. He greeted Rogers with the haughty demand, what was his business in that country, and how he dared enter it without his permission. Rogers informed him that the French were defeated, that Canada had surrendered, and that he was on his way to take possession of Detroit, and restore a general peace to white men and Indians alike. Pontiac listened with attention, but only replied that he should stand in the path of the English until morning. Having inquired if the strangers were in need of any thing which his country could afford, he withdrew, with his chiefs, at nightfall, to his own encampment; while the English, ill at ease, and suspecting treachery, stood well on their guard throughout the night.

In the morning, Pontiac returned to the camp with his attendant chiefs, and made his reply to Rogers's speech of the previous day. He was willing, he said, to live at peace with the English, and suffer them to remain in his country as long as they treated him with due respect and deference. The Indian chiefs and provincial officers smoked the calumet together, and perfect harmony seemed established between them.

Up to this time, Pontiac had been, in word and deed, the fast ally of the French; but it is easy to discern the motives that impelled him to renounce his old adherence. The American forest never produced a man more shrewd, politic, and ambitious. Ignorant as he was of what was passing in the world, he could clearly see that the French power was on the wane, and he knew his own interest too well to prop a falling cause. By making friends of the English, he hoped to gain powerful allies, who would aid his ambitious projects, and give him an increased influence over the tribes; and he flattered himself that the new-comers would treat him with the same respect which the French had always observed. In this, and all his other expectations of advantage from the English, he was doomed to disappointment.

A cold storm of rain set in, and the rangers were detained several days in their encampment. During this time, Rogers had several interviews with Pontiac, and was constrained to admire the native vigor of his intellect, no less than the singular control which he exercised over those around him.

On the twelfth of November, the detachment was again in motion, and within a few days they had reached the western end of Lake Erie. Here they heard that the Indians of Detroit were in arms against them, and that four hundred warriors lay in ambush at the entrance of the river to cut them off. But the powerful influence of Pontiac was exerted in behalf of his new friends. The warriors abandoned their design, and the rangers continued their progress towards Detroit, now within a short distance.

In the mean time, Lieutenant Brehm had been sent forward with a letter to Captain Belêtre, the commandant at Detroit, informing him that Canada had capitulated, that his garrison was included in the capitulation, and that an English detachment was approaching to relieve it. The Frenchman, in great wrath at the tidings, disregarded the message as an informal communication, and resolved to keep a hostile attitude to the last. He did his best to rouse the fury of the Indians. Among other devices, he displayed upon a pole, before the yelling multitude, the effigy of a crow pecking a man's head; the crow representing himself, and the head, observes Rogers, "being meant for my own." All his efforts were unavailing, and his faithless allies showed unequivocal symptoms of defection in the hour of need.

Rogers had now entered the mouth of the River Detroit, whence he sent forward Captain Campbell with a copy of the capitulation, and a letter from the Marquis de Vaudreuil, directing that the place should be given up, in accordance with the terms agreed upon between him and General Amherst. Belêtre was forced to yield, and with a very ill grace declared himself and his garrison at the disposal of the English commander.

The whale boats of the rangers moved slowly upwards between the low banks of the Detroit, until at length the green uniformity of marsh and forest was relieved by the Canadian houses, which began to appear on either bank, the outskirts of the secluded and isolated settlement. Before them, on the right side, they could see the village of the Wyandots, and on the left the clustered lodges of the Pottawattamies; while, a little beyond, the flag of France was flying for the last time above the bark roofs and weather-beaten palisades of the little fortified town.

The rangers landed on the opposite bank, and pitched their tents upon a meadow, while two officers, with a small detachment, went across the river to take possession of the place. In obedience to their summons, the French garrison defiled upon the plain, and laid down their arms. The fleur de lis was lowered from the flagstaff, and the cross of St. George rose aloft in its place, while seven hundred Indian warriors, lately the active allies of France, greeted the sight with a burst of triumphant yells. The Canadian militia were next called together and disarmed. The Indians looked on with amazement at their obsequious behavior, quite at a loss to understand why so many men should humble themselves before so few. Nothing is more effective in gaining the respect, or even attachment, of Indians than a display of power. The savage spectators conceived the loftiest idea of English prowess, and were astonished at the forbearance of the conquerors in not killing their vanquished enemies on the spot.

It was on the twenty-ninth of November, 1760, that Detroit fell into the hands of the English. The garrison were sent as prisoners down the lake, but the Canadian inhabitants were allowed to retain their farms and houses, on condition of swearing allegiance to the British crown. An officer was sent southward to take possession of the forts Miami and Ouatanon, which guarded the communication between Lake Erie and the Ohio; while Rogers himself, with a small party, proceeded northward to relieve the French garrison of Michillimackinac. The storms and gathering ice of Lake Huron forced him back without accomplishing his object; and Michillimackinac, with the three remoter posts of St. Marie, Green Bay, and St. Joseph, remained for a time in the hands of the French. During the next season, however, a detachment of the 60th regiment, then called the Royal Americans, took possession of them; and nothing now remained within the power of the French, except the few posts and settlements on the Mississippi and the Wabash, not included in the capitulation of Montreal.

The work of conquest was finished. The fertile wilderness beyond the Alleghanies, over which France had claimed sovereignty,—that boundless forest, with its tracery of interlacing streams, which, like veins and arteries, gave it life and nourishment,—had passed into the hands of her rival. It was by a few insignificant forts, separated by oceans of fresh water and uncounted leagues of forest, that the two great European powers, France first, and now England, endeavored to enforce their claims to this vast domain. There is something ludicrous in the disparity between the importance of the possession and the slenderness of the force employed to maintain it. A region embracing so many thousand miles of surface was consigned to the keeping of some five or six hundred men. Yet the force, small as it was, appeared adequate to its object, for there seemed no enemy to contend with. The hands of the French were tied by the capitulation, and little apprehension was felt from the red inhabitants of the woods. The lapse of two years sufficed to show how complete and fatal was the mistake.

ANGER OF THE INDIANS

1760 to 1763

The country was scarcely transferred to the English, when smothered murmurs of discontent began to be audible among the Indian tribes. From the head of the Potomac to Lake Superior, and from the Alleghanies to the Mississippi, in every wigwam and hamlet of the forest, a deep-rooted hatred of the English increased with rapid growth. Nor is this to be wondered at. We have seen with what sagacious policy the French had labored to ingratiate themselves with the Indians; and the slaughter of the Monongahela, with the horrible devastation of the western frontier, the outrages perpetrated at Oswego, and the massacre at Fort William Henry, bore witness to the success of their efforts. Even the Delawares and Shawanoes, the faithful allies of William Penn, had at length been seduced by their blandishments; and the Iroquois, the ancient enemies of Canada, had half forgotten their former hostility, and well-nigh taken part against the British colonists. The remote nations of the west had also joined in the war, descending in their canoes for hundreds of miles, to fight against the enemies of France. All these tribes entertained towards the English that rancorous enmity which an Indian always feels against those to whom he has been opposed in war.

Under these circumstances, it behooved the English to use the utmost care in their conduct towards the tribes. But even when the conflict with France was impending, and the alliance with the Indians was of the last importance, they had treated them with indifference and neglect. They were not likely to adopt a different course now that their friendship seemed a matter of no consequence. In truth, the intentions of the English were soon apparent. In the zeal for retrenchment, which prevailed after the close of hostilities, the presents which it had always been customary to give the Indians, at stated intervals, were either withheld altogether, or doled out with a niggardly and reluctant hand; while, to make the matter worse, the agents and officers of government often appropriated the presents to themselves, and afterwards sold them at an exorbitant price to the Indians. When the French had possession of the remote forts, they were accustomed, with a wise liberality, to supply the surrounding Indians with guns, ammunition, and clothing, until the latter had forgotten the weapons and garments of their forefathers, and depended on the white men for support. The sudden withholding of these supplies was, therefore, a grievous calamity. Want, suffering, and death, were the consequences; and this cause alone would have been enough to produce general discontent. But, unhappily, other grievances were superadded.

The English fur-trade had never been well regulated, and it was now in a worse condition than ever. Many of the traders, and those in their employ, were ruffians of the coarsest stamp, who vied with each other in rapacity, violence, and profligacy. They cheated, cursed, and plundered the Indians, and outraged their families; offering, when compared with the French traders, who were under better regulation, a most unfavorable example of the character of their nation.

The officers and soldiers of the garrisons did their full part in exciting the general resentment. Formerly, when the warriors came to the forts, they had been welcomed by the French with attention and respect. The inconvenience which their presence occasioned had been disregarded, and their peculiarities overlooked. But now they were received with cold looks and harsh words from the officers, and with oaths, menaces, and sometimes blows, from the reckless and brutal soldiers. When, after their troublesome and intrusive fashion, they were lounging everywhere about the fort, or lazily reclining in the shadow of the walls, they were met with muttered ejaculations of impatience, or abrupt orders to be gone, enforced, perhaps, by a touch from the butt of a sentinel's musket. These marks of contempt were unspeakably galling to their haughty spirit.

But what most contributed to the growing discontent of the tribes was the intrusion of settlers upon their lands, at all times a fruitful source of Indian hostility. Its effects, it is true, could only be felt by those whose country bordered upon the English settlements; but among these were the most powerful and influential of the tribes. The Delawares and Shawanoes, in particular, had by this time been roused to the highest pitch of exasperation. Their best lands had been invaded, and all remonstrance had been fruitless. They viewed with wrath and fear the steady progress of the white man, whose settlements had passed the Susquehanna, and were fast extending to the Alleghanies, eating away the forest like a spreading canker. The anger of the Delawares was abundantly shared by their ancient conquerors, the Six Nations. The threatened occupation of Wyoming by settlers from Connecticut gave great umbrage to the confederacy. The Senecas were more especially incensed at English intrusion, since, from their position, they were farthest removed from the soothing influence of Sir William Johnson, and most exposed to the seductions of the French; while the Mohawks, another member of the confederacy, were justly alarmed at seeing the better part of their lands patented out without their consent. Some Christian Indians of the Oneida tribe, in the simplicity of their hearts, sent an earnest petition to Sir William Johnson, that the English forts within the limits of the Six Nations might be removed, or, as the petition expresses it, kicked out of the way.

The discontent of the Indians gave great satisfaction to the French, who saw in it an assurance of safe and bloody vengeance on their conquerors. Canada, it is true, was gone beyond hope of recovery; but they still might hope to revenge its loss. Interest, moreover, as well as passion, prompted them to inflame the resentment of the Indians; for most of the inhabitants of the French settlements upon the lakes and the Mississippi were engaged in the fur-trade, and, fearing the English as formidable rivals, they would gladly have seen them driven out of the country. Traders, habitans, coureurs de bois, and all classes of this singular population, accordingly dispersed themselves among the villages of the Indians, or held councils with them in the secret places of the woods, urging them to take up arms against the English. They exhibited the conduct of the latter in its worst light, and spared neither misrepresentation nor falsehood. They told their excited hearers that the English had formed a deliberate scheme to root out the whole Indian race, and, with that design, had already begun to hem them in with settlements on the one hand, and a chain of forts on the other. Among other atrocious plans for their destruction, they had instigated the Cherokees to attack and destroy the tribes of the Ohio valley. These groundless calumnies found ready belief. The French declared, in addition, that the King of France had of late years fallen asleep; that, during his slumbers, the English had seized upon Canada; but that he was now awake again, and that his armies were advancing up the St. Lawrence and the Mississippi, to drive out the intruders from the country of his red children. To these fabrications was added the more substantial encouragement of arms, ammunition, clothing, and provisions, which the French trading companies, if not the officers of the crown, distributed with a liberal hand.

The fierce passions of the Indians, excited by their wrongs, real or imagined, and exasperated by the representations of the French, were yet farther wrought upon by influences of another kind. A prophet rose among the Delawares. This man may serve as a counterpart to the famous Shawanoe prophet, who figured so conspicuously in the Indian outbreak, under Tecumseh, immediately before the war with England in 1812. Many other parallel instances might be shown, as the great susceptibility of the Indians to superstitious impressions renders the advent of a prophet among them no very rare occurrence. In the present instance, the inspired Delaware seems to have been rather an enthusiast than an impostor; or perhaps he combined both characters. The objects of his mission were not wholly political. By means of certain external observances, most of them sufficiently frivolous and absurd, his disciples were to strengthen and purify their natures, and make themselves acceptable to the Great Spirit, whose messenger he proclaimed himself to be. He also enjoined them to lay aside the weapons and clothing which they received from the white men, and return to the primitive life of their ancestors. By so doing, and by strictly observing his other precepts, the tribes would soon be restored to their ancient greatness and power, and be enabled to drive out the white men who infested their territory. The prophet had many followers. Indians came from far and near, and gathered together in large encampments to listen to his exhortations. His fame spread even to the nations of the northern lakes; but though his disciples followed most of his injunctions, flinging away flint and steel, and making copious use of emetics, with other observances equally troublesome, yet the requisition to abandon the use of fire-arms was too inconvenient to be complied with.

With so many causes to irritate their restless and warlike spirit, it could not be supposed that the Indians would long remain quiet. Accordingly, in the summer of the year 1761, Captain Campbell, then commanding at Detroit, received information that a deputation of Senecas had come to the neighboring village of the Wyandots for the purpose of instigating the latter to destroy him and his garrison. On farther inquiry, the plot proved to be general; and Niagara, Fort Pitt, and other posts, were to share the fate of Detroit. Campbell instantly despatched messengers to Sir Jeffrey Amherst, and the commanding officers of the different forts; and, by this timely discovery, the conspiracy was nipped in the bud. During the following summer, 1762, another similar design was detected and suppressed. They proved to be the precursors of a tempest. When, early in 1763, it was announced to the tribes that the King of France had ceded all their country to the King of England, without even asking their leave, a ferment of indignation at once became apparent among them; and, within a few weeks, a plot was matured, such as was never, before or since, conceived or executed by a North American Indian. It was determined to attack all the English forts upon the same day; then, having destroyed their garrisons, to turn upon the defenceless frontier, and ravage and lay waste the settlements, until, as many of the Indians fondly believed, the English should all be driven into the sea, and the country restored to its primitive owners.

It is difficult to determine which tribe was first to raise the cry of war. There were many who might have done so, for all the savages in the backwoods were ripe for an outbreak, and the movement seemed almost simultaneous. The Delawares and Senecas were the most incensed, and Kiashuta, a chief of the latter, was perhaps foremost to apply the torch; but, if this was the case, he touched fire to materials already on the point of igniting. It belonged to a greater chief than he to give method and order to what would else have been a wild burst of fury, and convert desultory attacks into a formidable and protracted war. But for Pontiac, the whole might have ended in a few troublesome inroads upon the frontier, and a little whooping and yelling under the walls of Fort Pitt.

Pontiac, as already mentioned, was principal chief of the Ottawas. The Ottawas, Ojibwas, and Pottawattamies, had long been united in a loose kind of confederacy, of which he was the virtual head. Over those around him his authority was almost despotic, and his power extended far beyond the limits of the three united tribes. His influence was great among all the nations of the Illinois country; while, from the sources of the Ohio to those of the Mississippi, and, indeed, to the farthest boundaries of the wide-spread Algonquin race, his name was known and respected.

The fact that Pontiac was born the son of a chief would in no degree account for the extent of his power; for, among Indians, many a chief's son sinks back into insignificance, while the offspring of a common warrior may succeed to his place. Among all the wild tribes of the continent, personal merit is indispensable to gaining or preserving dignity. Courage, resolution, address, and eloquence are sure passports to distinction. With all these Pontiac was pre-eminently endowed, and it was chiefly to them, urged to their highest activity by a vehement ambition, that he owed his greatness. He possessed a commanding energy and force of mind, and in subtlety and craft could match the best of his wily race. But, though capable of acts of magnanimity, he was a thorough savage, with a wider range of intellect than those around him, but sharing all their passions and prejudices, their fierceness and treachery. His faults were the faults of his race; and they cannot eclipse his nobler qualities. His memory is still cherished among the remnants of many Algonquin tribes, and the celebrated Tecumseh adopted him for his model, proving himself no unworthy imitator.

Pontiac was now about fifty years old. Until Major Rogers came into the country, he had been, from motives probably both of interest and inclination, a firm friend of the French. Not long before the French war broke out, he had saved the garrison of Detroit from the imminent peril of an attack from some of the discontented tribes of the north. During the war, he had fought on the side of France. It is said that he commanded the Ottawas at the memorable defeat of Braddock; and it is certain that he was treated with much honor by the French officers, and received especial marks of esteem from the Marquis of Montcalm.

We have seen how, when the tide of affairs changed, the subtle and ambitious chief trimmed his bark to the current, and gave the hand of friendship to the English. That he was disappointed in their treatment of him, and in all the hopes that he had formed from their alliance, is sufficiently evident from one of his speeches. A new light soon began to dawn upon his untaught but powerful mind, and he saw the altered posture of affairs under its true aspect.

It was a momentous and gloomy crisis for the Indian race, for never before had they been exposed to such imminent and pressing danger. With the downfall of Canada, the tribes had sunk at once from their position of importance. Hitherto the two rival European nations had kept each other in check upon the American continent, and the Indians had, in some measure, held the balance of power between them. To conciliate their good will and gain their alliance, to avoid offending them by injustice and encroachment, was the policy both of the French and English. But now the face of affairs was changed. The English had gained an undisputed ascendency, and the Indians, no longer important as allies, were treated as mere barbarians, who might be trampled upon with impunity. Abandoned to their own feeble resources and divided strength, they must fast recede, and dwindle away before the steady progress of the colonial power. Already their best hunting-grounds were invaded, and from the eastern ridges of the Alleghanies they might see, from far and near, the smoke of the settlers' clearings, rising in tall columns from the dark-green bosom of the forest. The doom of the race was sealed, and no human power could avert it; but they, in their ignorance, believed otherwise, and vainly thought that, by a desperate effort, they might yet uproot and overthrow the growing strength of their destroyers.

It would be idle to suppose that the great mass of the Indians understood, in its full extent, the danger which threatened their race. With them, the war was a mere outbreak of fury, and they turned against their enemies with as little reason or forecast as a panther when he leaps at the throat of the hunter. Goaded by wrongs and indignities, they struck for revenge, and for relief from the evil of the moment. But the mind of Pontiac could embrace a wider and deeper view. The peril of the times was unfolded in its full extent before him, and he resolved to unite the tribes in one grand effort to avert it. He did not, like many of his people, entertain the absurd idea that the Indians, by their unaided strength, could drive the English into the sea. He adopted the only plan consistent with reason, that of restoring the French ascendency in the west, and once more opposing a check to British encroachment. With views like these, he lent a greedy ear to the plausible falsehoods of the Canadians, who assured him that the armies of King Louis were already advancing to recover Canada, and that the French and their red brethren, fighting side by side, would drive the English dogs back within their own narrow limits.

Revolving these thoughts, and remembering that his own ambitious views might be advanced by the hostilities he meditated, Pontiac no longer hesitated. Revenge, ambition, and patriotism wrought upon him alike, and he resolved on war. At the close of the year 1762, he sent ambassadors to the different nations. They visited the country of the Ohio and its tributaries, passed northward to the region of the upper lakes, and the borders of the river Ottawa; and far southward towards the mouth of the Mississippi. Bearing with them the war-belt of wampum, broad and long, as the importance of the message demanded, and the tomahawk stained red, in token of war, they went from camp to camp, and village to village. Wherever they appeared, the sachems and old men assembled, to hear the words of the great Pontiac. Then the chief of the embassy flung down the tomahawk on the ground before them, and holding the war-belt in his hand, delivered, with vehement gesture, word for word, the speech with which he was charged. It was heard everywhere with approval; the belt was accepted, the hatchet snatched up, and the assembled chiefs stood pledged to take part in the war. The blow was to be struck at a certain time in the month of May following, to be indicated by the changes of the moon. The tribes were to rise together, each destroying the English garrison in its neighborhood, and then, with a general rush, the whole were to turn against the settlements of the frontier.

The tribes, thus banded together against the English, comprised, with a few unimportant exceptions, the whole Algonquin stock, to whom were united the Wyandots, the Senecas, and several tribes of the lower Mississippi. The Senecas were the only members of the Iroquois confederacy who joined in the league, the rest being kept quiet by the influence of Sir William Johnson, whose utmost exertions, however, were barely sufficient to allay their irritation.

While thus on the very eve of an outbreak, the Indians concealed their designs with the dissimulation of their race. The warriors still lounged about the forts, with calm, impenetrable faces, begging, as usual, for tobacco, gunpowder, and whiskey. Now and then, some slight intimation of danger would startle the garrisons from their security. An English trader, coming in from the Indian villages, would report that, from their manner and behavior, he suspected them of brooding mischief; or some scoundrel half-breed would be heard boasting in his cups that before next summer he would have English hair to fringe his hunting-frock. On one occasion, the plot was nearly discovered. Early in March, 1763, Ensign Holmes, commanding at Fort Miami, was told by a friendly Indian that the warriors in the neighboring village had lately received a war-belt, with a message urging them to destroy him and his garrison, and that this they were preparing to do. Holmes called the Indians together, and boldly charged them with their design. They did as Indians on such occasions have often done, confessed their fault with much apparent contrition, laid the blame on a neighboring tribe, and professed eternal friendship to their brethren, the English. Holmes writes to report his discovery to Major Gladwyn, who, in his turn, sends the information to Sir Jeffrey Amherst, expressing his opinion that there has been a general irritation among the Indians, but that the affair will soon blow over, and that, in the neighborhood of his own post, the savages were perfectly tranquil. Within cannon shot of the deluded officer's palisades, was the village of Pontiac himself, the arch enemy of the English, and prime mover in the plot.

With the approach of spring, the Indians, coming in from their wintering grounds, began to appear in small parties about the various forts; but now they seldom entered them, encamping at a little distance in the woods. They were fast pushing their preparations for the meditated blow, and waiting with stifled eagerness for the appointed hour.

INDIAN PREPARATION

1763

I interrupt the progress of the narrative to glance for a moment at the Indians in their military capacity, and observe how far they were qualified to prosecute the formidable war into which they were about to plunge.
A people living chiefly by the chase, and therefore, of necessity, thinly and widely scattered; divided into numerous tribes, held together by no strong principle of cohesion, and with no central government to combine their strength, could act with little efficiency against such an enemy as was now opposed to them. Loose and disjointed as a whole, the government even of individual tribes, and of their smallest separate communities, was too feeble to deserve the name. There were, it is true, chiefs whose office was in a manner hereditary; but their authority was wholly of a moral nature, and enforced by no compulsory law. Their province was to advise, and not to command. Their influence, such as it was, is chiefly to be ascribed to the principle of hero-worship, natural to the Indian character, and to the reverence for age, which belongs to a state of society where a patriarchal element largely prevails. It was their office to declare war and make peace; but when war was declared, they had no power to carry the declaration into effect. The warriors fought if they chose to do so; but if, on the contrary, they preferred to remain quiet, no man could force them to raise the hatchet. The war-chief, whose part it was to lead them to battle, was a mere partisan, whom his bravery and exploits had led to distinction. If he thought proper, he sang his war-song and danced his war-dance; and as many of the young men as were disposed to follow him, gathered around and enlisted themselves under him. Over these volunteers he had no legal

authority, and they could desert him at any moment, with no other penalty than disgrace. When several war parties, of different bands or tribes, were united in a common enterprise, their chiefs elected a leader, who was nominally to command the whole; but unless this leader was a man of uncommon reputation and ability, his commands were disregarded, and his authority was a cipher. Among his followers, every latent element of discord, pride, jealousy, and ancient half-smothered feuds, were ready at any moment to break out, and tear the whole asunder. His warriors would often desert in bodies; and many an Indian army, before reaching the enemy's country, has been known to dwindle away until it was reduced to a mere scalping party.

To twist a rope of sand would be as easy a task as to form a permanent and effective army of such materials. The wild love of freedom, and impatience of all control, which mark the Indian race, render them utterly intolerant of military discipline. Partly from their individual character, and partly from this absence of subordination, spring results highly unfavorable to continued and extended military operations. Indian warriors, when acting in large masses, are to the last degree wayward, capricious, and unstable; infirm of purpose as a mob of children, and devoid of providence and foresight. To provide supplies for a campaign forms no part of their system. Hence the blow must be struck at once, or not struck at all; and to postpone victory is to insure defeat. It is when acting in small, detached parties, that the Indian warrior puts forth his energies, and displays his admirable address, endurance, and intrepidity. It is then that he becomes a truly formidable enemy. Fired with the hope of winning scalps, he is stanch as a bloodhound. No hardship can divert him from his purpose, and no danger subdue his patient and cautious courage.

From their inveterate passion for war, the Indians are always prompt enough to engage in it; and on the present occasion, the prevailing irritation gave ample assurance that they would not remain idle. While there was little risk that they would capture any strong and well-defended fort, or carry any important position, there was, on the other hand, every reason to apprehend wide-spread havoc, and a destructive war of detail. That the war might be carried on with effect, it was the part of the Indian leaders to work upon the passions of their people, and keep alive their irritation; to whet their native appetite for blood and glory, and cheer them on to the attack; to guard against all that might quench their ardor, or cool their fierceness; to avoid pitched battles; never to fight except under advantage; and to avail themselves of all the aid which craft and treachery could afford. The very circumstances which unfitted the Indians for continued and concentrated attack were, in another view, highly advantageous, by preventing the enemy from assailing them with vital effect. It was no easy task to penetrate tangled woods in search of a foe, alert and active as a lynx, who would seldom stand and fight, whose deadly shot and triumphant whoop were the first and often the last tokens of his presence, and who, at the approach of a hostile force, would vanish into the black recesses of forests and pine-swamps, only to renew his attacks with unabated ardor. There were no forts to capture, no magazines to destroy, and little property to seize upon. No warfare could be more perilous and harassing in its prosecution, or less satisfactory in its results.

The English colonies at this time were but ill fitted to bear the brunt of the impending war. The army which had conquered Canada was broken up and dissolved; the provincials were disbanded, and most of the regulars sent home. A few fragments of regiments, miserably wasted by war and sickness, had just arrived from the West Indies; and of these, several were already ordered to England, to be disbanded. There remained barely troops enough to furnish feeble garrisons for the various forts on the frontier and in the Indian country. At the head of this dilapidated army was Sir Jeffrey Amherst, who had achieved the reduction of Canada, and clinched the nail which Wolfe had driven. In some respects he was well fitted for the emergency; but, on the other hand, he held the Indians in supreme contempt, and his arbitrary treatment of them and total want of every quality of conciliation where they were concerned, had had no little share in exciting them to war.

While the war was on the eve of breaking out, an event occurred which had afterwards an important effect upon its progress,—the signing of the treaty of peace at Paris, on the tenth of February, 1763. By this treaty France resigned her claims to the territories east of the Mississippi, and that great148 river now became the western boundary of the British colonial possessions. In portioning out her new acquisitions into separate governments, England left the valley of the Ohio and the adjacent regions as an Indian domain, and by the proclamation of the seventh of October following, the intrusion of settlers upon these lands was strictly prohibited. Could these just and necessary measures have been sooner adopted, it is probable that the Indian war might have been prevented, or, at all events, rendered less general and violent, for the treaty would have made it apparent that the French could never repossess themselves of Canada, and would have proved the futility of every hope which the Indians entertained of assistance from that quarter, while, at the same time, the royal proclamation would have tended to tranquillize their minds, by removing the chief cause of irritation. But the remedy came too late, and served only to inflame the evil. While the sovereigns of France, England, and Spain, were signing the treaty at Paris, countless Indian warriors in the American forests were singing the war-song, and whetting their scalping-knives.

Throughout the western wilderness, in a hundred camps and villages, were celebrated the savage rites of war. Warriors, women, and children were alike eager and excited; magicians consulted their oracles, and prepared charms to insure success; while the war-chief, his body painted black from head to foot, concealed himself in the solitude of rocks and caverns, or the dark recesses of the forest. Here, fasting and praying, he calls day and night upon the Great Spirit, consulting his dreams, to draw from them auguries of good or evil; and if, perchance, a vision of the great war-eagle seems to hover over him with expanded wings, he exults in the full conviction of triumph. When a few days have elapsed, he emerges from his retreat, and the people discover him descending from the woods, and approaching their camp, black as a demon of war, and shrunken with fasting and vigil. They flock around and listen to his wild harangue. He calls on them to avenge the blood of their slaughtered relatives; he assures them that the Great Spirit is on their side, and that victory is certain. With exulting cries they disperse to their wigwams, to array themselves in the savage decorations of the war-dress. An old man now passes through the camp, and invites the warriors to a feast in the name of the chief. They gather from all quarters to his wigwam, where they find him seated, no longer covered with black, but adorned with the startling and fantastic blazonry of the war-paint. Those who join in the feast pledge themselves, by so doing, to follow him against the enemy. The guests seat themselves on the ground, in a circle around the wigwam, and the flesh of dogs is placed in wooden dishes before them, while the chief, though goaded by the pangs of his long, unbroken fast, sits smoking his pipe with unmoved countenance, and takes no part in the feast. Night has now closed in; and the rough clearing is illumined by the blaze of fires and burning pine-knots, casting their deep red glare upon the dusky boughs of the surrounding forest, and upon the wild multitude who, fluttering with feathers and bedaubed with paint, have gathered for the celebration of the war-dance. A painted post is driven into the ground, and the crowd form a wide circle around it. The chief leaps into the vacant space, brandishing his hatchet as if rushing upon an enemy, and, in a loud, vehement tone, chants his own exploits and those of his ancestors, enacting the deeds which he describes, yelling the war-whoop, throwing himself into all the postures of actual fight, striking the post as if it were an enemy, and tearing the scalp from the head of the imaginary victim. Warrior after warrior follows his example, until the whole assembly, as if fired with sudden frenzy, rush together into the ring, leaping, stamping, and whooping, brandishing knives and hatchets in the fire-light, hacking and stabbing the air, and breaking at intervals into a burst of ferocious yells, which sounds for miles away over the lonely, midnight forest.

In the morning, the warriors prepare to depart. They leave the camp in single file, still decorated with all their finery of paint, feathers, and scalp-locks; and, as they enter the woods, the chief fires his gun, the warrior behind follows his example, and the discharges pass in slow succession from front to rear, the salute concluding with a general whoop. They encamp at no great distance from the village, and divest themselves of their much-prized ornaments, which are carried back by the women, who have followed them for this purpose. The warriors pursue their journey, clad in the rough attire of hard service, and move silently and stealthily through the forest towards the hapless garrison, or defenceless settlement, which they have marked as their prey.

The woods were now filled with war-parties such as this, and soon the first tokens of the approaching tempest began to alarm the unhappy settlers of the frontier. At first, some trader or hunter, weak and emaciated, would come in from the forest, and relate that his companions had been butchered in the Indian villages, and that he alone had escaped. Next succeeded vague and uncertain rumors of forts attacked and garrisons slaughtered; and soon after, a report gained ground that every post throughout the Indian country had been taken, and every soldier killed. Close upon these tidings came the enemy himself. The Indian war-parties broke out of the woods like gangs of wolves, murdering, burning, and laying waste; while hundreds of terror-stricken families, abandoning their homes, fled for refuge towards the older settlements, and all was misery and ruin.

Passing over, for the present, this portion of the war, we will penetrate at once into the heart of the Indian country, and observe those passages of the conflict which took place under the auspices of Pontiac himself,—the siege of Detroit, and the capture of the interior posts and garrisons.

THE COUNCIL AT THE RIVER ECORCES

1763

To begin the war was reserved by Pontiac as his own peculiar privilege. With the first opening of spring his preparations were complete. His light-footed messengers, with their wampum belts and gifts of tobacco, visited many a lonely hunting camp in the gloom of the northern woods, and called chiefs and warriors to attend the general meeting. The appointed spot was on the banks of the little River Ecorces, not far from Detroit. Thither went Pontiac himself, with his squaws and his children. Band after band came straggling in from every side, until the meadow was thickly dotted with their frail wigwams. Here were idle warriors smoking and laughing in groups, or beguiling the lazy hours with gambling, feasting, or doubtful stories of their own martial exploits. Here were youthful gallants, bedizened with all the foppery of beads, feathers, and hawks' bells, but held as yet in light esteem, since they had slain no enemy, and taken no scalp. Here too were young damsels, radiant with bears' oil, ruddy with vermilion, and versed in all the arts of forest coquetry; shrivelled hags, with limbs of wire, and the voices of screech-owls; and troops of naked children, with small, black, mischievous eyes, roaming along the outskirts of the woods.

The great Roman historian observes of the ancient Germans, that when summoned to a public meeting, they would lag behind the appointed time in order to show their independence. The remark holds true, and perhaps with greater emphasis, of the American Indians; and thus it happened, that several days elapsed before the assembly was complete. In such a motley concourse of barbarians, where different bands and different tribes were mustered on one common camp ground, it would need all the art of a prudent leader to prevent their dormant jealousies from starting into open strife. No people are more prompt to quarrel, and none more prone, in the fierce excitement of the present, to forget the purpose of the future; yet, through good fortune, or the wisdom of Pontiac, no rupture occurred; and at length the last loiterer appeared, and farther delay was needless.

The council took place on the twenty-seventh of April. On that morning, several old men, the heralds of the camp, passed to and fro among the lodges, calling the warriors, in a loud voice, to attend the meeting.

In accordance with the summons, they issued from their cabins: the tall, naked figures of the wild Ojibwas, with quivers slung at their backs, and light war-clubs resting in the hollow of their arms; Ottawas, wrapped close in their gaudy blankets; Wyandots, fluttering in painted shirts, their heads adorned with feathers, and their leggins garnished with bells. All were soon seated in a wide circle upon the grass, row within row, a grave and silent assembly. Each savage countenance seemed carved in wood, and none could have detected the ferocious passions hidden beneath that immovable mask. Pipes with ornamented stems were lighted, and passed from hand to hand.

Then Pontiac rose, and walked forward into the midst of the council. According to Canadian tradition, he was not above the middle height, though his muscular figure was cast in a mould of remarkable symmetry and vigor. His complexion was darker than is usual with his race, and his features, though by no means regular, had a bold and stern expression; while his habitual bearing was imperious and peremptory, like that of a man accustomed to sweep away all opposition by the force of his impetuous will. His ordinary attire was that of the primitive savage,—a scanty cincture girt about his loins, and his long, black hair flowing loosely at his back; but on occasions like this he was wont to appear as befitted his power and character, and he stood doubtless before the council plumed and painted in the full costume of war.

Looking round upon his wild auditors he began to speak, with fierce gesture, and a loud, impassioned voice; and at every pause, deep, guttural ejaculations of assent and approval responded to his words. He inveighed against the arrogance, rapacity, and injustice, of the English, and contrasted them with the French, whom they had driven from the soil. He declared that the British commandant had treated him with neglect and contempt; that the soldiers of the garrison had abused the Indians; and that one of them had struck a follower of his own. He represented the danger that would arise from the supremacy of the English. They had expelled the French, and now they only waited for a pretext to turn upon the Indians and destroy them. Then, holding out a broad belt of wampum, he told the council that he had received it from their great father the King of France, in token that he had heard the voice of his red children; that his sleep was at an end; and that his great war canoes would soon sail up the St. Lawrence, to win back Canada, and wreak vengeance on his enemies. The Indians and their French brethren would fight once more side by side, as they had always fought; they would strike the English as they had struck them many moons ago, when their great army marched down the Monongahela, and they had shot them from their ambush, like a flock of pigeons in the woods. Having roused in his warlike listeners their native thirst for blood and vengeance, he next addressed himself to their superstition, and told the following tale. Its precise origin is not easy to determine. It is possible that the Delaware prophet, mentioned in a former chapter, may have had some part in it; or it might have been the offspring of Pontiac's heated imagination, during his period of fasting and dreaming. That he deliberately invented it for the sake of the effect it would produce, is the least probable conclusion of all; for it evidently proceeds from the superstitious mind of an Indian, brooding upon the evil days in which his lot was cast, and turning for relief to the mysterious Author of his being. It is, at all events, a characteristic specimen of the Indian legendary tales, and, like many of them, bears an allegoric significancy. Yet he who endeavors to interpret an Indian allegory through all its erratic windings and puerile inconsistencies, has undertaken no enviable task.

"A Delaware Indian," said Pontiac, "conceived an eager desire to learn wisdom from the Master of Life; but, being ignorant where to find him, he had recourse to fasting, dreaming, and magical incantations. By these means it was revealed to him, that, by moving forward in a straight, undeviating course, he would reach the abode of the Great Spirit. He told his purpose to no one, and having provided the equipments of a hunter,—gun, powder-horn, ammunition, and a kettle for preparing his food,—he set out on his errand. For some time he journeyed on in high hope and confidence. On the evening of the eighth day, he stopped by the side of a brook at the edge of a meadow, where he began to make ready his evening meal, when, looking up, he saw three large openings in the woods before him, and three well-beaten paths which entered them. He was much surprised; but his wonder increased, when, after it had grown dark, the three paths were more clearly visible than ever. Remembering the important object of his journey, he could neither rest nor sleep; and, leaving his fire, he crossed the meadow, and entered the largest of the three openings. He had advanced but a short distance into the forest, when a bright flame sprang out of the ground before him, and arrested his steps. In great amazement, he turned back, and entered the second path, where the same wonderful phenomenon again encountered him; and now, in terror and bewilderment, yet still resolved to persevere, he took the last of the three paths. On this he journeyed a whole day without interruption, when at length, emerging from the forest, he saw before him a vast mountain, of dazzling whiteness. So precipitous was the ascent, that the Indian thought it hopeless to go farther, and looked around him in despair: at that moment, he saw, seated at some distance above, the figure of a beautiful woman arrayed in white, who arose as he looked upon her, and thus accosted him: 'How can you hope, encumbered as you are, to succeed in your design? Go down to the foot of the mountain, throw away your gun, your ammunition, your provisions, and your clothing; wash yourself in the stream which flows there, and you will then be prepared to stand before the Master of Life.' The Indian obeyed, and again began to ascend among the rocks, while the woman, seeing him still discouraged, laughed at his faintness of heart, and told him that, if he wished for success, he must climb by the aid of one hand and one foot only. After great toil and suffering, he at length found himself at the summit. The woman had disappeared, and he was left alone. A rich and beautiful plain lay before him, and at a little distance he saw three great villages, far superior to the squalid wigwams of the Delawares. As he approached the largest, and stood hesitating whether he should enter, a man gorgeously attired stepped forth, and, taking him by the hand, welcomed him to the celestial abode. He then conducted him into the presence of the Great Spirit, where the Indian stood confounded at the unspeakable splendor which surrounded him. The Great Spirit bade him be seated, and thus addressed him:—

"'I am the Maker of heaven and earth, the trees, lakes, rivers, and all things else. I am the Maker of mankind; and because I love you, you must do my will. The land on which you live I have made for you, and not for others. Why do you suffer the white men to dwell among you? My children, you have forgotten the customs and traditions of your forefathers. Why do you not clothe yourselves in skins, as they did, and use the bows and arrows, and the stone-pointed lances, which they used? You have bought guns, knives, kettles, and blankets, from the white men, until you can no longer do without them; and, what is worse, you have drunk the poison fire-water, which turns you into fools. Fling all these things away; live as your wise forefathers lived before you. And as for these English,—these dogs dressed in red, who have come to rob you of your hunting-grounds, and drive away the game,—you must lift the hatchet against them. Wipe them from the face of the earth, and then you will win my favor back again, and once more be happy and prosperous. The children of your great father, the King of France, are not like the English. Never forget that they are your brethren. They are very dear to me, for they love the red men, and understand the true mode of worshipping me,'"

The Great Spirit next gave his hearer various precepts of morality and religion, such as the prohibition to marry more than one wife; and a warning against the practice of magic, which is worshipping the devil. A prayer, embodying the substance of all that he had heard, was then presented to the Delaware. It was cut in hieroglyphics upon a wooden stick, after the custom of his people; and he was directed to send copies of it to all the Indian villages.

The adventurer now departed, and, returning to the earth, reported all the wonders he had seen in the celestial regions.

Such was the tale told by Pontiac to the council; and it is worthy of notice, that not he alone, but many of the most notable men who have arisen among the Indians, have been opponents of civilization, and stanch advocates of primitive barbarism. Red Jacket and Tecumseh would gladly have brought back their people to the rude simplicity of their original condition. There is nothing progressive in the rigid, inflexible nature of an Indian. He will not open his mind to the idea of improvement; and nearly every change that has been forced upon him has been a change for the worse.

Many other speeches were doubtless made in the council, but no record of them has been preserved. All present were eager to attack the British fort; and Pontiac told them, in conclusion, that on the second of May he would gain admittance, with a party of his warriors, on pretence of dancing the calumet dance before the garrison; that they would take note of the strength of the fortification; and that he would then summon another council to determine the mode of attack.

The assembly now dissolved, and all the evening the women were employed in loading the canoes, which were drawn up on the bank of the stream. The encampments broke up at so early an hour, that when the sun rose, the savage swarm had melted away; the secluded scene was restored to its wonted silence and solitude, and nothing remained but the slender framework of several hundred cabins, with fragments of broken utensils, pieces of cloth, and scraps of hide, scattered over the trampled grass; while the smouldering embers of numberless fires mingled their dark smoke with the white mist which rose from the little river.

Every spring, after the winter hunt was over, the Indians were accustomed to return to their villages, or permanent encampments, in the vicinity of Detroit; and, accordingly, after the council had broken up, they made their appearance as usual about the fort. On the first of May, Pontiac came to the gate with forty men of the Ottawa tribe, and asked permission to enter and dance the calumet dance, before the officers of the garrison. After some hesitation, he was admitted; and proceeding to the corner of the street, where stood the house of the commandant, Major Gladwyn, he and thirty of his warriors began their dance, each recounting his own exploits, and boasting himself the bravest of mankind. The officers and men gathered around them; while, in the mean time, the remaining ten of the Ottawas strolled about the fort, observing every thing it contained. When the dance was over, they all quietly withdrew, not a suspicion of their designs having arisen in the minds of the English.

After a few days had elapsed, Pontiac's messengers again passed among the

Indian cabins, calling the principal chiefs to another council, in the Pottawattamie village. Here there was a large structure of bark, erected for the public use on occasions like the present. A hundred chiefs were seated around this dusky council-house, the fire in the centre shedding its fitful light upon their dark, naked forms, while the pipe passed from hand to hand. To prevent interruption, Pontiac had stationed young men as sentinels, near the house. He once more addressed the chiefs; inciting them to hostility against the English, and concluding by the proposal of his plan for destroying Detroit. It was as follows: Pontiac would demand a council with the commandant concerning matters of great importance; and on this pretext he flattered himself that he and his principal chiefs would gain ready admittance within the fort. They were all to carry weapons concealed beneath their blankets. While in the act of addressing the commandant in the council-room, Pontiac was to make a certain signal, upon which the chiefs were to raise the war-whoop, rush upon the officers present, and strike them down. The other Indians, waiting meanwhile at the gate, or loitering among the houses, on hearing the yells and firing within the building, were to assail the astonished and half-armed soldiers; and thus Detroit would fall an easy prey.

In opening this plan of treachery, Pontiac spoke rather as a counsellor than as a commander. Haughty as he was, he had too much sagacity to wound the pride of a body of men over whom he had no other control than that derived from his personal character and influence. No one was hardy enough to venture opposition to the proposal of their great leader. His plan was eagerly adopted. Hoarse ejaculations of applause echoed his speech; and, gathering their blankets around them, the chiefs withdrew to their respective villages, to prepare for the destruction of the unsuspecting garrison.

DETROIT

1763

To the credulity of mankind each great calamity has its dire prognostics. Signs and portents in the heavens, the vision of an Indian bow, and the figure of a scalp imprinted on the disk of the moon, warned the New England Puritans of impending war. The apparitions passed away, and Philip of Mount Hope burst from the forest with his Narragansett warriors. In October, 1762, thick clouds of inky blackness gathered above the fort and settlement of Detroit. The river darkened beneath the awful shadows, and the forest was wrapped in double gloom. Drops of rain began to fall, of strong, sulphurous odor, and so deeply colored that the people, it is said, collected them and used them for writing. A literary and philosophical journal of the time seeks to explain this strange phenomenon on some principle of physical science; but the simple Canadians held a different faith. Throughout the winter, the shower of black rain was the foremost topic of their fireside talk; and forebodings of impending evil disturbed the breast of many a timorous matron.

La Motte-Cadillac was the founder of Detroit. In the year 1701, he planted the little military colony, which time has transformed into a thriving American city. At an earlier date, some feeble efforts had been made to secure the possession of this important pass; and when La Hontan visited the lakes, a small post, called Fort St. Joseph, was standing near the present site of Fort Gratiot. The wandering Jesuits, too, made frequent sojourns upon the borders of the Detroit, and baptized the savage children whom they found there.

Fort St. Joseph was abandoned in the year 1688. The establishment of Cadillac was destined to a better fate, and soon rose to distinguished importance among the western outposts of Canada. Indeed, the site was formed by nature for prosperity; and a bad government and a thriftless people could not prevent the increase of the colony. At the close of the French war, as Major Rogers tells us, the place contained twenty-five hundred inhabitants. The centre of the settlement was the fortified town, currently called the Fort, to distinguish it from the straggling dwellings along the river banks. It stood on the western margin of the river, covering a small part of the ground now occupied by the city of Detroit, and contained about a hundred houses, compactly pressed together, and surrounded by a palisade. Both above and below the fort, the banks of the stream were lined on both sides with small Canadian dwellings, extending at various intervals for nearly eight miles. Each had its garden and its orchard, and each was enclosed by a fence of rounded pickets. To the soldier or the trader, fresh from the harsh scenery and ambushed perils of the surrounding wilds, the secluded settlement was welcome as an oasis in the desert.

The Canadian is usually a happy man. Life sits lightly upon him; he laughs at its hardships, and soon forgets its sorrows. A lover of roving and adventure, of the frolic and the dance, he is little troubled with thoughts of the past or the future, and little plagued with avarice or ambition. At Detroit, all his propensities found ample scope. Aloof from the world, the simple colonists shared none of its pleasures and excitements, and were free from many of its cares. Nor were luxuries wanting which civilization might have envied them. The forests teemed with game, the marshes with wild fowl, and the rivers with fish. The apples and pears of the old Canadian orchards are even to this day held in esteem. The poorer inhabitants made wine from the fruit of the wild grape, which grew profusely in the woods, while the wealthier class procured a better quality from Montreal, in exchange for the canoe loads of furs which they sent down with every year. Here, as elsewhere in Canada, the long winter was a season of social enjoyment; and when, in summer and autumn, the traders and voyageurs, the coureurs de bois, and half-breeds, gathered from the distant forests of the north-west, the whole settlement was alive with dancing and feasting, drinking, gaming, and carousing.

Fort and SettlementS of Detroit, A. D. 1763
Larger.

Within the limits of the settlement were three large Indian villages. On the western shore, a little below the fort, were the lodges of the Pottawattamies; nearly opposite, on the eastern side, was the village of the Wyandots; and on the same side, five miles higher up, Pontiac's band of Ottawas had fixed their abode. The settlers had always maintained the best terms with their savage neighbors. In truth, there was much congeniality between the red man and the Canadian. Their harmony was seldom broken; and among the woods and wilds of the northern lakes roamed many a lawless half-breed, the mongrel offspring of the colonists of Detroit and the Indian squaws.

We have already seen how, in an evil hour for the Canadians, a party of British troops took possession of Detroit, towards the close of the year 1760. The British garrison, consisting partly of regulars and partly of provincial rangers, was now quartered in a well-built range of barracks within the town or fort. The latter, as already mentioned, contained about a hundred small houses. Its form was nearly square, and the palisade which surrounded it was about twenty-five feet high. At each corner was a wooden bastion, and a blockhouse was erected over each gateway. The houses were small, chiefly built of wood, and roofed with bark or a thatch of straw. The streets also were extremely narrow, though a wide passage way, known as the chemin du ronde, surrounded the town, between the houses and the palisade. Besides the barracks, the only public buildings were a council-house and a rude little church.

The garrison consisted of a hundred and twenty soldiers, with about forty fur-traders and engagés; but the latter, as well as the Canadian inhabitants of the place, could little be trusted, in the event of an Indian outbreak. Two small, armed schooners, the Beaver and the Gladwyn, lay anchored in the stream, and several light pieces of artillery were mounted on the bastions.

Such was Detroit,—a place whose defences could have opposed no resistance to a civilized enemy; and yet, far removed as it was from the hope of speedy succor, it could only rely, in the terrible struggles that awaited it, upon its own slight strength and feeble resources.

Standing on the water bastion of Detroit, a pleasant landscape spread before the eye. The river, about half a mile wide, almost washed the foot of the stockade; and either bank was lined with the white Canadian cottages. The joyous sparkling of the bright blue water; the green luxuriance of the woods; the white dwellings, looking out from the foliage; and, in the distance, the Indian wigwams curling their smoke against the sky,—all were mingled in one broad scene of wild and rural beauty.

Pontiac, the Satan of this forest paradise, was accustomed to spend the early part of the summer upon a small island at the opening of the Lake St. Clair, hidden from view by the high woods that covered the intervening Isle au Cochon. "The king and lord of all this country," as Rogers calls him, lived in no royal state. His cabin was a small, oven-shaped structure of bark and rushes. Here he dwelt, with his squaws and children; and here, doubtless, he might often have been seen, lounging, half-naked, on a rush mat, or a bear-skin, like any ordinary warrior. We may fancy the current of his thoughts, the turmoil of his uncurbed passions, as he revolved the treacheries which, to his savage mind, seemed fair and honorable. At one moment, his fierce heart would burn with the anticipation of vengeance on the detested English; at another, he would meditate how he best might turn the approaching tumults to the furtherance of his own ambitious schemes. Yet we may believe that Pontiac was not a stranger to the high emotion of the patriot hero, the champion not merely of his nation's rights, but of the very existence of his race. He did not dream how desperate a game he was about to play. He hourly flattered himself with the futile hope of aid from France, and thought in his ignorance that the British colonies must give way before the rush of his savage warriors; when, in truth, all the combined tribes of the forest might have chafed in vain rage against the rock-like strength of the Anglo-Saxon.

Looking across an intervening arm of the river, Pontiac could see on its eastern bank the numerous lodges of his Ottawa tribesmen, half hidden among the ragged growth of trees and bushes. On the afternoon of the fifth of May, a Canadian woman, the wife of St. Aubin, one of the principal settlers, crossed over from the western side, and visited the Ottawa village, to obtain from the Indians a supply of maple sugar and venison. She was surprised at finding several of the warriors engaged in filing off the muzzles of their guns, so as to reduce them, stock and all, to the length of about a yard. Returning home in the evening, she mentioned what she had seen to several of her neighbors. Upon this, one of them, the blacksmith of the village, remarked that many of the Indians had lately visited his shop, and attempted to borrow files and saws for a purpose which they would not explain. These circumstances excited the suspicion of the experienced Canadians. Doubtless there were many in the settlement who might, had they chosen, have revealed the plot; but it is no less certain that the more numerous and respectable class in the little community had too deep an interest in the preservation of peace, to countenance the designs of Pontiac. M. Gouin, an old and wealthy settler, went to the commandant, and conjured him to stand upon his guard; but Gladwyn, a man of fearless temper, gave no heed to the friendly advice.

In the Pottawattamie village, if there be truth in tradition, lived an Ojibwa girl, who could boast a larger share of beauty than is common in the wigwam. She had attracted the eye of Gladwyn. He had formed a connection with her, and she had become much attached to him. On the afternoon of the sixth, Catharine—for so the officers called her—came to the fort, and repaired to Gladwyn's quarters, bringing with her a pair of elk-skin moccasons, ornamented with porcupine work, which he had requested her to make. There was something unusual in her look and manner. Her face was sad and downcast. She said little, and soon left the room; but the sentinel at the door saw her still lingering at the street corner, though the hour for closing the gates was nearly come. At length she attracted the notice of Gladwyn himself; and calling her to him, he pressed her to declare what was weighing upon her mind. Still she remained for a long time silent, and it was only after much urgency and many promises not to betray her, that she revealed her momentous secret.

To-morrow, she said, Pontiac will come to the fort with sixty of his chiefs. Each will be armed with a gun, cut short, and hidden under his blanket. Pontiac will demand to hold a council; and after he has delivered his speech, he will offer a peace-belt of wampum, holding it in a reversed position. This will be the signal of attack. The chiefs will spring up and fire upon the officers, and the Indians in the street will fall upon the garrison. Every Englishman will be killed, but not the scalp of a single Frenchman will be touched.

Such is the story told in 1768 to the traveller Carver at Detroit, and preserved in local tradition, but not sustained by contemporary letters or diaries. What is certain is, that Gladwyn received secret information, on the night of the sixth of May, that an attempt would be made on the morrow to capture the fort by treachery. He called some of his officers, and told them what he had heard. The defences of the place were feeble and extensive, and the garrison by far too weak to repel a general assault. The force of the Indians at this time is variously estimated at from six hundred to two thousand; and the commandant greatly feared that some wild impulse might precipitate their plan, and that they would storm the fort before the morning. Every preparation was made to meet the sudden emergency. Half the garrison were ordered under arms, and all the officers prepared to spend the night upon the ramparts.

The day closed, and the hues of sunset faded. Only a dusky redness lingered in the west, and the darkening earth seemed her dull self again. Then night descended, heavy and black, on the fierce Indians and the sleepless English. From sunset till dawn, an anxious watch was kept from the slender palisades of Detroit. The soldiers were still ignorant of the danger; and the sentinels did not know why their numbers were doubled, or why, with such unwonted vigilance, their officers repeatedly visited their posts. Again and again Gladwyn mounted his wooden ramparts, and looked forth into the gloom. There seemed nothing but repose and peace in the soft, moist air of the warm spring evening, with the piping of frogs along the river bank, just roused from their torpor by the genial influence of May. But, at intervals, as the night wind swept across the bastion, it bore sounds of fearful portent to the ear, the sullen booming of the Indian drum and the wild chorus of quavering yells, as the warriors, around their distant camp-fires, danced the war-dance, in preparation for the morrow's work.

TREACHERY OF PONTIAC

1763

The night passed without alarm. The sun rose upon fresh fields and newly budding woods, and scarcely had the morning mists dissolved, when the garrison could see a fleet of birch canoes crossing the river from the eastern shore, within range of cannon shot above the fort. Only two or three warriors appeared in each, but all moved slowly, and seemed deeply laden. In truth, they were full of savages, lying flat on their faces, that their numbers might not excite the suspicion of the English.

At an early hour the open common behind the fort was thronged with squaws, children, and warriors, some naked, and others fantastically arrayed in their barbarous finery. All seemed restless and uneasy, moving hither and thither, in apparent preparation for a general game of ball. Many tall warriors, wrapped in their blankets, were seen stalking towards the fort, and casting malignant furtive glances upward at the palisades. Then, with an air of assumed indifference, they would move towards the gate. They were all admitted; for Gladwyn, who, in this instance at least, showed some knowledge of Indian character, chose to convince his crafty foe that, though their plot was detected, their hostility was despised.

The whole garrison was ordered under arms. Sterling, and the other English fur-traders, closed their storehouses and armed their men, and all in cool confidence stood waiting the result.

Meanwhile, Pontiac, who had crossed with the canoes from the eastern shore, was approaching along the river road, at the head of his sixty chiefs, all gravely marching in Indian file. A Canadian settler, named Beaufait, had been that morning to the fort. He was now returning homewards, and as he reached the bridge which led over the stream then called Parent's Creek, he saw the chiefs in the act of crossing from the farther bank. He stood aside to give them room. As the last Indian passed, Beaufait recognized him as an old friend and associate. The savage greeted him with the usual ejaculation, opened for an instant the folds of his blanket, disclosed the hidden gun, and, with an emphatic gesture towards the fort, indicated the purpose to which he meant to apply it.

At ten o'clock, the great war-chief, with his treacherous followers, reached the fort, and the gateway was thronged with their savage faces. All were wrapped to the throat in colored blankets. Some were crested with hawk, eagle, or raven plumes; others had shaved their heads, leaving only the fluttering scalp-lock on the crown; while others, again, wore their long, black hair flowing loosely at their backs, or wildly hanging about their brows like a lion's mane. Their bold yet crafty features, their cheeks besmeared with ochre and vermilion, white lead and soot, their keen, deep-set eyes gleaming in their sockets, like those of rattlesnakes, gave them an aspect grim, uncouth, and horrible. For the most part, they were tall, strong men, and all had a gait and bearing of peculiar stateliness.

As Pontiac entered, it is said that he started, and that a deep ejaculation half escaped from his breast. Well might his stoicism fail, for at a glance he read the ruin of his plot. On either hand, within the gateway, stood ranks of soldiers and hedges of glittering steel. The swarthy engagés of the fur-traders, armed to the teeth, stood in groups at the street corners, and the measured tap of a drum fell ominously on the ear. Soon regaining his composure, Pontiac strode forward into the narrow street; and his chiefs filed after him in silence, while the scared faces of women and children looked out from the windows as they passed. Their rigid muscles betrayed no sign of emotion; yet, looking closely, one might have seen their small eyes glance from side to side with restless scrutiny.

Traversing the entire width of the little town, they reached the door of the council-house, a large building standing near the margin of the river. On entering, they saw Gladwyn, with several of his officers, seated in readiness to receive them, and the observant chiefs did not fail to remark that every Englishman wore a sword at his side, and a pair of pistols in his belt. The conspirators eyed each other with uneasy glances. "Why," demanded Pontiac, "do I see so many of my father's young men standing in the street with their guns?" Gladwyn replied through his interpreter, La Butte, that he had ordered the soldiers under arms for the sake of exercise and discipline. With much delay and many signs of distrust, the chiefs at length sat down on the mats prepared for them; and, after the customary pause, Pontiac rose to speak. Holding in his hand the wampum belt which was to have given the fatal signal, he addressed the commandant, professing strong attachment to the English, and declaring, in Indian phrase, that he had come to smoke the pipe of peace, and brighten the chain of friendship. The officers watched him keenly as he uttered these hollow words, fearing lest, though conscious that his designs were suspected, he might still attempt to accomplish them. And once, it is said, he raised the wampum belt as if about to give the signal of attack. But at that instant Gladwyn signed slightly with his hand. The sudden clash of arms sounded from the passage without, and a drum rolling the charge filled the council-room with its stunning din. At this, Pontiac stood like one confounded. Some writers will have it, that Gladwyn, rising from his seat, drew the chief's blanket aside, exposed the hidden gun, and sternly rebuked him for his treachery. But the commandant wished only to prevent the consummation of the plot, without bringing on an open rupture. His own letters affirm that he and his officers remained seated as before. Pontiac, seeing his unruffled brow and his calm eye fixed steadfastly upon him, knew not what to think, and soon sat down in amazement and perplexity. Another pause ensued, and Gladwyn commenced a brief reply. He assured the chiefs that friendship and protection should be extended towards them as long as they continued to deserve it, but threatened ample vengeance for the first act of aggression. The council then broke up; but, before leaving the room, Pontiac told the officers that he would return in a few days, with his squaws and children, for he wished that they should all shake hands with their fathers the English. To this new piece of treachery Gladwyn deigned no reply. The gates of the fort, which had been closed during the conference, were again flung open, and the baffled savages were suffered to depart, rejoiced, no doubt, to breathe once more the free air of the open fields.

Gladwyn has been censured, and perhaps with justice, for not detaining the chiefs as hostages for the good conduct of their followers. An entrapped wolf meets no quarter from the huntsman; and a savage, caught in his treachery, has no claim to forbearance. Perhaps the commandant feared lest, should he arrest the chiefs when gathered at a public council, and guiltless as yet of open violence, the act might be interpreted as cowardly and dishonorable. He was ignorant, moreover, of the true nature of the plot. In his view, the whole affair was one of those impulsive outbreaks so common among Indians; and he trusted that, could an immediate rupture be averted, the threatening clouds would soon blow over.

Here, and elsewhere, the conduct of Pontiac is marked with the blackest treachery; and one cannot but lament that a commanding and magnanimous nature should be stained with the odious vice of cowards and traitors. He could govern, with almost despotic sway, a race unruly as the winds. In generous thought and deed, he rivalled the heroes of ancient story; and craft and cunning might well seem alien to a mind like his. Yet Pontiac was a thorough savage, and in him stand forth, in strongest light and shadow, the native faults and virtues of the Indian race. All children, says Sir Walter Scott, are naturally liars; and truth and honor are developments of later education. Barbarism is to civilization what childhood is to maturity; and all savages, whatever may be their country, their color, or their lineage, are prone to treachery and deceit. The barbarous ancestors of our own frank and manly race are no less obnoxious to the charge than those of the cat-like Bengalee; for in this childhood of society brave men and cowards are treacherous alike.

The Indian differs widely from the European in his notion of military virtue. In his view, artifice is wisdom; and he honors the skill that can circumvent, no less than the valor that can subdue, an adversary. The object of war, he argues, is to destroy the enemy. To accomplish this end, all means are honorable; and it is folly, not bravery, to incur a needless risk. Had Pontiac ordered his followers to storm the palisades of Detroit, not one of them would have obeyed him. They might, indeed, after their strange superstition, have reverenced him as a madman; but, from that hour, his fame as a war-chief would have sunk forever.

Balked in his treachery, the great chief withdrew to his village, enraged and mortified, yet still resolved to persevere. That Gladwyn had suffered him to escape, was to his mind an ample proof either of cowardice or ignorance. The latter supposition seemed the more probable; and he resolved to visit the English once more, and convince them, if possible, that their suspicions against him were unfounded. Early on the following morning, he repaired to the fort with three of his chiefs, bearing in his hand the sacred calumet, or pipe of peace, its bowl carved in stone, and its stem adorned with feathers. Offering it to the commandant, he addressed him and his officers to the following effect: "My fathers, evil birds have sung lies in your ear. We that stand before you are friends of the English. We love them as our brothers; and, to prove our love, we have come this day to smoke the pipe of peace." At his departure, he gave the pipe to Captain Campbell, second in command, as a farther pledge of his sincerity.

That afternoon, the better to cover his designs, Pontiac called the young men of all the tribes to a game of ball, which took place, with great noise and shouting, on the neighboring fields. At nightfall, the garrison were startled by a burst of loud, shrill yells. The drums beat to arms, and the troops were ordered to their posts; but the alarm was caused only by the victors in the ball-play, who were announcing their success by these discordant outcries. Meanwhile, Pontiac was in the Pottawattamie village, consulting with the chiefs of that tribe, and with the Wyandots, by what means they might compass the ruin of the English.

Early on the following morning, Monday, the ninth of May, the French inhabitants went in procession to the principal church of the settlement, which stood near the river bank, about half a mile above the fort. Having heard mass, they all returned before eleven o'clock, without discovering any signs that the Indians meditated an immediate act of hostility. Scarcely, however, had they done so, when the common behind the fort was once more thronged with Indians of all the four tribes; and Pontiac, advancing from among the multitude, approached the gate. It was closed and barred against him. He shouted to the sentinels, and demanded why he was refused admittance. Gladwyn himself replied, that the great chief might enter, if he chose, but that the crowd he had brought with him must remain outside. Pontiac rejoined, that he wished all his warriors to enjoy the fragrance of the friendly calumet. Gladwyn's answer was more concise than courteous, and imported that he would have none of his rabble in the fort. Thus repulsed, Pontiac threw off the mask which he had worn so long. With a grin of hate and rage, he turned abruptly from the gate, and strode towards his followers, who, in great multitudes, lay flat upon the ground, just beyond reach of gunshot. At his approach, they all leaped up and ran off, "yelping," in the words of an eye-witness, "like so many devils."

Looking out from the loopholes, the garrison could see them running in a body towards the house of an old English woman, who lived, with her family, on a distant part of the common. They beat down the doors, and rushed tumultuously in. A moment more, and the mournful scalp-yell told the fate of the wretched inmates. Another large body ran, yelling, to the river bank, and, leaping into their canoes, paddled with all speed to the Isle au Cochon, where dwelt an Englishman, named Fisher, formerly a sergeant of the regulars.

They soon dragged him from the hiding-place where he had sought refuge, murdered him on the spot, took his scalp, and made great rejoicings over this miserable trophy of brutal malice. On the following day, several Canadians crossed over to the island to inter the body, which they accomplished, as they thought, very effectually. Tradition, however, relates, as undoubted truth, that when, a few days after, some of the party returned to the spot, they beheld the pale hands of the dead man thrust above the ground, in an attitude of eager entreaty. Having once more covered the refractory members with earth, they departed, in great wonder and awe; but what was their amazement, when, on returning a second time, they saw the hands protruding as before. At this, they repaired in horror to the priest, who hastened to the spot, sprinkled the grave with holy water, and performed over it the neglected rites of burial. Thenceforth, says the tradition, the corpse of the murdered soldier slept in peace.

Pontiac had borne no part in the wolfish deeds of his followers. When he saw his plan defeated, he turned towards the shore; and no man durst approach him, for he was terrible in his rage. Pushing a canoe from the bank, he urged it with vigorous strokes, against the current, towards the Ottawa village, on the farther side. As he drew near, he shouted to the inmates. None remained in the lodges but women, children, and old men, who all came flocking out at the sound of his imperious voice. Pointing across the water, he ordered that all should prepare to move the camp to the western shore, that the river might no longer interpose a barrier between his followers and the English. The squaws labored with eager alacrity to obey him. Provisions, utensils, weapons, and even the bark covering to the lodges, were carried to the shore; and before evening all was ready for embarkation. Meantime, the warriors had come dropping in from their bloody work, until, at nightfall, nearly all had returned. Then Pontiac, hideous in his war-paint, leaped into the central area of the village. Brandishing his tomahawk, and stamping on the ground, he recounted his former exploits, and denounced vengeance on the English. The Indians flocked about him. Warrior after warrior caught the fierce contagion, and soon the ring was filled with dancers, circling round and round with frantic gesture, and startling the distant garrison with unearthly yells.

The war-dance over, the work of embarkation was commenced, and long before morning the transfer was complete. The whole Ottawa population crossed the river, and pitched their wigwams on the western side, just above the mouth of the little stream then known as Parent's Creek, but since named Bloody Run, from the scenes of terror which it witnessed.

During the evening, fresh tidings of disaster reached the fort. A Canadian, named Desnoyers, came down the river in a birch canoe, and, landing at the water-gate, brought news that two English officers, Sir Robert Davers and Captain Robertson, had been waylaid and murdered by the Indians, above Lake St. Clair. The Canadian declared, moreover, that Pontiac had just been joined by a formidable band of Ojibwas, from the Bay of Saginaw. These were a peculiarly ferocious horde, and their wretched descendants still retain the character.

Every Englishman in the fort, whether trader or soldier, was now ordered under arms. No man lay down to sleep, and Gladwyn himself walked the ramparts throughout the night.

All was quiet till the approach of dawn. But as the first dim redness tinged the east, and fields and woods grew visible in the morning twilight, suddenly the war-whoop rose on every side at once. As wolves assail the wounded bison, howling their gathering cries across the wintry prairie, so the fierce Indians, pealing their terrific yells, came bounding naked to the assault. The men hastened to their posts. And truly it was time; for not the Ottawas alone, but the whole barbarian swarm—Wyandots, Pottawattamies, and Ojibwas—were upon them, and bullets rapped hard and fast against the palisades. The soldiers looked from the loopholes, thinking to see their assailants gathering for a rush against the feeble barrier. But, though their clamors filled the air, and their guns blazed thick and hot, yet very few were visible. Some were ensconced behind barns and fences, some skulked among bushes, and some lay flat in hollows of the ground; while those who could find no shelter were leaping about with the agility of monkeys, to dodge the shot of the fort. Each had filled his mouth with bullets, for the convenience of loading, and each was charging and firing without suspending these agile gymnastics for a moment. There was one low hill, at no great distance from the fort, behind which countless black heads of Indians alternately appeared and vanished; while, all along the ridge, their guns emitted incessant white puffs of smoke. Every loophole was a target for their bullets; but the fire was returned with steadiness, and not without effect. The Canadian engagés of the fur-traders retorted the Indian war-whoops with outcries not less discordant, while the British and provincials paid back the clamor of the enemy with musket and rifle balls. Within half gunshot of the palisades was a cluster of outbuildings, behind which a host of Indians found shelter. A cannon was brought to bear upon them, loaded with red-hot spikes. They were soon wrapped in flames, upon which the disconcerted savages broke away in a body, and ran off yelping, followed by a shout of laughter from the soldiers.

For six hours, the attack was unabated; but as the day advanced, the assailants grew weary of their futile efforts. Their fire slackened, their clamors died away, and the garrison was left once more in peace, though from time to time a solitary shot, or lonely whoop, still showed the presence of some lingering savage, loath to be balked of his revenge. Among the garrison, only five men had been wounded, while the cautious enemy had suffered but trifling loss.

Gladwyn was still convinced that the whole affair was a sudden ebullition, which would soon subside; and being, moreover, in great want of provisions, he resolved to open negotiations with the Indians, under cover of which he might obtain the necessary supplies. The interpreter, La Butte, who, like most of his countrymen, might be said to hold a neutral position between the English and the Indians, was despatched to the camp of Pontiac, to demand the reasons of his conduct, and declare that the commandant was ready to redress any real grievance of which he might complain. Two old Canadians of Detroit, Chapeton and Godefroy, earnest to forward the negotiation, offered to accompany him. The gates were opened for their departure, and many other inhabitants of the place took this opportunity of leaving it, alleging as their motive, that they did not wish to see the approaching slaughter of the English.

Reaching the Indian Camp, the three ambassadors were received by Pontiac with great apparent kindness. La Butte delivered his message, and the two Canadians labored to dissuade the chief, for his own good and for theirs, from pursuing his hostile purposes. Pontiac stood listening, armed with the true impenetrability of an Indian. At every proposal, he uttered an ejaculation of assent, partly from a strange notion of courtesy peculiar to his race, and partly from the deep dissimulation which seems native to their blood. Yet with all this seeming acquiescence, the heart of the savage was unmoved as a rock. The Canadians were completely deceived. Leaving Chapeton and Godefroy to continue the conference and push the fancied advantage, La Butte hastened back to the fort. He reported the happy issue of his mission, and added that peace might readily be had by making the Indians a few presents, for which they are always rapaciously eager. When, however, he returned to the Indian camp, he found, to his chagrin, that his companions had made no progress in the negotiation. Though still professing a strong desire for peace, Pontiac had evaded every definite proposal. At La Butte's appearance, all the chiefs withdrew to consult among themselves. They returned after a short debate, and Pontiac declared that, out of their earnest desire for firm and lasting peace, they wished to hold council with their English fathers themselves. With this view, they were especially desirous that Captain Campbell, second in command, should visit their camp. This veteran officer, from his just, upright, and manly character, had gained the confidence of the Indians. To the Canadians the proposal seemed a natural one, and returning to the fort, they laid it before the commandant. Gladwyn suspected treachery, but Captain Campbell urgently asked permission to comply with the request of Pontiac. He felt, he said, no fear of the Indians, with whom he had always maintained the most friendly terms. Gladwyn, with some hesitation, acceded; and Campbell left the fort, accompanied by a junior officer, Lieutenant M'Dougal, and attended by La Butte and several other Canadians.

In the mean time, M. Gouin, anxious to learn what was passing, had entered the Indian camp, and, moving from lodge to lodge, soon saw and heard enough to convince him that the two British officers were advancing into the lion's jaws. He hastened to despatch two messengers to warn them of the peril. The party had scarcely left the gate when they were met by these men, breathless with running; but the warning came too late. Once embarked on the embassy, the officers would not be diverted from it; and passing up the river road, they approached the little wooden bridge that led over Parent's Creek. Crossing this bridge, and ascending a rising ground beyond, they saw before them the wide-spread camp of the Ottawas. A dark multitude gathered along its outskirts, and no sooner did they recognize the red uniform of the officers, than they all raised at once a horrible outcry of whoops and howlings. Indeed, they seemed disposed to give the ambassadors the reception usually accorded to captives taken in war; for the women seized sticks, stones, and clubs, and ran towards Campbell and his companion, as if to make them pass the cruel ordeal of running the gauntlet. Pontiac came forward, and his voice allayed the tumult. He shook the officers by the hand, and, turning, led the way through the camp. It was a confused assemblage of huts, chiefly of a conical or half-spherical shape, and constructed of a slender framework covered with rush mats or sheets of birch-bark. Many of the graceful birch canoes, used by the Indians of the upper lakes, were lying here and there among paddles, fish-spears, and blackened kettles slung above the embers of the fires. The camp was full of lean, wolfish dogs, who, roused by the clamor of their owners, kept up a discordant baying as the strangers passed. Pontiac paused before the entrance of a large lodge, and, entering, pointed to several mats placed on the ground, at the side opposite the opening. Here, obedient to his signal, the two officers sat down. Instantly the lodge was thronged with savages. Some, and these were for the most part chiefs, or old men, seated themselves on the ground before the strangers; while the remaining space was filled by a dense crowd, crouching or standing erect, and peering over each other's shoulders. At their first entrance, Pontiac had spoken a few words. A pause then ensued, broken at length by Campbell, who from his seat addressed the Indians in a short speech. It was heard in perfect silence, and no reply was made. For a full hour, the unfortunate officers saw before them the same concourse of dark, inscrutable faces, bending an unwavering gaze upon them. Some were passing out, and others coming in to supply their places, and indulge their curiosity by a sight of the Englishmen. At length, Captain Campbell, conscious, no doubt, of the danger in which he was placed, resolved fully to ascertain his true position, and, rising to his feet, declared his intention of returning to the fort. Pontiac made a sign that he should resume his seat. "My father," he said, "will sleep to-night in the lodges of his red children." The gray-haired soldier and his companion were betrayed into the hands of their enemies.

Many of the Indians were eager to kill the captives on the spot, but Pontiac would not carry his treachery so far. He protected them from injury and insult, and conducted them to the house of M. Meloche, near Parent's Creek, where good quarters were assigned them, and as much liberty allowed as was consistent with safe custody. The peril of their situation was diminished by the circumstance that two Indians, who, several days before, had been detained at the fort for some slight offence, still remained prisoners in the power of the commandant.

Late in the evening, La Butte, the interpreter, returned to the fort. His face wore a sad and downcast look, which sufficiently expressed the melancholy tidings that he brought. On hearing his account, some of the officers suspected, though probably without ground, that he was privy to the detention of the two ambassadors; and La Butte, feeling himself an object of distrust, lingered about the streets, sullen and silent, like the Indians among whom his rough life had been spent.

PONTIAC AT THE SIEGE OF DETROIT

1763

On the morning after the detention of the officers, Pontiac crossed over, with several of his chiefs, to the Wyandot village. A part of this tribe, influenced by Father Pothier, their Jesuit priest, had refused to take up arms against the English; but, being now threatened with destruction if they should longer remain neutral, they were forced to join the rest. They stipulated, however, that they should be allowed time to hear mass, before dancing the war-dance. To this condition Pontiac readily agreed, "although," observes the chronicler in the fulness of his horror and detestation, "he himself had no manner of worship, and cared not for festivals or Sundays." These nominal Christians of Father Pothier's flock, together with the other Wyandots, soon distinguished themselves in the war; fighting better, it was said, than all the other Indians,—an instance of the marked superiority of the Iroquois over the Algonquin stock.

Having secured these new allies, Pontiac prepared to resume his operations with fresh vigor; and to this intent, he made an improved disposition of his forces. Some of the Pottawattamies were ordered to lie in wait along the river bank, below the fort; while others concealed themselves in the woods, in order to intercept any Englishman who might approach by land or water. Another band of the same tribe were to conceal themselves in the neighborhood of the fort, when no general attack was going forward, in order to shoot down any soldier or trader who might chance to expose his person. On the eleventh of May, when these arrangements were complete, several Canadians came early in the morning to the fort, to offer what they called friendly advice. It was to the effect that the garrison should at once abandon the place, as it would be stormed within an hour by fifteen hundred Indians. Gladwyn refused, whereupon the Canadians departed; and soon after some six hundred Indians began a brisk fusillade, which they kept up till seven o'clock in the evening. A Canadian then appeared, bearing a summons from Pontiac, demanding the surrender of the fort, and promising that the English should go unmolested on board their vessels, leaving all their arms and effects behind. Gladwyn again gave a flat refusal.

On the evening of that day, the officers met to consider what course of conduct the emergency required; and, as one of them writes, the commandant was almost alone in the opinion that they ought still to defend the place. It seemed to the rest that the only course remaining was to embark and sail for Niagara. Their condition appeared desperate; for, on the shortest allowance, they had scarcely provision enough to sustain the garrison three weeks, within which time there was little hope of succor. The houses being, moreover, of wood, and chiefly thatched with straw, might be set on fire with burning missiles. But the chief apprehensions of the officers arose from their dread that the enemy would make a general onset, and cut or burn their way through the pickets,—a mode of attack to which resistance would be unavailing. Their anxiety on this score was relieved by a Canadian in the fort, who had spent half his life among Indians, and who now assured the commandant that every maxim of their warfare was opposed to such a measure. Indeed, an Indian's idea of military honor widely differs, as before observed, from that of a white man; for he holds it to consist no less in a wary regard to his own life than in the courage and impetuosity with which he assails his enemy. His constant aim is to gain advantages without incurring loss. He sets an inestimable value on the lives of his own party, and deems a victory dearly purchased by the death of a single warrior. A war-chief attains the summit of his renown when he can boast that he has brought home a score of scalps without the loss of a man; and his reputation is wofully abridged if the mournful wailings of the women mingle with the exulting yells of the warriors. Yet, with all his subtlety and caution, the Indian is not a coward, and, in his own way of fighting, often exhibits no ordinary courage. Stealing alone into the heart of an enemy's country, he prowls around the hostile village, watching every movement; and when night sets in, he enters a lodge, and calmly stirs the decaying embers, that, by their light, he may select his sleeping victims. With cool deliberation he deals the mortal thrust, kills foe after foe, and tears away scalp after scalp, until at length an alarm is given; then, with a wild yell, he bounds out into the darkness, and is gone.

Time passed on, and brought little change and no relief to the harassed and endangered garrison. Day after day the Indians continued their attacks, until their war-cries and the rattle of their guns became familiar sounds. For many weeks, no man lay down to sleep, except in his clothes, and with his weapons by his side. Parties of volunteers sallied, from time to time, to burn the outbuildings which gave shelter to the enemy. They cut down orchard trees, and levelled fences, until the ground about the fort was clear and open, and the enemy had no cover left from whence to fire. The two vessels in the river, sweeping the northern and southern curtains of the works with their fire, deterred the Indians from approaching those points, and gave material aid to the garrison. Still, worming their way through the grass, sheltering themselves behind every rising ground, the pertinacious savages would crawl close to the palisade, and shoot arrows, tipped with burning tow, upon the roofs of the houses; but cisterns and tanks of water were everywhere provided against such an emergency, and these attempts proved abortive. The little church, which stood near the palisade, was particularly exposed, and would probably have been set on fire, had not the priest of the settlement threatened Pontiac with the vengeance of the Great Spirit, should he be guilty of such sacrilege. Pontiac, who was filled with eagerness to get possession of the garrison, neglected no expedient that his savage tactics could supply. He went farther, and begged the French inhabitants to teach him the European method of attacking a fortified place by regular approaches; but the rude Canadians knew as little of the matter as he; or if, by chance, a few were better informed, they wisely preferred to conceal their knowledge. Soon after the first attack, the Ottawa chief had sent in to Gladwyn a summons to surrender, assuring him that, if the place were at once given up, he might embark on board the vessels, with all his men; but that, if he persisted in his defence, he would treat him as Indians treat each other; that is, he would burn him alive. To this Gladwyn made answer that he cared nothing for his threats. The attacks were now renewed with increased activity, and the assailants were soon after inspired with fresh ardor by the arrival of a hundred and twenty Ojibwa warriors from Grand River. Every man in the fort, officers, soldiers, traders, and engagés, now slept upon the ramparts; even in stormy weather none were allowed to withdraw to their quarters; yet a spirit of confidence and cheerfulness still prevailed among the weary garrison.

Meanwhile, great efforts were made to procure a supply of provisions. Every house was examined, and all that could serve for food, even grease and tallow, was collected and placed in the public storehouse, compensation having first been made to the owners. Notwithstanding these precautions Detroit must have been abandoned or destroyed, but for the assistance of a few friendly Canadians, and especially of M. Baby, a prominent habitant, who lived on the opposite side of the river, and provided the garrison with cattle, hogs, and other supplies. These, under cover of night, were carried from his farm to the fort in boats, the Indians long remaining ignorant of what was going forward.

They, on their part, began to suffer from hunger. Thinking to have taken Detroit at a single stroke, they had neglected, with their usual improvidence, to provide against the exigencies of a siege; and now, in small parties, they would visit the Canadian families along the river shore, passing from house to house, demanding provisions, and threatening violence in case of refusal. This was the more annoying, since the food thus obtained was wasted with characteristic recklessness. Unable to endure it longer, the Canadians appointed a deputation of fifteen of the eldest among them to wait upon Pontiac, and complain of his followers' conduct. The meeting took place at a Canadian house, probably that of M. Meloche, where the great chief had made his headquarters, and where the prisoners, Campbell and M'Dougal, were confined.

When Pontiac saw the deputation approaching along the river road, he was seized with an exceeding eagerness to know the purpose of their visit; for having long desired to gain the Canadians as allies against the English, and made several advances to that effect, he hoped that their present errand might relate to the object next his heart. So strong was his curiosity, that, forgetting the ordinary rule of Indian dignity and decorum, he asked the business on which they had come before they themselves had communicated it. The Canadians replied, that they wished the chiefs to be convened, for they were about to speak upon a matter of much importance. Pontiac instantly despatched messengers to the different camps and villages. The chiefs, soon arriving at his summons, entered the apartment, where they seated themselves upon the floor, having first gone through the necessary formality of shaking hands with the Canadian deputies. After a suitable pause, the eldest of the French rose, and heavily complained of the outrages which they had committed. "You pretend," he said, "to be friends of the French, and yet you plunder us of our hogs and cattle, you trample upon our fields of young corn, and when you enter our houses, you enter with tomahawk raised. When your French father comes from Montreal with his great army, he will hear of what you have done, and, instead of shaking hands with you as brethren, he will punish you as enemies."

Pontiac sat with his eyes riveted upon the ground, listening to every word that was spoken. When the speaker had concluded, he returned the following answer:—

"Brothers:

"We have never wished to do you harm, nor allow any to be done you; but among us there are many young men who, though strictly watched, find opportunities of mischief. It is not to revenge myself alone that I make war on the English. It is to revenge you, my Brothers. When the English insulted us, they insulted you also. I know that they have taken away your arms, and made you sign a paper which they have sent home to their country. Therefore you are left defenceless; and I mean now to revenge your cause and my own together. I mean to destroy the English, and leave not one upon our lands. You do not know the reasons from which I act. I have told you those only which concern yourselves; but you will learn all in time. You will cease then to think me a fool. I know, my brothers, that there are many among you who take part with the English. I am sorry for it, for their own sakes; for when our Father arrives, I shall point them out to him, and they will see whether they or I have most reason to be satisfied with the part we have acted.

"I do not doubt, my Brothers, that this war is very troublesome to you, for our warriors are continually passing and repassing through your settlement. I am sorry for it. Do not think that I approve of the damage that is done by them; and, as a proof of this, remember the war with the Foxes, and the part which I took in it. It is now seventeen years since the Ojibwas of Michillimackinac, combined with the Sacs and Foxes, came down to destroy you. Who then defended you? Was it not I and my young men? Mickinac, great chief of all these nations, said in council that he would carry to his village the head of your commandant—that he would eat his heart and drink his blood. Did I not take your part? Did I not go to his camp, and say to him, that if he wished to kill the French, he must first kill me and my warriors? Did I not assist you in routing them and driving them away? And now you think that I would turn my arms against you! No, my Brothers; I am the same French Pontiac who assisted you seventeen years ago. I am a Frenchman, and I wish to die a Frenchman; and I now repeat to you that you and I are one—that it is for both our interests that I should be avenged. Let me alone. I do not ask you for aid, for it is not in your power to give it. I only ask provisions for myself and men. Yet, if you are inclined to assist me, I shall not refuse you. It would please me, and you yourselves would be sooner rid of your troubles; for I promise you, that, as soon as the English are driven out, we will go back to our villages, and there await the arrival of our French Father. You have heard what I have to say; remain at peace, and I will watch that no harm shall be done to you, either by my men or by the other Indians."

This speech is reported by a writer whose chief characteristic is the scrupulous accuracy with which he has chronicled minute details without interest or importance. He neglects, moreover, no opportunity of casting ignominy and contempt upon the name of Pontiac. His mind is of so dull and commonplace an order as to exclude the supposition that he himself is author of the words which he ascribes to the Ottawa chief, and the speech may probably be taken as a literal translation of the original.

As soon as the council broke up, Pontiac took measures for bringing the disorders complained of to a close, while, at the same time, he provided sustenance for his warriors; and, in doing this, he displayed a policy and forecast scarcely paralleled in the history of his race. He first forbade the commission of farther outrage. He next visited in turn the families of the Canadians, and, inspecting the property belonging to them, he assigned to each the share of provisions which it must furnish for the support of the Indians. The contributions thus levied were all collected at the house of Meloche, near Parent's Creek, whence they were regularly issued, as the exigence required, to the savages of the different camps. As the character and habits of an Indian but ill qualify him to act the part of commissary, Pontiac in this matter availed himself of French assistance.

On the river bank, not far from the house of Meloche, lived an old Canadian, named Quilleriez, a man of exceeding vanity and self-conceit, and noted in the settlement for the gayety of his attire. He wore moccasons of the most elaborate pattern, and a sash plentifully garnished with beads and wampum. He was continually intermeddling in the affairs of the Indians, being anxious to be regarded as the leader or director among them. Of this man Pontiac evidently made a tool, employing him, together with several others, to discharge, beneath his eye, the duties of his novel commissariat. Anxious to avoid offending the French, yet unable to make compensation for the provisions he had exacted, Pontiac had recourse to a remarkable expedient, suggested, no doubt, by one of these European assistants. He issued promissory notes, drawn upon birch-bark, and signed with the figure of an otter, the totem to which he belonged; and we are told by a trustworthy authority that they were all faithfully redeemed. In this, as in several other instances, he exhibits an openness of mind and a power of adaptation not a little extraordinary among a people whose intellect will rarely leave the narrow and deeply cut channels in which it has run for ages, who reject instruction, and adhere with rigid tenacity to ancient ideas and usages. Pontiac always exhibited an eager desire for knowledge. Rogers represents him as earnest to learn the military art as practised among Europeans, and as inquiring curiously into the mode of making cloth, knives, and the other articles of Indian trade. Of his keen and subtle genius we have the following singular testimony from the pen of General Gage: "From a paragraph of M. D'Abbadie's letter, there is reason to judge of Pontiac, not only as a savage possessed of the most refined cunning and treachery natural to the Indians, but as a person of extraordinary abilities. He says that he keeps two secretaries, one to write for him, and the other to read the letters he receives, and he manages them so as to keep each of them ignorant of what is transacted by the other."

Major Rogers, a man familiar with the Indians, and an acute judge of mankind, speaks in the highest terms of Pontiac's character and talents. "He puts on," he says, "an air of majesty and princely grandeur, and is greatly honored and revered by his subjects."

In the present instance, few durst infringe the command he had given, that the property of the Canadians should be respected; indeed, it is said that none of his followers would cross the cultivated fields, but always followed the beaten paths; in such awe did they stand of his displeasure.

Pontiac's position was very different from that of an ordinary military leader. When we remember that his authority, little sanctioned by law or usage, was derived chiefly from the force of his own individual mind, and that it was exercised over a people singularly impatient of restraint, we may better appreciate the commanding energy that could hold control over spirits so intractable.

The glaring faults of Pontiac's character have already appeared too clearly. He was artful and treacherous, bold, fierce, ambitious, and revengeful; yet the following anecdotes will evince that noble and generous thought was no stranger to the savage hero of this dark forest tragedy. Some time after the period of which we have been speaking, Rogers came up to Detroit, with a detachment of troops, and, on landing, sent a bottle of brandy, by a friendly Indian, as a present to Pontiac. The Indians had always been suspicious that the English meant to poison them. Those around the chief, endeavored to persuade him that the brandy was drugged. Pontiac listened to what they said, and, as soon as they had concluded, poured out a cup of the liquor, and immediately drank it, saying that the man whose life he had saved had no power to kill him. He referred to his having prevented the Indians from attacking Rogers and his party when on their way to demand the surrender of Detroit. The story may serve as a counterpart to the well-known anecdote of Alexander the Great and his physician.

Pontiac had been an old friend of Baby; and one evening, at an early period of the siege, he entered his house, and, seating himself by the fire, looked for some time steadily at the embers. At length, raising his head, he said he had heard that the English had offered the Canadian a bushel of silver for the scalp of his friend. Baby declared that the story was false, and protested that he would never betray him. Pontiac for a moment keenly studied his features. "My brother has spoken the truth," he said, "and I will show that I believe him." He remained in the house through the evening, and, at its close, wrapped himself in his blanket, and lay down upon a bench, where he slept in full confidence till morning.

Another anecdote, from the same source, will exhibit the power which he exercised over the minds of his followers. A few young Wyandots were in the habit of coming, night after night, to the house of Baby, to steal hogs and cattle. The latter complained of the theft to Pontiac, and desired his protection. Being at that time ignorant of the intercourse between Baby and the English, Pontiac hastened to the assistance of his friend, and, arriving about nightfall at the house, walked to and fro among the barns and enclosures. At a late hour, he distinguished the dark forms of the plunderers stealing through the gloom. "Go back to your village, you Wyandot dogs," said the Ottawa chief; "if you tread again on this man's land, you shall die." They slunk back abashed; and from that time forward the Canadian's property was safe. The Ottawas had no political connection with the

Wyandots, who speak a language radically distinct. Over them he could claim no legitimate authority; yet his powerful spirit forced respect and obedience from all who approached him.

ROUT OF CUYLER'S DETACHMENT

1763

While perils were thickening around the garrison of Detroit, the British commander-in-chief at New York remained ignorant of its danger. Indeed, an unwonted quiet had prevailed, of late, along the borders and about the neighboring forts. With the opening of spring, a strong detachment had been sent up the lakes, with a supply of provisions and ammunition for the use of Detroit and the other western posts. The boats of this convoy were now pursuing their course along the northern shore of Lake Erie; and Gladwyn's garrison, aware of their approach, awaited their arrival with an anxiety which every day increased.

Day after day passed on, and the red cross of St. George still floated above Detroit. The keen-eyed watchfulness of the Indians had never abated; and woe to the soldier who showed his head above the palisades, or exposed his person before a loophole. Strong in his delusive hope of French assistance, Pontiac had sent messengers to M. Neyon, commandant at the Illinois, earnestly requesting that a force of regular troops might be sent to his aid; and Gladwyn, on his side, had ordered one of the vessels to Niagara, to hasten forward the expected convoy. The schooner set sail; but on the next day, as she lay becalmed at the entrance of Lake Erie, a multitude of canoes suddenly darted out upon her from the neighboring shores. In the prow of the foremost the Indians had placed their prisoner, Captain Campbell, with the dastardly purpose of interposing him as a screen between themselves and the fire of the English. But the brave old man called out to the crew to do their duty, without regard to him. Happily, at that moment a fresh breeze sprang up; the flapping sails stretched to the wind, and the schooner bore prosperously on her course towards Niagara, leaving the savage flotilla far behind.

The fort, or rather town, of Detroit had, by this time, lost its wonted vivacity and life. Its narrow streets were gloomy and silent. Here and there strolled a Canadian, in red cap and gaudy sash; the weary sentinel walked to and fro before the quarters of the commandant; an officer, perhaps, passed along with rapid step and anxious face; or an Indian girl, the mate of some soldier or trader, moved silently by, in her finery of beads and vermilion. Such an aspect as this the town must have presented on the morning of the thirtieth of May, when, at about nine o'clock, the voice of the sentinel sounded from the south-east bastion; and loud exclamations, in the direction of the river, roused Detroit from its lethargy. Instantly the place was astir. Soldiers, traders, and habitants, hurrying through the water-gate, thronged the canoe wharf and the narrow strand without. The half-wild coureurs de bois, the tall and sinewy provincials, and the stately British soldiers, stood crowded together, their uniforms soiled and worn, and their faces haggard with unremitted watching. Yet all alike wore an animated and joyous look. The long expected convoy was full in sight. On the farther side of the river, at some distance below the fort, a line of boats was rounding the woody projection, then called Montreal Point, their oars flashing in the sun, and the red flag of England flying from the stern of the foremost. The toils and dangers of the garrison were drawing to an end. With one accord, they broke into three hearty cheers, again and again repeated, while a cannon, glancing from the bastion, sent its loud voice of defiance to the enemy, and welcome to approaching friends. But suddenly every cheek grew pale with horror. Dark naked figures were seen rising, with wild gesture, in the boats, while, in place of the answering salute, the distant yell of the war-whoop fell faintly on their ears. The convoy was in the hands of the enemy. The boats had all been taken, and the troops of the detachment slain or made captive. Officers and men stood gazing in mournful silence, when an incident occurred which caused them to forget the general calamity in the absorbing interest of the moment.

Leaving the disappointed garrison, we will pass over to the principal victims of this deplorable misfortune. In each of the boats, of which there were eighteen, two or more of the captured soldiers, deprived of their weapons, were compelled to act as rowers, guarded by several armed savages, while many other Indians, for the sake of farther security, followed the boats along the shore. In the foremost, as it happened, there were four soldiers and only three Indians. The larger of the two vessels still lay anchored in the stream, about a bow-shot from the fort, while her companion, as we have seen, had gone down to Niagara to hasten up this very re-enforcement. As the boat came opposite this vessel, the soldier who acted as steersman conceived a daring plan of escape. The principal Indian sat immediately in front of another of the soldiers. The steersman called, in English, to his comrade to seize the savage and throw him overboard. The man answered that he was not strong enough; on which the steersman directed him to change places with him, as if fatigued with rowing, a movement which would excite no suspicion on the part of their guard. As the bold soldier stepped forward, as if to take his companion's oar, he suddenly seized the Indian by the hair, and, griping with the other hand the girdle at his waist, lifted him by main force, and flung him into the river. The boat rocked till the water surged over her gunwale. The Indian held fast to his enemy's clothes, and, drawing himself upward as he trailed alongside, stabbed him again and again with his knife, and then dragged him overboard. Both went down the swift current, rising and sinking; and, as some relate, perished, grappled in each other's arms. The two remaining Indians leaped out of the boat. The prisoners turned, and pulled for the distant vessel, shouting aloud for aid. The Indians on shore opened a heavy fire upon them, and many canoes paddled swiftly in pursuit. The men strained with desperate strength. A fate inexpressibly horrible was the alternative. The bullets hissed thickly around their heads; one of them was soon wounded, and the light birch canoes gained on them with fearful rapidity. Escape seemed hopeless, when the report of a cannon burst from the side of the vessel. The ball flew close past the boat, beating the water in a line of foam, and narrowly missing the foremost canoe. At this, the pursuers drew back in dismay; and the Indians on shore, being farther saluted by a second shot, ceased firing, and scattered among the bushes. The prisoners soon reached the vessel, where they were greeted as men snatched from the jaws of fate; "a living monument," writes an officer of the garrison, "that Fortune favors the brave."

They related many particulars of the catastrophe which had befallen them and their companions. Lieutenant Cuyler had left Fort Niagara as early as the thirteenth of May, and embarked from Fort Schlosser, just above the falls, with ninety-six men and a plentiful supply of provisions and ammunition. Day after day he had coasted the northern shore of Lake Erie, and seen neither friend nor foe amid those lonely forests and waters, until, on the twenty-eighth of the month, he landed at Point Pelée, not far from the mouth of the River Detroit. The boats were drawn on the beach, and the party prepared to encamp. A man and a boy went to gather firewood at a short distance from the spot, when an Indian leaped out of the woods, seized the boy by the hair, and tomahawked him. The man ran into camp with the alarm. Cuyler immediately formed his soldiers into a semicircle before the boats. He had scarcely done so when the enemy opened their fire. For an instant, there was a hot blaze of musketry on both sides; then the Indians broke out of the woods in a body, and rushed fiercely upon the centre of the line, which gave way in every part; the men flinging down their guns, running in a blind panic to the boats, and struggling with ill-directed efforts to shove them into the water. Five were set afloat, and pushed off from the shore, crowded with the terrified soldiers. Cuyler, seeing himself, as he says, deserted by his men, waded up to his neck in the lake, and climbed into one of the retreating boats. The Indians, on their part, pushing two more afloat, went in pursuit of the fugitives, three boat-loads of whom allowed themselves to be recaptured without resistance; but the remaining two, in one of which was Cuyler himself, made their escape. They rowed all night, and landed in the morning upon a small island. Between thirty and forty men, some of whom were wounded, were crowded in these two boats; the rest, about sixty in number, being killed or taken. Cuyler now made for Sandusky, which, on his arrival, he found burnt to the ground. Immediately leaving the spot, he rowed along the south shore to Presqu' Isle, from whence he proceeded to Niagara and reported his loss to Major Wilkins, the commanding officer.

The actors in this bold and well-executed stroke were the Wyandots, who, for some days, had lain in ambush at the mouth of the river, to intercept trading boats or parties of troops. Seeing the fright and confusion of Cuyler's men, they had forgotten their usual caution, and rushed upon them in the manner described. The ammunition, provisions, and other articles, taken in this attack, formed a valuable prize; but, unfortunately, there was, among the rest, a great quantity of whiskey. This the Indians seized, and carried to their respective camps, which, throughout the night, presented a scene of savage revelry and riot. The liquor was poured into vessels of birch-bark, or any thing capable of containing it; and the Indians, crowding around, scooped it up in their cups and ladles, and quaffed the raw whiskey like water. While some sat apart, wailing and moaning in maudlin drunkenness, others were maddened to the ferocity of wild beasts. Dormant jealousies were awakened, old forgotten quarrels kindled afresh, and, had not the squaws taken the precaution of hiding all the weapons they could find before the debauch began, much blood would, no doubt, have been spilt. As it was, the savages were not entirely without means of indulging their drunken rage. Many were wounded, of whom two died in the morning; and several others had their noses bitten off,—a singular mode of revenge, much in vogue upon similar occasions, among the Indians of the upper lakes. The English were gainers by this scene of riot; for late in the evening, two Indians, in all the valor and vain-glory of drunkenness, came running directly towards the fort, boasting their prowess in a loud voice; but being greeted with two rifle bullets, they leaped into the air like a pair of wounded bucks, and fell dead on their tracks.

It will not be proper to pass over in silence the fate of the unfortunate men taken prisoners in this affair. After night had set in, several Canadians came to the fort, bringing vague and awful reports of the scenes that had been enacted at the Indian camp. The soldiers gathered round them, and, frozen with horror, listened to the appalling narrative. A cloud of deep gloom sank down upon the garrison, and none could help reflecting how thin and frail a barrier protected them from a similar fate. On the following day, and for several succeeding days, they beheld frightful confirmation of the rumors they had heard. Naked corpses, gashed with knives and scorched with fire, floated down on the pure waters of the Detroit, whose fish came up to nibble at the clotted blood that clung to their ghastly faces.

Late one afternoon, at about this period of the siege, the garrison were again greeted with the dismal cry of death, and a line of naked warriors was seen issuing from the woods, which, like a wall of foliage, rose beyond the pastures in rear of the fort. Each savage was painted black, and each bore a scalp fluttering from the end of a pole. It was but too clear that some new disaster had befallen; and in truth, before nightfall, one La Brosse, a Canadian, came to the gate with the tidings that Fort Sandusky had been taken, and all its garrison slain or made captive. This post had been attacked by the band of Wyandots living in its neighborhood, aided by a detachment of their brethren from Detroit. Among the few survivors of the slaughter was the commanding officer, Ensign Paully, who had been brought prisoner to Detroit, bound hand and foot, and solaced on the passage with the expectation of being burnt alive. On landing near the camp of Pontiac, he was surrounded by a crowd of Indians, chiefly squaws and children, who pelted him with stones, sticks, and gravel, forcing him to dance and sing, though by no means in a cheerful strain. A worse infliction seemed in store for him, when happily an old woman, whose husband had lately died, chose to adopt him in place of the deceased warrior. Seeing no alternative but the stake, Paully accepted the proposal; and, having been first plunged in the river, that the white blood might be washed from his veins, he was conducted to the lodge of the widow, and treated thenceforth with all the consideration due to an Ottawa warrior.

Gladwyn soon received a letter from him, through one of the Canadian inhabitants, giving a full account of the capture of Fort Sandusky. On the sixteenth of May—such was the substance of the communication—Paully was informed that seven Indians were waiting at the gate to speak with him. As several of the number were well known to him, he ordered them, without hesitation, to be admitted. Arriving at his quarters, two of the treacherous visitors seated themselves on each side of the commandant, while the rest were disposed in various parts of the room. The pipes were lighted, and the conversation began, when an Indian, who stood in the doorway, suddenly made a signal by raising his head. Upon this, the astonished officer was instantly pounced upon and disarmed; while, at the same moment, a confused noise of shrieks and yells, the firing of guns, and the hurried tramp of feet, sounded from the area of the fort without. It soon ceased, however, and Paully, led by his captors from the room, saw the parade ground strown with the corpses of his murdered garrison. At nightfall, he was conducted to the margin of the lake, where several birch canoes lay in readiness; and as, amid thick darkness, the party pushed out from shore, the captive saw the fort, lately under his command, bursting on all sides into sheets of flame.

Soon after these tidings of the loss of Sandusky, Gladwyn's garrison heard the scarcely less unwelcome news that the strength of their besiegers had been re-enforced by two strong bands of Ojibwas. Pontiac's forces in the vicinity of Detroit now amounted, according to Canadian computation, to about eight hundred and twenty warriors. Of these, two hundred and fifty were Ottawas, commanded by himself in person; one hundred and fifty were Pottawattamies, under Ninivay; fifty were Wyandots, under Takee; two hundred were Ojibwas, under Wasson; and added to these were a hundred and seventy of the same tribe, under their chief, Sekahos. As the warriors brought their squaws and children with them, the whole number of savages congregated about Detroit no doubt exceeded three thousand; and the neighboring fields and meadows must have presented a picturesque and stirring scene.

The sleepless garrison, worn by fatigue and ill fare, and harassed by constant petty attacks, were yet farther saddened by the news of disaster which thickened from every quarter. Of all the small posts scattered at intervals through the vast wilderness to the westward of Niagara and Fort Pitt, it soon appeared that Detroit alone had been able to sustain itself. For the rest, there was but one unvaried tale of calamity and ruin. On the fifteenth of June, a number of Pottawattamies were seen approaching the gate of the fort, bringing with them four English prisoners, who proved to be Ensign Schlosser, lately commanding at St. Joseph's, together with three private soldiers. The Indians wished to exchange them for several of their own tribe, who had been for nearly two months prisoners in the fort. After some delay, this was effected; and the garrison then learned the unhappy fate of their comrades at St. Joseph's. This post stood at the mouth of the River St. Joseph's, near the head of Lake Michigan, a spot which had long been the site of a Roman Catholic mission. Here, among the forests, swamps, and ocean-like waters, at an unmeasured distance from any abode of civilized man, the indefatigable Jesuits had labored more than half a century for the spiritual good of the Pottawattamies, who lived in great numbers near the margin of the lake. As early as the year 1712, as Father Marest informs us, the mission was in a thriving state, and around it had gathered a little colony of the forest-loving Canadians. Here, too, the French government had established a military post, whose garrison, at the period of our narrative, had been supplanted by Ensign Schlosser, with his command of fourteen men, a mere handful, in the heart of a wilderness swarming with insidious enemies. They seem, however, to have apprehended no danger, when, on the twenty-fifth of May, early in the morning, the officer was informed that a large party of the Pottawattamies of Detroit had come to pay a visit to their relatives at St. Joseph's. Presently, a chief, named Washashe, with three or four followers, came to his quarters, as if to hold a friendly "talk;" and immediately after a Canadian came in with intelligence that the fort was surrounded by Indians, who evidently had hostile intentions. At this, Schlosser ran out of the apartment, and crossing the parade, which was full of Indians and Canadians, hastily entered the barracks. These were also crowded with savages, very insolent and disorderly. Calling upon his sergeant to get the men under arms, he hastened out again to the parade, and endeavored to muster the Canadians together; but while busying himself with these somewhat unwilling auxiliaries, he heard a wild cry from within the barracks. Instantly all the Indians in the fort rushed to the gate, tomahawked the sentinel, and opened a free passage to their comrades without. In less than two minutes, as the officer declares, the fort was plundered, eleven men were killed, and himself, with the three survivors, made prisoners, and bound fast. They then conducted him to Detroit, where he was exchanged as we have already seen.

Three days after these tidings reached Detroit, Father Jonois, a Jesuit priest of the Ottawa mission near Michillimackinac, came to Pontiac's camp, together with the son of Minavavana, great chief of the Ojibwas, and several other Indians. On the following morning, he appeared at the gate of the fort, bringing a letter from Captain Etherington, commandant at Michillimackinac. The commencement of the letter was as follows:—

"Michillimackinac, 12 June, 1763.

"Sir:

"Notwithstanding what I wrote you in my last, that all the savages were arrived, and that every thing seemed in perfect tranquillity, yet on the second instant the Chippeways, who live in a plain near this fort, assembled to play ball, as they had done almost every day since their arrival. They played from morning till noon; then, throwing their ball close to the gate, and observing Lieutenant Lesley and me a few paces out of it, they came behind us, seized and carried us into the woods.

"In the mean time, the rest rushed into the fort, where they found their squaws, whom they had previously planted there, with their hatchets hid under their blankets, which they took, and in an instant killed Lieutenant Jamet, and fifteen rank and file, and a trader named Tracy. They wounded two, and took the rest of the garrison prisoners, five of whom they have since killed.

"They made prisoners all the English traders, and robbed them of every thing they had; but they offered no violence to the persons or property of any of the Frenchmen."

Captain Etherington next related some particulars of the massacre at

Michillimackinac, sufficiently startling, as will soon appear. He spoke in high terms of the character and conduct of Father Jonois, and requested that Gladwyn would send all the troops he could spare up Lake Huron, that the post might be recaptured from the Indians, and garrisoned afresh. Gladwyn, being scarcely able to defend himself, could do nothing for the relief of his brother officer, and the Jesuit set out on his long and toilsome canoe voyage back to Michillimackinac. The loss of this place was a very serious misfortune, for, next to Detroit, it was the most important post on the upper lakes.

The next news which came in was that of the loss of Ouatanon, a fort situated upon the Wabash, a little below the site of the present town of La Fayette. Gladwyn received a letter from its commanding officer, Lieutenant Jenkins, informing him that, on the first of June, he and several of his men had been made prisoners by stratagem, on which the rest of the garrison had surrendered. The Indians, however, apologized for their conduct, declaring that they acted contrary to their own inclinations, and that the surrounding tribes compelled them to take up the hatchet. These excuses, so consolatory to the sufferers, might probably have been founded in truth, for these savages were of a character less ferocious than many of the others, and as they were farther removed from the settlements, they had not felt to an equal degree the effects of English insolence and encroachment.

Close upon these tidings came the news that Fort Miami was taken. This post, standing on the River Maumee, was commanded by Ensign Holmes. And here I cannot but remark on the forlorn situation of these officers, isolated in the wilderness, hundreds of miles, in some instances, from any congenial associates, separated from every human being except the rude soldiers under their command, and the white or red savages who ranged the surrounding woods. Holmes suspected the intention of the Indians, and was therefore on his guard, when, on the twenty-seventh of May, a young Indian girl, who lived with him, came to tell him that a squaw lay dangerously ill in a wigwam near the fort, and urged him to come to her relief. Having confidence in the girl, Holmes forgot his caution and followed her out of the fort. Pitched at the edge of a meadow, hidden from view by an intervening spur of the woodland, stood a great number of Indian wigwams. When Holmes came in sight of them, his treacherous conductress pointed out that in which the sick woman lay. He walked on without suspicion; but, as he drew near, two guns flashed from behind the hut, and stretched him lifeless on the grass. The shots were heard at the fort, and the sergeant rashly went out to learn the reason of the firing. He was immediately taken prisoner, amid exulting yells and whoopings. The soldiers in the fort climbed upon the palisades, to look out, when Godefroy, a Canadian, and two other white men, made their appearance, and summoned them to surrender; promising that, if they did so, their lives should be spared, but that otherwise they would all be killed without mercy. The men, being in great terror, and without a leader, soon threw open the gate, and gave themselves up as prisoners.

Had detachments of Rogers's Rangers garrisoned these posts, or had they been held by such men as the Rocky Mountain trappers of the present day, wary, skilful, and almost ignorant of fear, some of them might, perhaps, have been saved; but the soldiers of the 60th Regiment, though many of them were of provincial birth, were not suited by habits and discipline for this kind of service.

The loss of Presqu' Isle will close this catalogue of calamity. Rumors of it first reached Detroit on the twentieth of June, and, two days after, the garrison heard those dismal cries announcing scalps and prisoners, which, of late, had grown mournfully familiar to their ears. Indians were seen passing in numbers along the opposite bank of the river, leading several English prisoners, who proved to be Ensign Christie, the commanding officer at Presqu' Isle, with those of his soldiers who survived.

On the third of June, Christie, then safely ensconced in the fort which he commanded, had written as follows to his superior officer, Lieutenant Gordon, at Venango: "This morning Lieutenant Cuyler of Queen's Company of Rangers came here, and gave me the following melancholy account of his whole party being cut off by a large body of Indians at the mouth of the Detroit River." Here follows the story of Cuyler's disaster, and Christie closes as follows: "I have sent to Niagara a letter to the Major, desiring some more ammunition and provisions, and have kept six men of Lieutenant Cuyler's, as I expect a visit from the hell-hounds. I have ordered everybody here to move into the blockhouse, and shall be ready for them, come when they will."

Fort Presqu' Isle stood on the southern shore of Lake Erie, at the site of the present town of Erie. It was an important post to be commanded by an Ensign, for it controlled the communication between the lake and Fort Pitt; but the blockhouse, to which Christie alludes, was supposed to make it impregnable against Indians. This blockhouse, a very large and strong one, stood at an angle of the fort, and was built of massive logs, with the projecting upper story usual in such structures, by means of which a vertical fire could be had upon the heads of assailants, through openings in the projecting part of the floor, like the machicoulis of a mediæval castle. It had also a kind of bastion, from which one or more of its walls could be covered by a flank fire. The roof was of shingles, and might easily be set on fire; but at the top was a sentry-box or look-out, from which water could be thrown. On one side was the lake, and on the other a small stream which entered it. Unfortunately, the bank of this stream rose in a high steep ridge within forty yards of the blockhouse, thus affording a cover to assailants, while the bank of the lake offered them similar advantages on another side.

After his visit from Cuyler, Christie, whose garrison now consisted of twenty-seven men, prepared for a stubborn defence. The doors of the blockhouse, and the sentry-box at the top, were lined to make them bullet-proof; the angles of the roof were covered with green turf as a protection against fire-arrows, and gutters of bark were laid in such a manner that streams of water could be sent to every part. His expectation of a "visit from the hell-hounds" proved to be perfectly well founded. About two hundred of them had left Detroit expressly for this object. At early dawn on the fifteenth of June, they were first discovered stealthily crossing the mouth of the little stream, where the bateaux were drawn up, and crawling under cover of the banks of the lake and of the adjacent saw-pits. When the sun rose, they showed themselves, and began their customary yelling. Christie, with a very unnecessary reluctance to begin the fray, ordered his men not to fire till the Indians had set the example. The consequence was, that they were close to the blockhouse before they received the fire of the garrison; and many of them sprang into the ditch, whence, being well sheltered, they fired at the loopholes, and amused themselves by throwing stones and handfuls of gravel, or, what was more to the purpose, fire-balls of pitch. Some got into the fort and sheltered themselves behind the bakery and other buildings, whence they kept up a brisk fire; while others pulled down a small outhouse of plank, of which they made a movable breastwork, and approached under cover of it by pushing it before them. At the same time, great numbers of them lay close behind the ridges by the stream, keeping up a rattling fire into every loophole, and shooting burning arrows against the roof and sides of the blockhouse. Some were extinguished with water, while many dropped out harmless after burning a small hole. The Indians now rolled logs to the top of the ridges, where they made three strong breastworks, from behind which they could discharge their shot and throw their fireworks with greater effect. Sometimes they would try to dart across the intervening space and shelter themselves with their companions in the ditch, but all who attempted it were killed or wounded. And now the hard-beset little garrison could see them throwing up earth and stones behind the nearest breastwork. Their implacable foes were undermining the blockhouse. There was little time to reflect on this new danger; for another, more imminent, soon threatened them. The barrels of water, always kept in the building, were nearly emptied in extinguishing the frequent fires; and though there was a well close at hand, in the parade ground, it was death to approach it. The only resource was to dig a subterranean passage to it. The floor was torn up; and while some of the men fired their heated muskets from the loopholes, the rest labored stoutly at this cheerless task. Before it was half finished, the roof was on fire again, and all the water that remained was poured down to extinguish it. In a few moments, the cry of fire was again raised, when a soldier, at imminent risk of his life, tore off the burning shingles and averted the danger.

By this time it was evening. The garrison had had not a moment's rest since the sun rose. Darkness brought little relief, for guns flashed all night from the Indian intrenchments. In the morning, however, there was a respite. The Indians were ominously quiet, being employed, it seems, in pushing their subterranean approaches, and preparing fresh means for firing the blockhouse. In the afternoon the attack began again. They set fire to the house of the commanding officer, which stood close at hand, and which they had reached by means of their trenches. The pine logs blazed fiercely, and the wind blew the flame against the bastion of the blockhouse, which scorched, blackened, and at last took fire; but the garrison had by this time dug a passage to the well, and, half stifled as they were, they plied their water-buckets with such good will that the fire was subdued, while the blazing house soon sank to a glowing pile of embers. The men, who had behaved throughout with great spirit, were now, in the words of their officer, "exhausted to the greatest extremity;" yet they still kept up their forlorn defence, toiling and fighting without pause within the wooden walls of their dim prison, where the close and heated air was thick with the smoke of gunpowder. The firing on both sides lasted through the rest of the day, and did not cease till midnight, at which hour a voice was heard to call out, in French, from the enemy's intrenchments, warning the garrison that farther resistance would be useless, since preparations were made for setting the blockhouse on fire, above and below at once. Christie demanded if there were any among them who spoke English; upon which, a man in the Indian dress came out from behind the breastwork. He was a soldier, who, having been made prisoner early in the French war, had since lived among the savages, and now espoused their cause, fighting with them against his own countrymen. He said that if they yielded, their lives should be spared; but if they fought longer, they must all be burnt alive. Christie told them to wait till morning for his answer. They assented, and suspended their fire. Christie now asked his men, if we may believe the testimony of two of them, "whether they chose to give up the blockhouse, or remain in it and be burnt alive?" They replied that they would stay as long as they could bear the heat, and then fight their way through. A third witness, Edward Smyth, apparently a corporal, testifies that all but two of them were for holding out. He says that when his opinion was asked, he replied that, having but one life to lose, he would be governed by the rest; but that at the same time he reminded them of the recent treachery at Detroit, and of the butchery at Fort William Henry, adding that, in his belief, they themselves could expect no better usage.

When morning came, Christie sent out two soldiers as if to treat with the enemy, but, in reality, as he says, to learn the truth of what they had told him respecting their preparations to burn the blockhouse. On reaching the breastwork, the soldiers made a signal, by which their officer saw that his worst fears were well founded. In pursuance of their orders, they then demanded that two of the principal chiefs should meet with Christie midway between the breastwork and the blockhouse. The chiefs appeared accordingly; and Christie, going out, yielded up the blockhouse; having first stipulated that the lives of all the garrison should be spared, and that they might retire unmolested to the nearest post. The soldiers, pale and haggard, like men who had passed through a fiery ordeal, now issued from their scorched and bullet-pierced stronghold. A scene of plunder instantly began. Benjamin Gray, a Scotch soldier, who had just been employed, on Christie's order, in carrying presents to the Indians, seeing the confusion, and hearing a scream from a sergeant's wife, the only woman in the garrison, sprang off into the woods and succeeded in making his way to Fort Pitt with news of the disaster. It is needless to say that no faith was kept with the rest, and they had good cause to be thankful that they were not butchered on the spot. After being detained for some time in the neighborhood, they were carried prisoners to Detroit, where Christie soon after made his escape, and gained the fort in safety.

After Presqu' Isle was taken, the neighboring posts of Le Bœuf and Venango shared its fate; while farther southward, at the forks of the Ohio, a host of Delaware and Shawanoe warriors were gathering around Fort Pitt, and blood and havoc reigned along the whole frontier.

THE INDIANS CONTINUE TO BLOCKADE DETROIT

1763

We return once more to Detroit and its beleaguered garrison. On the nineteenth of June, a rumor reached them that one of the vessels had been seen near Turkey Island, some miles below the fort, but that, the wind failing her, she had dropped down with the current, to wait a more favorable opportunity. It may be remembered that this vessel had, several weeks before, gone down Lake Erie to hasten the advance of Cuyler's expected detachment. Passing these troops on her way, she had held her course to Niagara; and here she had remained until the return of Cuyler, with the remnant of his men, made known the catastrophe that had befallen him. This officer, and the survivors of his party, with a few other troops spared from the garrison of Niagara, were ordered to embark in her, and make the best of their way back to Detroit. They had done so, and now, as we have seen, were almost within sight of the fort; but the critical part of the undertaking yet remained. The river channel was in some places narrow, and more than eight hundred Indians were on the alert to intercept their passage.

For several days, the officers at Detroit heard nothing farther of the vessel, when, on the twenty-third, a great commotion was visible among the Indians, large parties of whom were seen to pass along the outskirts of the woods, behind the fort. The cause of these movements was unknown till evening, when M. Baby came in with intelligence that the vessel was again attempting to ascend the river, and that all the Indians had gone to attack her. Upon this, two cannon were fired, that those on board might know that the fort still held out. This done, all remained in much anxiety awaiting the result.

The schooner, late that afternoon, began to move slowly upward, with a gentle breeze, between the main shore and the long-extended margin of Fighting Island. About sixty men were crowded on board, of whom only ten or twelve were visible on deck; the officer having ordered the rest to lie hidden below, in hope that the Indians, encouraged by this apparent weakness, might make an open attack. Just before reaching the narrowest part of the channel, the wind died away, and the anchor was dropped. Immediately above, and within gunshot of the vessel, the Indians had made a breastwork of logs, carefully concealed by bushes, on the shore of Turkey Island. Here they lay in force, waiting for the schooner to pass. Ignorant of this, but still cautious and wary, the crew kept a strict watch from the moment the sun went down.

Hours wore on, and nothing had broken the deep repose of the night. The current gurgled with a monotonous sound around the bows of the schooner, and on either hand the wooded shores lay amid the obscurity, black and silent as the grave. At length, the sentinel could discern, in the distance, various moving objects upon the dark surface of the water. The men were ordered up from below, and all took their posts in perfect silence. The blow of a hammer on the mast was to be the signal to fire. The Indians, gliding stealthily over the water in their birch canoes, had, by this time, approached within a few rods of their fancied prize, when suddenly the dark side of the slumbering vessel burst into a blaze of cannon and musketry, which illumined the night like a flash of lightning. Grape- and musket-shot flew tearing among the canoes, destroying several of them, killing fourteen Indians, wounding as many more, and driving the rest in consternation to the shore. Recovering from their surprise, they began to fire upon the vessel from behind their breastwork; upon which she weighed anchor, and dropped down once more beyond their reach, into the broad river below. Several days afterwards, she again attempted to ascend. This time, she met with better success; for, though the Indians fired at her constantly from the shore, no man was hurt, and at length she left behind her the perilous channels of the Islands. As she passed the Wyandot village, she sent a shower of grape among its yelping inhabitants, by which several were killed; and then, furling her sails, lay peacefully at anchor by the side of her companion vessel, abreast of the fort.

The schooner brought to the garrison a much-needed supply of men, ammunition, and provisions. She brought, also, the important tidings that peace was at length concluded between France and England. The bloody and momentous struggle of the French war, which had shaken North America since the year 1755, had indeed been virtually closed by the victory on the Plains of Abraham, and the junction of the three British armies at

Montreal. Yet up to this time, its embers had continued to burn, till at length peace was completely established by formal treaty between the hostile powers. France resigned her ambitious project of empire in America, and ceded Canada and the region of the lakes to her successful rival. By this treaty, the Canadians of Detroit were placed in a new position. Hitherto they had been, as it were, prisoners on capitulation, neutral spectators of the quarrel between their British conquerors and the Indians; but now their allegiance was transferred from the crown of France to that of Britain, and they were subjects of the English king. To many of them the change was extremely odious, for they cordially hated the British. They went about among the settlers and the Indians, declaring that the pretended news of peace was only an invention of Major Gladwyn; that the king of France would never abandon his children; and that a great French army was even then ascending the St. Lawrence, while another was approaching from the country of the Illinois. This oft-repeated falsehood was implicitly believed by the Indians, who continued firm in the faith that their Great Father was about to awake from his sleep, and wreak his vengeance upon the insolent English, who had intruded on his domain.

Pontiac himself clung fast to this delusive hope; yet he was greatly vexed at the safe arrival of the vessel, and the assistance she had brought to the obstinate defenders of Detroit. He exerted himself with fresh zeal to gain possession of the place, and attempted to terrify Gladwyn into submission. He sent a message, in which he strongly urged him to surrender, adding, by way of stimulus, that eight hundred more Ojibwas were every day expected, and that, on their arrival, all his influence could not prevent them from taking the scalp of every Englishman in the fort. To this friendly advice Gladwyn returned a brief and contemptuous answer.

Pontiac, having long been anxious to gain the Canadians as auxiliaries in the war, now determined on a final effort to effect his object. For this purpose, he sent messages to the principal inhabitants, inviting them to meet him in council. In the Ottawa camp, there was a vacant spot, quite level, and encircled by the huts of the Indians. Here mats were spread for the reception of the deputies, who soon convened, and took their seats in a wide ring. One part was occupied by the Canadians, among whom were several whose withered, leathery features proclaimed them the patriarchs of the secluded little settlement. Opposite these sat the stern-visaged Pontiac, with his chiefs on either hand, while the intervening portions of the circle were filled by Canadians and Indians promiscuously mingled. Standing on the outside, and looking over the heads of this more dignified assemblage, was a motley throng of Indians and Canadians, half-breeds, trappers, and voyageurs, in wild and picturesque, though very dirty attire. Conspicuous among them were numerous Indian dandies, a large class in every aboriginal community, where they hold about the same relative position as do their counterparts in civilized society. They were wrapped in the gayest blankets, their necks adorned with beads, their cheeks daubed with vermilion, and their ears hung with pendants. They stood sedately looking on, with evident self-complacency, yet ashamed and afraid to take their places among the aged chiefs and warriors of repute.

All was silent, and several pipes were passing round from hand to hand, when Pontiac rose, and threw down a war-belt at the feet of the Canadians.

"My brothers," he said, "how long will you suffer this bad flesh to remain upon your lands? I have told you before, and I now tell you again, that when I took up the hatchet, it was for your good. This year the English must all perish throughout Canada. The Master of Life commands it; and you, who know him better than we, wish to oppose his will. Until now I have said nothing on this matter. I have not urged you to take part with us in the war. It would have been enough had you been content to sit quiet on your mats, looking on, while we were fighting for you. But you have not done so. You call yourselves our friends, and yet you assist the English with provisions, and go about as spies among our villages. This must not continue. You must be either wholly French or wholly English. If you are French, take up that war-belt, and lift the hatchet with us; but if you are English, then we declare war upon you. My brothers, I know this is a hard thing. We are all alike children of our Great Father the King of France, and it is hard to fight among brethren for the sake of dogs. But there is no choice. Look upon the belt, and let us hear your answer."

One of the Canadians, having suspected the purpose of Pontiac, had brought with him, not the treaty of peace, but a copy of the capitulation of Montreal with its dependencies, including Detroit. Pride, or some other motive, restrained him from confessing that the Canadians were no longer children of the King of France, and he determined to keep up the old delusion that a French army was on its way to win back Canada, and chastise the English invaders. He began his speech in reply to Pontiac by professing great love for the Indians, and a strong desire to aid them in the war. "But, my brothers," he added, holding out the articles of capitulation, "you must first untie the knot with which our Great Father, the King, has bound us. In this paper, he tells all his Canadian children to sit quiet and obey the English until he comes, because he wishes to punish his enemies himself. We dare not disobey him, for he would then be angry with us. And you, my brothers, who speak of making war upon us if we do not do as you wish, do you think you could escape his wrath, if you should raise the hatchet against his French children? He would treat you as enemies, and not as friends, and you would have to fight both English and French at once. Tell us, my brothers, what can you reply to this?"

Pontiac for a moment sat silent, mortified, and perplexed; but his purpose was not destined to be wholly defeated. "Among the French," says the writer of the diary, "were many infamous characters, who, having no property, cared nothing what became of them." Those mentioned in these opprobrious terms were a collection of trappers, voyageurs, and nondescript vagabonds of the forest, who were seated with the council, or stood looking on, variously attired in greasy shirts, Indian leggins, and red woollen caps. Not a few among them, however, had thought proper to adopt the style of dress and ornament peculiar to the red men, who were their usual associates, and appeared among their comrades with paint rubbed on their cheeks, and feathers dangling from their hair. Indeed, they aimed to identify themselves with the Indians, a transformation by which they gained nothing; for these renegade whites were held in light esteem, both by those of their own color and the savages themselves. They were for the most part a light and frivolous crew, little to be relied on for energy or stability; though among them were men of hard and ruffian features, the ringleaders and bullies of the voyageurs, and even a terror to the Bourgeois himself. It was one of these who now took up the war-belt, and declared that he and his comrades were ready to raise the hatchet for Pontiac. The better class of Canadians were shocked at this proceeding, and vainly protested against it. Pontiac, on his part, was much pleased at such an accession to his forces, and he and his chiefs shook hands, in turn, with each of their new auxiliaries. The council had been protracted to a late hour. It was dark before the assembly dissolved, "so that," as the chronicler observes, "these new Indians had no opportunity of displaying their exploits that day." They remained in the Indian camp all night, being afraid of the reception they might meet among their fellow-whites in the settlement. The whole of the following morning was employed in giving them a feast of welcome. For this entertainment a large number of dogs were killed, and served up to the guests; none of whom, according to the Indian custom on such formal occasions, were permitted to take their leave until they had eaten the whole of the enormous portion placed before them. Pontiac derived little advantage from his Canadian allies, most of whom, fearing the resentment of the English and the other inhabitants, fled, before the war was over, to the country of the Illinois. On the night succeeding the feast, a party of the renegades, joined by about an equal number of Indians, approached the fort, and intrenched themselves, in order to fire upon the garrison. At daybreak, they were observed, the gate was thrown open, and a file of men, headed by Lieutenant Hay, sallied to dislodge them. This was effected without much difficulty. The Canadians fled with such despatch, that all of them escaped unhurt, though two of the Indians were shot.

It happened that among the English was a soldier who had been prisoner, for several years, among the Delawares, and who, while he had learned to hate the whole race, at the same time had acquired many of their habits and practices. He now ran forward, and, kneeling on the body of one of the dead savages, tore away the scalp, and shook it, with an exultant cry, towards the fugitives. This act, as afterwards appeared, excited great rage among the Indians.

Lieutenant Hay and his party, after their successful sally, had retired to the fort; when, at about four o'clock in the afternoon, a man was seen running towards it, closely pursued by Indians. On his arriving within gunshot, they gave over the chase, and the fugitive came panting beneath the stockade, where a wicket was flung open to receive him. He proved to be the commandant of Sandusky, who, having, as before mentioned, been adopted by the Indians, and married to an old squaw, now seized the first opportunity of escaping from her embraces.

Through him, the garrison learned the unhappy tidings that Captain Campbell was killed. This gentleman, from his high personal character, no less than his merit as an officer, was held in general esteem; and his fate excited a feeling of anger and grief among all the English in Detroit. It appeared that the Indian killed and scalped, in the skirmish of that morning, was nephew to Wasson, chief of the Ojibwas. On hearing of his death, the enraged uncle had immediately blackened his face in sign of revenge, called together a party of his followers, and repairing to the house of Meloche, where Captain Campbell was kept prisoner, had seized upon him, and bound him fast to a neighboring fence, where they shot him to death with arrows. Others say that they tomahawked him on the spot; but all agree that his body was mutilated in a barbarous manner. His heart is said to have been eaten by his murderers, to make them courageous; a practice not uncommon among Indians, after killing an enemy of acknowledged bravery. The corpse was thrown into the river, and afterwards brought to shore and buried by the Canadians. According to one authority, Pontiac was privy to this act; but a second, equally credible, represents him as ignorant of it, and declares that Wasson fled to Saginaw to escape his fury; while a third affirms that the Ojibwas carried off Campbell by force from before the eyes of the great chief. The other captive, M'Dougal, had previously escaped.

The two armed schooners, anchored opposite the fort, were now become objects of awe and aversion to the Indians. This is not to be wondered at, for, besides aiding in the defence of the place, by sweeping two sides of it with their fire, they often caused great terror and annoyance to the besiegers. Several times they had left their anchorage, and, taking up a convenient position, had battered the Indian camps and villages with no little effect. Once in particular,—and this was the first attempt of the kind,—Gladwyn himself, with several of his officers, had embarked on board the smaller vessel, while a fresh breeze was blowing from the northwest. The Indians, on the banks, stood watching her as she tacked from shore to shore, and pressed their hands against their mouths in amazement, thinking that magic power alone could enable her thus to make her way against wind and current. Making a long reach from the opposite shore, she came on directly towards the camp of Pontiac, her sails swelling, her masts leaning over till the black muzzles of her guns almost touched the river. The Indians watched her in astonishment. On she came, till their fierce hearts exulted in the idea that she would run ashore within their clutches, when suddenly a shout of command was heard on board, her progress was arrested, she rose upright, and her sails flapped and fluttered as if tearing loose from their fastenings. Steadily she came round, broadside to the shore; then, leaning once more to the wind, bore away gallantly on the other tack. She did not go far. The wondering spectators, quite at a loss to understand her movements, soon heard the hoarse rattling of her cable, as the anchor dragged it out, and saw her furling her vast white wings. As they looked unsuspectingly on, a puff of smoke was emitted from her side; a loud report followed; then another and another; and the balls, rushing over their heads, flew through the midst of their camp, and tore wildly among the forest-trees beyond. All was terror and consternation. The startled warriors bounded away on all sides; the squaws snatched up their children, and fled screaming; and, with a general chorus of yells, the whole encampment scattered in such haste, that little damage was done, except knocking to pieces their frail cabins of bark.

This attack was followed by others of a similar kind; and now the Indians seemed resolved to turn all their energies to the destruction of the vessel which caused them such annoyance. On the night of the tenth of July, they sent down a blazing raft, formed of two boats, secured together with a rope, and filled with pitch-pine, birch-bark, and other combustibles, which, by good fortune, missed the vessel, and floated down the stream without doing injury. All was quiet throughout the following night; but about two o'clock on the morning of the twelfth, the sentinel on duty saw a glowing spark of fire on the surface of the river, at some distance above. It grew larger and brighter; it rose in a forked flame, and at length burst forth into a broad conflagration. In this instance, too, fortune favored the vessel; for the raft, which was larger than the former, passed down between her and the fort, brightly gilding her tracery of ropes and spars, lighting up the old palisades and bastions of Detroit, disclosing the white Canadian farms and houses along the shore, and revealing the dusky margin of the forest behind. It showed, too, a dark group of naked spectators, who stood on the bank to watch the effect of their artifice, when a cannon flashed, a loud report broke the stillness, and before the smoke of the gun had risen, these curious observers had vanished. The raft floated down, its flames crackling and glaring wide through the night, until it was burnt to the water's edge, and its last hissing embers were quenched in the river.

Though twice defeated, the Indians would not abandon their plan, but, soon after this second failure, began another raft, of different construction from the former, and so large that they thought it certain to take effect. Gladwyn, on his part, provided boats which were moored by chains at some distance above the vessels, and made other preparations of defence, so effectual that the Indians, after working four days upon the raft, gave over their undertaking as useless. About this time, a party of Shawanoe and Delaware Indians arrived at Detroit, and were received by the Wyandots with a salute of musketry, which occasioned some alarm among the English, who knew nothing of its cause. They reported the progress of the war in the south and east; and, a few days after, an Abenaki, from Lower Canada, also made his appearance, bringing to the Indians the flattering falsehood that their Great Father, the King of France, was at that moment advancing up the St. Lawrence with his army. It may here be observed, that the name of Father, given to the Kings of France and England, was a mere title of courtesy or policy; for, in his haughty independence, the Indian yields submission to no man.

It was now between two and three months since the siege began; and if one is disposed to think slightingly of the warriors whose numbers could avail so little against a handful of half-starved English and provincials, he has only to recollect, that where barbarism has been arrayed against civilization, disorder against discipline, and ungoverned fury against considerate valor, such has seldom failed to be the result.

At the siege of Detroit, the Indians displayed a high degree of comparative steadiness and perseverance; and their history cannot furnish another instance of so large a force persisting so long in the attack of a fortified place. Their good conduct may be ascribed to their deep rage against the English, to their hope of speedy aid from the French, and to the controlling spirit of Pontiac, which held them to their work. The Indian is but ill qualified for such attempts, having too much caution for an assault by storm, and too little patience for a blockade. The Wyandots and Pottawattamies had shown, from the beginning, less zeal than the other nations; and now, like children, they began to tire of the task they had undertaken. A deputation of the Wyandots came to the fort, and begged for peace, which was granted them; but when the Pottawattamies came on the same errand, they insisted, as a preliminary, that some of their people, who were detained prisoners by the English, should first be given up. Gladwyn demanded, on his part, that the English captives known to be in their village should be brought to the fort, and three of them were accordingly produced. As these were but a small part of the whole, the deputies were sharply rebuked for their duplicity, and told to go back for the rest. They withdrew angry and mortified; but, on the following day, a fresh deputation of chiefs made their appearance, bringing with them six prisoners. Having repaired to the council-room, they were met by Gladwyn, attended only by one or two officers. The Indians detained in the fort were about to be given up, and a treaty concluded, when one of the prisoners declared that there were several others still remaining in the Pottawattamie village. Upon this, the conference was broken off, and the deputies ordered instantly to depart. On being thus a second time defeated, they were goaded to such a pitch of rage, that, as afterwards became known, they formed the desperate resolution of killing Gladwyn on the spot, and then making their escape in the best way they could; but, happily, at that moment the commandant observed an Ottawa among them, and, resolving to seize him, called upon the guard without to assist in doing so. A file of soldiers entered, and the chiefs, seeing it impossible to execute their design, withdrew from the fort, with black and sullen brows. A day or two afterwards, however, they returned with the rest of the prisoners, on which peace was granted them, and their people set at liberty.

THE FIGHT OF BLOODY BRIDGE

1763

From the time when peace was concluded with the Wyandots and Pottawattamies until the end of July, little worthy of notice took place at Detroit. The fort was still watched closely by the Ottawas and Ojibwas, who almost daily assailed it with petty attacks. In the mean time, unknown to the garrison, a strong re-enforcement was coming to their aid. Captain Dalzell had left Niagara with twenty-two barges, bearing two hundred and eighty men, with several small cannon, and a fresh supply of provisions and ammunition.

Coasting the south shore of Lake Erie, they soon reached Presqu' Isle, where they found the scorched and battered blockhouse captured a few weeks before, and saw with surprise the mines and intrenchments made by the Indians in assailing it. Thence, proceeding on their voyage, they reached Sandusky on the twenty-sixth of July; and here they marched inland to the neighboring village of the Wyandots, which they burnt to the ground, at the same time destroying the corn, which this tribe, more provident than most of the others, had planted there in the spring. Dalzell then steered northward for the mouth of the Detroit, which he reached on the evening of the twenty-eighth, and cautiously ascended under cover of night. "It was fortunate," writes Gladwyn, "that they were not discovered, in which case they must have been destroyed or taken, as the Indians, being emboldened by their late successes, fight much better than we could have expected."

On the morning of the twenty-ninth, the whole country around Detroit was covered by a sea of fog, the precursor of a hot and sultry day; but at sunrise its surface began to heave and toss, and, parting at intervals, disclosed the dark and burnished surface of the river; then lightly rolling, fold upon fold, the mists melted rapidly away, the last remnant clinging sluggishly along the margin of the forests. Now, for the first time, the garrison could discern the approaching convoy. Still they remained in suspense, fearing lest it might have met the fate of the former detachment; but a salute from the fort was answered by a swivel from the boats, and at once all apprehension passed away. The convoy soon reached a point in the river midway between the villages of the Wyandots and the Pottawattamies. About a fortnight before, as we have seen, these capricious savages had made a treaty of peace, which they now saw fit to break, opening a hot fire upon the boats from either bank. It was answered by swivels and musketry; but before the short engagement was over, fifteen of the English were killed or wounded. This danger passed, boat after boat came to shore, and landed its men amid the cheers of the garrison. The detachment was composed of soldiers from the 55th and 80th Regiments, with twenty independent rangers, commanded by Major Rogers; and as the barracks in the place were too small to receive them, they were all quartered upon the inhabitants.

Scarcely were these arrangements made, when a great smoke was seen rising from the Wyandot village across the river, and the inhabitants, apparently in much consternation, were observed paddling down stream with their household utensils, and even their dogs. It was supposed that they had abandoned and burned their huts; but in truth, it was only an artifice of these Indians, who had set fire to some old canoes and other refuse piled in front of their village, after which the warriors, having concealed the women and children, returned and lay in ambush among the bushes, hoping to lure some of the English within reach of their guns. None of them, however, fell into the snare.

Captain Dalzell was the same officer who was the companion of Israel Putnam in some of the most adventurous passages of that rough veteran's life; but more recently he had acted as aide-de-camp to Sir Jeffrey Amherst. On the day of his arrival, he had a conference with Gladwyn, at the quarters of the latter, and strongly insisted that the time was come when an irrecoverable blow might be struck at Pontiac. He requested permission to march out on the following night, and attack the Indian camp. Gladwyn, better acquainted with the position of affairs, and perhaps more cautious by nature, was averse to the attempt; but Dalzell urged his request so strenuously that the commandant yielded to his representations, and gave a tardy consent.

Pontiac had recently removed his camp from its old position near the mouth of Parent's Creek, and was now posted several miles above, behind a great marsh, which protected the Indian huts from the cannon of the vessel. On the afternoon of the thirtieth, orders were issued and preparations made for the meditated attack. Through the inexcusable carelessness of some of the officers, the design became known to a few Canadians, the bad result of which will appear in the sequel.

About two o'clock on the morning of the thirty-first of July, the gates were thrown open in silence, and the detachment, two hundred and fifty in number, passed noiselessly out. They filed two deep along the road, while two large bateaux, each bearing a swivel on the bow, rowed up the river abreast of them. Lieutenant Brown led the advance guard of twenty-five men; the centre was commanded by Captain Gray, and the rear by Captain Grant. The night was still, close, and sultry, and the men marched in light undress. On their right was the dark and gleaming surface of the river, with a margin of sand intervening, and on their left a succession of Canadian houses, with barns, orchards, and cornfields, from whence the clamorous barking of watch-dogs saluted them as they passed. The inhabitants, roused from sleep, looked from the windows in astonishment and alarm. An old man has told the writer how, when a child, he climbed on the roof of his father's house, to look down on the glimmering bayonets, and how, long after the troops had passed, their heavy and measured tramp sounded from afar, through the still night. Thus the English moved forward to the attack, little thinking that, behind houses and enclosures, Indian scouts watched every yard of their progress—little suspecting that Pontiac, apprised by the Canadians of their plan, had broken up his camp, and was coming against them with all his warriors, armed and painted for battle.

A mile and a half from the fort, Parent's Creek, ever since that night called Bloody Run, descended through a wild and rough hollow, and entered the Detroit amid a growth of rank grass and sedge. Only a few rods from its mouth, the road crossed it by a narrow wooden bridge, not existing at the present day. Just beyond this bridge, the land rose in abrupt ridges, parallel to the stream. Along their summits were rude intrenchments made by Pontiac to protect his camp, which had formerly occupied the ground immediately beyond. Here, too, were many piles of firewood belonging to the Canadians, besides strong picket fences, enclosing orchards and gardens connected with the neighboring houses. Behind fences, wood-piles, and intrenchments, crouched an unknown number of Indian warriors with levelled guns. They lay silent as snakes, for now they could hear the distant tramp of the approaching column.

The sky was overcast, and the night exceedingly dark. As the English drew near the dangerous pass, they could discern the oft-mentioned house of Meloche upon a rising ground to the left, while in front the bridge was dimly visible, and the ridges beyond it seemed like a wall of undistinguished blackness. They pushed rapidly forward, not wholly unsuspicious of danger. The advance guard were half way over the bridge, and the main body just entering upon it, when a horrible burst of yells rose in their front, and the Indian guns blazed forth in a general discharge. Half the advanced party were shot down; the appalled survivors shrank back aghast. The confusion reached even the main body, and the whole recoiled together; but Dalzell raised his clear voice above the din, advanced to the front, rallied the men, and led them forward to the attack. Again the Indians poured in their volley, and again the English hesitated; but Dalzell shouted from the van, and, in the madness of mingled rage and fear, they charged at a run across the bridge and up the heights beyond. Not an Indian was there to oppose them. In vain the furious soldiers sought their enemy behind fences and intrenchments. The active savages had fled; yet still their guns flashed thick through the gloom, and their war-cry rose with undiminished clamor. The English pushed forward amid the pitchy darkness, quite ignorant of their way, and soon became involved in a maze of outhouses and enclosures. At every pause they made, the retiring enemy would gather to renew the attack, firing back hotly upon the front and flanks. To advance farther would be useless, and the only alternative was to withdraw and wait for daylight. Captain Grant, with his company, recrossed the bridge, and took up his station on the road. The rest followed, a small party remaining to hold the enemy in check while the dead and wounded were placed on board the two bateaux which had rowed up to the bridge during the action. This task was commenced amid a sharp fire from both sides; and before it was completed, heavy volleys were heard from the rear, where Captain Grant was stationed. A great force of Indians had fired upon him from the house of Meloche and the neighboring orchards. Grant pushed up the hill, and drove them from the orchards at the point of the bayonet—drove them, also, from the house, and, entering it, found two Canadians within. These men told him that the Indians were bent on cutting off the English from the fort, and that they had gone in great numbers to occupy the houses which commanded the road below. It was now evident that instant retreat was necessary; and the command being issued to that effect, the men fell back into marching order, and slowly began their retrograde movement. Grant was now in the van, and Dalzell at the rear. Some of the Indians followed, keeping up a scattering and distant fire; and from time to time the rear faced about, to throw back a volley of musketry at the pursuers. Having proceeded in this manner for half a mile, they reached a point where, close upon the right, were many barns and outhouses, with strong picket fences. Behind these, and in a newly dug cellar close at hand, lay concealed a great multitude of Indians. They suffered the advanced party to pass unmolested; but when the centre and rear came opposite their ambuscade, they raised a frightful yell, and poured a volley among them. The men had well-nigh fallen into a panic. The river ran close on their left, and the only avenue of escape lay along the road in front. Breaking their ranks, they crowded upon one another in blind eagerness to escape the storm of bullets; and but for the presence of Dalzell, the retreat would have been turned into a flight. "The enemy," writes an officer who was in the fight, "marked him for his extraordinary bravery;" and he had already received two severe wounds. Yet his exertions did not slacken for a moment. Some of the soldiers he rebuked, some he threatened, and some he beat with the flat of his sword; till at length order was partially restored, and the fire of the enemy returned with effect. Though it was near daybreak, the dawn was obscured by a thick fog, and little could be seen of the Indians, except the incessant flashes of their guns amid the mist, while hundreds of voices, mingled in one appalling yell, confused the faculties of the men, and drowned the shout of command. The enemy had taken possession of a house, from the windows of which they fired down upon the English. Major Rogers, with some of his provincial rangers, burst the door with an axe, rushed in, and expelled them. Captain Gray was ordered to dislodge a large party from behind some neighboring fences. He charged them with his company, but fell, mortally wounded, in the attempt. They gave way, however; and now, the fire of the Indians being much diminished, the retreat was resumed. No sooner had the men faced about, than the savages came darting through the mist upon their flank and rear, cutting down stragglers, and scalping the fallen. At a little distance lay a sergeant of the 55th, helplessly wounded, raising himself on his hands, and gazing with a look of despair after his retiring comrades. The sight caught the eye of Dalzell. That gallant soldier, in the true spirit of heroism, ran out, amid the firing, to rescue the wounded man, when a shot struck him, and he fell dead. Few observed his fate, and none durst turn back to recover his body. The detachment pressed on, greatly harassed by the pursuing Indians. Their loss would have been much more severe, had not Major Rogers taken possession of another house, which commanded the road, and covered the retreat of the party.

He entered it with some of his own men, while many panic-stricken regulars broke in after him, in their eagerness to gain a temporary shelter. The house was a large and strong one, and the women of the neighborhood had crowded into the cellar for refuge. While some of the soldiers looked in blind terror for a place of concealment, others seized upon a keg of whiskey in one of the rooms and quaffed the liquor with eager thirst; while others, again, piled packs of furs, furniture, and all else within their reach, against the windows, to serve as a barricade. Panting and breathless, their faces moist with sweat and blackened with gunpowder, they thrust their muskets through the openings, and fired out upon the whooping assailants. At intervals, a bullet flew sharply whizzing through a crevice, striking down a man, perchance, or rapping harmlessly against the partitions. Old Campau, the master of the house, stood on a trap-door to prevent the frightened soldiers from seeking shelter among the women in the cellar. A ball grazed his gray head, and buried itself in the wall, where a few years since it might still have been seen. The screams of the half-stifled women below, the quavering war-whoops without, the shouts and curses of the soldiers, mingled in a scene of clamorous confusion, and it was long before the authority of Rogers could restore order.

In the mean time, Captain Grant, with his advanced party, had moved forward about half a mile, where he found some orchards and enclosures, by means of which he could maintain himself until the centre and rear should arrive. From this point he detached all the men he could spare to occupy the houses below; and as soldiers soon began to come in from the rear, he was enabled to re-enforce these detachments, until a complete line of communication was established with the fort, and the retreat effectually secured. Within an hour, the whole party had arrived, with the exception of Rogers and his men, who were quite unable to come off, being besieged in the house of Campau, by full two hundred Indians. The two armed bateaux had gone down to the fort, laden with the dead and wounded. They now returned, and, in obedience to an order from Grant, proceeded up the river to a point opposite Campau's house, where they opened a fire of swivels, which swept the ground above and below it, and completely scattered the assailants. Rogers and his party now came out, and marched down the road, to unite themselves with Grant. The two bateaux accompanied them closely, and, by a constant fire, restrained the Indians from making an attack. Scarcely had Rogers left the house at one door, when the enemy entered it at another, to obtain the scalps from two or three corpses left behind. Foremost of them all, a withered old squaw rushed in, with a shrill scream, and, slashing open one of the dead bodies with her knife, scooped up the blood between her hands, and quaffed it with a ferocious ecstasy.

Grant resumed his retreat as soon as Rogers had arrived, falling back from house to house, joined in succession by the parties sent to garrison each. The Indians, in great numbers, stood whooping and yelling, at a vain distance, unable to make an attack, so well did Grant choose his positions, and so steadily and coolly conduct the retreat. About eight o'clock, after six hours of marching and combat, the detachment entered once more within the sheltering palisades of Detroit.

In this action, the English lost fifty-nine men killed and wounded. The loss of the Indians could not be ascertained, but it certainly did not exceed fifteen or twenty. At the beginning of the fight, their numbers were probably much inferior to those of the English; but fresh parties were continually joining them, until seven or eight hundred warriors must have been present.

The Ojibwas and Ottawas alone formed the ambuscade at the bridge, under Pontiac's command; for the Wyandots and Pottawattamies came later to the scene of action, crossing the river in their canoes, or passing round through the woods behind the fort, to take part in the fray.

In speaking of the fight of Bloody Bridge, an able writer in the Annual Register for the year 1763 observes, with justice, that although in European warfare it would be deemed a mere skirmish, yet in a conflict with the American savages, it rises to the importance of a pitched battle; since these people, being thinly scattered over a great extent of country, are accustomed to conduct their warfare by detail, and never take the field in any great force.

The Indians were greatly elated by their success. Runners were sent out for several hundred miles, through the surrounding woods, to spread tidings of the victory; and re-enforcements soon began to come in to swell the force of Pontiac. "Fresh warriors," writes Gladwyn, "arrive almost every day, and I believe that I shall soon be besieged by upwards of a thousand." The English, on their part, were well prepared for resistance, since the garrison now comprised more than three hundred effective men; and no one entertained a doubt of their ultimate success in defending the place. Day after day passed on; a few skirmishes took place, and a few men were killed, but nothing worthy of notice occurred, until the night of the fourth of September, at which time was achieved one of the most memorable feats which the chronicles of that day can boast.

The schooner Gladwyn, the smaller of the two armed vessels so often mentioned, had been sent down to Niagara with letters and despatches. She was now returning, having on board Horst, her master, Jacobs, her mate, and a crew of ten men, all of whom were provincials, besides six Iroquois Indians, supposed to be friendly to the English. On the night of the third, she entered the River Detroit; and in the morning the six Indians asked to be set on shore, a request which was foolishly granted. They disappeared in the woods, and probably reported to Pontiac's warriors the small numbers of the crew. The vessel stood up the river until nightfall, when, the wind failing, she was compelled to anchor about nine miles below the fort. The men on board watched with anxious vigilance; and as night came on, they listened to every sound which broke the stillness, from the strange cry of the night-hawk, wheeling above their heads, to the bark of the fox from the woods on shore. The night set in with darkness so complete, that at the distance of a few rods nothing could be discerned. Meantime, three hundred and fifty Indians, in their birch canoes, glided silently down with the current, and were close upon the vessel before they were seen. There was only time to fire a single cannon-shot among them, before they were beneath her bows, and clambering up her sides, holding their knives clinched fast between their teeth. The crew gave them a close fire of musketry, without any effect; then, flinging down their guns, they seized the spears and hatchets with which they were all provided, and met the assailants with such furious energy and courage, that in the space of two or three minutes they had killed and wounded more than twice their own number. But the Indians were only checked for a moment. The master of the vessel was killed, several of the crew were disabled, and the assailants were leaping over the bulwarks, when Jacobs, the mate, called out to blow up the schooner. This desperate command saved her and her crew. Some Wyandots, who had gained the deck, caught the meaning of his words, and gave the alarm to their companions. Instantly every Indian leaped overboard in a panic, and the whole were seen diving and swimming off in all directions, to escape the threatened explosion. The schooner was cleared of her assailants, who did not dare to renew the attack; and on the following morning she sailed for the fort, which she reached without molestation. Six of her crew escaped unhurt. Of the remainder, two were killed, and four seriously wounded, while the Indians had seven men killed upon the spot, and nearly twenty wounded, of whom eight were known to have died within a few days after. As the action was very brief, the fierceness of the struggle is sufficiently apparent from the loss on both sides. "The appearance of the men," says an eye-witness who saw them on their arrival, "was enough to convince every one of their bravery; they being as bloody as butchers, and their bayonets, spears, and cutlasses, blood to the hilt." The survivors of the crew were afterwards rewarded as their courage deserved.

And now, taking leave, for a time, of the garrison of Detroit, whose fortunes we have followed so long, we will turn to observe the progress of events in a quarter of the wilderness yet more wild and remote.

MICHILLIMACKINAC

1763

In the spring of the year 1763, before the war broke out, several English traders went up to Michillimackinac, some adopting the old route of the Ottawa, and others that of Detroit and the lakes. We will follow one of the latter on his adventurous progress. Passing the fort and settlement of Detroit, he soon enters Lake St. Clair, which seems like a broad basin filled to overflowing, while, along its far distant verge, a faint line of forest separates the water from the sky. He crosses the lake, and his voyageurs next urge his canoe against the current of the great river above. At length, Lake Huron opens before him, stretching its liquid expanse, like an ocean, to the farthest horizon. His canoe skirts the eastern shore of Michigan, where the forest rises like a wall from the water's edge; and as he advances northward, an endless line of stiff and shaggy fir-trees, hung with long mosses, fringes the shore with an aspect of monotonous desolation. In the space of two or three weeks, if his Canadians labor well, and no accident occur, the trader approaches the end of his voyage. Passing on his right the extensive Island of Bois Blanc, he sees, nearly in front, the beautiful Mackinaw, rising, with its white cliffs and green foliage, from the broad breast of the waters. He does not steer towards it, for at that day the Indians were its only tenants, but keeps along the main shore to the left, while his voyageurs raise their song and chorus. Doubling a point, he sees before him the red flag of England swelling lazily in the wind, and the palisades and wooden bastions of Fort Michillimackinac standing close upon the margin of the lake. On the beach, canoes are drawn up, and Canadians and Indians are idly lounging. A little beyond the fort is a cluster of the white Canadian houses, roofed with bark, and protected by fences of strong round pickets.

The trader enters at the gate, and sees before him an extensive square area, surrounded by high palisades. Numerous houses, barracks, and other buildings, form a smaller square within, and in the vacant space which they enclose appear the red uniforms of British soldiers, the gray coats of Canadians, and the gaudy Indian blankets, mingled in picturesque confusion; while a multitude of squaws, with children of every hue, stroll restlessly about the place. Such was Fort Michillimackinac in 1763. Its name, which, in the Algonquin tongue, signifies the Great Turtle, was first, from a fancied resemblance, applied to the neighboring island, and thence to the fort.

Though buried in a wilderness, Michillimackinac was still of no recent origin. As early as 1671, the Jesuits had established a mission near the place, and a military force was not long in following; for, under the French dominion, the priest and the soldier went hand in hand. Neither toil, nor suffering, nor all the terrors of the wilderness, could damp the zeal of the undaunted missionary; and the restless ambition of France was always on the alert to seize every point of vantage, and avail itself of every means to gain ascendency over the forest tribes. Besides Michillimackinac, there were two other posts in this northern region, Green Bay, and the Sault Ste. Marie. Both were founded at an early period, and both presented the same characteristic features—a mission-house, a fort, and a cluster of Canadian dwellings. They had been originally garrisoned by small parties of militia, who, bringing their families with them, settled on the spot, and were founders of these little colonies. Michillimackinac, much the largest of the three, contained thirty families within the palisades of the fort, and about as many more without. Besides its military value, it was important as a centre of the fur-trade; for it was here that the traders engaged their men, and sent out their goods in canoes, under the charge of subordinates, to the more distant regions of the Mississippi and the North-west.

During the greater part of the year, the garrison and the settlers were completely isolated—cut off from all connection with the world; and, indeed, so great was the distance, and so serious the perils, which separated the three sister posts of the northern lakes, that often, through the whole winter, all intercourse was stopped between them.

It is difficult for the imagination adequately to conceive the extent of these fresh-water oceans, and vast regions of forest, which, at the date of our narrative, were the domain of nature, a mighty hunting and fishing ground, for the sustenance of a few wandering tribes. One might journey among them for days, and even weeks together, without beholding a human face. The Indians near Michillimackinac were the Ojibwas and Ottawas, the former of whom claimed the eastern section of Michigan, and the latter the western, their respective portions being separated by a line drawn southward from the fort itself. The principal village of the Ojibwas contained about a hundred warriors, and stood upon the Island of Michillimackinac, now called Mackinaw. There was another smaller village near the head of Thunder Bay. The Ottawas, to the number of two hundred and fifty warriors, lived at the settlement of L'Arbre Croche, on the shores of Lake Michigan, some distance west of the fort. This place was then the seat of the old Jesuit mission of St. Ignace, originally placed, by Father Marquette, on the northern side of the straits. Many of the Ottawas were nominal Catholics. They were all somewhat improved from their original savage condition, living in log houses, and cultivating corn and vegetables to such an extent as to supply the fort with provisions, besides satisfying their own wants. The Ojibwas, on the other hand, were not in the least degree removed from their primitive barbarism.

These two tribes, with most of the other neighboring Indians, were strongly hostile to the English. Many of their warriors had fought against them in the late war, for France had summoned allies from the farthest corners of the wilderness, to aid her in her struggle. This feeling of hostility was excited to a higher pitch by the influence of the Canadians, who disliked the English, not merely as national enemies, but also as rivals in the fur-trade, and were extremely jealous of their intrusion upon the lakes. The following incidents, which occurred in the autumn of the year 1761, will illustrate the state of feeling which prevailed:—

At that time, although Michillimackinac had been surrendered, and the French garrison removed, no English troops had yet arrived to supply their place, and the Canadians were the only tenants of the fort. An adventurous trader, Alexander Henry, who, with one or two others, was the pioneer of the English fur-trade in this region, came to Michillimackinac by the route of the Ottawa. On the way, he was several times warned to turn back, and assured of death if he proceeded; and, at length, was compelled for safety to assume the disguise of a Canadian voyageur. When his canoes, laden with goods, reached the fort, he was very coldly received by its inhabitants, who did all in their power to alarm and discourage him. Soon after his arrival, he received the very unwelcome information, that a large number of Ojibwas, from the neighboring villages, were coming, in their canoes, to call upon him. Under ordinary circumstances, such a visitation, though disagreeable enough, would excite neither anxiety nor surprise; for the Indians, when in their villages, lead so monotonous an existence, that they are ready to snatch at the least occasion of excitement, and the prospect of a few trifling presents, and a few pipes of tobacco, is often a sufficient inducement for a journey of several days. But in the present instance there was serious cause of apprehension, since Canadians and Frenchmen were alike hostile to the solitary trader. The story could not be better told than in his own words.

"At two o'clock in the afternoon, the Chippewas (Ojibwas) came to the house, about sixty in number, and headed by Minavavana, their chief. They walked in single file, each with his tomahawk in one hand and scalping-knife in the other. Their bodies were naked from the waist upward, except in a few examples, where blankets were thrown loosely over the shoulders. Their faces were painted with charcoal, worked up with grease, their bodies with white clay, in patterns of various fancies. Some had feathers thrust through their noses, and their heads decorated with the same. It is unnecessary to dwell on the sensations with which I beheld the approach of this uncouth, if not frightful assemblage.

"The chief entered first, and the rest followed without noise. On receiving a sign from the former, the latter seated themselves on the floor.

"Minavavana appeared to be about fifty years of age. He was six feet in height, and had in his countenance an indescribable mixture of good and evil. Looking steadfastly at me, where I sat in ceremony, with an interpreter on either hand, and several Canadians behind me, he entered, at the same time, into conversation with Campion, inquiring how long it was since I left Montreal, and observing that the English, as it would seem, were brave men, and not afraid of death, since they dared to come, as I had done, fearlessly among their enemies.

"The Indians now gravely smoked their pipes, while I inwardly endured the tortures of suspense. At length, the pipes being finished, as well as a long pause, by which they were succeeded, Minavavana, taking a few strings of wampum in his hand, began the following speech:—

"'Englishman, it is to you that I speak, and I demand your attention.

"'Englishman, you know that the French King is our father. He promised to be such; and we, in return, promised to be his children. This promise we have kept.

"'Englishman, it is you that have made war with this our father. You are his enemy; and how, then, could you have the boldness to venture among us, his children? You know that his enemies are ours.

"'Englishman, we are informed that our father, the King of France, is old and infirm; and that, being fatigued with making war upon your nation, he is fallen asleep. During his sleep you have taken advantage of him, and possessed yourselves of Canada. But his nap is almost at an end. I think I hear him already stirring, and inquiring for his children, the Indians; and when he does awake, what must become of you? He will destroy you utterly.

"'Englishman, although you have conquered the French, you have not yet conquered us. We are not your slaves. These lakes, these woods and mountains, were left to us by our ancestors. They are our inheritance; and we will part with them to none. Your nation supposes that we, like the white people, cannot live without bread, and pork, and beef! But you ought to know that He, the Great Spirit and Master of Life, has provided food for us in these spacious lakes, and on these woody mountains.

"'Englishman, our father, the King of France, employed our young men to make war upon your nation. In this warfare many of them have been killed; and it is our custom to retaliate until such time as the spirits of the slain are satisfied. But the spirits of the slain are to be satisfied in either of two ways; the first is by the spilling of the blood of the nation by which they fell; the other, by covering the bodies of the dead, and thus allaying the resentment of their relations. This is done by making presents.

"'Englishman, your king has never sent us any presents, nor entered into any treaty with us; wherefore he and we are still at war; and, until he does these things, we must consider that we have no other father nor friend, among the white men, than the King of France; but for you, we have taken into consideration that you have ventured your life among us, in the expectation that we should not molest you. You do not come armed, with an intention to make war; you come in peace, to trade with us, and supply us with necessaries, of which we are in much want. We shall regard you, therefore, as a brother; and you may sleep tranquilly, without fear of the Chippewas. As a token of our friendship, we present you this pipe to smoke.'

"As Minavavana uttered these words, an Indian presented me with a pipe, which, after I had drawn the smoke three times, was carried to the chief, and after him to every person in the room. This ceremony ended, the chief arose, and gave me his hand, in which he was followed by all the rest."

These tokens of friendship were suitably acknowledged by the trader, who made a formal reply to Minavavana's speech. To this succeeded a request for whiskey on the part of the Indians, with which Henry unwillingly complied; and, having distributed several small additional presents, he beheld, with profound satisfaction, the departure of his guests. Scarcely had he ceased to congratulate himself on having thus got rid of the Ojibwas, or, as he calls them, the Chippewas, when a more formidable invasion once more menaced him with destruction. Two hundred L'Arbre Croche Ottawas came in a body to the fort, and summoned Henry, together with Goddard and Solomons, two other traders, who had just arrived, to meet them in council. Here they informed their startled auditors that they must distribute their goods among the Indians, adding a worthless promise to pay them in the spring, and threatening force in case of a refusal. Being allowed until the next morning to reflect on what they had heard, the traders resolved on resistance, and, accordingly, arming about thirty of their men with muskets, they barricaded themselves in the house occupied by Henry, and kept strict watch all night. The Ottawas, however, did not venture an attack. On the following day, the Canadians, with pretended sympathy, strongly advised compliance with the demand; but the three traders resolutely held out, and kept possession of their stronghold till night, when, to their surprise and joy, the news arrived that the body of troops known to be on their way towards the fort were, at that moment, encamped within a few miles of it. Another night of watching and anxiety succeeded; but at sunrise, the Ottawas launched their canoes and departed, while, immediately after, the boats of the English detachment were seen to approach the landing-place. Michillimackinac received a strong garrison; and for a time, at least, the traders were safe.

Time passed on, and the hostile feelings of the Indians towards the English did not diminish. It necessarily follows, from the extremely loose character of Indian government,—if indeed the name government be applicable at all,—that the separate members of the same tribe have little political connection, and are often united merely by the social tie of totemship. Thus the Ottawas at L'Arbre Croche were quite independent of those at Detroit. They had a chief of their own, who by no means acknowledged the authority of Pontiac, though the high reputation of this great warrior everywhere attached respect and influence to his name. The same relations subsisted between the Ojibwas of Michillimackinac and their more southern tribesmen; and the latter might declare war and make peace without at all involving the former.

The name of the Ottawa chief at L'Arbre Croche has not survived in history or tradition. The chief of the Ojibwas, however, is still remembered by the remnants of his people, and was the same whom Henry calls Minavavana, or, as the Canadians entitled him, by way of distinction, Le Grand Sauteur, or the Great Ojibwa. He lived in the little village of Thunder Bay, though his power was acknowledged by the Indians of the neighboring islands. That his mind was of no common order is sufficiently evinced by his speech to Henry; but he had not the commanding spirit of Pontiac. His influence seems not to have extended beyond his own tribe. He could not, or at least he did not, control the erratic forces of an Indian community, and turn them into one broad current of steady and united energy. Hence, in the events about to be described, the natural instability of the Indian character was abundantly displayed.

In the spring of the year 1763, Pontiac, in compassing his grand scheme of hostility, sent, among the rest, to the Indians of Michillimackinac, inviting them to aid him in the war. His messengers, bearing in their hands the war-belt of black and purple wampum, appeared before the assembled warriors, flung at their feet a hatchet painted red, and delivered the speech with which they had been charged. The warlike auditory answered with ejaculations of applause, and, taking up the blood-red hatchet, pledged themselves to join in the contest. Before the end of May, news reached the Ojibwas that Pontiac had already struck the English at Detroit. This wrought them up to a high pitch of excitement and emulation, and they resolved that peace should last no longer. Their numbers were at this time more than doubled by several bands of their wandering people, who had gathered at Michillimackinac from far and near, attracted probably by rumors of impending war. Being, perhaps, jealous of the Ottawas, or willing to gain all the glory and plunder to themselves, they determined to attack the fort, without communicating the design to their neighbors of L'Arbre Croche.

At this time there were about thirty-five men, with their officers, in garrison at Michillimackinac. Warning of the tempest that impended had been clearly given; enough, had it been heeded, to have averted the fatal disaster. Several of the Canadians least hostile to the English had thrown out hints of approaching danger, and one of them had even told Captain Etherington, the commandant, that the Indians had formed a design to destroy, not only his garrison, but all the English on the lakes. With a folly, of which, at this period, there were several parallel instances among the British officers in America, Etherington not only turned a deaf ear to what he heard, but threatened to send prisoner to Detroit the next person who should disturb the fort with such tidings. Henry, the trader, who was at this time in the place, had also seen occasion to distrust the Indians; but on communicating his suspicions to the commandant, the latter treated them with total disregard. Henry accuses himself of sharing this officer's infatuation. That his person was in danger, had been plainly intimated to him, under the following curious circumstances:—

An Ojibwa chief, named Wawatam, had conceived for him one of those friendly attachments which often form so pleasing a feature in the Indian character. It was about a year since Henry had first met with this man. One morning, Wawatam had entered his house, and placing before him, on the ground, a large present of furs and dried meat, delivered a speech to the following effect: Early in life, he said, he had withdrawn, after the ancient usage of his people, to fast and pray in solitude, that he might propitiate the Great Spirit, and learn the future career marked out for him. In the course of his dreams and visions on this occasion, it was revealed to him that, in after years, he should meet a white man, who should be to him a friend and brother. No sooner had he seen Henry, than the irrepressible conviction rose up within him, that he was the man whom the Great Spirit had indicated, and that the dream was now fulfilled. Henry replied to the speech with suitable acknowledgments of gratitude, made a present in his turn, smoked a pipe with Wawatam, and, as the latter soon after left the fort, speedily forgot his Indian friend and brother altogether. Many months had elapsed since the occurrence of this very characteristic incident, when, on the second of June, Henry's door was pushed open without ceremony, and the dark figure of Wawatam glided silently in. He said that he was just returned from his wintering ground. Henry, at length recollecting him, inquired after the success of his hunt; but the Indian, without replying, sat down with a dejected air, and expressed his surprise and regret at finding his brother still in the fort. He said that he was going on the next day to the Sault Ste. Marie, and that he wished Henry to go with him. He then asked if the English had heard no bad news, and said that through the winter he himself had been much disturbed by the singing of evil birds. Seeing that Henry gave little attention to what he said, he at length went away with a sad and mournful face. On the next morning he came again, together with his squaw, and, offering the trader a present of dried meat, again pressed him to go with him, in the afternoon, to the Sault Ste. Marie. When Henry demanded his reason for such urgency, he asked if his brother did not know that many bad Indians, who had never shown themselves at the fort, were encamped in the woods around it. To-morrow, he said, they are coming to ask for whiskey, and would all get drunk, so that it would be dangerous to remain. Wawatam let fall, in addition, various other hints, which, but for Henry's imperfect knowledge of the Algonquin language, could hardly have failed to draw his attention. As it was, however, his friend's words were spoken in vain; and at length, after long and persevering efforts, he and his squaw took their departure, but not, as Henry declares, before each had let fall some tears. Among the Indian women, the practice of weeping and wailing is universal upon all occasions of sorrowful emotion; and the kind-hearted squaw, as she took down her husband's lodge, and loaded his canoe for departure, did not cease to sob and moan aloud.

On this same afternoon, Henry remembers that the fort was full of Indians, moving about among the soldiers with a great appearance of friendship. Many of them came to his house, to purchase knives and small hatchets, often asking to see silver bracelets, and other ornaments, with the intention, as afterwards appeared, of learning their places of deposit, in order the more easily to lay hand on them at the moment of pillage. As the afternoon drew to a close, the visitors quietly went away; and many of the unhappy garrison saw for the last time the sun go down behind the waters of Lake Michigan.

THE MASSACRE

1763

The following morning was warm and sultry. It was the fourth of June, the birthday of King George. The discipline of the garrison was relaxed, and some license allowed to the soldiers. Encamped in the woods, not far off, were a large number of Ojibwas, lately arrived; while several bands of the Sac Indians, from the River Wisconsin, had also erected their lodges in the vicinity. Early in the morning, many Ojibwas came to the fort, inviting officers and soldiers to come out and see a grand game of ball, which was to be played between their nation and the Sacs. In consequence, the place was soon deserted by half its tenants. An outline of Michillimackinac, as far as tradition has preserved its general features, has already been given; and it is easy to conceive, with sufficient accuracy, the appearance it must have presented on this eventful morning. The houses and barracks were so ranged as to form a quadrangle, enclosing an extensive area, upon which their doors all opened, while behind rose the tall palisades, forming a large external square. The picturesque Canadian houses, with their rude porticoes, and projecting roofs of bark, sufficiently indicated the occupations of their inhabitants; for birch canoes were lying near many of them, and fishing-nets were stretched to dry in the sun. Women and children were moving about the doors; knots of Canadian voyageurs reclined on the ground, smoking and conversing; soldiers were lounging listlessly at the doors and windows of the barracks, or strolling in careless undress about the area.

Without the fort the scene was of a very different character. The gates were wide open, and soldiers were collected in groups under the shadow of the palisades, watching the Indian ball-play. Most of them were without arms, and mingled among them were a great number of Canadians, while a multitude of Indian squaws, wrapped in blankets, were conspicuous in the crowd.

Captain Etherington and Lieutenant Leslie stood near the gate, the former indulging his inveterate English propensity; for, as Henry informs us, he had promised the Ojibwas that he would bet on their side against the Sacs. Indian chiefs and warriors were also among the spectators, intent, apparently, on watching the game, but with thoughts, in fact, far otherwise employed.

The plain in front was covered by the ball-players. The game in which they were engaged, called baggattaway by the Ojibwas, is still, as it always has been, a favorite with many Indian tribes. At either extremity of the ground, a tall post was planted, marking the stations of the rival parties. The object of each was to defend its own post, and drive the ball to that of its adversary. Hundreds of lithe and agile figures were leaping and bounding upon the plain. Each was nearly naked, his loose black hair flying in the wind, and each bore in his hand a bat of a form peculiar to this game. At one moment the whole were crowded together, a dense throng of combatants, all struggling for the ball; at the next, they were scattered again, and running over the ground like hounds in full cry. Each, in his excitement, yelled and shouted at the height of his voice. Rushing and striking, tripping their adversaries, or hurling them to the ground, they pursued the animating contest amid the laughter and applause of the spectators. Suddenly, from the midst of the multitude, the ball soared into the air, and, descending in a wide curve, fell near the pickets of the fort. This was no chance stroke. It was part of a preconcerted stratagem to insure the surprise and destruction of the garrison. As if in pursuit of the ball, the players turned and came rushing, a maddened and tumultuous throng, towards the gate. In a moment they had reached it. The amazed English had no time to think or act. The shrill cries of the ball-players were changed to the ferocious war-whoop. The warriors snatched from the squaws the hatchets, which the latter, with this design, had concealed beneath their blankets. Some of the Indians assailed the spectators without, while others rushed into the fort, and all was carnage and confusion. At the outset, several strong hands had fastened their gripe upon Etherington and Leslie, and led them away from the scene of massacre towards the woods. Within the area of the fort, the men were slaughtered without mercy. But here the task of description may well be resigned to the pen of the trader, Henry.

"I did not go myself to see the match which was now to be played without the fort, because, there being a canoe prepared to depart on the following day for Montreal, I employed myself in writing letters to my friends; and even when a fellow-trader, Mr. Tracy, happened to call upon me, saying that another canoe had just arrived from Detroit, and proposing that I should go with him to the beach, to inquire the news, it so happened that I still remained to finish my letters; promising to follow Mr. Tracy in the course of a few minutes. Mr. Tracy had not gone more than twenty paces from my door, when I heard an Indian war-cry, and a noise of general confusion.

"Going instantly to my window, I saw a crowd of Indians, within the fort, furiously cutting down and scalping every Englishman they found: in particular, I witnessed the fate of Lieutenant Jamette.

"I had, in the room in which I was, a fowling-piece, loaded with swan shot. This I immediately seized, and held it for a few minutes, waiting to hear the drum beat to arms. In this dreadful interval I saw several of my countrymen fall, and more than one struggling between the knees of an Indian, who, holding him in this manner, scalped him while yet living.

"At length, disappointed in the hope of seeing resistance made to the enemy, and sensible, of course, that no effort of my own unassisted arm could avail against four hundred Indians, I thought only of seeking shelter amid the slaughter which was raging. I observed many of the Canadian inhabitants of the fort calmly looking on, neither opposing the Indians nor suffering injury; and from this circumstance, I conceived a hope of finding security in their houses.

"Between the yard door of my own house and that of M. Langlade, my next neighbor, there was only a low fence, over which I easily climbed. At my entrance, I found the whole family at the windows, gazing at the scene of blood before them. I addressed myself immediately to M. Langlade, begging that he would put me into some place of safety until the heat of the affair should be over; an act of charity by which he might, perhaps, preserve me from the general massacre; but while I uttered my petition, M. Langlade, who had looked for a moment at me, turned again to the window, shrugging his shoulders, and intimating that he could do nothing for me— 'Que voudriez-vous que j'en ferais?'

"This was a moment for despair; but the next a Pani woman, a slave of M. Langlade's, beckoned me to follow her. She brought me to a door, which she opened, desiring me to enter, and telling me that it led to the garret, where I must go and conceal myself. I joyfully obeyed her directions; and she, having followed me up to the garret door, locked it after me, and, with great presence of mind, took away the key.

"This shelter obtained, if shelter I could hope to find it, I was naturally anxious to know what might still be passing without. Through an aperture, which afforded me a view of the area of the fort, I beheld, in shapes the foulest and most terrible, the ferocious triumphs of barbarian conquerors. The dead were scalped and mangled; the dying were writhing and shrieking under the unsatiated knife and tomahawk; and from the bodies of some, ripped open, their butchers were drinking the blood, scooped up in the hollow of joined hands, and quaffed amid shouts of rage and victory. I was shaken not only with horror, but with fear. The sufferings which I witnessed I seemed on the point of experiencing. No long time elapsed before every one being destroyed who could be found, there was a general cry of 'All is finished.' At the same instant I heard some of the Indians enter the house where I was.

"The garret was separated from the room below only by a layer of single boards, at once the flooring of the one and the ceiling of the other. I could, therefore, hear every thing that passed; and the Indians no sooner came in than they inquired whether or not any Englishmen were in the house. M. Langlade replied, that 'he could not say, he did not know of any,' answers in which he did not exceed the truth; for the Pani woman had not only hidden me by stealth, but kept my secret and her own. M. Langlade was, therefore, as I presume, as far from a wish to destroy me as he was careless about saving me, when he added to these answers, that 'they might examine for themselves, and would soon be satisfied as to the object of their question.' Saying this, he brought them to the garret door.

"The state of my mind will be imagined. Arrived at the door, some delay was occasioned by the absence of the key; and a few moments were thus allowed me, in which to look around for a hiding-place. In one corner of the garret was a heap of those vessels of birch-bark used in maple-sugar making.

"The door was unlocked and opening, and the Indians ascending the stairs, before I had completely crept into a small opening which presented itself at one end of the heap. An instant after, four Indians entered the room, all armed with tomahawks, and all besmeared with blood, upon every part of their bodies.

"The die appeared to be cast. I could scarcely breathe; but I thought the throbbing of my heart occasioned a noise loud enough to betray me. The Indians walked in every direction about the garret; and one of them approached me so closely, that, at a particular moment had he put forth his hand, he must have touched me. Still I remained undiscovered; a circumstance to which the dark color of my clothes, and the want of light, in a room which had no window in the corner in which I was, must have contributed. In a word, after taking several turns in the room, during which they told M. Langlade how many they had killed, and how many scalps they had taken, they returned downstairs; and I, with sensations not to be expressed, heard the door, which was the barrier between me and my fate, locked for the second time.

"There was a feather bed on the floor; and on this, exhausted as I was by the agitation of my mind, I threw myself down and fell asleep. In this state I remained till the dusk of the evening, when I was awakened by a second opening of the door. The person that now entered was M. Langlade's wife, who was much surprised at finding me, but advised me not to be uneasy, observing that the Indians had killed most of the English, but that she hoped I might myself escape. A shower of rain having begun to fall, she had come to stop a hole in the roof. On her going away, I begged her to send me a little water to drink, which she did.

"As night was now advancing, I continued to lie on the bed, ruminating on my condition, but unable to discover a resource from which I could hope for life. A flight to Detroit had no probable chance of success. The distance from Michillimackinac was four hundred miles; I was without provisions, and the whole length of the road lay through Indian countries, countries of an enemy in arms, where the first man whom I should meet would kill me. To stay where I was, threatened nearly the same issue. As before, fatigue of mind, and not tranquillity, suspended my cares, and procured me farther sleep.

"The respite which sleep afforded me during the night was put an end to by the return of morning. I was again on the rack of apprehension. At sunrise, I heard the family stirring; and, presently after, Indian voices, informing M. Langlade that they had not found my hapless self among the dead, and they supposed me to be somewhere concealed. M. Langlade appeared, from what followed, to be, by this time, acquainted with the place of my retreat; of which, no doubt, he had been informed by his wife. The poor woman, as soon as the Indians mentioned me, declared to her husband, in the French tongue, that he should no longer keep me in his house, but deliver me up to my pursuers; giving as a reason for this measure, that, should the Indians discover his instrumentality in my concealment, they might revenge it on her children, and that it was better that I should die than they. M. Langlade resisted, at first, this sentence of his wife, but soon suffered her to prevail, informing the Indians that he had been told I was in his house; that I had come there without his knowledge, and that he would put me into their hands. This was no sooner expressed than he began to ascend the stairs, the Indians following upon his heels.

"I now resigned myself to the fate with which I was menaced; and, regarding every effort at concealment as vain, I rose from the bed, and presented myself full in view to the Indians, who were entering the room. They were all in a state of intoxication, and entirely naked, except about the middle. One of them, named Wenniway, whom I had previously known, and who was upwards of six feet in height, had his entire face and body covered with charcoal and grease, only that a white spot, of two inches in diameter, encircled either eye. This man, walking up to me, seized me, with one hand, by the collar of the coat, while in the other he held a large carving-knife, as if to plunge it into my breast; his eyes, meanwhile, were fixed steadfastly on mine. At length, after some seconds of the most anxious suspense, he dropped his arm, saying, 'I won't kill you!' To this he added, that he had been frequently engaged in wars against the English, and had brought away many scalps; that, on a certain occasion, he had lost a brother, whose name was Musinigon, and that I should be called after him.

"A reprieve, upon any terms, placed me among the living, and gave me back the sustaining voice of hope; but Wenniway ordered me downstairs, and there informing me that I was to be taken to his cabin, where, and indeed everywhere else, the Indians were all mad with liquor, death again was threatened, and not as possible only, but as certain. I mentioned my fears on this subject to M. Langlade, begging him to represent the danger to my master. M. Langlade, in this instance, did not withhold his compassion; and Wenniway immediately consented that I should remain where I was, until he found another opportunity to take me away."

Scarcely, however, had he been gone an hour, when an Indian came to the house, and directed Henry to follow him to the Ojibwa camp. Henry knew this man, who was largely in his debt, and some time before, on the trader's asking him for payment, the Indian had declared, in a significant tone, that he would pay him soon. There seemed at present good ground to suspect his intention; but, having no choice, Henry was obliged to follow him. The Indian led the way out of the gate; but, instead of going towards the camp, he moved with a quick step in the direction of the bushes and sand-hills behind the fort. At this, Henry's suspicions were confirmed. He refused to proceed farther, and plainly told his conductor that he believed he meant to kill him. The Indian coolly replied that he was quite right in thinking so, and at the same time, seizing the prisoner by the arm, raised his knife to strike him in the breast. Henry parried the blow, flung the Indian from him, and ran for his life. He gained the gate of the fort, his enemy close at his heels, and, seeing Wenniway standing in the centre of the area, called upon him for protection. The chief ordered the Indian to desist; but the latter, who was foaming at the mouth with rage, still continued to pursue Henry, vainly striking at him with his knife. Seeing the door of Langlade's house wide open, the trader darted in, and at length found himself in safety. He retired once more to his garret, and lay down, feeling, as he declares, a sort of conviction that no Indian had power to harm him.

This confidence was somewhat shaken when, early in the night, he was startled from sleep by the opening of the door. A light gleamed in upon him, and he was summoned to descend. He did so, when, to his surprise and joy, he found, in the room below, Captain Etherington, Lieutenant Leslie, and Mr. Bostwick, a trader, together with Father Jonois, the Jesuit priest from L'Arbre Croche. The Indians were bent on enjoying that night a grand debauch upon the liquor they had seized; and the chiefs, well knowing the extreme danger to which the prisoners would be exposed during these revels, had conveyed them all into the fort, and placed them in charge of the Canadians.

Including officers, soldiers, and traders, they amounted to about twenty men, being nearly all who had escaped the massacre.

When Henry entered the room, he found his three companions in misfortune engaged in anxious debate. These men had supped full of horrors; yet they were almost on the point of risking a renewal of the bloodshed from which they had just escaped. The temptation was a strong one. The fort was this evening actually in the hands of the white men. The Indians, with their ordinary recklessness and improvidence, had neglected even to place a guard within the palisades. They were now, one and all, in their camp, mad with liquor, and the fort was occupied by twenty Englishmen, and about three hundred Canadians, principally voyageurs. To close the gates, and set the Indians at defiance, seemed no very difficult matter. It might have been attempted, but for the dissuasions of the Jesuit, who had acted throughout the part of a true friend of humanity, and who now strongly represented the probability that the Canadians would prove treacherous, and the certainty that a failure would involve destruction to every Englishman in the place. The idea was therefore abandoned, and Captain Etherington, with his companions, that night shared Henry's garret, where they passed the time in condoling with each other on their common misfortune.

A party of Indians came to the house in the morning, and ordered Henry to follow them out. The weather had changed, and a cold storm had set in. In the dreary and forlorn area of the fort were a few of the Indian conquerors, though the main body were still in their camp, not yet recovered from the effects of their last night's carouse. Henry's conductors led him to a house, where, in a room almost dark, he saw two traders and a soldier imprisoned. They were released, and directed to follow the party. The whole then proceeded together to the lake shore, where they were to embark for the Isles du Castor. A chilling wind blew strongly from the north-east, and the lake was covered with mists, and tossing angrily. Henry stood shivering on the beach, with no other upper garment than a shirt, drenched with the cold rain. He asked Langlade, who was near him, for a blanket, which the latter refused unless security were given for payment. Another Canadian proved more merciful, and Henry received a covering from the weather. With his three companions, guarded by seven Indians, he embarked in the canoe, the soldier being tied by his neck to one of the cross-bars of the vessel. The thick mists and the tempestuous weather compelled them to coast the shore, close beneath the wet dripping forests. In this manner they had proceeded about eighteen miles, and were approaching L'Arbre Croche, when an Ottawa Indian came out of the woods, and called to them from the beach, inquiring the news, and asking who were their prisoners. Some conversation followed, in the course of which the canoe approached the shore, where the water was very shallow. All at once, a loud yell was heard, and a hundred Ottawas, rising from among the trees and bushes, rushed into the water, and seized upon the canoe and prisoners. The astonished Ojibwas remonstrated in vain. The four Englishmen were taken from them, and led in safety to the shore. Good will to the prisoners, however, had by no means prompted the Ottawas to this very unexpected proceeding. They were jealous and angry that the Ojibwas should have taken the fort without giving them an opportunity to share in the plunder; and they now took this summary mode of asserting their rights.

The chiefs, however, shook Henry and his companions by the hand, professing great good will, assuring them, at the same time, that the Ojibwas were carrying them to the Isles du Castor merely to kill and eat them. The four prisoners, the sport of so many changing fortunes, soon found themselves embarked in an Ottawa canoe, and on their way back to Michillimackinac. They were not alone. A flotilla of canoes accompanied them, bearing a great number of Ottawa warriors; and before the day was over, the whole had arrived at the fort. At this time, the principal Ojibwa encampment was near the woods, in full sight of the landing-place. Its occupants, astonished at this singular movement on the part of their rivals, stood looking on in silent amazement, while the Ottawa warriors, well armed, filed into the fort, and took possession of it.

This conduct is not difficult to explain, when we take into consideration the peculiarities of the Indian character. Pride and jealousy are always strong and active elements in it. The Ottawas deemed themselves insulted because the Ojibwas had undertaken an enterprise of such importance without consulting them, or asking their assistance. It may be added, that the Indians of L'Arbre Croche were somewhat less hostile to the English than the neighboring tribes; for the great influence of the priest Jonois seems always to have been exerted on the side of peace.

The English prisoners looked upon the new-comers as champions and protectors, and conceived hopes from their interference not destined to be fully realized. On the morning after their arrival, the Ojibwa chiefs invited the principal men of the Ottawas to hold a council with them, in a building within the fort. They placed upon the floor a valuable present of goods, which were part of the plunder they had taken; and their great war-chief, Minavavana, who had conducted the attack, rose and addressed the Ottawas.

Their conduct, he said, had greatly surprised him. They had betrayed the common cause, and opposed the will of the Great Spirit, who had decreed that every Englishman must die. Excepting them, all the Indians had raised the hatchet. Pontiac had taken Detroit, and every other fort had also been destroyed. The English were meeting with destruction throughout the whole world, and the King of France was awakened from his sleep. He exhorted them, in conclusion, no longer to espouse the cause of the English, but, like their brethren, to lift the hatchet against them.

When Minavavana had concluded his speech, the council adjourned until the next day; a custom common among Indians, in order that the auditors may have time to ponder with due deliberation upon what they have heard. At the next meeting, the Ottawas expressed a readiness to concur with the views of the Ojibwas. Thus the difference between the two tribes was at length amicably adjusted. The Ottawas returned to the Ojibwas some of the prisoners whom they had taken from them; still, however, retaining the officers and several of the soldiers. These they soon after carried to L'Arbre Croche, where they were treated with kindness, probably owing to the influence of Father Jonois. The priest went down to Detroit with a letter from Captain Etherington, acquainting Major Gladwyn with the loss of Michillimackinac, and entreating that a force might be sent immediately to his aid. The letter, as we have seen, was safely delivered; but Gladwyn was, of course, unable to render the required assistance.

Though the Ottawas and Ojibwas had come to terms, they still looked on each other with distrust, and it is said that the former never forgot the slight that had been put upon them. The Ojibwas took the prisoners who had been returned to them from the fort, and carried them to one of their small villages, which stood near the shore, at no great distance to the south-east. Among the other lodges was a large one, of the kind often seen in Indian villages, erected for use on public occasions, such as dances, feasts, or councils. It was now to serve as a prison. The soldiers were bound together, two and two, and farther secured by long ropes tied round their necks, and fastened to the pole which supported the lodge in the centre. Henry and the other traders escaped this rigorous treatment. The spacious lodge was soon filled with Indians, who came to look at their captives, and gratify themselves by deriding and jeering at them. At the head of the lodge sat the great war-chief Minavavana, side by side with Henry's master, Wenniway. Things had remained for some time in this position, when Henry observed an Indian stooping to enter at the low aperture which served for a door, and, to his great joy, recognized his friend and brother, Wawatam, whom he had last seen on the day before the massacre. Wawatam said nothing; but, as he passed the trader, he shook him by the hand, in token of encouragement, and, proceeding to the head of the lodge, sat down with Wenniway and the war-chief. After he had smoked with them for a while in silence, he rose and went out again. Very soon he came back, followed by his squaw, who brought in her hands a valuable present, which she laid at the feet of the two chiefs. Wawatam then addressed them in the following speech:—

"Friends and relations, what is it that I shall say? You know what I feel. You all have friends, and brothers, and children, whom as yourselves you love; and you,—what would you experience, did you, like me, behold your dearest friend—your brother—in the condition of a slave; a slave, exposed every moment to insult, and to menaces of death? This case, as you all know, is mine. See there, [pointing to Henry,] my friend and brother among slaves,—himself a slave!

"You all well know that, long before the war began, I adopted him as my brother. From that moment he became one of my family, so that no change of circumstances could break the cord which fastened us together.

"He is my brother; and because I am your relation, he is therefore your relation too; and how, being your relation, can he be your slave?

"On the day on which the war began, you were fearful lest, on this very account, I should reveal your secret. You requested, therefore, that I would leave the fort, and even cross the lake. I did so; but I did it with reluctance. I did it with reluctance, notwithstanding that you, Minavavana, who had the command in this enterprise, gave me your promise that you would protect my friend, delivering him from all danger, and giving him safely to me.

"The performance of this promise I now claim. I come not with empty hands to ask it. You, Minavavana, best know whether or not, as it respects yourself, you have kept your word; but I bring these goods to buy off every claim which any man among you all may have on my brother as his prisoner."

To this speech the war-chief returned a favorable answer. Wawatam's request was acceded to, the present was accepted, and the prisoner released. Henry soon found himself in the lodge of his friend, where furs were spread for him to lie upon, food and drink brought for his refreshment, and every thing done to promote his comfort that Indian hospitality could suggest. As he lay in the lodge, on the day after his release, he heard a loud noise from within the prison-house, which stood close at hand, and, looking through a crevice in the bark, he saw the dead bodies of seven soldiers dragged out. It appeared that a noted chief had just arrived from his wintering ground. Having come too late to take part in the grand achievement of his countrymen, he was anxious to manifest to all present his entire approval of what had been done, and with this design he had entered the lodge and despatched seven of the prisoners with his knife.

The Indians are not habitual cannibals. After a victory, however, it often happens that the bodies of their enemies are consumed at a formal war-feast—a superstitious rite, adapted, as they think, to increase their courage and hardihood. Such a feast took place on the present occasion, and most of the chiefs partook of it, though some of them, at least, did so with repugnance.

About a week had now elapsed since the massacre, and a revulsion of feeling began to take place among the Indians. Up to this time all had been triumph and exultation; but they now began to fear the consequences of their conduct. Indefinite and absurd rumors of an approaching attack from the English were afloat in the camp, and, in their growing uneasiness, they thought it expedient to shift their position to some point more capable of defence. Three hundred and fifty warriors, with their families and household effects, embarked in canoes for the Island of Michillimackinac, seven or eight miles distant. Wawatam, with his friend Henry, was of the number. Strong gusts of wind came from the north, and when the fleet of canoes was half way to the Island, it blew a gale, the waves pitching and tossing with such violence, that the frail and heavy-laden vessels were much endangered. Many voices were raised in prayer to the Great Spirit, and a dog was thrown into the lake, as a sacrifice to appease the angry manitou of the waters. The canoes weathered the storm, and soon drew near the island. Two squaws, in the same canoe with Henry, raised their voices in mournful wailing and lamentation. Late events had made him sensible to every impression of horror, and these dismal cries seemed ominous of some new disaster, until he learned that they were called forth by the recollection of dead relatives, whose graves were visible upon a neighboring point of the shore.

The Island of Michillimackinac, or Mackinaw, owing to its situation, its beauty, and the fish which the surrounding water supplied, had long been a favorite resort of Indians. It is about three miles wide. So clear are the waters of Lake Huron, which wash its shores, that one may count the pebbles at an incredible depth. The island is fenced round by white limestone cliffs, beautifully contrasting with the green foliage that half covers them, and in the centre the land rises in woody heights. The rock which forms its foundation assumes fantastic shapes—natural bridges, caverns, or sharp pinnacles, which at this day are pointed out as the curiosities of the region. In many of the caves have been found quantities of human bones, as if, at some period, the island had served as a grand depository for the dead; yet of these remains the present race of Indians can give no account. Legends and superstitions attached a mysterious celebrity to the place, and here, it was said, the fairies of Indian tradition might often be seen dancing upon the white rocks, or basking in the moonlight.

The Indians landed at the margin of a little bay. Unlading their canoes, and lifting them high and dry upon the beach, they began to erect their lodges, and before night had completed the work. Messengers arrived on the next day from Pontiac, informing them that he was besieging Detroit, and urging them to come to his aid. But their warlike ardor had well-nigh died out. A senseless alarm prevailed among them, and they now thought more of securing their own safety than of injuring the enemy. A vigilant watch was kept up all day, and the unusual precaution taken of placing guards at night. Their fears, however, did not prevent them from seizing two English trading canoes, which had come from Montreal by way of the Ottawa.

Among the booty found in them was a quantity of whiskey, and a general debauch was the immediate result. As night closed in, the dolorous chanting of drunken songs was heard from within the lodges, the prelude of a scene of riot; and Wawatam, knowing that his friend Henry's life would be in danger, privately led him out of the camp to a cavern in the hills, towards the interior of the island. Here the trader spent the night, in a solitude made doubly dreary by a sense of his forlorn and perilous situation. On waking in the morning, he found that he had been lying on human bones, which covered the floor of the cave. The place had anciently served as a charnel-house. Here he spent another solitary night, before his friend came to apprise him that he might return with safety to the camp.

Famine soon began among the Indians, who were sometimes without food for days together. No complaints were heard; but with faces blackened, in sign of sorrow, they patiently endured the privation with that resignation under inevitable suffering, which distinguishes the whole Indian race. They were at length compelled to cross over to the north shore of Lake Huron, where fish were more abundant; and here they remained until the end of summer, when they gradually dispersed, each family repairing to its winter hunting-grounds. Henry, painted and attired like an Indian, followed his friend Wawatam, and spent a lonely winter among the frozen forests, hunting the bear and moose for subsistence.

The posts of Green Bay and the Sault Ste. Marie did not share the fate of Michillimackinac. During the preceding winter, Ste. Marie had been partially destroyed by an accidental fire, and was therefore abandoned, the garrison withdrawing to Michillimackinac, where many of them perished in the massacre. The fort at Green Bay first received an English garrison in the year 1761, at the same time with the other posts of this region. The force consisted of seventeen men, of the 60th or Royal American regiment, commanded by Lieutenant Gorell. Though so few in number, their duties were of a very important character. In the neighborhood of Green Bay were numerous and powerful Indian tribes. The Menomonies lived at the mouth of Fox River, close to the fort. The Winnebagoes had several villages on the lake which bears their name, and the Sacs and Foxes were established on the River Wisconsin, in a large village composed of houses neatly built of logs and bark, and surrounded by fields of corn and vegetables. West of the Mississippi was the powerful nation of the Dahcotah, whose strength was loosely estimated at thirty thousand fighting men, and who, in the excess of their haughtiness, styled the surrounding tribes their dogs and slaves. The commandant of Green Bay was the representative of the British government, in communication with all these tribes. It devolved upon him to secure their friendship, and keep them at peace; and he was also intrusted, in a great measure, with the power of regulating the fur-trade among them. In the course of each season, parties of Indians, from every quarter, would come to the fort, each expecting to be received with speeches and presents.

Gorell seems to have acquitted himself with great judgment and prudence. On first arriving at the fort, he had found its defences decayed and ruinous, the Canadian inhabitants unfriendly, and many of the Indians disposed to hostility. His good conduct contributed to allay their irritation, and he was particularly successful in conciliating his immediate neighbors, the Menomonies. They had taken an active part in the late war between France and England, and their spirits were humbled by the losses they had sustained, as well as by recent ravages of the small-pox. Gorell summoned them to a council, and delivered a speech, in which he avoided wounding their pride, but at the same time assumed a tone of firmness and decision, such as can alone command an Indian's respect. He told them that the King of England had heard of their ill conduct, but that he was ready to forget all that had passed. If, however, they should again give him cause of complaint, he would send an army, numerous as the trees of the forest, and utterly destroy them. Flattering expressions of confidence and esteem succeeded, and the whole was enforced by the distribution of a few presents. The Menomonies replied by assurances of friendship, more sincerely made and faithfully kept than could have been expected. As Indians of the other tribes came from time to time to the fort, they met with a similar reception; and, in his whole intercourse with them, the constant aim of the commandant was to gain their good will. The result was most happy for himself and his garrison.

On the fifteenth of June, 1763, an Ottawa Indian brought to Gorell the following letter from Captain Etherington:—

"Michillimackinac, June 11, 1763.

"Dear Sir:

"This place was taken by surprise, on the second instant, by the Chippeways, [Ojibwas,] at which time Lieutenant Jamet and twenty [fifteen] more were killed, and all the rest taken prisoners; but our good friends, the Ottawas, have taken Lieutenant Lesley, me, and eleven men, out of their hands, and have promised to reinstate us again. You'll therefore, on the receipt of this, which I send by a canoe of Ottawas, set out with all your garrison, and what English traders you have with you, and come with the Indian who gives you this, who will conduct you safe to me. You must be sure to follow the instruction you receive from the bearer of this, as you are by no means to come to this post before you see me at the village, twenty miles from this.... I must once more beg you'll lose no time in coming to join me; at the same time, be very careful, and always be on your guard. I long much to see you, and am, dear sir,

"Your most humble serv't.

☐ Geo. Etherington.

"☐ ☐ J. Gorell,
☐ ☐ ☐ Royal Americans."

On receiving this letter, Gorell summoned the Menomonies to a council, told them what the Ojibwas had done, and said that he and his soldiers were going to Michillimackinac to restore order; adding, that during his absence he commended the fort to their care. Great numbers of the Winnebagoes and of the Sacs and Foxes afterwards arrived, and Gorell addressed them in nearly the same words. Presents were given them, and it soon appeared that the greater part were well disposed towards the English, though a few were inclined to prevent their departure, and even to threaten hostility. At this juncture, a fortunate incident occurred. A Dahcotah chief arrived with a message from his people to the following import: They had heard, he said, of the bad conduct of the Ojibwas. They hoped that the tribes of Green Bay would not follow their example, but, on the contrary, would protect the English garrison. Unless they did so, the Dahcotah would fall upon them, and take ample revenge. This auspicious interference must, no doubt, be ascribed to the hatred with which the Dahcotah had long regarded the Ojibwas. That the latter should espouse one side of the quarrel, was abundant reason to the Dahcotah for adopting the other.

Some of the Green Bay Indians were also at enmity with the Ojibwas, and all opposition to the departure of the English was now at an end. Indeed, some of the more friendly offered to escort the garrison on its way; and on the twenty-first of June, Gorell's party embarked in several bateaux, accompanied by ninety warriors in canoes. Approaching Isle du Castor, near the mouth of Green Bay, an alarm was given that the Ojibwas were lying there in ambush; on which the Menomonies raised the war-song, stripped themselves, and prepared to do battle in behalf of the English. The alarm, however, proved false; and, having crossed Lake Michigan in safety, the party arrived at the village of L'Arbre Croche on the thirtieth. The Ottawas came down to the beach, to salute them with a discharge of guns; and, on landing, they were presented with the pipe of peace. Captain Etherington and Lieutenant Leslie, with eleven men, were in the village, detained as prisoners, though treated with kindness. It was thought that the Ottawas intended to disarm the party of Gorell also; but the latter gave out that he would resist such an attempt, and his soldiers were permitted to retain their weapons.

Several succeeding days were occupied by the Indians in holding councils. Those from Green Bay requested the Ottawas to set their prisoners at liberty, and they at length assented. A difficulty still remained, as the Ojibwas had declared that they would prevent the English from passing down to Montreal. Their chiefs were therefore summoned; and being at this time, as we have seen, in a state of much alarm, they at length reluctantly yielded the point. On the eighteenth of July, the English, escorted by a fleet of Indian canoes, left L'Arbre Croche, and reaching, without interruption, the portage of the River Ottawa, descended to Montreal, where they all arrived in safety, on the thirteenth of August. Except the garrison of Detroit, not a British soldier now remained in the region of the lakes.

END OF VOL. I.

VOLUME II. CONSPIRACY OF PONTIAC

FRONTIER FORTS AND SETTLEMENTS

1763

We have followed the war to its farthest confines, and watched it in its remotest operations; not because there is any thing especially worthy to be chronicled in the capture of a backwoods fort, and the slaughter of a few soldiers, but because these acts exhibit some of the characteristic traits of the actors. It was along the line of the British frontier that the war raged with its most destructive violence. To destroy the garrisons, and then turn upon the settlements, had been the original plan of the Indians; and while Pontiac was pushing the siege of Detroit, and the smaller interior posts were treacherously assailed, the tempest was gathering which was soon to burst along the whole frontier.

In 1763, the British settlements did not extend beyond the Alleghanies. In the province of New York, they reached no farther than the German Flats, on the Mohawk. In Pennsylvania, the town of Bedford might be regarded as the extreme verge of the frontier, while the settlements of Virginia extended to a corresponding distance. Through the adjacent wilderness ran various lines of military posts, to make good the communication from point to point. One of the most important among these passed through the country of the Six Nations, and guarded the route between the northern colonies and Lake Ontario. This communication was formed by the Hudson, the Mohawk, Wood Creek, the Oneida Lake, and the River Oswego. It was defended by Forts Stanwix, Brewerton, Oswego, and two or three smaller posts. Near the western extremity of Lake Ontario stood Fort Niagara, at the mouth of the river whence it derived its name. It was a strong and extensive work, guarding the access to the whole interior country, both by way of the Oswego communication just mentioned, and by that of Canada and the St. Lawrence. From Fort Niagara the route lay by a portage beside the great falls to Presqu' Isle, on Lake Erie, where the town of Erie now stands. Thence the traveller could pass, by a short overland passage, to Fort Le Bœuf, on a branch of the Alleghany; thence, by water, to Venango; and thence, down the Alleghany, to Fort Pitt. This last-mentioned post stood on the present site of Pittsburg—the point of land formed by the confluence of the Alleghany and the Monongahela. Its position was as captivating to the eye of an artist as it was commanding in a military point of view. On the left, the Monongahela descended through a woody valley of singular beauty; on the right, flowed the Alleghany, beneath steep and lofty banks; and both united, in front, to form the broad Ohio, which, flanked by picturesque hills and declivities, began at this point its progress towards the Mississippi. The place already had its historic associations, though, as yet, their roughness was unmellowed by the lapse of time. It was here that the French had erected Fort du Quesne. Within a few miles, Braddock encountered his disastrous overthrow; and on the hill behind the fort, Grant's Highlanders and Lewis's Virginians had been surrounded and captured, though not without a stout resistance on the part of the latter.

Fort Pitt was built by General Stanwix, in the year 1759, upon the ruins of Fort du Quesne, destroyed by General Forbes. It was a strong fortification, with ramparts of earth, faced with brick on the side looking down the Ohio. Its walls have long since been levelled to the ground, and over their ruins have risen warehouses, and forges with countless chimneys, rolling up their black volumes of smoke. Where once the bark canoe lay on the strand, a throng of steamers now lie moored along the crowded levee.

Fort Pitt stood far aloof in the forest, and one might journey eastward full two hundred miles, before the English settlements began to thicken. Behind it lay a broken and woody tract; then succeeded the great barrier of the Alleghanies, traversing the country in successive ridges; and beyond these lay vast woods, extending to the Susquehanna. Eastward of this river, cabins of settlers became more numerous, until, in the neighborhood of Lancaster, the country assumed an appearance of prosperity and cultivation. Two roads led from Fort Pitt to the settlements, one of which was cut by General Braddock in his disastrous march across the mountains, from Cumberland, in the year 1755. The other, which was the more frequented, passed by Carlisle and Bedford, and was made by General Forbes, in 1758. Leaving the fort by this latter route, the traveller would find himself, after a journey of fifty-six miles, at the little post of Ligonier, whence he would soon reach Fort Bedford, about a hundred miles from Fort Pitt. It was nestled among mountains, and surrounded by clearings and log cabins. Passing several small posts and settlements, he would arrive at Carlisle, nearly a hundred miles farther east, a place resembling Bedford in its general aspect, although of greater extent. After leaving Fort Bedford, numerous houses of settlers were scattered here and there among the valleys, on each side of the road from Fort Pitt, so that the number of families beyond the Susquehanna amounted to several hundreds, thinly distributed over a great space. From Carlisle to Harris's Ferry, now Harrisburg, on the Susquehanna, was but a short distance; and from thence, the road led directly into the heart of the settlements. The frontiers of Virginia bore a general resemblance to those of Pennsylvania. It is not necessary at present to indicate minutely the position of their scattered settlements, and the small posts intended to protect them. Along these borders all had remained quiet, and nothing occurred to excite alarm or uneasiness. Captain Simeon Ecuyer, a brave Swiss officer, who commanded at Fort Pitt, had indeed received warnings of danger. On the fourth of May, he wrote to Colonel Bouquet at Philadelphia: "Major Gladwyn writes to tell me that I am surrounded by rascals. He complains a great deal of the Delawares and Shawanoes. It is this canaille who stir up the rest to mischief." At length, on the twenty-seventh, at about dusk in the evening, a party of Indians was seen descending the banks of the Alleghany, with laden pack-horses. They built fires, and encamped on the shore till daybreak, when they all crossed over to the fort, bringing with them a great quantity of valuable furs. These they sold to the traders, demanding, in exchange, bullets, hatchets, and gunpowder; but their conduct was so peculiar as to excite the just suspicion that they came either as spies or with some other insidious design. Hardly were they gone, when tidings came in that Colonel Clapham, with several persons, both men and women, had been murdered and scalped near the fort; and it was soon after discovered that the inhabitants of an Indian town, a few miles up the Alleghany, had totally abandoned their cabins, as if bent on some plan of mischief. On the next day, two soldiers were shot within a mile of the fort. An express was hastily sent to Venango, to warn the little garrison of danger; but he returned almost immediately, having been twice fired at, and severely wounded. A trader named Calhoun now came in from the Indian village of Tuscaroras, with intelligence of a yet more startling kind. At eleven o'clock on the night of the twenty-seventh, a chief named Shingas, with several of the principal warriors in the place, had come to Calhoun's cabin, and earnestly begged him to depart, declaring that they did not wish to see him killed before their eyes. The Ottawas and Ojibwas, they said, had taken up the hatchet, and captured Detroit, Sandusky, and all the forts of the interior. The Delawares and Shawanoes of the Ohio were following their example, and were murdering all the traders among them. Calhoun and the thirteen men in his employ lost no time in taking their departure. The Indians forced them to leave their guns behind, promising that they would give them three warriors to guide them in safety to Fort Pitt; but the whole proved a piece of characteristic dissimulation and treachery. The three guides led them into an ambuscade at the mouth of Beaver Creek. A volley of balls showered upon them; eleven were killed on the spot, and Calhoun and two others alone made their escape. "I see," writes Ecuyer to his colonel, "that the affair is general. I tremble for our outposts. I believe, from what I hear, that I am surrounded by Indians. I neglect nothing to give them a good reception; and I expect to be attacked to-morrow morning. Please God I may be. I am passably well prepared. Everybody is at work, and I do not sleep; but I tremble lest my messenger should be cut off."

The intelligence concerning the fate of the traders in the Indian villages proved but too true. They were slaughtered everywhere, without mercy, and often under circumstances of the foulest barbarity. A boy named M'Cullough, captured during the French war, and at this time a prisoner among the Indians, relates, in his published narrative, that he, with a party of Indian children, went out, one evening, to gaze with awe and wonder at the body of a trader, which lay by the side of the path, mangled with tomahawks, and stuck full of arrows. It was stated in the journals of the day, that more than a hundred traders fell victims, and that the property taken from them, or seized at the capture of the interior posts, amounted to an incredible sum.

The Moravian Loskiel relates that in the villages of the Hurons or Wyandots, meaning probably those of Sandusky, the traders were so numerous that the Indians were afraid to attack them openly, and had recourse to the following stratagem: They told their unsuspecting victims that the surrounding tribes had risen in arms, and were soon coming that way, bent on killing every Englishman they could find. The Wyandots averred that they would gladly protect their friends, the white men; but that it would be impossible to do so, unless the latter would consent, for the sake of appearances, to become their prisoners. In this case, they said, the hostile Indians would refrain from injuring them, and they should be set at liberty as soon as the danger was past. The traders fell into the snare. They gave up their arms, and, the better to carry out the deception, even consented to be bound; but no sooner was this accomplished, than their treacherous counsellors murdered them all in cold blood.

A curious incident, relating to this period, is given by the missionary Heckewelder. Strange as the story may appear, it is in strict accordance with Indian character and usage, and perhaps need not be rejected as wholly void of truth. The name of the person, to whom it relates, several times occurs in the manuscript journals and correspondence of officers in the Indian country. A trader named Chapman was made prisoner by the Indians near Detroit. For some time, he was protected by the humane interference of a Frenchman; but at length his captors resolved to burn him alive. He was tied to the stake, and the fire was kindled. As the heat grew intolerable, one of the Indians handed to him a bowl filled with broth. The wretched man, scorching with fiery thirst, eagerly snatched the vessel, and applied it to his lips; but the liquid was purposely made scalding hot. With a sudden burst of rage, he flung back the bowl and its contents into the face of the Indian. "He is mad! he is mad!" shouted the crowd; and though, the moment before, they had been keenly anticipating the delight of seeing him burn, they hastily put out the fire, released him from the stake, and set him at liberty. Such is the superstitious respect which the Indians entertain for every form of insanity.

While the alarming incidents just mentioned were occurring at Fort Pitt, the garrison of Fort Ligonier received yet more unequivocal tokens of hostility; for one morning a volley of bullets was sent among them, with no other effect, however, than killing a few horses. In the vicinity of Fort Bedford, several men were killed; on which the inhabitants were mustered and organized, and the garrison kept constantly on the alert. A few of the best woodsmen were formed into a company, dressed and painted like Indians. A party of the enemy suddenly appeared, whooping and brandishing their tomahawks, at the skirts of the forest; on which these counterfeit savages dashed upon them at full gallop, routing them in an instant, and driving them far through the woods.

At Fort Pitt every preparation was made for an attack. The houses and cabins outside the rampart were levelled to the ground, and every morning, at an hour before dawn, the drum beat, and the troops were ordered to their alarm posts. The garrison consisted of three hundred and thirty soldiers, traders, and backwoodsmen; and there were also in the fort about one hundred women, and a still greater number of children, most of them belonging to the families of settlers who were preparing to build their cabins in the neighborhood. "We are so crowded in the fort," writes Ecuyer to Colonel Bouquet, "that I fear disease; for, in spite of every care, I cannot keep the place as clean as I should like. Besides, the small-pox is among us; and I have therefore caused a hospital to be built under the drawbridge, out of range of musket-shot.... I am determined to hold my post, spare my men, and never expose them without necessity. This, I think, is what you require of me." The desultory outrages with which the war began, and which only served to put the garrison on their guard, prove that among the neighboring Indians there was no chief of sufficient power to curb their wayward temper, and force them to conform to any preconcerted plan. The authors of the mischief were unruly young warriors, fevered with eagerness to win the first scalp, and setting at defiance the authority of their elders. These petty annoyances, far from abating, continued for many successive days, and kept the garrison in a state of restless alarm. It was dangerous to venture outside the walls, and a few who attempted it were shot and scalped by lurking Indians. "They have the impudence," writes an officer, "to fire all night at our sentinels;" nor were these attacks confined to the night, for even during the day no man willingly exposed his head above the rampart. The surrounding woods were known to be full of prowling Indians, whose number seemed daily increasing, though as yet they had made no attempt at a general attack. At length, on the afternoon of the twenty-second of June, a party of them appeared at the farthest extremity of the cleared lands behind the fort, driving off the horses which were grazing there, and killing the cattle. No sooner was this accomplished than a general fire was opened upon the fort from every side at once, though at so great a distance that only two men were killed. The garrison replied by a discharge of howitzers, the shells of which, bursting in the midst of the Indians, greatly amazed and disconcerted them. As it grew dark, their fire slackened, though, throughout the night, the flash of guns was seen at frequent intervals, followed by the whooping of the invisible assailants.

At nine o'clock on the following morning, several Indians approached the fort with the utmost confidence, and took their stand at the outer edge of the ditch, where one of them, a Delaware, named the Turtle's Heart, addressed the garrison as follows:—

"My Brothers, we that stand here are your friends; but we have bad news to tell you. Six great nations of Indians have taken up the hatchet, and cut off all the English garrisons, excepting yours. They are now on their way to destroy you also.

"My Brothers, we are your friends, and we wish to save your lives. What we desire you to do is this: You must leave this fort, with all your women and children, and go down to the English settlements, where you will be safe. There are many bad Indians already here; but we will protect you from them. You must go at once, because if you wait till the six great nations arrive here, you will all be killed, and we can do nothing to protect you."

To this proposal, by which the Indians hoped to gain a safe and easy possession of the fort, Captain Ecuyer made the following reply. The vein of humor perceptible in it may serve to indicate that he was under no great apprehension for the safety of his garrison:—

"My Brothers, we are very grateful for your kindness, though we are convinced that you must be mistaken in what you have told us about the forts being captured. As for ourselves, we have plenty of provisions, and are able to keep the fort against all the nations of Indians that may dare to attack it. We are very well off in this place, and we mean to stay here.

"My Brothers, as you have shown yourselves such true friends, we feel bound in gratitude to inform you that an army of six thousand English will shortly arrive here, and that another army of three thousand is gone up the lakes, to punish the Ottawas and Ojibwas. A third has gone to the frontiers of Virginia, where they will be joined by your enemies, the Cherokees and

Catawbas, who are coming here to destroy you. Therefore take pity on your women and children, and get out of the way as soon as possible. We have told you this in confidence, out of our great solicitude lest any of you should be hurt; and we hope that you will not tell the other Indians, lest they should escape from our vengeance."

This politic invention of the three armies had an excellent effect, and so startled the Indians, that, on the next day, most of them withdrew from the neighborhood, and went to meet a great body of warriors, who were advancing from the westward to attack the fort. On the afternoon of the twenty-sixth, a soldier named Gray, belonging to the garrison of Presqu' Isle, came in with the report that, more than a week before, that little post had been furiously attacked by upwards of two hundred Indians from Detroit, that they had assailed it for three days, repeatedly setting it on fire, and had at length undermined it so completely, that the garrison was forced to capitulate, on condition of being allowed to retire in safety to Fort Pitt. No sooner, however, had they left their shelter, than the Indians fell upon them, and, as Gray declared, butchered them all, except himself and one other man, who darted into the woods, and escaped amid the confusion, hearing behind them, as they fled, the screams of their murdered comrades. This account proved erroneous, as the garrison were carried by their captors in safety to Detroit. Some time after this event, Captain Dalzell's detachment, on their way to Detroit, stopped at the place, and found, close to the ruined fort, the hair of several of the men, which had been shorn off, as a preliminary step in the process of painting and bedecking them like Indian warriors. From this it appears that some of the unfortunate soldiers were adopted on the spot into the tribes of their conquerors. In a previous chapter, a detailed account has been given of the defence of Presqu' Isle, and its capture.

Gray informed Captain Ecuyer that, a few days before the attack on the garrison, they had seen a schooner on the lake, approaching from the westward. She had sent a boat to shore with the tidings that Detroit had been beleaguered, for more than six weeks, by many hundred Indians, and that a detachment of ninety-six men had been attacked near that place, of whom only about thirty had escaped, the rest being either killed on the spot or put to death by slow torture. The panic-stricken soldier, in his flight from Presqu' Isle, had passed the spots where lately had stood the little forts of Le Bœuf and Venango. Both were burnt to the ground, and he surmised that the whole of their wretched garrisons had fallen victims. The disaster proved less fatal than his fears led him to suspect; for, on the same day on which he arrived, Ensign Price, the officer commanding at Le Bœuf, was seen approaching along the bank of the Alleghany, followed by seven haggard and half-famished soldiers. He and his men told the following story:

The available defences of Fort Le Bœuf consisted, at the time, of a single ill-constructed blockhouse, occupied by the ensign, with two corporals and eleven privates. They had only about twenty rounds of ammunition each; and the powder, moreover, was in a damaged condition. At nine or ten o'clock, on the morning of the eighteenth of June, a soldier told Price that he saw Indians approaching from the direction of Presqu' Isle. Price ran to the door, and, looking out, saw one of his men, apparently much frightened, shaking hands with five Indians. He held open the door till the man had entered, the five Indians following close, after having, in obedience to a sign from Price, left their weapons behind. They declared that they were going to fight the Cherokees, and begged for powder and ball. This being refused, they asked leave to sleep on the ground before the blockhouse. Price assented, on which one of them went off, but very soon returned with thirty more, who crowded before the window of the blockhouse, and begged for a kettle to cook their food. Price tried to give them one through the window, but the aperture proved too narrow, and they grew clamorous that he should open the door again. This he refused. They then went to a neighboring storehouse, pulled out some of the foundation stones, and got into the cellar; whence, by knocking away one or two planks immediately above the sill of the building, they could fire on the garrison in perfect safety, being below the range of shot from the loopholes of the blockhouse, which was not ten yards distant. Here they remained some hours, making their preparations, while the garrison waited in suspense, cooped up in their wooden citadel. Towards evening, they opened fire, and shot such a number of burning arrows against the side and roof of the blockhouse, that three times it was in flames. But the men worked desperately, and each time the fire was extinguished. A fourth time the alarm was given; and now the men on the roof came down in despair, crying out that they could not extinguish it, and calling on their officer for God's sake to let them leave the building, or they should all be burnt alive. Price behaved with great spirit. "We must fight as long as we can, and then die together," was his answer to the entreaties of his disheartened men. But he could not revive their drooping courage, and meanwhile the fire spread beyond all hope of mastering it. They implored him to let them go, and at length the brave young officer told them to save themselves if they could. It was time, for they were suffocating in their burning prison. There was a narrow window in the back of the blockhouse, through which, with the help of axes, they all got out; and, favored by the darkness,—for night had closed in,—escaped to the neighboring pine-swamp, while the Indians, to make assurance doubly sure, were still showering fire-arrows against the front of the blazing building. As the fugitives groped their way, in pitchy darkness, through the tangled intricacies of the swamp, they saw the sky behind them lurid with flames, and heard the reports of the Indians' guns, as these painted demons were leaping and yelling in front of the flaming blockhouse, firing into the loopholes, and exulting in the thought that their enemies were suffering the agonies of death within.

Presqu' Isle was but fifteen miles distant; but, from the direction in which his assailants had come, Price rightly judged that it had been captured, and therefore resolved to make his way, if possible, to Venango, and reinforce Lieutenant Gordon, who commanded there. A soldier named John Dortinger, who had been sixteen months at Le Bœuf, thought that he could guide the party, but lost the way in the darkness; so that, after struggling all night through swamps and forests, they found themselves at daybreak only two miles from their point of departure. Just before dawn, several of the men became separated from the rest. Price and those with him waited for some time, whistling, coughing, and making such other signals as they dared, to attract their attention, but without success, and they were forced to proceed without them. Their only provisions were three biscuits to a man. They pushed on all day, and reached Venango at one o'clock of the following night. Nothing remained but piles of smouldering embers, among which lay the half-burned bodies of its hapless garrison. They now continued their journey down the Alleghany. On the third night their last biscuit was consumed, and they were half dead with hunger and exhaustion before their eyes were gladdened at length by the friendly walls of Fort Pitt. Of those who had straggled from the party, all eventually appeared but two, who, spent with starvation, had been left behind, and no doubt perished.

Not a man remained alive to tell the fate of Venango. An Indian, who was present at its destruction, long afterwards described the scene to Sir William Johnson. A large body of Senecas gained entrance under pretence of friendship, then closed the gates, fell upon the garrison, and butchered them all except the commanding officer, Lieutenant Gordon, whom they forced to write, from their dictation, a statement of the grievances which had driven them to arms, and then tortured over a slow fire for several successive nights, till he expired. This done, they burned the place to the ground, and departed.

While Le Bœuf and Venango were thus assailed, Fort Ligonier was also attacked by a large body of Indians, who fired upon it with great fury and pertinacity, but were beaten off after a hard day's fighting. Fort Augusta, on the Susquehanna, was at the same time menaced; but the garrison being strengthened by a timely re-enforcement, the Indians abandoned their purpose. Carlisle, Bedford, and the small intermediate posts, all experienced some effects of savage hostility; while among the settlers, whose houses were scattered throughout the adjacent valleys, outrages were perpetrated, and sufferings endured, which defy all attempt at description.

At Fort Pitt, every preparation was made to repel the attack which was hourly expected. A part of the rampart, undermined by the spring floods, had fallen into the ditch; but, by dint of great labor, this injury was repaired. A line of palisades was erected along the ramparts; the barracks were made shot-proof, to protect the women and children; and, as the interior buildings were all of wood, a rude fire-engine was constructed, to extinguish any flames which might be kindled by the burning arrows of the Indians. Several weeks, however, elapsed without any determined attack from the enemy, who were engaged in their bloody work among the settlements and smaller posts. From the beginning of July until towards its close, nothing occurred except a series of petty and futile attacks, by which the Indians abundantly exhibited their malicious intentions, without doing harm to the garrison. During the whole of this time, the communication with the settlements was completely cut off, so that no letters were written from the fort, or, at all events, none reached their destination; and we are therefore left to depend upon a few meagre official reports, as our only sources of information.

On the twenty-sixth of July, a small party of Indians was seen approaching the gate, displaying a flag, which one of them had some time before received as a present from the English commander. On the strength of this token, they were admitted, and proved to be chiefs of distinction; among whom were Shingas, Turtle's Heart, and others, who had hitherto maintained an appearance of friendship. Being admitted to a council, one of them addressed Captain Ecuyer and his officers to the following effect:—

"Brothers, what we are about to say comes from our hearts, and not from our lips.

"Brothers, we wish to hold fast the chain of friendship—that ancient chain which our forefathers held with their brethren the English. You have let your end of the chain fall to the ground, but ours is still fast within our hands. Why do you complain that our young men have fired at your soldiers, and killed your cattle and your horses? You yourselves are the cause of this. You marched your armies into our country, and built forts here, though we told you, again and again, that we wished you to remove. My Brothers, this land is ours, and not yours.

"My Brothers, two days ago we received a great belt of wampum from the Ottawas of Detroit, and the message they sent us was in these words:—

"'Grandfathers the Delawares, by this belt we inform you that in a short time we intend to pass, in a very great body, through your country, on our way to strike the English at the forks of the Ohio. Grandfathers, you know us to be a headstrong people. We are determined to stop at nothing; and as we expect to be very hungry, we will seize and eat up every thing that comes in our way.'

"Brothers, you have heard the words of the Ottawas. If you leave this place immediately, and go home to your wives and children, no harm will come of it; but if you stay, you must blame yourselves alone for what may happen. Therefore we desire you to remove."

To the not wholly unreasonable statement of wrongs contained in this speech, Captain Ecuyer replied, by urging the shallow pretence that the forts were built for the purpose of supplying the Indians with clothes and ammunition. He then absolutely refused to leave the place. "I have," he said, "warriors, provisions, and ammunition, to defend it three years against all the Indians in the woods; and we shall never abandon it as long as a white man lives in America. I despise the Ottawas, and am very much surprised at our brothers the Delawares, for proposing to us to leave this place and go home. This is our home. You have attacked us without reason or provocation; you have murdered and plundered our warriors and traders; you have taken our horses and cattle; and at the same time you tell us your hearts are good towards your brethren the English. How can I have faith in you? Therefore, now, Brothers, I will advise you to go home to your towns, and take care of your wives and children. Moreover, I tell you that if any of you appear again about this fort, I will throw bombshells, which will burst and blow you to atoms, and fire cannon among you, loaded with a whole bag full of bullets. Therefore take care, for I don't want to hurt you."

The chiefs departed, much displeased with their reception. Though nobody in his senses could blame the course pursued by Captain Ecuyer, and though the building of forts in the Indian country could not be charged as a crime, except by the most overstrained casuistry, yet we cannot refrain from sympathizing with the intolerable hardship to which the progress of civilization subjected the unfortunate tenants of the wilderness, and which goes far to extenuate the perfidy and cruelty that marked their conduct throughout the whole course of the war.

Disappointed of gaining a bloodless possession of the fort, the Indians now, for the first time, began a general attack. On the night succeeding the conference, they approached in great numbers, under cover of the darkness, and completely surrounded it; many of them crawling under the banks of the two rivers, and, with incredible perseverance, digging, with their knives, holes in which they were completely sheltered from the fire of the fort. On one side, the whole bank was lined with these burrows, from each of which a bullet or an arrow was shot out whenever a soldier chanced to expose his head. At daybreak, a general fire was opened from every side, and continued without intermission until night, and through several succeeding days. No great harm was done, however. The soldiers lay close behind their parapet of logs, watching the movements of their subtle enemies, and paying back their shot with interest. The red uniforms of the Royal Americans mingled with the gray homespun of the border riflemen, or the fringed hunting-frocks of old Indian-fighters, wary and adroit as the red-skinned warriors themselves. They liked the sport, and were eager to sally from behind their defences, and bring their assailants to close quarters; but

Ecuyer was too wise to consent. He was among them, as well pleased as they, directing, encouraging, and applauding them in his broken English. An arrow flew over the rampart and wounded him in the leg; but, it seems, with no other result than to extort a passing execration. The Indians shot fire-arrows, too, from their burrows, but not one of them took effect. The yelling at times was terrific, and the women and children in the crowded barracks clung to each other in terror; but there was more noise than execution, and the assailants suffered more than the assailed. Three or four days after, Ecuyer wrote in French to his colonel, "They were all well under cover, and so were we. They did us no harm: nobody killed; seven wounded, and I myself slightly. Their attack lasted five days and five nights. We are certain of having killed and wounded twenty of them, without reckoning those we could not see. I let nobody fire till he had marked his man; and not an Indian could show his nose without being pricked with a bullet, for I have some good shots here.... Our men are doing admirably, regulars and the rest. All that they ask is to go out and fight. I am fortunate to have the honor of commanding such brave men. I only wish the Indians had ventured an assault. They would have remembered it to the thousandth generation!... I forgot to tell you that they threw fire-arrows to burn our works, but they could not reach the buildings, nor even the rampart. Only two arrows came into the fort, one of which had the insolence to make free with my left leg."

This letter was written on the second of August. On the day before the Indians had all decamped. An event, soon to be described, had put an end to the attack, and relieved the tired garrison of their presence.

THE WAR ON THE BORDERS

1763

Along the Western frontiers of Pennsylvania, Maryland, and Virginia, terror reigned supreme. The Indian scalping-parties were ranging everywhere, laying waste the settlements, destroying the harvests, and butchering men, women, and children, with ruthless fury. Many hundreds of wretched fugitives flocked for refuge to Carlisle and the other towns of the border, bringing tales of inconceivable horror. Strong parties of armed men, who went out to reconnoitre the country, found every habitation reduced to cinders, and the half-burned bodies of the inmates lying among the smouldering ruins; while here and there was seen some miserable wretch, scalped and tomahawked, but still alive and conscious. One writing from the midst of these scenes declares that, in his opinion, a thousand families were driven from their homes; that, on both sides of the Susquehanna, the woods were filled with fugitives, without shelter and without food; and that, unless the havoc were speedily checked, the western part of Pennsylvania would be totally deserted, and Lancaster become the frontier town.

While these scenes were enacted on the borders of Pennsylvania and the more southern provinces, the settlers in the valley of the Mohawk, and even along the Hudson, were menaced with destruction. Had not the Six Nations been kept tranquil by the exertions of Sir William Johnson, the most disastrous results must have ensued. The Senecas and a few of the Cayugas were the only members of the confederacy who took part in the war. Venango, as we have seen, was destroyed by a party of Senecas, who soon after made a feeble attack upon Niagara. They blockaded it for a few days, with no other effect than that of confining the garrison within the walls, and, soon despairing of success, abandoned the attempt.

In the mean time, Sir Jeffrey Amherst, the Commander-in-chief, was in a position far from enviable. He had reaped laurels; but if he hoped to enjoy them in peace, he was doomed to disappointment. A miserable war was suddenly thrown on his hands, barren of honors and fruitful of troubles; and this, too, at a time when he was almost bereft of resources. The armies which had conquered Canada were, as we have seen, disbanded or sent home, and nothing remained but a few fragments and skeletons of regiments lately arrived from the West Indies, enfeebled by disease and hard service. In one particular, however, he had reason to congratulate himself,—the character of the officers who commanded under his orders in Pennsylvania, Virginia, and Maryland. Colonel Henry Bouquet was a Swiss, of the Canton of Berne, who had followed the trade of war from boyhood. He had served first the King of Sardinia, and afterwards the republic of Holland; and when the French war began in 1755, he accepted the commission of lieutenant-colonel, in a regiment newly organized, under the direction of the Duke of Cumberland, expressly for American service. The commissions were to be given to foreigners as well as to Englishmen and provincials; and the ranks were to be filled chiefly from the German emigrants in Pennsylvania and other provinces. The men and officers of this regiment, known as the "Royal American," had now, for more than six years, been engaged in the rough and lonely service of the frontiers and forests; and when the Indian war broke out, it was chiefly they, who, like military hermits, held the detached outposts of the West. Bouquet, however, who was at this time colonel of the first battalion, had his headquarters at Philadelphia, where he was held in great esteem. His person was fine, and his bearing composed and dignified; perhaps somewhat austere, for he is said to have been more respected than loved by his officers. Nevertheless, their letters to him are very far from indicating any want of cordial relations. He was fond of the society of men of science, and wrote English better than most British officers of the time. Here and there, however, a passage in his letters suggests the inference, that the character of the gallant mercenary was toned to his profession, and to the unideal epoch in which he lived. Yet he was not the less an excellent soldier; indefatigable, faithful, full of resource, and without those arrogant prejudices which had impaired the efficiency of many good British officers, in the recent war, and of which Sir Jeffrey Amherst was a conspicuous example. He had acquired a practical knowledge of Indian warfare; and it is said that, in the course of the hazardous partisan service in which he was often engaged, when it was necessary to penetrate dark defiles and narrow passes, he was sometimes known to advance before his men, armed with a rifle, and acting the part of a scout.

Sir Jeffrey had long and persistently flattered himself that the Indian uprising was but a temporary ebullition, which would soon subside.

Bouquet sent him, on the fourth of June, a copy of a letter from Captain Ecuyer, at Fort Pitt, reporting the disturbances in that quarter. On the next day Bouquet wrote again, in a graver strain; and Amherst replied, from New York, on the sixth: "I gave immediate orders for completing the light infantry companies of the 17th, 42d, and 77th regiments. They are to assemble without loss of time, and to encamp on Staten Island, under Major Campbell, of the 42d.... Although I have thought proper to assemble this force, which I judge more than sufficient to quell any disturbances the whole Indian strength could raise, yet I am persuaded the alarm will end in nothing more than a rash attempt of what the Senecas have been threatening, and which we have heard of for some time past. As to their cutting off defenceless families, or even some of the small posts, it is certainly at all times in their power to effect such enterprises.... The post of Fort Pitt, or any of the others commanded by officers, can certainly never be in danger from such a wretched enemy.... I am only sorry that when such outrages are committed, the guilty should escape; for I am fully convinced the only true method of treating the savages is to keep them in proper subjection, and punish, without exception, the transgressors.... As I have no sort of dependence on the Assembly of Pennsylvania, I have taken such measures as will fully enable me to chastise any nation or tribe of Indians that dare to commit hostilities on his Majesty's subjects. I only wait to hear from you what farther steps the savages have taken; for I still think it cannot be any thing general, but the rash attempt of that turbulent tribe, the Senecas, who richly deserve a severe chastisement from our hands, for their treacherous behavior on many occasions."

On receiving this letter, Bouquet immediately wrote to Ecuyer at Fort Pitt: "The General has taken the necessary measures to chastise those infamous villains, and defers only to make them feel the weight of his resentment till he is better informed of their intentions." And having thus briefly despatched the business in hand, he proceeds to touch on the news of the day: "I give you joy of the success of our troops at the Manilla, where Captain George Ourry hath acquired the two best things in this world, glory and money. We hear of a great change in the ministry," etc.... "P. S. I have lent three pounds to the express. Please to stop it for me. The General expects that Mr. Croghan will proceed directly to Fort Pitt, when he will soon discover the causes of this sudden rupture and the intentions of these rascals."

Scarcely had Bouquet sent off the express-rider with this letter, when another came from Ecuyer with worse reports from the west. He forwarded it to Amherst, who wrote on receiving it: "I find by the intelligence enclosed in your letter that the affair of the Indians appears to be more general than I had apprehended, although I believe nothing of what is mentioned regarding the garrison of the Detroit being cut off. It is extremely inconvenient at this time; ... but I cannot defer sending you a reinforcement for the communication." Accordingly he ordered two companies of the 42d and 77th regiments to join Bouquet at Philadelphia. "If you think it necessary," he adds, "you will yourself proceed to Fort Pitt, that you may be the better enabled to put in execution the requisite orders for securing the communication and reducing the Indians to reason."

Amherst now bestirred himself to put such troops as he had into fighting order. The 80th regiment, Hopkins's company of Rangers, and a portion of the Royal Americans, were disbanded, and the men drafted to complete other broken corps. His plan was to push forward as many troops as possible to Niagara by way of Oswego, and to Presqu' Isle by way of Fort Pitt, and thence to send them up the lakes to take vengeance on the offending tribes.

Bouquet, recognizing at length the peril of the small outlying posts, like Venango and Le Bœuf, proposed to abandon them, and concentrate at Fort Pitt and Presqu' Isle; a movement which, could it have been executed in time, would have saved both blood and trouble. But Amherst would not consent. "I cannot think," he writes, "of giving them up at this time, if we can keep them, as such a step would give the Indians room to think themselves more formidable than they really are; and it would be much better we never attempted to take posts in what they call their country, if, upon every alarm, we abandon them.... It remains at present for us to take every precaution we can, by which we may put a stop, as soon as possible, to their committing any farther mischief, and to bring them to a proper subjection; for, without that, I never do expect that they will be quiet and orderly, as every act of kindness and generosity to those barbarians is looked upon as proceeding from our fears."

Bouquet next writes to report that, with the help of the two companies sent him, he has taken steps which he hopes will secure the communication to Fort Pitt and allay the fears of the country people, who are deserting their homes in a panic, though the enemy has not yet appeared east of the mountains. A few days later, on the twenty-third of June, Amherst writes, boiling with indignation. He had heard from Gladwyn of the investment of Detroit, and the murder of Sir Robert Davers and Lieutenant Robertson. "The villains after this," he says, "had the assurance to come with a Pipe of Peace, desiring admittance into the fort." He then commends the conduct of Gladwyn, but pursues: "I only regret that when the chief of the Ottawas and the other villains returned with the Pipe of Peace, they were not instantly put to death. I conclude Major Gladwyn was not apprised of the murder of Sir Robert Davers, Lieutenant Robertson, etc., at that time, or he certainly would have revenged their deaths by that method; and, indeed, I cannot but wish that whenever we have any of the savages in our power, who have in so treacherous a way committed any barbarities on our people, a quick retaliation may be made without the least exception or hesitation. I am determined," he continues, "to take every measure in my power, not only for securing and keeping entire possession of the country, but for punishing those barbarians who have thus perfidiously massacred his Majesty's subjects. To effect this most essential service, I intend to collect, agreeable to what I wrote you in my last, all the force I can at Presqu' Isle and Niagara, that I may push them forwards as occasion may require. I have therefore ordered the remains of the 42d and 77th regiments—the first consisting of two hundred and fourteen men, including officers, and the latter of one hundred and thirty-three, officers included—to march this evening or early to-morrow morning, under the command of Major Campbell of the 42d, who has my orders to send an officer before to acquaint you of his being on the march, and to obey such further directions as he may receive from you.... You will observe that I have now forwarded from hence every man that was here; for the small remains of the 17th regiment are already on their march up the Mohawk, and I have sent such of the 42d and 77th as were not able to march, to Albany, to relieve the company of the 55th at present there, who are to march immediately to Oswego."

Two days after, the twenty-fifth of June, he writes again to Bouquet: "All the troops from hence that could be collected are sent you; so that should the whole race of Indians take arms against us, I can do no more."

On the same day, Bouquet, who was on his way to the frontier, wrote to Amherst, from Lancaster: "I had this moment the honor of your Excellency's letter of the twenty-third instant, with the most welcome news of the preservation of the Detroit from the infernal treachery of the vilest of brutes. I regret sincerely the brave men they have so basely massacred, but hope that we shall soon take an adequate revenge on the barbarians. The reinforcement you have ordered this way, so considerable by the additional number of officers, will fully enable me to crush the little opposition they may dare to make along the road, and secure that part of the country against all their future attempts, till you think proper to order us to act in conjunction with the rest of your forces to extirpate that vermin from a country they have forfeited, and, with it, all claim to the rights of humanity."

Three days later the express-rider delivered the truculent letter, from which the above is taken, to Amherst at New York. He replied: "Last night I received your letter of the twenty-fifth, the contents of which please me very much,—your sentiments agreeing exactly with my own regarding the treatment the savages deserve from us ... I need only add that I wish to hear of no prisoners, should any of the villains be met with in arms; and whoever of those who were concerned in the murder of Sir Robert Davers, Lieutenant Robertson, etc., or were at the attack of the detachment going to the Detroit, and that may be hereafter taken, shall certainly be put to death."

Bouquet was now busy on the frontier in preparations for pushing forward to Fort Pitt with the troops sent him. After reaching the fort, with his wagon-trains of ammunition and supplies, he was to proceed to Venango and Le Bœuf, reinforce and provision them; and thence advance to Presqu' Isle to wait Amherst's orders for the despatch of his troops westward to Detroit, Michillimackinac, and the other distant garrisons, the fate of which was still unknown. He was encamped near Carlisle when, on the third of July, he heard what he styles the "fatal account of the loss of our posts at Presqu' Isle, Le Bœuf, and Venango." He at once sent the news to Amherst; who, though he persisted in his original plan of operations, became at length convinced of the formidable nature of the Indian outbreak, and felt bitterly the slenderness of his own resources. His correspondence, nevertheless, breathes a certain thick-headed, blustering arrogance, worthy of the successor of Braddock. In his contempt for the Indians, he finds fault with Captain Ecuyer at Fort Pitt for condescending to fire cannon at them, and with Lieutenant Blane at Fort Ligonier for burning some outhouses, under cover of which "so despicable an enemy" were firing at his garrison. This despicable enemy had, however, pushed him to such straits that he made, in a postscript to Bouquet, the following detestable suggestion:—

"Could it not be contrived to send the Small Pox among those disaffected tribes of Indians? We must on this occasion use every stratagem in our power to reduce them."

(Signed) J. A.

Bouquet replied, also in postscript:—

"I will try to inoculate the —— with some blankets that may fall in their hands, and take care not to get the disease myself. As it is a pity to expose good men against them, I wish we could make use of the Spanish method, to hunt them with English dogs, supported by rangers and some light horse, who would, I think, effectually extirpate or remove that vermin."

Amherst rejoined: "You will do well to try to inoculate the Indians by means of blankets, as well as to try every other method that can serve to extirpate this execrable race. I should be very glad your scheme for hunting them down by dogs could take effect, but England is at too great a distance to think of that at present."

(Signed) J. A.

There is no direct evidence that Bouquet carried into effect the shameful plan of infecting the Indians though, a few months after, the small-pox was known to have made havoc among the tribes of the Ohio. Certain it is, that he was perfectly capable of dealing with them by other means, worthy of a man and a soldier; and it is equally certain, that in relations with civilized men he was in a high degree honorable, humane, and kind.

The scenes which daily met his eye might well have moved him to pity as well as indignation. When he reached Carlisle, at the end of June, he found every building in the fort, every house, barn, and hovel, in the little town, crowded with the families of settlers, driven from their homes by the terror of the tomahawk. Wives made widows, children made orphans, wailed and moaned in anguish and despair. On the thirteenth of July he wrote to Amherst: "The list of the people known to be killed increases very fast every hour. The desolation of so many families, reduced to the last extremity of want and misery; the despair of those who have lost their parents, relations, and friends, with the cries of distracted women and children, who fill the streets,—form a scene painful to humanity, and impossible to describe." Rage alternated with grief. A Mohican and a Cayuga Indian, both well known as friendly and peaceable, came with their squaws and children to claim protection from the soldiers. "It was with the utmost difficulty," pursues Bouquet, "that I could prevail with the enraged multitude not to massacre them. I don't think them very safe in the gaol. They ought to be removed to Philadelphia."

Bouquet, on his part, was full of anxieties. On the road from Carlisle to Fort Pitt was a chain of four or five small forts, of which the most advanced and the most exposed were Fort Bedford and Fort Ligonier; the former commanded by Captain Lewis Ourry, and the latter by Lieutenant Archibald Blane. These officers kept up a precarious correspondence with him and each other, by means of express-riders, a service dangerous to the last degree and soon to become impracticable. It was of the utmost importance to hold these posts, which contained stores and munitions, the capture of which by the Indians would have led to the worst consequences. Ourry had no garrison worth the name; but at every Indian alarm the scared inhabitants would desert their farms, and gather for shelter around his fort, to disperse again when the alarm was over.

On the third of June, he writes to Bouquet: "No less than ninety-three families are now come in here for refuge, and more hourly arriving. I expect ten more before night." He adds that he had formed the men into two militia companies. "My returns," he pursues, "amount already to a hundred and fifty-five men. My regulars are increased by expresses, etc., to three corporals and nine privates; no despicable garrison!"

On the seventh, he sent another letter.... "As to myself, I find I can bear a good deal. Since the alarm I never lie down till about twelve, and am walking about the fort between two and three in the morning, turning out the guards and sending out patrols, before I suffer the gates to remain open.... My greatest difficulty is to keep my militia from straggling by twos and threes to their dear plantations, thereby exposing themselves to be scalped, and weakening my garrison by such numbers absenting themselves.

They are still in good spirits, but they don't know all the bad news. I shall use all means to prevail on them to stay till some troops come up. I long to see my Indian scouts come in with intelligence; but I long more to hear the Grenadiers' March, and see some more red-coats."

Ten days later, the face of affairs had changed. "I am now, as I foresaw, entirely deserted by the country people. No accident having happened here, they have gradually left me to return to their plantations; so that my whole force is reduced to twelve Royal Americans to guard the fort, and seven Indian prisoners. I should be very glad to see some troops come to my assistance. A fort with five bastions cannot be guarded, much less defended, by a dozen men; but I hope God will protect us."

On the next day, he writes again: "This moment I return from the parade. Some scalps taken up Dening's Creek yesterday, and to-day some families murdered and houses burnt, have restored me my militia.... Two or three other families are missing, and the houses are seen in flames. The people are all flocking in again."

Two days afterwards, he says that, while the countrymen were at drill on the parade, three Indians attempted to seize two little girls, close to the fort, but were driven off by a volley. "This," he pursues, "has added greatly to the panic of the people. With difficulty I can restrain them from murdering the Indian prisoners." And he concludes: "I can't help thinking that the enemy will collect, after cutting off the little posts one after another, leaving Fort Pitt as too tough a morsel, and bend their whole force upon the frontiers."

On the second of July, he describes an attack by about twenty Indians on a party of mowers, several of whom were killed. "This accident," he says, "has thrown the people into a great consternation, but such is their stupidity that they will do nothing right for their own preservation."

It was on the next day that he sent a mounted soldier to Bouquet with news of the loss of Presqu' Isle and its sister posts, which Blane, who had received it from Fort Pitt, had contrived to send him; though he himself, in his feeble little fort of Ligonier, buried in a sea of forests, hardly dared hope to maintain himself. Bouquet was greatly moved at the tidings, and his vexation betrayed him into injustice towards the defender of Presqu' Isle. "Humanity makes me hope that Christie is dead, as his scandalous capitulation, for a post of that consequence and so impregnable to savages, deserves the most severe punishment." He is equally vehement in regard to Blane, who appears to have intimated, in writing to Ourry, that he had himself had thoughts of capitulating, like Christie. "I shivered when you hinted to me Lieutenant Bl———'s intentions. Death and infamy would have been the reward he would expect, instead of the honor he has obtained by his prudence, courage, and resolution.... This is a most trying time.... You may be sure that all the expedition possible will be used for the relief of the few remaining posts."

As for Blane, the following extracts from his letters will show his position; though, when his affairs were at the worst, nothing was heard from him, as all his messengers were killed. On the fourth of June, he writes: "Thursday last my garrison was attacked by a body of Indians, about five in the morning; but as they only fired upon us from the skirts of the woods, I contented myself with giving them three cheers, without spending a single shot upon them. But as they still continued their popping upon the side next the town, I sent the sergeant of the Royal Americans, with a proper detachment, to fire the houses, which effectually disappointed them in their plan."

On the seventeenth, he writes to Bouquet: "I hope soon to see yourself, and live in daily hopes of a reinforcement.... Sunday last, a man straggling out was killed by the Indians; and Monday night three of them got under the n—— house, but were discovered. The darkness secured them their retreat.... I believe the communication between Fort Pitt and this is entirely cut off, having heard nothing from them since the thirtieth of May, though two expresses have gone from Bedford by this post."

On the twenty-eighth, he explains that he has not been able to report for some time, the road having been completely closed by the enemy. "On the twenty-first," he continues, "the Indians made a second attempt in a very serious manner, for near two hours, but with the like success as the first. They began with attempting to cut off the retreat of a small party of fifteen men, who, from their impatience to come at four Indians who showed themselves, in a great measure forced me to let them out. In the evening, I think above a hundred lay in ambush by the side of the creek, about four hundred yards from the fort; and, just as the party was returning pretty near where they lay, they rushed out, when they undoubtedly must have succeeded, had it not been for a deep morass which intervened. Immediately after, they began their attack; and I dare say they fired upwards of one thousand shot. Nobody received any damage. So far, my good fortune in dangers still attends me."

And here one cannot but give a moment's thought to those whose desperate duty it was to be the bearers of this correspondence of the officers of the forest outposts with their commander. They were usually soldiers, sometimes backwoodsmen, and occasionally a friendly Indian, who, disguising his attachment to the whites, could pass when others would infallibly have perished. If white men, they were always mounted; and it may well be supposed that their horses did not lag by the way. The profound solitude; the silence, broken only by the moan of the wind, the caw of the crow, or the cry of some prowling tenant of the waste; the mystery of the verdant labyrinth, which the anxious wayfarer strained his eyes in vain to penetrate; the consciousness that in every thicket, behind every rock, might lurk a foe more fierce and subtle than the cougar or the lynx; and the long hours of darkness, when, stretched on the cold ground, his excited fancy roamed in nightmare visions of a horror but too real and imminent,—such was the experience of many an unfortunate who never lived to tell it. If the messenger was an Indian, his greatest danger was from those who should have been his friends. Friendly Indians were told, whenever they approached a fort, to make themselves known by carrying green branches thrust into the muzzles of their guns; and an order was issued that the token should be respected. This gave them tolerable security as regarded soldiers, but not as regarded the enraged backwoodsmen, who would shoot without distinction at any thing with a red skin.

To return to Bouquet, who lay encamped at Carlisle, urging on his preparations, but met by obstacles at every step. Wagons and horses had been promised, but promises were broken, and all was vexation and delay. The province of Pennsylvania, from causes to be shown hereafter, would do nothing to aid the troops who were defending it; and even the people of the frontier, partly from the apathy and confusion of terror, and partly, it seems, from dislike and jealousy of the regulars, were backward and sluggish in co-operating with them. "I hope," writes Bouquet to Sir Jeffrey Amherst, "that we shall be able to save that infatuated people from destruction, notwithstanding all their endeavors to defeat your vigorous measures. I meet everywhere with the same backwardness, even among the most exposed of the inhabitants, which makes every thing move on heavily, and is disgusting to the last degree." And again: "I find myself utterly abandoned by the very people I am ordered to protect.... I have borne very patiently the ill-usage of this province, having still hopes that they will do something for us; and therefore have avoided to quarrel with them."

While, vexed and exasperated, Bouquet labored at his thankless task, remonstrated with provincial officials, or appealed to refractory farmers, the terror of the country people increased every day. When on Sunday, the third of July, Ourry's express rode into Carlisle with the disastrous news from Presqu' Isle and the other outposts, he stopped for a moment in the village street to water his horse. A crowd of countrymen were instantly about him, besieging him with questions. He told his ill-omened story; and added as, remounting, he rode towards Bouquet's tent, "The Indians will be here soon." All was now excitement and consternation. Messengers hastened out to spread the tidings; and every road and pathway leading into Carlisle was beset with the flying settlers, flocking thither for refuge. Soon rumors were heard that the Indians were come. Some of the fugitives had seen the smoke of burning houses rising from the valleys; and these reports were fearfully confirmed by the appearance of miserable wretches, who, half frantic with grief and dismay, had fled from blazing dwellings and slaughtered families. A party of the inhabitants armed themselves and went out, to warn the living and bury the dead. Reaching Shearman's Valley, they found fields laid waste, stacked wheat on fire, and the houses yet in flames; and they grew sick with horror at seeing a group of hogs tearing and devouring the bodies of the dead. As they advanced up the valley, every thing betokened the recent presence of the enemy, while columns of smoke, rising among the surrounding mountains, showed how general was the work of destruction.

On the preceding day, six men, assembled for reaping the harvest, had been seated at dinner at the house of Campbell, a settler on the Juniata. Four or five Indians suddenly burst the door, fired among them, and then beat down the survivors with the butts of their rifles. One young man leaped from his seat, snatched a gun which stood in a corner, discharged it into the breast of the warrior who was rushing upon him, and, leaping through an open window, made his escape. He fled through the forest to a settlement at some distance, where he related his story. Upon this, twelve young men volunteered to cross the mountain, and warn the inhabitants of the neighboring Tuscarora valley. On entering it, they found that the enemy had been there before them. Some of the houses were on fire, while others were still standing, with no tenants but the dead. Under the shed of a farmer, the Indians had been feasting on the flesh of the cattle they had killed, and the meat had not yet grown cold. Pursuing their course, the white men found the spot where several detached parties of the enemy had united almost immediately before; and they boldly resolved to follow, in order to ascertain what direction the marauders had taken. The trail led them up a deep and woody pass of the Tuscarora. Here the yell of the war-whoop and the din of fire-arms suddenly greeted them, and five of their number were shot down. Thirty warriors rose from their ambuscade, and rushed upon them. They gave one discharge, scattered, and ran for their lives. One of them, a boy named Charles Eliot, as he fled, plunging through the thickets, heard an Indian tearing the boughs behind him, in furious pursuit. He seized his powder-horn, poured the contents at random down the muzzle of his gun, threw in a bullet after them, without using the ramrod, and, wheeling about, discharged the piece into the breast of his pursuer. He saw the Indian shrink back and roll over into the bushes. He continued his flight; but a moment after, a voice called his name. Turning to the spot, he saw one of his comrades stretched helpless upon the ground. This man had been mortally wounded at the first fire, but had fled a few rods from the scene of blood, before his strength gave out. Eliot approached him. "Take my gun," said the dying frontiersman. "Whenever you see an Indian, kill him with it, and then I shall be satisfied." Eliot, with several others of the party, escaped, and finally reached Carlisle, where his story excited a spirit of uncontrollable wrath and vengeance among the fierce backwoodsmen. Several parties went out; and one of them, commanded by the sheriff of the place, encountered a band of Indians, routed them after a sharp fight, and brought in several scalps.

The surrounding country was by this time completely abandoned by the settlers, many of whom, not content with seeking refuge at Carlisle, continued their flight to the eastward, and, headed by the clergyman of that place, pushed on to Lancaster, and even to Philadelphia. Carlisle presented a most deplorable spectacle. A multitude of the refugees, unable to find shelter in the town, had encamped in the woods or on the adjacent fields, erecting huts of branches and bark, and living on such charity as the slender means of the townspeople could supply. Passing among them, one would have witnessed every form of human misery. In these wretched encampments were men, women, and children, bereft at one stroke of friends, of home, and the means of supporting life. Some stood aghast and bewildered at the sudden and fatal blow; others were sunk in the apathy of despair; others were weeping and moaning with irrepressible anguish. With not a few, the craven passion of fear drowned all other emotion, and day and night they were haunted with visions of the bloody knife and the reeking scalp; while in others, every faculty was absorbed by the burning thirst for vengeance, and mortal hatred against the whole Indian race.

THE BATTLE OF BUSHY RUN

1763

The miserable multitude were soon threatened with famine, and gathered in crowds around the tents of Bouquet, begging relief, which he had not the heart to refuse. After a delay of eighteen days, the chief obstacles were overcome. Wagons and draught animals had, little by little, been collected, and provisions gathered among the settlements to the eastward. At length all was ready, and Bouquet broke up his camp, and began his march. The force under his command did not exceed five hundred men, of whom the most effective were the Highlanders of the 42d regiment. The remnant of the 77th, which was also with him, was so enfeebled by West Indian exposures, that Amherst had at first pronounced it fit only for garrison duty, and nothing but necessity had induced him to employ it on this arduous service. As the heavy wagons of the convoy lumbered along the street of Carlisle, guarded by the bare-legged Highlanders, in kilts and plaids, the crowd gazed in anxious silence; for they knew that their all was at stake on the issue of this dubious enterprise. There was little to reassure them in the thin frames and haggard look of the worn-out veterans; still less in the sight of sixty invalid soldiers, who, unable to walk, were carried in wagons, to furnish a feeble reinforcement to the small garrisons along the route. The desponding rustics watched the last gleam of the bayonets, the last flutter of the tartans, as the rear files vanished in the woods; then returned to their hovels, prepared for tidings of defeat, and ready, when they heard them, to abandon the country, and fly beyond the Susquehanna.

In truth, the adventure was no boy's play. In that gloomy wilderness lay the bones of Braddock and the hundreds that perished with him. The number of the slain on that bloody day exceeded Bouquet's whole force; while the strength of the assailants was inferior to that of the swarms who now infested the forests. Bouquet's troops were, for the most part, as little accustomed to the backwoods as those of Braddock; but their commander had served seven years in America, and perfectly understood his work. He had attempted to engage a body of frontiersmen to join him on the march; but they preferred to remain for the defence of their families. He was therefore forced to employ the Highlanders as flankers, to protect his line of march and prevent surprise; but, singularly enough, these mountaineers were sure to lose themselves in the woods, and therefore proved useless. For a few days, however, his progress would be tolerably secure, at least from serious attack. His anxieties centred on Fort Ligonier, and he resolved to hazard the attempt to throw a reinforcement into it. Thirty of the best Highlanders were chosen, furnished with guides, and ordered to push forward with the utmost speed, avoiding the road, travelling by night on unfrequented paths, and lying close by day. The attempt succeeded. After resting several days at Bedford, where Ourry was expecting an attack, they again set out, found Fort Ligonier beset by Indians, and received a volley as they made for the gate; but entered safely, to the unspeakable relief of Blane and his beleaguered men.

Meanwhile, Bouquet's little army crept on its slow way along the Cumberland valley. Passing here and there a few scattered cabins, deserted or burnt to the ground, they reached the hamlet of Shippensburg, somewhat more than twenty miles from their point of departure. Here, as at Carlisle, was gathered a starving multitude, who had fled from the knife and the tomahawk. Beyond lay a solitude whence every settler had fled. They reached Fort Loudon, on the declivity of Cove Mountain, and climbed the wood-encumbered defiles beyond. Far on their right stretched the green ridges of the Tuscarora; and, in front, mountain beyond mountain was piled against the sky. Over rocky heights and through deep valleys, they reached at length Fort Littleton, a provincial post, in which, with incredible perversity, the government of Pennsylvania had refused to place a garrison. Not far distant was the feeble little port of the Juniata, empty like the other; for the two or three men who held it had been withdrawn by Ourry. On the twenty-fifth of July, they reached Bedford, hemmed in by encircling mountains. It was the frontier village and the centre of a scattered border population, the whole of which was now clustered in terror in and around the fort; for the neighboring woods were full of prowling savages. Ourry reported that for several weeks nothing had been heard from the westward, every messenger having been killed and the communication completely cut off. By the last intelligence Fort Pitt had been surrounded by Indians, and daily threatened with a general attack.

At Bedford, Bouquet had the good fortune to engage thirty backwoodsmen to accompany him. He lay encamped three days to rest men and animals, and then, leaving his invalids to garrison the fort, put out again into the sea of savage verdure that stretched beyond. The troops and convoy defiled along the road made by General Forbes in 1758, if the name of road can be given to a rugged track, hewn out by axemen through forests and swamps and up the steep acclivities of rugged mountains; shut in between impervious walls of trunks, boughs, and matted thickets, and overarched by a canopy of restless leaves. With difficulty and toil, the wagons dragged slowly on, by hill and hollow, through brook and quagmire, over roots, rocks, and stumps. Nature had formed the country for a war of ambuscades and surprises, and no pains were spared to guard against them. A band of backwoodsmen led the way, followed closely by the pioneers; the wagons and the cattle were in the centre, guarded by the regulars; and a rear guard of backwoodsmen closed the line of march. Frontier riflemen scoured the woods far in front and on either flank, and made surprise impossible. Thus they toiled heavily on till the main ridge of the Alleghanies, a mighty wall of green, rose up before them; and they began their zigzag progress up the woody heights amid the sweltering heats of July. The tongues of the panting oxen hung lolling from their jaws; while the pine-trees, scorching in the hot sun, diffused their resinous odors through the sultry air. At length from the windy summit the Highland soldiers could gaze around upon a boundless panorama of forest-covered mountains, wilder than their own native hills. Descending from the Alleghanies, they entered upon a country less rugged and formidable in itself, but beset with constantly increasing dangers. On the second of August, they reached Fort Ligonier, about fifty miles from Bedford, and a hundred and fifty from Carlisle. The Indians who were about the place vanished at their approach; but the garrison could furnish no intelligence of the motions and designs of the enemy, having been completely blockaded for weeks. In this uncertainty, Bouquet resolved to leave behind the oxen and wagons, which formed the most cumbrous part of the convoy, in order to advance with greater celerity, and oppose a better resistance in case of attack. Thus relieved, the army resumed its march on the fourth, taking with them three hundred and fifty pack-horses and a few cattle, and at nightfall encamped at no great distance from Ligonier. Within less than a day's march in advance lay the dangerous defiles of Turtle Creek, a stream flowing at the bottom of a deep hollow, flanked by steep declivities, along the foot of which the road at that time ran for some distance. Fearing that the enemy would lay an ambuscade at this place, Bouquet resolved to march on the following day as far as a small stream called Bushy Run; to rest here until night, and then, by a forced march, to cross Turtle Creek under cover of the darkness.

On the morning of the fifth, the tents were struck at an early hour, and the troops began their march through a country broken with hills and deep hollows, covered with the tall, dense forest, which spread for countless leagues around. By one o'clock, they had advanced seventeen miles; and the guides assured them that they were within half a mile of Bushy Run, their proposed resting-place. The tired soldiers were pressing forward with renewed alacrity, when suddenly the report of rifles from the front sent a thrill along the ranks; and, as they listened, the firing thickened into a fierce, sharp rattle; while shouts and whoops, deadened by the intervening forest, showed that the advance guard was hotly engaged. The two foremost companies were at once ordered forward to support it; but, far from abating, the fire grew so rapid and furious as to argue the presence of an enemy at once numerous and resolute. At this, the convoy was halted, the troops formed into line, and a general charge ordered. Bearing down through the forest with fixed bayonets, they drove the yelping assailants before them, and swept the ground clear. But at the very moment of success, a fresh burst of whoops and firing was heard from either flank; while a confused noise from the rear showed that the convoy was attacked. It was necessary instantly to fall back for its support. Driving off the assailants, the troops formed in a circle around the crowded and terrified horses. Though they were new to the work, and though the numbers and movements of the enemy, whose yelling resounded on every side, were concealed by the thick forest, yet no man lost his composure; and all displayed a steadiness which nothing but implicit confidence in their commander could have inspired. And now ensued a combat of a nature most harassing and discouraging. Again and again, now on this side and now on that, a crowd of Indians rushed up, pouring in a heavy fire, and striving, with furious outcries, to break into the circle. A well-directed volley met them, followed by a steady charge of the bayonet. They never waited an instant to receive the attack, but, leaping backwards from tree to tree, soon vanished from sight, only to renew their attack with unabated ferocity in another quarter. Such was their activity, that very few of them were hurt; while the British, less expert in bush-fighting, suffered severely. Thus the fight went on, without intermission, for seven hours, until the forest grew dark with approaching night. Upon this, the Indians gradually slackened their fire, and the exhausted soldiers found time to rest.

It was impossible to change their ground in the enemy's presence, and the troops were obliged to encamp upon the hill where the combat had taken place, though not a drop of water was to be found there. Fearing a night attack, Bouquet stationed numerous sentinels and outposts to guard against it; while the men lay down upon their arms, preserving the order they had maintained during the fight. Having completed the necessary arrangements, Bouquet, doubtful of surviving the battle of the morrow, wrote to Sir Jeffrey Amherst, in a few clear, concise words, an account of the day's events. His letter concludes as follows: "Whatever our fate may be, I thought it necessary to give your Excellency this early information, that you may, at all events, take such measures as you will think proper with the provinces, for their own safety, and the effectual relief of Fort Pitt; as, in case of another engagement, I fear insurmountable difficulties in protecting and transporting our provisions, being already so much weakened by the losses of this day, in men and horses, besides the additional necessity of carrying the wounded, whose situation is truly deplorable."

The condition of these unhappy men might well awaken sympathy. About sixty soldiers, besides several officers, had been killed or disabled. A space in the centre of the camp was prepared for the reception of the wounded, and surrounded by a wall of flour-bags from the convoy, affording some protection against the bullets which flew from all sides during the fight. Here they lay upon the ground, enduring agonies of thirst, and waiting, passive and helpless, the issue of the battle. Deprived of the animating thought that their lives and safety depended on their own exertions; surrounded by a wilderness, and by scenes to the horror of which no degree of familiarity could render the imagination callous, they must have endured mental sufferings, compared to which the pain of their wounds was slight. In the probable event of defeat, a fate inexpressibly horrible awaited them; while even victory would not ensure their safety, since any great increase in their numbers would render it impossible for their comrades to transport them. Nor was the condition of those who had hitherto escaped an enviable one. Though they were about equal in number to their assailants, yet the dexterity and alertness of the Indians, joined to the nature of the country, gave all the advantages of a greatly superior force. The enemy were, moreover, exulting in the fullest confidence of success; for it was in these very forests that, eight years before, they had nearly destroyed twice their number of the best British troops. Throughout the earlier part of the night, they kept up a dropping fire upon the camp; while, at short intervals, a wild whoop from the thick surrounding gloom told with what fierce eagerness they waited to glut their vengeance on the morrow. The camp remained in darkness, for it would have been dangerous to build fires within its precincts, to direct the aim of the lurking marksmen. Surrounded by such terrors, the men snatched a disturbed and broken sleep, recruiting their exhausted strength for the renewed struggle of the morning.

With the earliest dawn of day, and while the damp, cool forest was still involved in twilight, there rose around the camp a general burst of those horrible cries which form the ordinary prelude of an Indian battle. Instantly, from every side at once, the enemy opened their fire, approaching under cover of the trees and bushes, and levelling with a close and deadly aim. Often, as on the previous day, they would rush up with furious impetuosity, striving to break into the ring of troops. They were repulsed at every point; but the British, though constantly victorious, were beset with undiminished perils, while the violence of the enemy seemed every moment on the increase. True to their favorite tactics, they would never stand their ground when attacked, but vanish at the first gleam of the levelled bayonet, only to appear again the moment the danger was past. The troops, fatigued by the long march and equally long battle of the previous day, were maddened by the torments of thirst, "more intolerable," says their commander, "than the enemy's fire." They were fully conscious of the peril in which they stood, of wasting away by slow degrees beneath the shot of assailants at once so daring, so cautious, and so active, and upon whom it was impossible to inflict any decisive injury. The Indians saw their distress, and pressed them closer and closer, redoubling their yells and howlings; while some of them, sheltered behind trees, assailed the troops, in bad English, with abuse and derision.

Meanwhile the interior of the camp was a scene of confusion. The horses, secured in a crowd near the wall of flour-bags which covered the wounded, were often struck by the bullets, and wrought to the height of terror by the mingled din of whoops, shrieks, and firing. They would break away by half scores at a time, burst through the ring of troops and the outer circle of assailants, and scour madly up and down the hill-sides; while many of the drivers, overcome by the terrors of a scene in which they could bear no active part, hid themselves among the bushes, and could neither hear nor obey orders.

It was now about ten o'clock. Oppressed with heat, fatigue, and thirst, the distressed troops still maintained a weary and wavering defence, encircling the convoy in a yet unbroken ring. They were fast falling in their ranks, and the strength and spirits of the survivors had begun to flag. If the fortunes of the day were to be retrieved, the effort must be made at once; and happily the mind of the commander was equal to the emergency. In the midst of the confusion he conceived a masterly stratagem. Could the Indians be brought together in a body, and made to stand their ground when attacked, there could be little doubt of the result; and, to effect this object, Bouquet determined to increase their confidence, which had already mounted to an audacious pitch. Two companies of infantry, forming a part of the ring which had been exposed to the hottest fire, were ordered to fall back into the interior of the camp; while the troops on either hand joined their files across the vacant space, as if to cover the retreat of their comrades. These orders, given at a favorable moment, were executed with great promptness. The thin line of troops who took possession of the deserted part of the circle were, from their small numbers, brought closer in towards the centre. The Indians mistook these movements for a retreat. Confident that their time was come, they leaped up on all sides, from behind the trees and bushes, and, with infernal screeches, rushed headlong towards the spot, pouring in a heavy and galling fire. The shock was too violent to be long endured. The men struggled to maintain their posts; but the Indians seemed on the point of breaking into the heart of the camp, when the aspect of affairs was suddenly reversed. The two companies, who had apparently abandoned their position, were in fact destined to begin the attack; and they now sallied out from the circle at a point where a depression in the ground, joined to the thick growth of trees, concealed them from the eyes of the Indians. Making a short détour through the woods, they came round upon the flank of the furious assailants, and fired a close volley into the midst of the crowd. Numbers were seen to fall; yet though completely surprised, and utterly at a loss to understand the nature of the attack, the Indians faced about with the greatest intrepidity, and returned the fire. But the Highlanders, with yells as wild as their own, fell on them with the bayonet. The shock was irresistible, and they fled before the charging ranks in a tumultuous throng. Orders had been given to two other companies, occupying a contiguous part of the circle, to support the attack whenever a favorable moment should occur; and they had therefore advanced a little from their position, and lay close crouched in ambush. The fugitives, pressed by the Highland bayonets, passed directly across their front; upon which they rose, and poured among them a second volley, no less destructive than the first. This completed the rout. The four companies, uniting, drove the flying savages through the woods, giving them no time to rally or reload their empty rifles, killing many, and scattering the rest in hopeless confusion.

While this took place at one part of the circle, the troops and the savages had still maintained their respective positions at the other; but when the latter perceived the total rout of their comrades, and saw the troops advancing to assail them, they also lost heart, and fled. The discordant outcries which had so long deafened the ears of the English soon ceased altogether, and not a living Indian remained near the spot. About sixty corpses lay scattered over the ground. Among them were found those of several prominent chiefs, while the blood which stained the leaves of the bushes showed that numbers had fled wounded from the field. The soldiers took but one prisoner, whom they shot to death like a captive wolf. The loss of the British in the two battles surpassed that of the enemy, amounting to eight officers and one hundred and fifteen men.

Having been for some time detained by the necessity of making litters for the wounded, and destroying the stores which the flight of most of the horses made it impossible to transport, the army moved on, in the afternoon, to Bushy Run. Here they had scarcely formed their camp, when they were again fired upon by a body of Indians, who, however, were soon repulsed. On the next day they resumed their progress towards Fort Pitt, distant about twenty-five miles; and, though frequently annoyed on the march by petty attacks, they reached their destination, on the tenth, without serious loss. It was a joyful moment both to the troops and to the garrison.

The latter, it will be remembered, were left surrounded and hotly pressed by the Indians, who had beleaguered the place from the twenty-eighth of July to the first of August, when, hearing of Bouquet's approach, they had abandoned the siege, and marched to attack him. From this time, the garrison had seen nothing of them until the morning of the tenth, when, shortly before the army appeared, they had passed the fort in a body, raising the scalp-yell, and displaying their disgusting trophies to the view of the English.

The battle of Bushy Run was one of the best contested actions ever fought between white men and Indians. If there was any disparity of numbers, the advantage was on the side of the troops; and the Indians had displayed throughout a fierceness and intrepidity matched only by the steady valor with which they were met. In the provinces, the victory excited equal joy and admiration, especially among those who knew the incalculable difficulties of an Indian campaign. The Assembly of Pennsylvania passed a vote expressing their sense of the merits of Bouquet, and of the service he had rendered to the province. He soon after received the additional honor of the formal thanks of the King.

In many an Indian village, the women cut away their hair, gashed their limbs with knives, and uttered their dismal howlings of lamentation for the fallen. Yet, though surprised and dispirited, the rage of the Indians was too deep to be quenched, even by so signal a reverse; and their outrages upon the frontier were resumed with unabated ferocity. Fort Pitt, however, was effectually relieved; while the moral effect of the victory enabled the frontier settlers to encounter the enemy with a spirit which would have been wanting, had Bouquet sustained a defeat.

THE IROQUOIS

1763

While Bouquet was fighting the battle of Bushy Run, and Dalzell making his fatal sortie against the camp of Pontiac, Sir William Johnson was engaged in the more pacific yet more important task of securing the friendship and alliance of the Six Nations. After several preliminary conferences, he sent runners throughout the whole confederacy to invite deputies of the several tribes to meet him in council at Johnson Hall. The request was not declined. From the banks of the Mohawk; from the Oneida, Cayuga, and Tuscarora villages; from the valley of Onondaga, where, from immemorial time, had burned the great council-fire of the confederacy,—came chiefs and warriors, gathering to the place of meeting. The Senecas alone, the warlike tenants of the Genesee valley, refused to attend; for they were already in arms against the English. Besides the Iroquois, deputies came from the tribes dwelling along the St. Lawrence, and within the settled parts of Canada.

The council opened on the seventh of September. Despite their fair words, their attachment was doubtful; but Sir William Johnson, by a dexterous mingling of reasoning, threats, and promises, allayed their discontent, and banished the thoughts of war. They winced, however, when he informed them that, during the next season, an English army must pass through their country, on its way to punish the refractory tribes of the West. "Your foot is broad and heavy," said the speaker from Onondaga; "take care that you do not tread on us." Seeing the improved temper of his auditory, Johnson was led to hope for some farther advantage than that of mere neutrality. He accordingly urged the Iroquois to take up arms against the hostile tribes, and concluded his final harangue with the following figurative words: "I now deliver you a good English axe, which I desire you will give to the warriors of all your nations, with directions to use it against these covenant-breakers, by cutting off the bad links which have sullied the chain of friendship."

These words were confirmed by the presentation of a black war-belt of wampum, and the offer of a hatchet, which the Iroquois did not refuse to accept. That they would take any very active and strenuous part in the war, could not be expected; yet their bearing arms at all would prove of great advantage, by discouraging the hostile Indians who had looked upon the Iroquois as friends and abettors. Some months after the council, several small parties actually took the field; and, being stimulated by the prospect of reward, brought in a considerable number of scalps and prisoners.

Upon the persuasion of Sir William Johnson, the tribes of Canada were induced to send a message to the western Indians, exhorting them to bury the hatchet, while the Iroquois despatched an embassy of similar import to the Delawares on the Susquehanna. "Cousins the Delawares,"—thus ran the message,—"we have heard that many wild Indians in the West, who have tails like bears, have let fall the chain of friendship, and taken up the hatchet against our brethren the English. We desire you to hold fast the chain, and shut your ears against their words."

In spite of the friendly disposition to which the Iroquois had been brought, the province of New York suffered not a little from the attacks of the hostile tribes who ravaged the borders of Ulster, Orange, and Albany counties, and threatened to destroy the upper settlements of the Mohawk. Sir William Johnson was the object of their especial enmity, and he several times received intimations that he was about to be attacked. He armed his tenantry, surrounded his seat of Johnson Hall with a stockade, and garrisoned it with a party of soldiers, which Sir Jeffrey Amherst had ordered thither for his protection.

About this time, a singular incident occurred near the town of Goshen. Four or five men went out among the hills to shoot partridges, and, chancing to raise a large covey, they all fired their guns at nearly the same moment. The timorous inhabitants, hearing the reports, supposed that they came from an Indian war-party, and instantly fled in dismay, spreading the alarm as they went. The neighboring country was soon in a panic. The farmers cut the harness of their horses, and, leaving their carts and ploughs behind, galloped for their lives. Others, snatching up their children and their most valuable property, made with all speed for New England, not daring to pause until they had crossed the Hudson. For several days the neighborhood was abandoned, five hundred families having left their habitations and fled. Not long after this absurd affair, an event occurred of a widely different character. Allusion has before been made to the carrying-place of Niagara, which formed an essential link in the chain of communication between the province of New York and the interior country. Men and military stores were conveyed in boats up the River Niagara, as far as the present site of Lewiston. Thence a portage road, several miles in length, passed along the banks of the stream, and terminated at Fort Schlosser, above the cataract. This road traversed a region whose sublime features have gained for it a world-wide renown. The River Niagara, a short distance below the cataract, assumes an aspect scarcely less remarkable than that stupendous scene itself. Its channel is formed by a vast ravine, whose sides, now bare and weather-stained, now shaggy with forest-trees, rise in cliffs of appalling height and steepness. Along this chasm pour all the waters of the lakes, heaving their furious surges with the power of an ocean and the rage of a mountain torrent. About three miles below the cataract, the precipices which form the eastern wall of the ravine are broken by an abyss of awful depth and blackness, bearing at the present day the name of the Devil's Hole. In its shallowest part, the precipice sinks sheer down to the depth of eighty feet, where it meets a chaotic mass of rocks, descending with an abrupt declivity to unseen depths below. Within the cold and damp recesses of the gulf, a host of forest-trees have rooted themselves; and, standing on the perilous brink, one may look down upon the mingled foliage of ash, poplar, and maple, while, above them all, the spruce and fir shoot their sharp and rigid spires upward into sunlight. The roar of the convulsed river swells heavily on the ear; and, far below, its headlong waters, careering in foam, may be discerned through the openings of the matted foliage.

On the thirteenth of September, a numerous train of wagons and pack-horses proceeded from the lower landing to Fort Schlosser; and on the following morning set out on their return, guarded by an escort of twenty-four soldiers. They pursued their slow progress until they reached a point where the road passed along the brink of the Devil's Hole. The gulf yawned on their left, while on their right the road was skirted by low densely wooded hills. Suddenly they were greeted by the blaze and clatter of a hundred rifles. Then followed the startled cries of men, and the bounding of maddened horses. At the next instant, a host of Indians broke screeching from the woods, and rifle-butt and tomahawk finished the bloody work. All was over in a moment. Horses leaped the precipice; men were driven shrieking into the abyss; teams and wagons went over, crashing to atoms among the rocks below. Tradition relates that the drummer-boy of the detachment was caught, in his fall, among the branches of a tree, where he hung suspended by his drum-strap. Being but slightly injured, he disengaged himself, and, hiding in the recesses of the gulf, finally escaped. One of the teamsters also, who was wounded at the first fire, contrived to crawl into the woods, where he lay concealed till the Indians had left the place. Besides these two, the only survivor was Stedman, the conductor of the convoy;

who, being well mounted, and seeing the whole party forced helpless towards the precipice, wheeled his horse, and resolutely spurred through the crowd of Indians. One of them, it is said, seized his bridle; but he freed himself by a dexterous use of his knife, and plunged into the woods, untouched by the bullets which whistled about his head. Flying at full speed through the forest, he reached Fort Schlosser in safety.

The distant sound of the Indian rifles had been heard by a party of soldiers, who occupied a small fortified camp near the lower landing. Forming in haste, they advanced eagerly to the rescue. In anticipation of this movement, the Indians, who were nearly five hundred in number, had separated into two parties, one of which had stationed itself at the Devil's Hole, to waylay the convoy, while the other formed an ambuscade upon the road, a mile nearer the landing-place. The soldiers, marching precipitately, and huddled in a close body, were suddenly assailed by a volley of rifles, which stretched half their number dead upon the road. Then, rushing from the forest, the Indians cut down the survivors with merciless ferocity. A small remnant only escaped the massacre, and fled to Fort Niagara with the tidings. Major Wilkins, who commanded at this post, lost no time in marching to the spot, with nearly the whole strength of his garrison. Not an Indian was to be found. At the two places of ambuscade, about seventy dead bodies were counted, naked, scalpless, and so horribly mangled that many of them could not be recognized. All the wagons had been broken to pieces, and such of the horses as were not driven over the precipice had been carried off, laden, doubtless, with the plunder. The ambuscade of the Devil's Hole has gained a traditional immortality, adding fearful interest to a scene whose native horrors need no aid from the imagination.

The Seneca warriors, aided probably by some of the western Indians, were the authors of this unexpected attack. Their hostility did not end here. Several weeks afterwards, Major Wilkins, with a force of six hundred regulars, collected with great effort throughout the provinces, was advancing to the relief of Detroit. As the boats were slowly forcing their way upwards against the swift current above the falls of Niagara, they were assailed by a mere handful of Indians, thrown into confusion, and driven back to Fort Schlosser with serious loss. The next attempt was more fortunate, the boats reaching Lake Erie without farther attack; but the inauspicious opening of the expedition was followed by results yet more disastrous. As they approached their destination, a violent storm overtook them in the night. The frail bateaux, tossing upon the merciless waves of Lake Erie, were overset, driven ashore, and many of them dashed to pieces. About seventy men perished, all the ammunition and stores were destroyed, and the shattered flotilla was forced back to Niagara.

DESOLATION OF THE FRONTIERS

1763

The advancing frontiers of American civilization have always nurtured a class of men of striking and peculiar character. The best examples of this character have, perhaps, been found among the settlers of Western Virginia, and the hardy progeny who have sprung from that generous stock. The Virginian frontiersman was, as occasion called, a farmer, a hunter, and a warrior, by turns. The well-beloved rifle was seldom out of his hand; and he never deigned to lay aside the fringed frock, moccasons, and Indian leggins, which formed the appropriate costume of the forest ranger. Concerning the business, pleasures, and refinements of cultivated life, he knew little, and cared nothing; and his manners were usually rough and obtrusive to the last degree. Aloof from mankind, he lived in a world of his own, which, in his view, contained all that was deserving of admiration and praise. He looked upon himself and his compeers as models of prowess and manhood, nay, of all that is elegant and polite; and the forest gallant regarded with peculiar complacency his own half-savage dress, his swaggering gait, and his backwoods jargon. He was wilful, headstrong, and quarrelsome; frank, straightforward, and generous; brave as the bravest, and utterly intolerant of arbitrary control. His self-confidence mounted to audacity. Eminently capable of heroism, both in action and endurance, he viewed every species of effeminacy with supreme contempt; and, accustomed as he was to entire self-reliance, the mutual dependence of conventional life excited his especial scorn. With all his ignorance, he had a mind by nature quick, vigorous, and penetrating; and his mode of life, while it developed the daring energy of his character, wrought some of his faculties to a high degree of acuteness. Many of his traits have been reproduced in his offspring. From him have sprung those hardy men whose struggles and sufferings on the bloody ground of Kentucky will always form a striking page in American history; and that band of adventurers before whose headlong charge, in the valley of Chihuahua, neither breastworks, nor batteries, nor fivefold odds could avail for a moment.

At the period of Pontiac's war, the settlements of Virginia had extended as far as the Alleghanies, and several small towns had already sprung up beyond the Blue Ridge. The population of these beautiful valleys was, for the most part, thin and scattered; and the progress of settlement had been greatly retarded by Indian hostilities, which, during the early years of the French war, had thrown these borders into total confusion. They had contributed, however, to enhance the martial temper of the people, and give a warlike aspect to the whole frontier. At intervals, small stockade forts, containing houses and cabins, had been erected by the joint labor of the inhabitants; and hither, on occasion of alarm, the settlers of the neighborhood congregated for refuge, remaining in tolerable security till the danger was past. Many of the inhabitants were engaged for a great part of the year in hunting; an occupation upon which they entered with the keenest relish. Well versed in woodcraft, unsurpassed as marksmen, and practised in all the wiles of Indian war, they would have formed, under a more stringent organization, the best possible defence against a savage enemy; but each man came and went at his own sovereign will, and discipline and obedience were repugnant to all his habits.

The frontiers of Maryland and Virginia closely resembled each other; but those of Pennsylvania had peculiarities of their own. The population of this province was of a most motley complexion, being made up of members of various nations, and numerous religious sects: English, Irish, German, Swiss, Welsh, and Dutch; Quakers, Presbyterians, Lutherans, Dunkers, Mennonists, and Moravians. Nor is this catalogue by any means complete. The Quakers, to whose peaceful temper the rough frontier offered no attraction, were confined to the eastern parts of the province. Cumberland County, which lies west of the Susquehanna, and may be said to have formed the frontier, was then almost exclusively occupied by the Irish and their descendants; who, however, were neither of the Roman faith nor of Celtic origin, being emigrants from the colony of Scotch which forms a numerous and thrifty population in the north of Ireland. In religious faith, they were stanch and zealous Presbyterians. Long residence in the province had modified their national character, and imparted many of the peculiar traits of the American backwoodsman; yet the nature of their religious tenets produced a certain rigidity of temper and demeanor, from which the Virginian was wholly free. They were, nevertheless, hot-headed and turbulent, often setting law and authority at defiance. The counties east of the Susquehanna supported a mixed population, among which was conspicuous a swarm of German peasants; who had been inundating the country for many years past, and who for the most part were dull and ignorant boors, like some of their descendants. The Swiss and German sectaries called Mennonists, who were numerous in Lancaster County, professed, like the Quakers, principles of non-resistance, and refused to bear arms.

It was upon this mingled population, that the storm of Indian war was now descending with appalling fury,—a fury unparalleled through all past and succeeding years. For hundreds of miles from north to south, the country was wasted with fire and steel. It would be a task alike useless and revolting to explore, through all its details, this horrible monotony of blood and havoc. The country was filled with the wildest dismay. The people of Virginia betook themselves to their forts for refuge. Those of Pennsylvania, ill supplied with such asylums, fled by thousands, and crowded in upon the older settlements. The ranging parties who visited the scene of devastation beheld, among the ruined farms and plantations, sights of unspeakable horror; and discovered, in the depths of the forest, the half-consumed bodies of men and women, still bound fast to the trees, where they had perished in the fiery torture.

Among the numerous war-parties which were now ravaging the borders, none was more destructive than a band, about sixty in number, which ascended the Kenawha, and pursued its desolating course among the settlements about the sources of that river. They passed valley after valley, sometimes attacking the inhabitants by surprise, and sometimes murdering them under the mask of friendship, until they came to the little settlement of Greenbrier, where nearly a hundred of the people were assembled at the fortified house of Archibald Glendenning. Seeing two or three Indians approach, whom they recognized as former acquaintances, they suffered them to enter without distrust; but the new-comers were soon joined by others, until the entire party were gathered in and around the buildings. Some suspicion was now awakened; and, in order to propitiate the dangerous guests, they were presented with the carcass of an elk lately brought in by the hunters. They immediately cut it up, and began to feast upon it. The backwoodsmen, with their families, were assembled in one large room; and finding themselves mingled among the Indians, and embarrassed by the presence of the women and children, they remained indecisive and irresolute. Meanwhile, an old woman, who sat in a corner of the room, and who had lately received some slight accidental injury, asked one of the warriors if he could cure the wound. He replied that he thought he could, and, to make good his words, killed her with his tomahawk. This was the signal for a scene of general butchery. A few persons made their escape; the rest were killed or captured. Glendenning snatched up one of his children, and rushed from the house, but was shot dead as he leaped the fence. A negro woman gained a place of concealment, whither she was followed by her screaming child; and, fearing lest the cries of the boy should betray her, she turned and killed him at a blow. Among the prisoners was the wife of Glendenning, a woman of a most masculine spirit, who, far from being overpowered by what she had seen, was excited to the extremity of rage, charged her captors with treachery, cowardice, and ingratitude, and assailed them with a tempest of abuse. Neither the tomahawk, which they brandished over her head, nor the scalp of her murdered husband, with which they struck her in the face, could silence the undaunted virago. When the party began their retreat, bearing with them a great quantity of plunder packed on the horses they had stolen, Glendenning's wife, with her infant child, was placed among a long train of captives guarded before and behind by the Indians. As they defiled along a narrow path which led through a gap in the mountains, she handed the child to the woman behind her, and, leaving it to its fate, slipped into the bushes and escaped. Being well acquainted with the woods, she succeeded, before nightfall, in reaching the spot where the ruins of her dwelling had not yet ceased to burn. Here she sought out the body of her husband, and covered it with fence-rails, to protect it from the wolves. When her task was complete, and when night closed around her, the bold spirit which had hitherto borne her up suddenly gave way. The recollection of the horrors she had witnessed, the presence of the dead, the darkness, the solitude, and the gloom of the surrounding forest, wrought upon her till her terror rose to ecstasy; and she remained until daybreak, crouched among the bushes, haunted by the threatening apparition of an armed man, who, to her heated imagination, seemed constantly approaching to murder her.

Some time after the butchery at Glendenning's house, an outrage was perpetrated, unmatched, in its fiend-like atrocity, through all the annals of the war. In a solitary place, deep within the settled limits of Pennsylvania, stood a small school-house, one of those rude structures of logs which, to this day, may be seen in some of the remote northern districts of New England. A man chancing to pass by was struck by the unwonted silence; and, pushing open the door, he looked in. In the centre lay the master, scalped and lifeless, with a Bible clasped in his hand; while around the room were strewn the bodies of his pupils, nine in number, miserably mangled, though one of them still retained a spark of life. It was afterwards known that the deed was committed by three or four warriors from a village near the Ohio; and it is but just to observe that, when they returned home, their conduct was disapproved by some of the tribe.

Page after page might be filled with records like these, for the letters and journals of the day are replete with narratives no less tragical. Districts were depopulated, and the progress of the country put back for years. Those small and scattered settlements which formed the feeble van of advancing civilization were involved in general destruction, and the fate of one may stand for the fate of all. In many a woody valley of the Alleghanies, the axe and firebrand of the settlers had laid a wide space open to the sun. Here and there, about the clearing, stood rough dwellings of logs, surrounded by enclosures and cornfields; while, farther out towards the verge of the woods, the fallen trees still cumbered the ground. From the clay-built chimneys the smoke rose in steady columns against the dark verge of the forest; and the afternoon sun, which brightened the tops of the mountains, had already left the valley in shadow. Before many hours elapsed, the night was lighted up with the glare of blazing dwellings, and the forest rang with the shrieks of the murdered inmates.

Among the records of that day's sufferings and disasters, none are more striking than the narratives of those whose lives were spared that they might be borne captive to the Indian villages. Exposed to the extremity of hardship, they were urged forward with the assurance of being tomahawked or burnt in case their strength should fail them. Some made their escape from the clutches of their tormentors; but of these not a few found reason to repent their success, lost in a trackless wilderness, and perishing miserably from hunger and exposure. Such attempts could seldom be made in the neighborhood of the settlements. It was only when the party had penetrated deep into the forest that their vigilance began to relax, and their captives were bound and guarded with less rigorous severity. Then, perhaps, when encamped by the side of some mountain brook, and when the warriors lay lost in sleep around their fire, the prisoner would cut or burn asunder the cords that bound his wrists and ankles, and glide stealthily into the woods. With noiseless celerity he pursues his flight over the fallen trunks, through the dense undergrowth, and the thousand pitfalls and impediments of the forest; now striking the rough, hard trunk of a tree, now tripping among the insidious network of vines and brambles. All is darkness around him, and through the black masses of foliage above he can catch but dubious and uncertain glimpses of the dull sky. At length, he can hear the gurgle of a neighboring brook; and, turning towards it, he wades along its pebbly channel, fearing lest the soft mould and rotten wood of the forest might retain traces enough to direct the bloodhound instinct of his pursuers. With the dawn of the misty and cloudy morning, he is still pushing on his way, when his attention is caught by the spectral figure of an ancient birch-tree, which, with its white bark hanging about it in tatters, seems wofully familiar to his eye. Among the neighboring bushes, a blue smoke curls faintly upward; and, to his horror and amazement, he recognizes the very fire from which he had fled a few hours before, and the piles of spruce boughs upon which the warriors had slept. They have gone, however, and are ranging the forest, in keen pursuit of the fugitive, who, in his blind flight amid the darkness, had circled round to the very point whence he set out; a mistake not uncommon with careless or inexperienced travellers in the woods. Almost in despair, he leaves the ill-omened spot, and directs his course eastward with greater care; the bark of the trees, rougher and thicker on the northern side, furnishing a precarious clew for his guidance. Around and above him nothing can be seen but the same endless monotony of brown trunks and green leaves, closing him in with an impervious screen. He reaches the foot of a mountain, and toils upwards against the rugged declivity; but when he stands on the summit, the view is still shut out by impenetrable thickets. High above them all shoots up the tall, gaunt stem of a blasted pine-tree; and, in his eager longing for a view of the surrounding objects, he strains every muscle to ascend. Dark, wild, and lonely, the wilderness stretches around him, half hidden in clouds, half open to the sight, mountain and valley, crag and glistening stream; but nowhere can he discern the trace of human hand or any hope of rest and harborage. Before he can look for relief, league upon league must be passed, without food to sustain or weapon to defend him. He descends the mountain, forcing his way through the undergrowth of laurel-bushes; while the clouds sink lower, and a storm of sleet and rain descends upon the waste. Through such scenes, and under such exposures, he presses onward, sustaining life with the aid of roots and berries or the flesh of reptiles. Perhaps, in the last extremity, some party of Rangers find him, and bring him to a place of refuge; perhaps, by his own efforts, he reaches some frontier post, where rough lodging and rough fare seem to him unheard-of luxury; or perhaps, spent with fatigue and famine, he perishes in despair, a meagre banquet for the wolves.

Within two or three weeks after the war had broken out, the older towns and settlements of Pennsylvania were crowded with refugees from the deserted frontier, reduced, in many cases, to the extremity of destitution. Sermons were preached in their behalf at Philadelphia; the religious societies united for their relief, and liberal contributions were added by individuals. While private aid was thus generously bestowed upon the sufferers, the government showed no such promptness in arresting the public calamity. Early in July, Governor Hamilton had convoked the Assembly, and, representing the distress of the borders, had urged them to take measures of defence. But the provincial government of Pennsylvania was more conducive to prosperity in time of peace than to efficiency in time of war. The Quakers, who held a majority in the Assembly, were from principle and practice the reverse of warlike, and, regarding the Indians with a blind partiality, were reluctant to take measures against them. Proud, and with some reason, of the justice and humanity which had marked their conduct towards the Indian race, they had learned to regard themselves as its advocates and patrons, and their zeal was greatly sharpened by opposition and political prejudice. They now pretended that the accounts from the frontier were grossly exaggerated; and, finding this ground untenable, they alleged, with better show of reason, that the Indians were driven into hostility by the ill-treatment of the proprietaries and their partisans. They recognized, however, the necessity of defensive measures, and accordingly passed a bill for raising and equipping a force of seven hundred men, to be composed of frontier farmers, and to be kept in pay only during the time of harvest. They were not to leave the settled parts of the province to engage in offensive operations of any kind, nor even to perform garrison duty; their sole object being to enable the people to gather in their crops unmolested.

This force was divided into numerous small detached parties, who were stationed here and there at farm-houses and hamlets on both sides of the Susquehanna, with orders to range the woods daily from post to post, thus forming a feeble chain of defence across the whole frontier. The two companies assigned to Lancaster County were placed under the command of a clergyman, John Elder, pastor of the Presbyterian Church of Paxton; a man of worth and education, and held in great respect upon the borders. He discharged his military functions with address and judgment, drawing a cordon of troops across the front of the county, and preserving the inhabitants free from attack for a considerable time.

The feeble measures adopted by the Pennsylvania Assembly highly excited the wrath of Sir Jeffrey Amherst, and he did not hesitate to give his feelings an emphatic expression. "The conduct of the Pennsylvania legislature," he writes, "is altogether so infatuated and stupidly obstinate, that I want words to express my indignation thereat; but the colony of Virginia, I hope, will have the honor of not only driving the enemy from its own settlements, but that of protecting those of its neighbors who have not spirit to defend themselves."

Virginia did, in truth, exhibit a vigor and activity not unworthy of praise. Unlike Pennsylvania, she had the advantage of an existing militia law; and the House of Burgesses was neither embarrassed by scruples against the shedding of blood, nor by any peculiar tenderness towards the Indian race. The House, however, was not immediately summoned together; and the governor and council, without waiting to consult the Burgesses, called out a thousand of the militia, five hundred of whom were assigned to the command of Colonel Stephen, and an equal number to that of Major Lewis. The presence of these men, most of whom were woodsmen and hunters, restored order and confidence to the distracted borders; and the inhabitants, before pent up in their forts, or flying before the enemy, now took the field, in conjunction with the militia. Many severe actions were fought, but it seldom happened that the Indians could stand their ground against the border riflemen. The latter were uniformly victorious until the end of the summer; when Captains Moffat and Phillips, with sixty men, were lured into an ambuscade, and routed, with the loss of half their number. A few weeks after, they took an ample revenge. Learning by their scouts that more than a hundred warriors were encamped near Jackson's River, preparing to attack the settlements, they advanced secretly to the spot, and set upon them with such fury that the whole party broke away and fled; leaving weapons, provisions, articles of dress, and implements of magic, in the hands of the victors.

Meanwhile the frontier people of Pennsylvania, finding that they could hope for little aid from government, bestirred themselves with admirable spirit in their own defence. The march of Bouquet, and the victory of Bushy Run, caused a temporary lull in the storm, thus enabling some of the bolder inhabitants, who had fled to Shippensburg, Carlisle, and other places of refuge, to return to their farms, where they determined, if possible, to remain. With this resolution, the people of the Great Cove, and the adjacent valleys beyond Shippensburg, raised among themselves a small body of riflemen, which they placed under the command of James Smith; a man whose resolute and daring character, no less than the native vigor of his intellect, gave him great popularity and influence with the borderers. Having been, for several years, a prisoner among the Indians, he was thoroughly acquainted with their mode of fighting. He trained his men in the Indian tactics and discipline, and directed them to assume the dress of warriors, and paint their faces red and black, so that, in appearance, they were hardly distinguishable from the enemy. Thus equipped, they scoured the woods in front of the settlements, had various skirmishes with the enemy, and discharged their difficult task with such success that the inhabitants of the neighborhood were not again driven from their homes.

The attacks on the Pennsylvania frontier were known to proceed, in great measure, from several Indian villages, situated high up the west branch of the Susquehanna, and inhabited by a debauched rabble composed of various tribes, of whom the most conspicuous were Delawares. To root out this nest of banditti would be the most effectual means of protecting the settlements, and a hundred and ten men offered themselves for the enterprise. They marched about the end of August; but on their way along the banks of the Susquehanna, they encountered fifty warriors, advancing against the borders. The Indians had the first fire, and drove in the vanguard of the white men. A hot fight ensued. The warriors fought naked, painted black from head to foot; so that, as they leaped among the trees, they seemed to their opponents like demons of the forest. They were driven back with heavy loss; and the volunteers returned in triumph, though without accomplishing the object of the expedition; for which, indeed, their numbers were scarcely adequate.

Within a few weeks after their return, Colonel Armstrong, a veteran partisan of the French war, raised three hundred men, the best in

Cumberland County, with a view to the effectual destruction of the Susquehanna villages. Leaving their rendezvous at the crossings of the Juniata, about the first of October, they arrived on the sixth at the Great Island, high up the west branch. On or near this island were situated the principal villages of the enemy. But the Indians had vanished, abandoning their houses, their cornfields, their stolen horses and cattle, and the accumulated spoil of the settlements. Leaving a detachment to burn the towns and lay waste the fields, Armstrong, with the main body of his men, followed close on the trail of the fugitives; and, pursuing them through a rugged and difficult country, soon arrived at another village, thirty miles above the former. His scouts informed him that the place was full of Indians; and his men, forming a circle around it, rushed in upon the cabins at a given signal. The Indians were gone, having stolen away in such haste that the hominy and bear's meat, prepared for their meal, were found smoking upon their dishes of birch-bark. Having burned the place to the ground, the party returned to the Great Island; and, rejoining their companions, descended the Susquehanna, reaching Fort Augusta in a wretched condition, fatigued, half famished, and quarrelling among themselves.

Scarcely were they returned, when another expedition was set on foot, in which a portion of them were persuaded to take part. During the previous year, a body of settlers from Connecticut had possessed themselves of the valley of Wyoming, on the east branch of the Susquehanna, in defiance of the government of Pennsylvania, and to the great displeasure of the Indians. The object of the expedition was to remove these settlers, and destroy their corn and provisions, which might otherwise fall into the hands of the enemy. The party, composed chiefly of volunteers from Lancaster County, set out from Harris's Ferry, under the command of Major Clayton, and reached Wyoming on the seventeenth of October. They were too late. Two days before their arrival, a massacre had been perpetrated, the fitting precursor of that subsequent scene of blood which, embalmed in the poetic romance of Campbell, has made the name of Wyoming a household word. The settlement was a pile of ashes and cinders, and the bodies of its miserable inhabitants offered frightful proof of the cruelties inflicted upon them. A large war-party had fallen upon the place, killed and carried off more than twenty of the people, and driven the rest, men, women, and children, in terror to the mountains. Gaining a point which commanded the whole expanse of the valley below, the fugitives looked back, and saw the smoke rolling up in volumes from their burning homes; while the Indians could be discerned roaming about in quest of plunder, or feasting in groups upon the slaughtered cattle. One of the principal settlers, a man named Hopkins, was separated from the rest, and driven into the woods. Finding himself closely pursued, he crept into the hollow trunk of a fallen tree, while the Indians passed without observing him. They soon returned to the spot, and ranged the surrounding woods like hounds at fault; two of them approaching so near, that, as Hopkins declared, he could hear the bullets rattle in their pouches. The search was unavailing; but the fugitive did not venture from his place of concealment until extreme hunger forced him to return to the ruined settlement in search of food. The Indians had abandoned it some time before; and, having found means to restore his exhausted strength, he directed his course towards the settlements of the Delaware, which he reached after many days of wandering.

Having buried the dead bodies of those who had fallen in the massacre, Clayton and his party returned to the settlements. The Quakers, who seemed resolved that they would neither defend the people of the frontier nor allow them to defend themselves, vehemently inveighed against the several expeditions up the Susquehanna, and denounced them as seditious and murderous. Urged by their blind prejudice in favor of the Indians, they insisted that the bands of the Upper Susquehanna were friendly to the English; whereas, with the single exception of a few Moravian converts near Wyoming, who had not been molested by the whites, there could be no rational doubt that these savages nourished a rancorous and malignant hatred against the province. But the Quakers, removed by their situation from all fear of the tomahawk, securely vented their spite against the borderers, and doggedly closed their ears to the truth. Meanwhile, the people of the frontier besieged the Assembly with petitions for relief; but little heed was given to their complaints.

Sir Jeffrey Amherst had recently resigned his office of commander-in-chief; and General Gage, a man of less efficiency than his predecessor, was appointed to succeed him. Immediately before his departure for England, Amherst had reluctantly condescended to ask the several provinces for troops to march against the Indians early in the spring, and the first act of Gage was to confirm this requisition. New York was called upon to furnish fourteen hundred men, and New Jersey six hundred. The demand was granted, on condition that the New England provinces should also contribute a just proportion to the general defence. This condition was complied with, and the troops were raised.

Pennsylvania had been required to furnish a thousand men; but in this quarter many difficulties intervened. The Assembly of the province, never prompt to vote supplies for military purposes, was now embroiled in that obstinate quarrel with the proprietors, which for years past had clogged all the wheels of government. The proprietors insisted on certain pretended rights, which the Assembly strenuously opposed; and the governors, who represented the proprietary interest, were bound by imperative instructions to assert these claims, in spite of all opposition. On the present occasion, the chief point of dispute related to the taxation of the proprietary estates;

the governor, in conformity with his instructions, demanding that they should be assessed at a lower rate than other lands of equal value in the province. The Assembly stood their ground, and refused to remove the obnoxious clauses in the supply bill. Message after message passed between the House and the governor; mutual recrimination ensued, and ill blood was engendered. The frontiers might have been left to their misery but for certain events which, during the winter, threw the whole province into disorder, and acted like magic on the minds of the stubborn legislators.

These events may be ascribed, in some degree, to the renewed activity of the enemy; who, during a great part of the autumn, had left the borders in comparative quiet. As the winter closed in, their attacks became more frequent; and districts, repeopled during the interval of calm, were again made desolate. Again the valleys were illumined by the flames of burning houses, and families fled shivering through the biting air of the winter night, while the fires behind them shed a ruddy glow upon the snow-covered mountains. The scouts, who on snowshoes explored the track of the marauders, found the bodies of their victims lying in the forest, stripped naked, and frozen to marble hardness. The distress, wrath, and terror of the borderers produced results sufficiently remarkable to deserve a separate examination.

THE INDIANS RAISE THE SIEGE OF DETROIT

1763 to 1764

I return to the long-forgotten garrison of Detroit, which was left still beleaguered by an increasing multitude of savages, and disheartened by the defeat of Captain Dalzell's detachment. The schooner, so boldly defended by her crew against a force of more than twenty times their number, brought to the fort a much-needed supply of provisions. It was not, however, adequate to the wants of the garrison; and the whole were put upon the shortest possible allowance.

It was now the end of September. The Indians, with unexampled pertinacity, had pressed the siege since the beginning of May; but at length their constancy began to fail. The tidings had reached them that Major Wilkins, with a strong force, was on his way to Detroit. They feared the consequences of an attack, especially as their ammunition was almost exhausted; and, by this time, most of them were inclined to sue for peace, as the easiest mode of gaining safety for themselves, and at the same time lulling the English into security. They thought that by this means they might retire unmolested to their wintering grounds, and renew the war with good hope of success in the spring.

Accordingly, on the twelfth of October, Wapocomoguth, great chief of the Mississaugas, a branch of the Ojibwas, living within the present limits of Upper Canada, came to the fort with a pipe of peace. He began his speech to Major Gladwyn, with the glaring falsehood that he and his people had always been friends of the English. They were now, he added, anxious to conclude a formal treaty of lasting peace and amity. He next declared that he had been sent as deputy by the Pottawattamies, Ojibwas, and Wyandots, who had instructed him to say that they sincerely repented of their bad conduct, asked forgiveness, and humbly begged for peace. Gladwyn perfectly understood the hollowness of these professions, but the circumstances in which he was placed made it expedient to listen to their overtures. His garrison was threatened with famine, and it was impossible to procure provisions while completely surrounded by hostile Indians. He therefore replied, that, though he was not empowered to grant peace, he would still consent to a truce. The Mississauga deputy left the fort with this reply, and Gladwyn immediately took advantage of this lull in the storm to collect provisions among the Canadians; an attempt in which he succeeded so well that the fort was soon furnished with a tolerable supply for the winter.

The Ottawas alone, animated by Pontiac, had refused to ask for peace, and still persisted in a course of petty hostilities. They fired at intervals on the English foraging parties, until, on the thirty-first of October, an unexpected blow was given to the hopes of their great chief. French messengers came to Detroit with a letter from M. Neyon, commandant of Fort Chartres, the principal post in the Illinois country. This letter was one of those which, on demand of General Amherst, Neyon, with a very bad grace, had sent to the different Indian tribes. It assured Pontiac that he could expect no assistance from the French; that they and the English were now at peace, and regarded each other as brothers; and that the Indians had better abandon hostilities which could lead to no good result. The emotions of Pontiac at receiving this message may be conceived. His long-cherished hopes of assistance from the French were swept away at once, and he saw himself and his people thrown back upon their own slender resources. His cause was lost. At least, there was no present hope for him but in dissimulation. True to his Indian nature, he would put on a mask of peace, and bide his time. On the day after the arrival of the message from Neyon, Gladwyn wrote as follows to Amherst: "This moment I received a message from Pondiac, telling me that he should send to all the nations concerned in the war to bury the hatchet; and he hopes your Excellency will forget what has passed."

Having soothed the English commander with these hollow overtures, Pontiac withdrew with some of his chiefs to the Maumee, to stir up the Indians in that quarter, and renew the war in the spring.

About the middle of November, not many days after Pontiac's departure, two friendly Wyandot Indians from the ancient settlement at Lorette, near Quebec, crossed the river, and asked admittance into the fort. One of them then unslung his powder-horn, and, taking out a false bottom, disclosed a closely folded letter, which he gave to Major Gladwyn. The letter was from Major Wilkins, and contained the disastrous news that the detachment under his command had been overtaken by a storm, that many of the boats had been wrecked, that seventy men had perished, that all the stores and ammunition had been destroyed, and the detachment forced to return to Niagara. This intelligence had an effect upon the garrison which rendered the prospect of the cold and cheerless winter yet more dreary and forlorn.

The summer had long since drawn to a close, and the verdant landscape around Detroit had undergone an ominous transformation. Touched by the first October frosts, the forest glowed like a bed of tulips; and, all along the river bank, the painted foliage, brightened by the autumnal sun, reflected its mingled colors upon the dark water below. The western wind was fraught with life and exhilaration; and in the clear, sharp air, the form of the fish-hawk, sailing over the distant headland, seemed almost within range of the sportsman's gun.

A week or two elapsed, and then succeeded that gentler season which bears among us the name of the Indian summer; when a light haze rests upon the morning landscape, and the many-colored woods seem wrapped in the thin drapery of a veil; when the air is mild and calm as that of early June, and at evening the sun goes down amid a warm, voluptuous beauty, that may well outrival the softest tints of Italy. But through all the still and breathless afternoon the leaves have fallen fast in the woods, like flakes of snow; and every thing betokens that the last melancholy change is at hand. And, in truth, on the morrow the sky is overspread with cold and stormy clouds; and a raw, piercing wind blows angrily from the north-east. The shivering sentinel quickens his step along the rampart, and the half-naked Indian folds his tattered blanket close around him. The shrivelled leaves are blown from the trees, and soon the gusts are whistling and howling amid gray, naked twigs and mossy branches. Here and there, indeed, the beech-tree, as the wind sweeps among its rigid boughs, shakes its pale assemblage of crisp and rustling leaves. The pines and firs, with their rough tops of dark evergreen, bend and moan in the wind; and the crow caws sullenly, as, struggling against the gusts, he flaps his black wings above the denuded woods.

The vicinity of Detroit was now almost abandoned by its besiegers, who had scattered among the forests to seek sustenance through the winter for themselves and their families. Unlike the buffalo-hunting tribes of the western plains, they could not at this season remain together in large bodies. The comparative scarcity of game forced them to separate into small bands, or even into single families. Some steered their canoes far northward, across Lake Huron; while others turned westward, and struck into the great wilderness of Michigan. Wandering among forests, bleak, cheerless, and choked with snow, now famishing with want, now cloyed with repletion, they passed the dull, cold winter. The chase yielded their only subsistence; and the slender lodges, borne on the backs of the squaws, were their only shelter. Encamped at intervals by the margin of some frozen lake, surrounded by all that is most stern and dreary in the aspects of nature, they were subjected to every hardship, and endured all with stubborn stoicism. Sometimes, during the frosty night, they were gathered in groups about the flickering lodge-fire, listening to traditions of their forefathers, and wild tales of magic and incantation. Perhaps, before the season was past, some bloody feud broke out among them; perhaps they were assailed by their ancient enemies the Dahcotah; or perhaps some sinister omen or evil dream spread more terror through the camp than the presence of an actual danger would have awakened. With the return of spring, the scattered parties once more united, and moved towards Detroit, to indulge their unforgotten hatred against the English.

Detroit had been the central point of the Indian operations; its capture had been their favorite project; around it they had concentrated their greatest force, and the failure of the attempt proved disastrous to their cause. Upon the Six Nations, more especially, it produced a marked effect. The friendly tribes of this confederacy were confirmed in their friendship, while the hostile Senecas began to lose heart. Availing himself of this state of things, Sir William Johnson, about the middle of the winter, persuaded a number of Six Nation warriors, by dint of gifts and promises, to go out against the enemy. He stimulated their zeal by offering rewards of fifty dollars for the heads of the two principal Delaware chiefs. Two hundred of them, accompanied by a few provincials, left the Oneida country during the month of February, and directed their course southward. They had been out but a few days, when they found an encampment of forty Delawares, commanded by a formidable chief, known as Captain Bull, who, with his warriors, was on his way to attack the settlements. They surrounded the camp undiscovered, during the night, and at dawn of day raised the war-whoop and rushed in. The astonished Delawares had no time to snatch their arms. They were all made prisoners, taken to Albany, and thence sent down to New York, where they were conducted, under a strong guard, to the common jail; the mob crowding round them as they passed, and admiring the sullen ferocity of their countenances. Not long after this success, Captain Montour, with a party of provincials and Six Nation warriors, destroyed the town of Kanestio, and other hostile villages, on the upper branches of the Susquehanna. This blow, inflicted by supposed friends, produced more effect upon the enemy than greater reverses would have done, if encountered at the hands of the English alone.

The calamities which overwhelmed the borders of the middle provinces were not unfelt at the south. It was happy for the people of the Carolinas that the Cherokees, who had broken out against them three years before, had at that time received a chastisement which they could never forget, and from which they had not yet begun to recover. They were thus compelled to remain comparatively quiet; while the ancient feud between them and the northern tribes would, under any circumstances, have prevented their uniting with the latter. The contagion of the war reached them, however, and they perpetrated numerous murders; while the neighboring nation of the Creeks rose in open hostility, and committed formidable ravages. Towards the north, the Indian tribes were compelled, by their position, to remain tranquil, yet they showed many signs of uneasiness; and those of Nova Scotia caused great alarm, by mustering in large bodies in the neighborhood of Halifax. The excitement among them was temporary, and they dispersed without attempting mischief.

THE PAXTON MEN

1763

Along the thinly settled borders, two thousand persons had been killed, or carried off, and nearly an equal number of families driven from their homes. The frontier people of Pennsylvania, goaded to desperation by long-continued suffering, were divided between rage against the Indians, and resentment against the Quakers, who had yielded them cold sympathy and inefficient aid. The horror and fear, grief and fury, with which these men looked upon the mangled remains of friends and relatives, set language at defiance. They were of a rude and hardy stamp, hunters, scouts, rangers, Indian traders, and backwoods farmers, who had grown up with arms in their hands, and been trained under all the influences of the warlike frontier. They fiercely complained that they were interposed as a barrier between the rest of the province and a ferocious enemy; and that they were sacrificed to the safety of men who looked with indifference on their miseries, and lost no opportunity to extenuate and smooth away the cruelties of their destroyers. They declared that the Quakers would go farther to befriend a murdering Delaware than to succor a fellow-countryman; that they loved red blood better than white, and a pagan better than a Presbyterian. The Pennsylvania borderers were, as we have seen, chiefly the descendants of Presbyterian emigrants from the north of Ireland. They had inherited some portion of their forefathers' sectarian zeal, which, while it did nothing to soften the barbarity of their manners, served to inflame their animosity against the Quakers, and added bitterness to their just complaints. It supplied, moreover, a convenient sanction for the indulgence of their hatred and vengeance; for, in the general turmoil of their passions, fanaticism too was awakened, and they interpreted the command that

Joshua should destroy the heathen into an injunction that they should exterminate the Indians.

The prevailing excitement was not confined to the vulgar. Even the clergy and the chief magistrates shared it; and while they lamented the excess of the popular resentment, they maintained that the general complaints were founded in justice. Viewing all the circumstances, it is not greatly to be wondered at that some of the more violent class were inflamed to the commission of atrocities which bear no very favorable comparison with those of the Indians themselves.

It is not easy for those living in the tranquillity of polished life fully to conceive the depth and force of that unquenchable, indiscriminate hate, which Indian outrages can awaken in those who have suffered them. The chronicles of the American borders are filled with the deeds of men, who, having lost all by the merciless tomahawk, have lived for vengeance alone; and such men will never cease to exist so long as a hostile tribe remains within striking distance of an American settlement. Never was this hatred more deep or more general than on the Pennsylvania frontier at this period; and never, perhaps, did so many collateral causes unite to inflame it to madness. It was not long in finding a vent.

Near the Susquehanna, and at no great distance from the town of Lancaster, was a spot known as the Manor of Conestoga; where a small band of Indians, speaking the Iroquois tongue, had been seated since the first settlement of the province. William Penn had visited and made a treaty with them, which had been confirmed by several succeeding governors, so that the band had always remained on terms of friendship with the English. Yet, like other Indian communities in the neighborhood of the whites, they had dwindled in numbers and prosperity, until they were reduced to twenty persons; who inhabited a cluster of squalid cabins, and lived by beggary and the sale of brooms, baskets, and wooden ladles, made by the women. The men spent a small part of their time in hunting, and lounged away the rest in idleness. In the immediate neighborhood, they were commonly regarded as harmless vagabonds; but elsewhere a more unfavorable opinion was entertained, and they were looked upon as secretly abetting the enemy, acting as spies, giving shelter to scalping-parties, and even aiding them in their depredations. That these suspicions were not wholly unfounded is shown by a conclusive mass of evidence, though it is probable that the treachery was confined to one or two individuals. The exasperated frontiersmen were not in a mood to discriminate, and the innocent were destined to share the fate of the guilty.

On the east bank of the Susquehanna, at some distance above Conestoga, stood the little town of Paxton; a place which, since the French war, had occupied a position of extreme exposure. In the year 1755 the Indians had burned it to the ground, killing many of the inhabitants, and reducing the rest to poverty. It had since been rebuilt; but its tenants were the relatives of those who had perished, and the bitterness of the recollection was enhanced by the sense of their own more recent sufferings. Mention has before been made of John Elder, the Presbyterian minister of this place; a man whose worth, good sense, and superior education gave him the character of counsellor and director throughout the neighborhood, and caused him to be known and esteemed even in Philadelphia. His position was a peculiar one. From the rough pulpit of his little church, he had often preached to an assembly of armed men, while scouts and sentinels were stationed without, to give warning of the enemy's approach. The men of Paxton, under the auspices of their pastor, formed themselves into a body of rangers, who became noted for their zeal and efficiency in defending the borders. One of their principal leaders was Matthew Smith, a man who had influence and popularity among his associates, and was not without pretensions to education; while he shared a full proportion of the general hatred against Indians, and suspicion against the band of Conestoga.

Towards the middle of December, a scout came to the house of Smith, and reported that an Indian, known to have committed depredations in the neighborhood, had been traced to Conestoga. Smith's resolution was taken at once. He called five of his companions; and, having armed and mounted, they set out for the Indian settlement. They reached it early in the night; and Smith, leaving his horse in charge of the others, crawled forward, rifle in hand, to reconnoitre; when he saw, or fancied he saw, a number of armed warriors in the cabins. Upon this discovery he withdrew, and rejoined his associates. Believing themselves too weak for an attack, the party returned to Paxton. Their blood was up, and they determined to extirpate the Conestogas. Messengers went abroad through the neighborhood; and, on the following day, about fifty armed and mounted men, chiefly from the towns of Paxton and Donegal, assembled at the place agreed upon. Led by Matthew Smith, they took the road to Conestoga, where they arrived a little before daybreak, on the morning of the fourteenth. As they drew near, they discerned the light of a fire in one of the cabins, gleaming across the snow. Leaving their horses in the forest, they separated into small parties, and advanced on several sides at once. Though they moved with some caution, the sound of their footsteps or their voices caught the ear of an Indian; and they saw him issue from one of the cabins, and walk forward in the direction of the noise. He came so near that one of the men fancied that he recognized him. "He is the one that killed my mother," he exclaimed with an oath; and, firing his rifle, brought the Indian down. With a general shout, the furious ruffians burst into the cabins, and shot, stabbed, and hacked to death all whom they found there. It happened that only six Indians were in the place; the rest, in accordance with their vagrant habits, being scattered about the neighborhood. Thus baulked of their complete vengeance, the murderers seized upon what little booty they could find, set the cabins on fire, and departed at dawn of day.

The morning was cold and murky. Snow was falling, and already lay deep upon the ground; and, as they urged their horses through the drifts, they were met by one Thomas Wright, who, struck by their appearance, stopped to converse with them. They freely told him what they had done; and, on his expressing surprise and horror, one of them demanded if he believed in the Bible, and if the Scripture did not command that the heathen should be destroyed.

They soon after separated, dispersing among the farmhouses, to procure food for themselves and their horses. Several rode to the house of Robert Barber, a prominent settler in the neighborhood; who, seeing the strangers stamping their feet and shaking the snow from their blanket coats, invited them to enter, and offered them refreshment. Having remained for a short time seated before his fire, they remounted and rode off through the snowstorm. A boy of the family, who had gone to look at the horses of the visitors, came in and declared that he had seen a tomahawk, covered with blood, hanging from each man's saddle; and that a small gun, belonging to one of the Indian children, had been leaning against the fence. Barber at once guessed the truth, and, with several of his neighbors, proceeded to the Indian settlement, where they found the solid log cabins still on fire. They buried the remains of the victims, which Barber compared in appearance to half-burnt logs. While they were thus engaged, the sheriff of Lancaster, with a party of men, arrived on the spot; and the first care of the officer was to send through the neighborhood to collect the Indians, fourteen in number, who had escaped the massacre. This was soon accomplished. The unhappy survivors, learning the fate of their friends and relatives, were in great terror for their own lives, and earnestly begged protection. They were conducted to Lancaster, where, amid great excitement, they were lodged in the county jail, a strong stone building, which it was thought would afford the surest refuge.

An express was despatched to Philadelphia with news of the massacre; on hearing which, the governor issued a proclamation denouncing the act, and offering a reward for the discovery of the perpetrators. Undaunted by this measure, and enraged that any of their victims should have escaped, the Paxton men determined to continue the work they had begun. In this resolution they were confirmed by the prevailing impression, that an Indian known to have murdered the relatives of one of their number was among those who had received the protection of the magistrates at Lancaster. They sent forward a spy to gain intelligence, and, on his return, once more met at their rendezvous. On this occasion, their nominal leader was Lazarus Stewart, who was esteemed upon the borders as a brave and active young man; and who, there is strong reason to believe, entertained no worse design than that of seizing the obnoxious Indian, carrying him to Carlisle, and there putting him to death, in case he should be identified as the murderer. Most of his followers, however, hardened amidst war and bloodshed, were bent on indiscriminate slaughter; a purpose which they concealed from their more moderate associates.

Early on the twenty-seventh of December, the party, about fifty in number, left Paxton on their desperate errand. Elder had used all his influence to divert them from their design; and now, seeing them depart, he mounted his horse, overtook them, and addressed them with the most earnest remonstrance. Finding his words unheeded, he drew up his horse across the narrow road in front, and charged them, on his authority as their pastor, to return. Upon this, Matthew Smith rode forward, and, pointing his rifle at the breast of Elder's horse, threatened to fire unless he drew him aside, and gave room to pass. The clergyman was forced to comply, and the party proceeded.

At about three o'clock in the afternoon, the rioters, armed with rifle, knife, and tomahawk, rode at a gallop into Lancaster; turned their horses into the yard of the public house, ran to the jail, burst open the door, and rushed tumultuously in. The fourteen Indians were in a small yard adjacent to the building, surrounded by high stone walls. Hearing the shouts of the mob, and startled by the apparition of armed men in the doorway, two or three of them snatched up billets of wood in self-defence. Whatever may have been the purpose of the Paxton men, this show of resistance banished every thought of forbearance; and the foremost, rushing forward, fired their rifles among the crowd of Indians. In a moment more, the yard was filled with ruffians, shouting, cursing, and firing upon the cowering wretches; holding the muzzles of their pieces, in some instances, so near their victims' heads that the brains were scattered by the explosion. The work was soon finished. The bodies of men, women, and children, mangled with outrageous brutality, lay scattered about the yard; and the murderers were gone.

When the first alarm was given, the magistrates were in the church, attending the Christmas service, which had been postponed on the twenty-fifth. The door was flung open, and the voice of a man half breathless was heard in broken exclamations, "Murder—the jail—the Paxton Boys—the Indians."

The assembly broke up in disorder, and Shippen, the principal magistrate, hastened towards the scene of riot; but, before he could reach it, all was finished, and the murderers were galloping in a body from the town. The sheriff and the coroner had mingled among the rioters, aiding and abetting them, as their enemies affirm, but, according to their own statement, vainly risking their lives to restore order. A company of Highland soldiers, on their way from Fort Pitt to Philadelphia, were encamped near the town.

Their commander, Captain Robertson, afterwards declared that he put himself in the way of the magistrates, expecting that they would call upon him to aid the civil authority; while, on the contrary, several of the inhabitants testify, that, when they urged him to interfere, he replied with an oath that his men had suffered enough from Indians already, and should not stir hand or foot to save them. Be this as it may, it seems certain that neither soldiers nor magistrates, with their best exertions, could have availed to prevent the massacre; for so well was the plan concerted, that, within ten or twelve minutes after the alarm, the Indians were dead, and the murderers mounted to depart.

The people crowded into the jail-yard to gaze upon the miserable spectacle; and, when their curiosity was sated, the bodies were gathered together, and buried not far from the town, where they reposed three quarters of a century; until, at length, the bones were disinterred in preparing the foundation for a railroad.

The tidings of this massacre threw the country into a ferment. Various opinions were expressed; but, in the border counties, even the most sober and moderate regarded it, not as a wilful and deliberate crime, but as the mistaken act of rash men, fevered to desperation by wrongs and sufferings.

When the news reached Philadelphia, a clamorous outcry rose from the Quakers, who could find no words to express their horror and detestation. They assailed not the rioters only, but the whole Presbyterian sect, with a tempest of abuse, not the less virulent for being vented in the name of philanthropy and religion. The governor again issued a proclamation, offering rewards for the detection and arrest of the murderers; but the latter, far from shrinking into concealment, proclaimed their deed in the face of day, boasted the achievement, and defended it by reason and Scripture. So great was the excitement in the frontier counties, and so deep the sympathy with the rioters, that to arrest them would have required the employment of a strong military force, an experiment far too dangerous to be tried. Nothing of the kind was attempted until nearly eight years afterwards, when Lazarus Stewart was apprehended on the charge of murdering the Indians of Conestoga. Learning that his trial was to take place, not in the county where the act was committed, but in Philadelphia, and thence judging that his condemnation was certain, he broke jail and escaped. Having written a declaration to justify his conduct, he called his old associates around him, set the provincial government of Pennsylvania at defiance, and withdrew to Wyoming with his band. Here he joined the settlers recently arrived from Connecticut, and thenceforth played a conspicuous part in the eventful history of that remarkable spot.

After the massacre at Conestoga, the excitement in the frontier counties, far from subsiding, increased in violence daily; and various circumstances conspired to inflame it. The principal of these was the course pursued by the provincial government towards the Christian Indians attached to the Moravian missions. Many years had elapsed since the Moravians began the task of converting the Indians of Pennsylvania, and their steadfast energy and regulated zeal had been crowned with success. Several thriving settlements of their converts had sprung up in the valley of the Lehigh, when the opening of the French war, in 1755, involved them in unlooked-for calamities. These unhappy neutrals, between the French and Indians on the one side, and the English on the other, excited the enmity of both; and while from the west they were threatened by the hatchets of their own countrymen, they were menaced on the east by the no less formidable vengeance of the white settlers, who, in their distress and terror, never doubted that the Moravian converts were in league with the enemy. The popular rage against them at length grew so furious, that their destruction was resolved upon. The settlers assembled and advanced against the Moravian community of Gnadenhutten; but the French and Indians gained the first blow, and, descending upon the doomed settlement, utterly destroyed it. This disaster, deplorable as it was in itself, proved the safety of the other Moravian settlements, by making it fully apparent that their inhabitants were not in league with the enemy. They were suffered to remain unmolested for several years; but with the murders that ushered in Pontiac's war, in 1763, the former suspicion revived, and the expediency of destroying the Moravian Indians was openly debated. Towards the end of the summer, several outrages were committed upon the settlers in the neighborhood, and the Moravian Indians were loudly accused of taking part in them. These charges were never fully confuted; and, taking into view the harsh treatment which the converts had always experienced from the whites, it is highly probable that some of them were disposed to sympathize with their heathen countrymen, who are known to have courted their alliance. The Moravians had, however, excited in their converts a high degree of religious enthusiasm; which, directed as it was by the teachings of the missionaries, went farther than any thing else could have done to soften their national prejudices, and wean them from their warlike habits.

About three months before the massacre at Conestoga, a party of drunken Rangers, fired by the general resentment against the Moravian Indians, murdered several of them, both men and women, whom they found sleeping in a barn. Not long after, the same party of Rangers were, in their turn, surprised and killed, some peaceful settlers of the neighborhood sharing their fate. This act was at once ascribed, justly or unjustly, to the vengeance of the converted Indians, relatives of the murdered; and the frontier people, who, like the Paxton men, were chiefly Scotch and Irish Presbyterians, resolved that the objects of their suspicion should live no longer. At this time, the Moravian converts consisted of two communities, those of Nain and Wecquetank, near the Lehigh; and to these may be added a third, at Wyalusing, near Wyoming. The latter, from its distant situation, was, for the present, safe; but the two former were in imminent peril, and the inhabitants, in mortal terror for their lives, stood day and night on the watch.

At length, about the tenth of October, a gang of armed men approached Wecquetank, and encamped in the woods, at no great distance. They intended to make their attack under favor of the darkness; but before evening a storm, which to the missionaries seemed providential, descended with such violence, that the fires of the hostile camp were extinguished in a moment, the ammunition of the men wet, and the plan defeated.

After so narrow an escape, it was apparent that flight was the only resource. The terrified congregation of Wecquetank broke up on the following day; and, under the charge of their missionary, Bernard Grube, removed to the Moravian town of Nazareth, where it was hoped they might remain in safety.

In the mean time, the charges against the Moravian converts had been laid before the provincial Assembly; and, to secure the safety of the frontier people, it was judged expedient to disarm the suspected Indians, and remove them to a part of the province where it would be beyond their power to do mischief. The motion was passed in the Assembly with little dissent; the Quakers supporting it from regard to the safety of the Indians, and their opponents from regard to the safety of the whites. The order for removal reached its destination on the sixth of November; and the Indians, reluctantly yielding up their arms, prepared for departure. When a sermon had been preached before the united congregations, and a hymn sung in which all took part, the unfortunate exiles set out on their forlorn pilgrimage; the aged, the young, the sick, and the blind, borne in wagons, while the rest journeyed on foot. Their total number, including the band from Wyalusing, which joined them after they reached Philadelphia, was about a hundred and forty. At every village and hamlet which they passed on their way, they were greeted with threats and curses; nor did the temper of the people improve as they advanced, for, when they came to Germantown, the mob could scarcely be restrained from attacking them. On reaching Philadelphia, they were conducted, amidst the yells and hootings of the rabble, to the barracks, which had been intended to receive them; but the soldiers, who outdid the mob in their hatred of Indians, refused to admit them, and set the orders of the governor at defiance. From ten o'clock in the morning until three in the afternoon, the persecuted exiles remained drawn up in the square before the barracks, surrounded by a multitude who never ceased to abuse and threaten them; but wherever the broad hat of a Quaker was seen in the crowd, there they felt the assurance of a friend,—a friend, who, both out of love for them, and aversion to their enemies, would spare no efforts in their behalf. The soldiers continued refractory, and the Indians were at length ordered to proceed. As they moved down the street, shrinking together in their terror, the mob about them grew so angry and clamorous, that to their missionaries they seemed like a flock of sheep in the midst of howling wolves. A body-guard of Quakers gathered around, protecting them from the crowd, and speaking words of sympathy and encouragement. Thus they proceeded to Province Island, below the city, where they were lodged in waste buildings, prepared in haste for their reception, and where the Quakers still attended them, with every office of kindness and friendship.

THE RIOTERS MARCH ON PHILADELPHIA

1764

The Conestoga murders did not take place until some weeks after the removal of the Moravian converts to Philadelphia; and the rioters, as they rode, flushed with success, out of Lancaster, after the achievement of their exploit, were heard to boast that they would soon visit the city and finish their work, by killing the Indians whom it had taken under its protection. It was soon but too apparent that this design was seriously entertained by the people of the frontier. They had tasted blood, and they craved more. It seemed to them intolerable, that, while their sufferings were unheeded, and their wounded and destitute friends uncared for, they should be taxed to support those whom they regarded as authors of their calamities, or, in their own angry words, "to maintain them through the winter, that they may scalp and butcher us in the spring." In their blind rage, they would not see that the Moravian Indians had been removed to Philadelphia, in part, at least, with a view to the safety of the borders. To their enmity against Indians was added a resentment, scarcely less vehement, against the Quakers, whose sectarian principles they hated and despised. They complained, too, of political grievances, alleging that the five frontier counties were inadequately represented in the Assembly, and that from thence arose the undue influence of the Quakers in the councils of the province.
The excited people soon began to assemble at taverns and other places of resort, recounting their grievances, real or imaginary; relating frightful stories of Indian atrocities, and launching fierce invectives against the Quakers. Political agitators harangued them on their violated rights; self-constituted preachers urged the duty of destroying the heathen, forgetting

that the Moravian Indians were Christians, and their exasperated hearers were soon ripe for any rash attempt. They resolved to assemble and march in arms to Philadelphia. On a former occasion, they had sent thither a wagon laden with the mangled corpses of their friends and relatives, who had fallen by Indian butchery; but the hideous spectacle had failed of the intended effect, and the Assembly had still turned a deaf ear to their entreaties for more effective aid. Appeals to sympathy had been thrown away, and they now resolved to try the efficacy of their rifles.

They mustered under their popular leaders, prominent among whom was Matthew Smith, who had led the murderers at Conestoga; and, towards the end of January, took the road to Philadelphia, in force variously estimated at from five hundred to fifteen hundred men. Their avowed purpose was to kill the Moravian Indians; but what vague designs they may have entertained to change the government, and eject the Quakers from a share in it, must remain a matter of uncertainty. Feeble as they were in numbers, their enterprise was not so hopeless as might at first appear, for they counted on aid from the mob of the city, while a numerous party, comprising the members of the Presbyterian sect, were expected to give them secret support, or at least to stand neutral in the quarrel. The Quakers, who were their most determined enemies, could not take arms against them without glaring violation of the principles which they had so often and loudly professed; and even should they thus fly in the face of conscience, the warlike borderers would stand in little fear of such unpractised warriors. They pursued their march in high confidence, applauded by the inhabitants, and hourly increasing in numbers.

Startling rumors of the danger soon reached Philadelphia, spreading alarm among the citizens. The Quakers, especially, had reason to fear, both for themselves and for the Indians, of whom it was their pride to be esteemed the champions. These pacific sectaries found themselves in a new and embarrassing position, for hitherto they had been able to assert their principles at no great risk to person or property. The appalling tempest, which, during the French war, had desolated the rest of the province, had been unfelt near Philadelphia; and while the inhabitants to the westward had been slaughtered by hundreds, scarcely a Quaker had been hurt. Under these circumstances, the aversion of the sect to warlike measures had been a fruitful source of difficulty. It is true that, on several occasions, they had voted supplies for the public defence; but unwilling to place on record such a testimony of inconsistency, they had granted the money, not for the avowed purpose of raising and arming soldiers, but under the title of a gift to the crown. They were now to be deprived of even this poor subterfuge, and subjected to the dilemma of suffering their friends to be slain and themselves to be plundered, or openly appealing to arms.

Their embarrassment was increased by the exaggerated ideas which prevailed among the ignorant and timorous respecting the size and strength of the borderers, their ferocity of temper, and their wonderful skill as marksmen. Quiet citizens, whose knowledge was confined to the narrow limits of their firesides and shops, listened horror-stricken to these reports; the prevalence of which is somewhat surprising, when it is considered that, at the present day, the district whence the dreaded rioters came may be reached from Philadelphia within a few hours.

Tidings of the massacre in Lancaster jail had arrived at Philadelphia on the twenty-ninth of December, and with them came the rumor that numerous armed mobs were already on their march to the city. Terror and confusion were universal; and, as the place was defenceless, no other expedient suggested itself than the pitiful one of removing the objects of popular resentment beyond reach of danger. Boats were sent to Province Island, and the Indians ordered to embark and proceed with all haste down the river; but, the rumor proving groundless, a messenger was despatched to recall the fugitives. The assurance that, for a time at least, the city was safe, restored some measure of tranquillity; but, as intelligence of an alarming kind came in daily from the country, Governor Penn sent to General Gage an earnest request for a detachment of regulars to repel the rioters; and, in the interval, means to avert the threatened danger were eagerly sought. A proposal was laid before the Assembly to embark the Indians and send them to England; but the scheme was judged inexpedient, and another, of equal weakness, adopted in its place. It was determined to send the refugees to New York, and place them under the protection of the Indian Superintendent, Sir William Johnson; a plan as hastily executed as timidly conceived. At midnight, on the fourth of January, no measures having been taken to gain the consent of either the government of New York or Johnson himself, the Indians were ordered to leave the island and proceed to the city; where they arrived a little before daybreak, passing in mournful procession, thinly clad and shivering with cold, through the silent streets. The Moravian Brethren supplied them with food; and Fox, the commissary, with great humanity, distributed blankets among them. Before they could resume their progress, the city was astir; and as they passed the suburbs, they were pelted and hooted at by the mob. Captain Robertson's Highlanders, who had just arrived from Lancaster, were ordered to escort them. These soldiers, who had their own reasons for hating Indians, treated them at first with no less insolence and rudeness than the populace; but at length, overcome by the meekness and patience of the sufferers, they changed their conduct, and assumed a tone of sympathy and kindness.

Thus escorted, the refugees pursued their dreary progress through the country, greeted on all sides by the threats and curses of the people. When they reached Trenton, they were received by Apty, the commissary at that place, under whose charge they continued their journey towards Amboy, where several small vessels had been provided to carry them to New York. Arriving at Amboy, however, Apty, to his great surprise, received a letter from Governor Colden of New York, forbidding him to bring the Indians within the limits of that province. A second letter, from General Gage to Captain Robertson, conveyed orders to prevent their advance; and a third, to the owners of the vessels, threatened heavy penalties if they should bring the Indians to the city. The charges of treachery against the Moravian Indians, the burden their presence would occasion, and the danger of popular disturbance, were the chief causes which induced the government of New York to adopt this course; a course that might have been foreseen from the beginning.

Thus disappointed in their hopes of escape, the hapless Indians remained several days lodged in the barracks at Amboy, where they passed much of their time in religious services. A message, however, soon came from the Governor of New Jersey, requiring them to leave that province; and they were compelled reluctantly to retrace their steps to Philadelphia. A detachment of a hundred and seventy soldiers had arrived, sent by General Gage in compliance with the request of Governor Penn; and under the protection of these troops, the exiles began their backward journey. On the twenty-fourth of January, they reached Philadelphia, where they were lodged at the barracks within the city; the soldiers, forgetful of former prejudice, no longer refusing them entrance.

The return of the Indians, banishing the hope of repose with which the citizens had flattered themselves, and the tidings of danger coming in quick succession from the country, made it apparent that no time must be lost; and the Assembly, laying aside their scruples, unanimously passed a bill providing means for the public defence. The pacific city displayed a scene of unwonted bustle. All who held property, or regarded the public order, might, it should seem, have felt a deep interest in the issue; yet a numerous and highly respectable class stood idle spectators, or showed at best but a lukewarm zeal. These were the Presbyterians, who had naturally felt a strong sympathy with their suffering brethren of the frontier. To this they added a deep bitterness against the Quaker, greatly increased by a charge, most uncharitably brought by the latter against the whole Presbyterian sect, of conniving at and abetting the murders at Conestoga and Lancaster. They regarded the Paxton men as victims of Quaker neglect and injustice, and showed a strong disposition to palliate, or excuse altogether, the violence of which they had been guilty. Many of them, indeed, were secretly inclined to favor the designs of the advancing rioters; hoping that by their means the public grievances would be redressed, the Quaker faction put down, and the social and political balance of the state restored.

Whatever may have been the sentiments of the Presbyterians and of the city mob, the rest of the inhabitants bestirred themselves for defence with all the alacrity of fright. The Quakers were especially conspicuous for their zeal. Nothing more was heard of the duty of non-resistance. The city was ransacked for arms, and the Assembly passed a vote, extending the English riot act to the province, the Quaker members heartily concurring in the measure. Franklin, whose energy and practical talents made his services invaluable, was the moving spirit of the day; and under his auspices the citizens were formed into military companies, six of which were of infantry, one of artillery, and two of horse. Besides this force, several thousands of the inhabitants, including many Quakers, held themselves ready to appear in arms at a moment's notice.

These preparations were yet incomplete, when, on the fourth of February, couriers came in with the announcement that the Paxton men, horse and foot, were already within a short distance of the city. Proclamation was made through the streets, and the people were called to arms. A mob of citizen soldiers repaired in great excitement to the barracks, where the Indians were lodged, under protection of the handful of regulars. Here the crowd remained all night, drenched with the rain, and in a dismal condition. On the following day, Sunday, a barricade was thrown up across the great square enclosed by the barracks; and eight cannon, to which four more were afterwards added, were planted to sweep the adjacent streets. These pieces were discharged, to convey to the rioters an idea of the reception prepared for them; but whatever effect the explosion may have produced on the ears for which it was intended, the new and appalling sounds struck the Indians in the barracks with speechless terror. While the city assumed this martial attitude, its rulers thought proper to adopt the safer though less glorious course of conciliation; and a deputation of clergymen was sent out to meet the rioters, and pacify them by reason and Scripture. Towards night, as all remained quiet and nothing was heard from the enemy, the turmoil began to subside, the citizen soldiers dispersed, the regulars withdrew into quarters, and the city recovered something of the ordinary repose of a Sabbath evening.

Through the early part of the night, the quiet was undisturbed; but at about two o'clock in the morning, the clang of bells and the rolling of drums startled the people from their slumbers, and countless voices from the street echoed the alarm. Immediately, in obedience to the previous day's orders, lighted candles were placed in every window, till the streets seemed illuminated for a festival. The citizen soldiers, with more zeal than order, mustered under their officers. The governor, dreading an irruption of the mob, repaired to the house of Franklin; and the city was filled with the jangling of bells, and the no less vehement clamor of tongues. A great multitude gathered before the barracks, where it was supposed the attack would be made; and among them was seen many a Quaker, with musket in hand. Some of the more consistent of the sect, unwilling to take arms with their less scrupulous brethren, went into the barracks to console and reassure the Indians; who, however, showed much more composure than their comforters, and sat waiting the result with invincible calmness. Several hours of suspense and excitement passed, when it was recollected, that, though the other ferries of the Schuylkill had been secured, a crossing place, known as the Swedes' Ford, had been left open; and a party at once set out to correct this unlucky oversight. Scarcely were they gone, when a cry rose among the crowd before the barracks, and a general exclamation was heard that the Paxton Boys were coming. In fact, a band of horsemen was seen advancing up Second Street. The people crowded to get out of the way; the troops fell into such order as they could; a cannon was pointed full at the horsemen, and the gunner was about to apply the match, when a man ran out from the crowd, and covered the touch-hole with his hat. The cry of a false alarm was heard, and it was soon apparent to all that the supposed Paxton Boys were a troop of German butchers and carters, who had come to aid in defence of the city, and had nearly paid dear for their patriotic zeal. The tumult of this alarm was hardly over, when a fresh commotion was raised by the return of the men who had gone to secure the Swedes' Ford, and who reported that they had been too late; that the rioters had crossed the river, and were already at Germantown. Those who had crossed proved to be the van of the Paxton men, two hundred in number, and commanded by Matthew Smith; who, learning what welcome was prepared for them, thought it prudent to remain quietly at Germantown, instead of marching forward to certain destruction. In the afternoon, many of the inhabitants gathered courage, and went out to visit them. They found nothing very extraordinary in the aspect of the rioters, who, in the words of a writer of the day, were "a set of fellows in blanket coats and moccasons, like our Indian traders or back country wagoners, all armed with rifles and tomahawks, and some with pistols stuck in their belts." They received their visitors with a courtesy which might doubtless be ascribed, in great measure, to their knowledge of the warlike preparations within the city; and the report made by the adventurers, on their return, greatly tended to allay the general excitement.

The alarm, however, was again raised on the following day; and the cry to arms once more resounded through the city of peace. The citizen soldiers mustered with exemplary despatch; but their ardor was quenched by a storm of rain, which drove them all under shelter. A neighboring Quaker meeting-house happened to be open, and a company of the volunteers betook themselves in haste to this convenient asylum. Forthwith, the place was bristling with bayonets; and the walls, which had listened so often to angry denunciations against war, now echoed the clang of weapons,—an unspeakable scandal to the elders of the sect, and an occasion of pitiless satire to the Presbyterians.

This alarm proving groundless, like all the others, the governor and council proceeded to the execution of a design which they had formed the day before. They had resolved, in pursuance of their timid policy, to open negotiations with the rioters, and persuade them, if possible, to depart peacefully. Many of the citizens protested against the plan, and the soldiers volunteered to attack the Paxton men; but none were so vehement as the Quakers, who held that fire and steel were the only welcome that should be accorded to such violators of the public peace, and audacious blasphemers of the society of Friends. The plan was nevertheless sustained; and Franklin, with three other citizens of character and influence, set out for Germantown. The rioters received them with marks of respect; and, after a long conference, the leaders of the mob were so far wrought upon as to give over their hostile designs, the futility of which was now sufficiently apparent. An assurance was given, on the part of the government, that their complaints should have a hearing; and safety was guaranteed to those of their number who should enter the city as their representatives and advocates. For this purpose, Matthew Smith and James Gibson were appointed by the general voice; and two papers, a "Declaration" and a "Remonstrance," were drawn up, addressed to the governor and Assembly. With this assurance that their cause should be represented, the rioters signified their willingness to return home, glad to escape so easily from an affair which had begun to threaten worse consequences.

Towards evening, the commissioners, returning to the city, reported the success of their negotiations. Upon this, the citizen soldiers were convened in front of the court house, and addressed by a member of the council. He thanked them for their zeal, and assured them there was no farther occasion for their services; since the Paxton men, though falsely represented as enemies of government, were in fact its friends, entertaining no worse design than that of gaining relief to their sufferings, without injury to the city or its inhabitants. The people, ill satisfied with what they heard, returned in no placid temper to their homes. On the morrow, the good effect of the treaty was apparent in a general reopening of schools, shops, and warehouses, and a return to the usual activity of business, which had been wholly suspended for some days. The security was not of long duration. Before noon, an uproar more tumultuous than ever, a cry to arms, and a general exclamation that the Paxton Boys had broken the treaty and were entering the town, startled the indignant citizens. The streets were filled in an instant with a rabble of armed merchants and shopmen, who for once were fully bent on slaughter, and resolved to put an end to the long-protracted evil. Quiet was again restored; when it was found that the alarm was caused by about thirty of the frontiersmen, who, with singular audacity, were riding into the city on a visit of curiosity. As their deportment was inoffensive, it was thought unwise to molest them. Several of these visitors had openly boasted of the part they had taken in the Conestoga murders, and a large reward had been offered for their apprehension; yet such was the state of factions in the city, and such the dread of the frontiersmen, that no man dared lay hand on the criminals. The party proceeded to the barracks, where they requested to see the Indians, declaring that they could point out several who had been in the battle against Colonel Bouquet, or engaged in other acts of open hostility. The request was granted, but no discovery made. Upon this, it was rumored abroad that the Quakers had removed the guilty individuals to screen them from just punishment; an accusation which, for a time, excited much ill blood between the rival factions.

The thirty frontiersmen withdrew from the city, and soon followed the example of their companions, who had begun to move homeward, leaving their leaders, Smith and Gibson, to adjust their differences with the government. Their departure gave great relief to the people of the neighborhood, to whom they had, at times, conducted themselves after a fashion somewhat uncivil and barbarous; uttering hideous outcries, in imitation of the war-whoop; knocking down peaceable citizens, and pretending to scalp them; thrusting their guns in at windows, and committing unheard-of ravages among hen-roosts and hog-pens.

Though the city was now safe from all external danger, contentions sprang up within its precincts, which, though by no means as perilous, were not less clamorous and angry than those menaced from an irruption of the rioters. The rival factions turned savagely upon each other; while the more philosophic citizens stood laughing by, and ridiculed them both. The Presbyterians grew furious, the Quakers dogged and spiteful. Pamphlets, farces, dialogues, and poems came forth in quick succession. These sometimes exhibited a few traces of wit, and even of reasoning; but abuse was the favorite weapon, and it is difficult to say which of the combatants handled it with the greater freedom and dexterity. The Quakers accused the Presbyterians of conniving at the act of murderers, of perverting Scripture for their defence, and of aiding the rioters with counsel and money in their audacious attempt against the public peace. The Presbyterians, on their part, with about equal justice, charged the Quakers with leaguing themselves with the common enemy and exciting them to war. They held up to scorn those accommodating principles which denied the aid of arms to suffering fellow-countrymen, but justified their use at the first call of self-interest. The Quaker warrior, in his sober garb of ostentatious simplicity, his prim person adorned with military trappings, and his hands grasping a musket which threatened more peril to himself than to his enemy, was a subject of ridicule too tempting to be overlooked.

While this paper warfare was raging in the city, the representatives of the frontiersmen, Smith and Gibson, had laid before the Assembly the memorial, entitled the Remonstrance; and to this a second paper, styled a Declaration, was soon afterwards added. Various grievances were specified, for which redress was demanded. It was urged that those counties where the Quaker interest prevailed sent to the Assembly more than their due share of representatives. The memorialists bitterly complained of a law, then before the Assembly, by which those charged with murdering Indians were to be brought to trial, not in the district where the act was committed, but in one of the three eastern counties. They represented the Moravian converts as enemies in disguise, and denounced the policy which yielded them protection and support while the sick and wounded of the frontiers were cruelly abandoned to their misery. They begged that a suitable reward might be offered for scalps, since the want of such encouragement had "damped the spirits of many brave men." Angry invectives against the Quakers succeeded. To the "villany, infatuation, and influence of a certain faction, that have got the political reins in their hands, and tamely tyrannize over the other good subjects of the province," were to be ascribed, urged the memorialists, the intolerable evils which afflicted the people. The Quakers, they insisted, had held private treaties with the Indians, encouraged them to hostile acts, and excused their cruelties on the charitable plea that this was their method of making war.

The memorials were laid before a committee, who recommended that a public conference should be held with Smith and Gibson, to consider the grounds of complaint. To this the governor, in view of the illegal position assumed by the frontiersmen, would not give his consent; an assertion of dignity that would have done him more honor had he made it when the rioters were in arms before the city, at which time he had shown an abundant alacrity to negotiate. It was intimated to Smith and Gibson that they might leave Philadelphia; and the Assembly soon after became involved in its inevitable quarrels with the governor, relative to the granting of supplies for the service of the ensuing campaign. The supply bill passed, as mentioned in a former chapter; and the consequent military preparations, together with a threatened renewal of the war on the part of the enemy, engrossed the minds of the frontier people, and caused the excitements of the winter to be forgotten. No action on the two memorials was ever taken by the Assembly; and the memorable Paxton riots had no other definite result than that of exposing the weakness and distraction of the provincial government, and demonstrating the folly and absurdity of all principles of non-resistance.

Yet to the student of human nature these events supply abundant food for reflection. In the frontiersman, goaded by the madness of his misery to deeds akin to those by which he suffered, and half believing that, in the perpetration of these atrocities, he was but the minister of divine vengeance; in the Quaker, absorbed by one narrow philanthropy, and closing his ears to the outcries of his wretched countrymen; in the Presbyterian, urged by party spirit and sectarian zeal to countenance the crimes of rioters and murderers,—in each and all of these lies an embodied satire, which may find its application in every age of the world, and every condition of society.

The Moravian Indians, the occasion—and, at least, as regards most of them, the innocent occasion—of the tumult, remained for a full year in the barracks of Philadelphia. There they endured frightful sufferings from the small-pox, which destroyed more than a third of their number. After the conclusion of peace, they were permitted to depart; and, having thanked the governor for his protection and care, they withdrew to the banks of the Susquehanna, where, under the direction of the missionaries, they once more formed a prosperous settlement.

BRADSTREET'S ARMY ON THE LAKES

1764

The campaign of 1763, a year of disaster to the English colonies, was throughout of a defensive nature, and no important blow had been struck against the enemy. With the opening of the following spring, preparations were made to renew the war on a more decisive plan. Before the commencement of hostilities, Sir William Johnson and his deputy, George Croghan, severally addressed to the lords of trade memorials, setting forth the character, temper, and resources of the Indian tribes, and suggesting the course of conduct which they judged it expedient to pursue. They represented that, before the conquest of Canada, all the tribes, jealous of French encroachment, had looked to the English to befriend and protect them; but that now one general feeling of distrust and hatred filled them all. They added that the neglect and injustice of the British government, the outrages of ruffian borderers and debauched traders, and the insolence of English soldiers, had aggravated this feeling, and given double effect to the restless machinations of the defeated French; who, to revenge themselves on their conquerors, were constantly stirring up the Indians to war. A race so brave and tenacious of liberty, so wild and erratic in their habits, dwelling in a country so savage and inaccessible, could not be exterminated or reduced to subjection without an immoderate expenditure of men, money, and time. The true policy of the British government was therefore to conciliate; to soothe their jealous pride, galled by injuries and insults; to gratify them by presents, and treat them with a respect and attention to which their haughty spirit would not fail to respond. We ought, they said, to make the Indians our friends; and, by a just, consistent, and straightforward course, seek to gain their esteem, and wean them from their partiality to the

French. To remove the constant irritation which arose from the intrusion of the white inhabitants on their territory, Croghan urged the expediency of purchasing a large tract of land to the westward of the English settlements; thus confining the tribes to remoter hunting-grounds. For a moderate sum the Indians would part with as much land as might be required. A little more, laid out in annual presents, would keep them in good temper; and by judicious management all hostile collision might be prevented, till, by the extension of the settlements, it should become expedient to make yet another purchase.

This plan was afterwards carried into execution by the British government. Founded as it is upon the supposition that the Indian tribes must gradually dwindle and waste away, it might well have awakened the utmost fears of that unhappy people. Yet none but an enthusiast or fanatic could condemn it as iniquitous. To reclaim the Indians from their savage state has again and again been attempted, and each attempt has failed. Their intractable, unchanging character leaves no other alternative than their gradual extinction, or the abandonment of the western world to eternal barbarism; and of this and other similar plans, whether the offspring of British or American legislation, it may alike be said that sentimental philanthropy will find it easier to cavil at than to amend them.

Now, turning from the Indians, let us observe the temper of those whose present business it was to cudgel them into good behavior; that is to say, the British officers, of high and low degree. They seem to have been in a mood of universal discontent, not in the least surprising when one considers that they were forced to wage, with crippled resources, an arduous, profitless, and inglorious war; while perverse and jealous legislatures added gall to their bitterness, and taxed their patience to its utmost endurance. The impossible requirements of the commander-in-chief were sometimes joined to their other vexations. Sir Jeffrey Amherst, who had, as we have seen, but a slight opinion of Indians, and possibly of everybody else except a British nobleman and a British soldier, expected much of his officers; and was at times unreasonable in his anticipations of a prompt "vengeance on the barbarians." Thus he had no sooner heard of the loss of Michillimackinac, Miami, and other western outposts, than he sent orders to Gladwyn to re-establish them at once. Gladwyn, who had scarcely force enough to maintain himself at Detroit, thereupon writes to his friend Bouquet: "The last I received from the General is of the second July, in which I am ordered to establish the outposts immediately. At the time I received these orders, I knew it was impossible to comply with any part of them: the event shows I was right. I am heartily wearied of my command, and I have signified the same to Colonel Amherst (Sir Jeffrey's adjutant). I hope I shall be relieved soon; if not, I intend to quit the service, for I would not choose to be any longer exposed to the villany and treachery of the settlement and Indians."

Two or three weeks before the above was written, George Croghan, Sir William Johnson's deputy, who had long lived on the frontier, and was as well versed in Indian affairs as the commander-in-chief was ignorant of them, wrote to Colonel Bouquet:—"Seven tribes in Canada have offered their services to act with the King's troops; but the General seems determined to neither accept of Indians' services, nor provincials'.... I have resigned out of the service, and will start for England about the beginning of December. Sir Jeffrey Amherst would not give his consent; so I made my resignation in writing, and gave my reasons for so doing. Had I continued, I could be of no more service than I have been these eighteen months past; which was none at all, as no regard was had to any intelligence I sent, no more than to my opinion." Croghan, who could not be spared, was induced, on Gage's accession to the command, to withdraw his resignation and retain his post.

Next, we have a series of complaints from Lieutenant Blane of Fort Ligonier; who congratulates Bouquet on his recent victory at Bushy Run, and adds: "I have now to beg that I may not be left any longer in this forlorn way, for I can assure you the fatigue I have gone through begins to get the better of me. I must therefore beg that you will appoint me, by the return of the convoy, a proper garrison.... My present situation is fifty times worse than ever." And again, on the seventeenth of September: "I must beg leave to recommend to your particular attention the sick soldiers here; as there is neither surgeon nor medicine, it would really be charity to order them up. I must also beg leave to ask what you intend to do with the poor starved militia, who have neither shirts, shoes, nor any thing else. I am sorry you can do nothing for the poor inhabitants.... I really get heartily tired of this post." He endured it some two months more, and then breaks out again on the twenty-fourth of November: "I intend going home by the first opportunity, being pretty much tired of a service that's so little worth any man's time; and the more so, as I cannot but think I have been particularly unlucky in it."

Now follow the letters, written in French, of the gallant Swiss, Captain Ecuyer, always lively and entertaining even in his discontent. He writes to Bouquet from Bedford, on the thirteenth of November. Like other officers on the frontier, he complains of the settlers, who, notwithstanding their fear of the enemy, always did their best to shelter deserters; and he gives a list of eighteen soldiers who had deserted within five days: "I have been twenty-two years in service, and I never in my life saw any thing equal to it,—a gang of mutineers, bandits, cut-throats, especially the grenadiers. I have been obliged, after all the patience imaginable, to have two of them whipped on the spot, without court-martial. One wanted to kill the sergeant and the other wanted to kill me.... For God's sake, let me go and raise cabbages. You can do it if you will, and I shall thank you eternally for it. Don't refuse, I beg you. Besides, my health is not very good; and I don't know if I can go up again to Fort Pitt with this convoy."

Bouquet himself was no better satisfied than his correspondents. On the twentieth of June, 1764, he wrote to Gage, Amherst's successor: "I flatter myself that you will do me the favor to have me relieved from this command, the burden and fatigues of which I begin to feel my strength very unequal to."

Gage knew better than to relieve him, and Bouquet was forced to resign himself to another year of bush-fighting. The plan of the summer's campaign had been settled; and he was to be the most important, if not the most conspicuous, actor in it. It had been resolved to march two armies from different points into the heart of the Indian country. The first, under Bouquet, was to advance from Fort Pitt into the midst of the Delaware and Shawanoe settlements of the valley of the Ohio. The other, under Colonel Bradstreet, was to pass up the lakes, and force the tribes of Detroit, and the regions beyond, to unconditional submission.

The name of Bradstreet was already well known in America. At a dark and ill-omened period of the French war, he had crossed Lake Ontario with a force of three thousand provincials, and captured Fort Frontenac, a formidable stronghold of the French, commanding the outlet of the lake. He had distinguished himself, moreover, by his gallant conduct in a skirmish with the French and Indians on the River Oswego. These exploits had gained for him a reputation beyond his merits. He was a man of more activity than judgment, self-willed, vain, and eager for notoriety; qualities which became sufficiently apparent before the end of the campaign.

Several of the northern provinces furnished troops for the expedition; but these levies did not arrive until after the appointed time; and, as the service promised neither honor nor advantage, they were of very indifferent quality, looking, according to an officer of the expedition, more like candidates for a hospital than like men fit for the arduous duty before them. The rendezvous of the troops was at Albany, and thence they took their departure about the end of June. Adopting the usual military route to the westward, they passed up the Mohawk, crossed the Oneida Lake, and descended the Onondaga. The boats and bateaux, crowded with men, passed between the war-worn defences of Oswego, which guarded the mouth of the river on either hand, and, issuing forth upon Lake Ontario, steered in long procession over its restless waters. A storm threw the flotilla into confusion; and several days elapsed before the ramparts of Fort Niagara rose in sight, breaking the tedious monotony of the forest-covered shores. The troops landed beneath its walls. The surrounding plains were soon dotted with the white tents of the little army, whose strength, far inferior to the original design, did not exceed twelve hundred men.

A striking spectacle greeted them on their landing. Hundreds of Indian cabins were clustered along the skirts of the forest, and a countless multitude of savages, in all the picturesque variety of their barbaric costume, were roaming over the fields, or lounging about the shores of the lake. Towards the close of the previous winter, Sir William Johnson had despatched Indian messengers to the tribes far and near, warning them of the impending blow; and urging all who were friendly to the English, or disposed to make peace while there was yet time, to meet him at Niagara, and listen to his words. Throughout the winter, the sufferings of the Indians had been great and general. The suspension of the fur-trade; the consequent want of ammunition, clothing, and other articles of necessity; the failure of expected aid from the French; and, above all, the knowledge that some of their own people had taken up arms for the English, combined to quench their thirst for war. Johnson's messengers had therefore been received with unexpected favor, and many had complied with his invitation. Some came to protest their friendship for the English; others hoped, by an early submission, to atone for past misconduct. Some came as spies; while others, again, were lured by the hope of receiving presents, and especially a draught of English milk, that is to say, a dram of whiskey. The trader, Alexander Henry, the same who so narrowly escaped the massacre at Michillimackinac, was with a party of Ojibwas at the Sault Ste. Marie, when a canoe, filled with warriors, arrived, bringing the message of Sir William Johnson. A council was called; and the principal messenger, offering a belt of wampum, spoke as follows: "My friends and brothers, I am come with this belt from our great father, Sir William Johnson. He desired me to come to you, as his ambassador, and tell you that he is making a great feast at Fort Niagara; that his kettles are all ready, and his fires lighted. He invites you to partake of the feast, in common with your friends, the Six Nations, who have all made peace with the English. He advises you to seize this opportunity of doing the same, as you cannot otherwise fail of being destroyed; for the English are on their march with a great army, which will be joined by different nations of Indians. In a word, before the fall of the leaf they will be at Michillimackinac, and the Six Nations with them."

The Ojibwas had been debating whether they should go to Detroit, to the assistance of Pontiac, who had just sent them a message to that effect; but the speech of Johnson's messenger turned the current of their thoughts. Most of them were in favor of accepting the invitation; but, distrusting mere human wisdom in a crisis so important, they resolved, before taking a decisive step, to invoke the superior intelligence of the Great Turtle, the chief of all the spirits. A huge wigwam was erected, capable of containing the whole population of the little village. In the centre, a sort of tabernacle was constructed by driving posts into the ground, and closely covering them with hides. With the arrival of night, the propitious time for consulting their oracle, all the warriors assembled in the spacious wigwam, half lighted by the lurid glare of fires, and waited, in suspense and awe, the issue of the invocation. The medicine man, or magician, stripped almost naked, now entered the central tabernacle, which was barely large enough to receive him, and carefully closed the aperture. At once the whole structure began to shake with a violence which threatened its demolition; and a confusion of horrible sounds, shrieks, howls, yells, and moans of anguish, mingled with articulate words, sounded in hideous discord from within. This outrageous clamor, which announced to the horror-stricken spectators the presence of a host of evil spirits, ceased as suddenly as it had begun. A low, feeble sound, like the whine of a young puppy, was next heard within the recess; upon which the warriors raised a cry of joy, and hailed it as the voice of the Great Turtle—the spirit who never lied. The magician soon announced that the spirit was ready to answer any question which might be proposed. On this, the chief warrior stepped forward; and, having propitiated the Great Turtle by a present of tobacco thrust through a small hole in the tabernacle, inquired if the English were in reality preparing to attack the Indians, and if the troops were already come to Niagara. Once more the tabernacle was violently shaken, a loud yell was heard, and it was apparent to all that the spirit was gone. A pause of anxious expectation ensued; when, after the lapse of a quarter of an hour, the weak, puppy-like voice of the Great Turtle was again heard addressing the magician in a language unknown to the auditors. When the spirit ceased speaking, the magician interpreted his words. During the short interval of his departure, he had crossed Lake Huron, visited Niagara, and descended the St. Lawrence to Montreal. Few soldiers had as yet reached Niagara; but as he flew down the St. Lawrence, he had seen the water covered with boats, all filled with English warriors, coming to make war on the Indians. Having obtained this answer to his first question, the chief ventured to propose another; and inquired if he and his people, should they accept the invitation of Sir William Johnson, would be well received at Niagara. The answer was most satisfactory. "Sir William Johnson," said the spirit, "will fill your canoes with presents; with blankets, kettles, guns, gunpowder and shot; and large barrels of rum, such as the stoutest of the Indians will not be able to lift; and every man will return in safety to his family." This grateful response produced a general outburst of acclamations; and, with cries of joy, many voices were heard to exclaim, "I will go too! I will go too!"

They set out, accordingly, for Niagara; and thither also numerous bands of warriors were tending, urged by similar messages, and encouraged, it may be, by similar responses of their oracles. Crossing fresh-water oceans in their birch canoes, and threading the devious windings of solitary streams, they came flocking to the common centre of attraction. Such a concourse of savages has seldom been seen in America. Menomonies, Ottawas, Ojibwas, Mississaugas, from the north; Caughnawagas from Canada, even Wyandots from Detroit, together with a host of Iroquois, were congregated round Fort Niagara to the number of more than two thousand warriors; many of whom had brought with them their women and children. Even the Sacs, the Foxes, and the Winnebagoes had sent their deputies; and the Osages, a tribe beyond the Mississippi, had their representative in this general meeting.

Though the assembled multitude consisted, for the most part, of the more pacific members of the tribes represented, yet their friendly disposition was by no means certain. Several straggling soldiers were shot at in the neighborhood, and it soon became apparent that the utmost precaution must be taken to avert a rupture. The troops were kept always on their guard; while the black muzzles of the cannon, thrust from the bastions of the fort, struck a wholesome awe into the savage throng below.

Although so many had attended the meeting, there were still numerous tribes, and portions of tribes, who maintained a rancorous, unwavering hostility. The Delawares and Shawanoes, however, against whom Bouquet, with the army of the south, was then in the act of advancing, sent a message to the effect, that, though they had no fear of the English, and though they regarded them as old women, and held them in contempt, yet, out of pity for their sufferings, they were willing to treat of peace. To this insolent missive Johnson made no answer; and, indeed, those who sent it were, at this very time, renewing the bloody work of the preceding year along the borders of Pennsylvania and Virginia. The Senecas, that numerous and warlike people, to whose savage enmity were to be ascribed the massacre at the Devil's Hole, and other disasters of the last summer, had recently made a preliminary treaty with Sir William Johnson, and at the same time pledged themselves to appear at Niagara to ratify and complete it. They broke their promise; and it soon became known that they had leagued themselves with a large band of hostile Delawares, who had visited their country. Upon this, a messenger was sent to them, threatening that, unless they instantly came to Niagara, the English would march upon them and burn their villages. The menace had full effect; and a large body of these formidable warriors appeared at the English camp, bringing fourteen prisoners, besides several deserters and runaway slaves. A peace was concluded, on condition that they should never again attack the English, and that they should cede to the British crown a strip of land, between the Lakes Erie and Ontario, four miles in width, on both sides of the River, or Strait, of Niagara. A treaty was next made with a deputation of Wyandots from Detroit, on condition of the delivery of prisoners, and the preservation of friendship for the future. Councils were next held, in turn, with each of the various tribes assembled around the fort, some of whom craved forgiveness for the hostile acts they had committed, and deprecated the vengeance of the English; while others alleged their innocence, urged their extreme wants and necessities, and begged that English traders might once more be allowed to visit them. The council-room in the fort was crowded from morning till night; and the wearisome formalities of such occasions, the speeches made and replied to, and the final shaking of hands, smoking of pipes, and serving out of whiskey, engrossed the time of the superintendent for many successive days.

Among the Indians present were a band of Ottawas from Michillimackinac, and remoter settlements, beyond Lake Michigan, and a band of Menomonies from Green Bay. The former, it will be remembered, had done good service to the English, by rescuing the survivors of the garrison of Michillimackinac from the clutches of the Ojibwas; and the latter had deserved no less at their hands, by the protection they had extended to Lieutenant Gorell, and the garrison at Green Bay. Conscious of their merits, they had come to Niagara in full confidence of a favorable reception. Nor were they disappointed; for Johnson met them with a cordial welcome, and greeted them as friends and brothers. They, on their part, were not wanting in expressions of pleasure; and one of their orators exclaimed, in the figurative language of his people, "When our brother came to meet us, the storms ceased, the lake became smooth, and the whole face of nature was changed."

They disowned all connection or privity with the designs of Pontiac. "Brother," said one of the Ottawa chiefs, "you must not imagine I am acquainted with the cause of the war. I only heard a little bird whistle an account of it, and, on going to Michillimackinac, I found your people killed; upon which I sent our priest to inquire into the matter. On the priest's return, he brought me no favorable account, but a war-hatchet from Pontiac, which I scarcely looked on, and immediately threw away."

Another of the Ottawas, a chief of the remoter band of Lake Michigan, spoke to a similar effect, as follows: "We are not of the same people as those residing about Michillimackinac; we only heard at a distance that the enemy were killing your soldiers, on which we covered our heads, and I resolved not to suffer my people to engage in the war. I gathered them together, and made them sit still. In the spring, on uncovering my head, I perceived that they had again begun a war, and that the sky was all cloudy in that quarter."

The superintendent thanked them for their fidelity to the English; reminded them that their true interest lay in the preservation of peace, and concluded with a gift of food and clothing, and a permission, denied to all the rest, to open a traffic with the traders, who had already begun to assemble at the fort. "And now, my brother," said a warrior, as the council was about to break up, "we beg that you will tell us where we can find some rum to comfort us; for it is long since we have tasted any, and we are very thirsty." This honest request was not refused. The liquor was distributed, and a more copious supply promised for the future; upon which the deputation departed, and repaired to their encampment, much pleased with their reception.

Throughout these conferences, one point of policy was constantly adhered to. No general council was held. Separate treaties were made, in order to promote mutual jealousies and rivalries, and discourage the feeling of union, and of a common cause among the widely scattered tribes. Johnson at length completed his task, and, on the sixth of August, set sail for Oswego. The march of the army had hitherto been delayed by rumors of hostile designs on the part of the Indians, who, it was said, had formed a scheme for attacking Fort Niagara, as soon as the troops should have left the ground. Now, however, when the concourse was melting away, and the tribes departing for their distant homes, it was thought that the danger was past, and that the army might safely resume its progress. They advanced, accordingly, to Fort Schlosser, above the cataract, whither their boats and bateaux had been sent before them, craned up the rocks at Lewiston, and dragged by oxen over the rough portage road. The troops had been joined by three hundred friendly Indians, and an equal number of Canadians. The appearance of the latter in arms would, it was thought, have great effect on the minds of the enemy, who had always looked upon them as friends and supporters. Of the Indian allies, the greater part were Iroquois, and the remainder, about a hundred in number, Ojibwas and Mississaugas; the former being the same who had recently arrived from the Sault Ste. Marie, bringing with them their prisoner, Alexander Henry. Henry was easily persuaded to accompany the expedition; and the command of the Ojibwas and Mississaugas was assigned to him—"To me," writes the adventurous trader, "whose best hope it had lately been to live by their forbearance." His long-continued sufferings and dangers hardly deserved to be rewarded by so great a misfortune as that of commanding a body of Indian warriors; an evil from which, however, he was soon to be relieved. The army had hardly begun its march, when nearly all his followers ran off, judging it wiser to return home with the arms and clothing given them for the expedition, than to make war against their own countrymen and relatives. Fourteen warriors still remained; but on the following night, when the army lay at Fort Schlosser, having contrived by some means to obtain liquor, they created such a commotion in the camp, by yelling and firing their guns, as to excite the utmost indignation of the commander. They received from him, in consequence, a reproof so harsh and ill judged, that most of them went home in disgust; and Henry found his Indian battalion suddenly dwindled to four or five vagabond hunters. A large number of Iroquois still followed the army, the strength of which, farther increased by a re-enforcement of

Highlanders, was now very considerable.

The troops left Fort Schlosser on the eighth. Their boats and bateaux pushed out into the Niagara, whose expanded waters reposed in a serenity soon to be exchanged for the wild roar and tumultuous struggle of the rapids and the cataract. They coasted along the southern shore of Lake Erie until the twelfth, when, in the neighborhood of Presqu' Isle, they were overtaken by a storm of rain, which forced them to drag their boats on shore, and pitch their tents in the dripping forest. Before the day closed, word was brought that strange Indians were near the camp. They soon made their appearance, proclaiming themselves to be chiefs and deputies of the Delawares and Shawanoes, empowered to beg for peace in the name of their respective tribes. Various opinions were entertained of the visitors. The Indian allies wished to kill them, and many of the officers believed them to be spies. There was no proof of their pretended character of deputies; and, for all that appeared to the contrary, they might be a mere straggling party of warriors. Their professions of an earnest desire for peace were contradicted by the fact that they brought with them but one small belt of wampum; a pledge no less indispensable in a treaty with these tribes than seals and signatures in a convention of European sovereigns. Bradstreet knew, or ought to have known, the character of the treacherous enemy with whom he had to deal. He knew that the Shawanoes and Delawares had shown, throughout the war, a ferocious and relentless hostility; that they had sent an insolent message to Niagara; and, finally, that in his own instructions he was enjoined to deal sternly with them, and not be duped by pretended overtures. Yet, in spite of the suspicious character of the self-styled deputies, in spite of the sullen wrath of his Indian allies, and the murmured dissent of his officers, he listened to their proposals, and entered into a preliminary treaty. He pledged himself to refrain from attacking the Delawares and Shawanoes, on condition that within twenty-five days the deputies should again meet him at Sandusky, in order to yield up their prisoners, and conclude a definite treaty of peace. It afterwards appeared—and this, indeed, might have been suspected at the time—that the sole object of the overtures was to retard the action of the army until the season should be too far advanced to prosecute the campaign. At this very moment, the Delaware and Shawanoe war-parties were murdering and scalping along the frontiers; and the work of havoc continued for weeks, until it was checked at length by the operations of Colonel Bouquet.

Bradstreet was not satisfied with the promise he had made to abandon his own hostile designs. He consummated his folly and presumption by despatching a messenger to his superior officer, Colonel Bouquet, informing him that the Delawares and Shawanoes had been reduced to submission without his aid, and that he might withdraw his troops, as there was no need of his advancing farther. Bouquet, astonished and indignant,

paid no attention to this communication, but pursued his march as before.
The course pursued by Bradstreet in this affair—a course which can only be ascribed to the vain ambition of finishing the war without the aid of others—drew upon him the severe censures of the commander-in-chief, who, on hearing of the treaty, at once annulled it. Bradstreet has been accused of having exceeded his orders, in promising to conclude a definite treaty with the Indians, a power which was vested in Sir William Johnson alone; but as upon this point his instructions were not explicit, he may be spared the full weight of this additional charge.

Having, as he thought, accomplished not only a great part of his own task, but also the whole of that which had been assigned to Colonel Bouquet, Bradstreet resumed his progress westward, and in a few days reached Sandusky. He had been ordered to attack the Wyandots, Ottawas, and Miamis, dwelling near this place; but at his approach, these Indians, hastening to avert the danger, sent a deputation to meet him, promising that, if he would refrain from attacking them, they would follow him to Detroit, and there conclude a treaty. Bradstreet thought proper to trust this slippery promise; though, with little loss of time, he might have reduced them, on the spot, to a much more effectual submission. He now bent his course for Detroit, leaving the Indians of Sandusky much delighted, and probably no less surprised, at the success of their embassy. Before his departure, however, he despatched Captain Morris, with several Canadians and friendly Indians, to the Illinois, in order to persuade the savages of that region to treat of peace with the English. The measure was in a high degree ill advised and rash, promising but doubtful advantage, and exposing the life of a valuable officer to imminent risk. The sequel of Morris's adventure will soon appear.

The English boats now entered the mouth of the Detroit, and on the twenty-sixth of August came within sight of the fort and adjacent settlements. The inhabitants of the Wyandot village on the right, who, it will be remembered, had recently made a treaty of peace at Niagara, ran down to the shore, shouting, whooping, and firing their guns,—a greeting more noisy than sincere,—while the cannon of the garrison echoed salutation from the opposite shore, and cheer on cheer, deep and heartfelt, pealed welcome from the crowded ramparts.

Well might Gladwyn's beleaguered soldiers rejoice at the approaching succor. They had been beset for more than fifteen months by their wily enemy; and though there were times when not an Indian could be seen, yet woe to the soldier who should wander into the forest in search of game, or stroll too far beyond range of the cannon. Throughout the preceding winter, they had been left in comparative quiet; but with the opening spring the Indians had resumed their pertinacious hostilities; not, however, with the same activity and vigor as during the preceding summer. The messages of Sir William Johnson, and the tidings of Bradstreet's intended expedition, had had great effect upon their minds, and some of them had begged abjectly for peace; but still the garrison were harassed by frequent alarms, and days and nights of watchfulness were their unvarying lot. Cut off for months together from all communication with their race; pent up in an irksome imprisonment; ill supplied with provisions, and with clothing worn threadbare, they hailed with delight the prospect of a return to the world from which they had been banished so long. The army had no sooner landed than the garrison was relieved, and fresh troops substituted in their place. Bradstreet's next care was to inquire into the conduct of the Canadian inhabitants of Detroit, and punish such of them as had given aid to the Indians. A few only were found guilty, the more culpable having fled to the Illinois on the approach of the army.

Pontiac too was gone. The great war-chief, his vengeance unslaked, and his purpose unshaken, had retired, as we have seen, to the banks of the Maumee, whence he sent a haughty defiance to the English commander. The Indian villages near Detroit were half emptied of their inhabitants, many of whom still followed the desperate fortunes of their indomitable leader. Those who remained were, for the most part, brought by famine and misery to a sincere desire for peace, and readily obeyed the summons of Bradstreet to meet him in council.

The council was held in the open air, on the morning of the seventh of September, with all the accompaniments of military display which could inspire awe and respect among the assembled savages. The tribes, or rather fragments of tribes, represented at this meeting, were the Ottawas, Ojibwas, Pottawattamies, Miamis, Sacs, and Wyandots. The Indians of Sandusky kept imperfectly the promise they had made, the Wyandots of that place alone sending a full deputation; while the other tribes were merely represented by the Ojibwa chief Wasson. This man, who was the principal chief of his tribe, and the most prominent orator on the present occasion, rose and opened the council.

"My brother," he said, addressing Bradstreet, "last year God forsook us. God has now opened our eyes, and we desire to be heard. It is God's will our hearts are altered. It was God's will you had such fine weather to come to us. It is God's will also there should be peace and tranquillity over the face of the earth and of the waters."

Having delivered this exordium, Wasson frankly confessed that the tribes which he represented were all justly chargeable with the war, and now deeply regretted their delinquency. It is common with Indians, when accused of acts of violence, to lay the blame upon the unbridled recklessness of their young warriors; and this excuse is often perfectly sound and valid; but since, in the case of a premeditated and long-continued war, it was glaringly inadmissible, they now reversed the usual course, and made scapegoats of the old chiefs and warriors, who, as they declared, had led the people astray by sinister counsel and bad example.

Bradstreet would grant peace only on condition that they should become subjects of the King of England, and acknowledge that he held over their country a sovereignty as ample and complete as over any other part of his dominions. Nothing could be more impolitic and absurd than this demand. The smallest attempt at an invasion of their liberties has always been regarded by the Indians with extreme jealousy, and a prominent cause of the war had been an undue assumption of authority on the part of the English. This article of the treaty, could its purport have been fully understood, might have kindled afresh the quarrel which it sought to extinguish; but happily not a savage present was able to comprehend it. Subjection and sovereignty are ideas which never enter into the mind of an Indian, and therefore his language has no words to express them. Most of the western tribes, it is true, had been accustomed to call themselves children of the King of France; but the words were a mere compliment, conveying no sense of any political relation whatever. Yet it was solely by means of this harmless metaphor that the condition in question could be explained to the assembled chiefs. Thus interpreted, it met with a ready assent; since, in their eyes, it involved no concession beyond a mere unmeaning change of forms and words. They promised, in future, to call the English king father, instead of brother; unconscious of any obligation which so trifling a change could impose, and mentally reserving a full right to make war on him or his people, whenever it should suit their convenience. When Bradstreet returned from his expedition, he boasted that he had reduced the tribes of Detroit to terms of more complete submission than any other Indians had ever before yielded; but the truth was soon detected and exposed by those conversant with Indian affairs.

At this council, Bradstreet was guilty of the bad policy and bad taste of speaking through the medium of a French interpreter; so that most of his own officers, as well as the Iroquois allies, who were strangers to the Algonquin language, remained in ignorance of all that passed. The latter were highly indignant, and refused to become parties to the treaty, or go through the usual ceremony of shaking hands with the chiefs of Detroit, insisting that they had not heard their speeches, and knew not whether they were friends or enemies. In another particular, also, Bradstreet gave great offence. From some unexplained impulse or motive, he cut to pieces, with a hatchet, a belt of wampum which was about to be used in the council; and all the Indians present, both friends and enemies, were alike incensed at this rude violation of the ancient pledge of faith, which, in their eyes, was invested with something of a sacred character.

Having settled the affairs of Detroit, Bradstreet despatched Captain Howard, with a strong detachment, to take possession of Michillimackinac, which had remained unoccupied since its capture in the preceding summer. Howard effected his object without resistance, and, at the same time, sent parties of troops to reoccupy the deserted posts of Green Bay and Sault Ste. Marie. Thus, after the interval of more than a year, the flag of England was again displayed among the solitudes of the northern wilderness.

While Bradstreet's army lay encamped on the fields near Detroit, Captain Morris, with a few Iroquois and Canadian attendants, was pursuing his adventurous embassy to the country of the Illinois. Morris, who has left us his portrait, prefixed to a little volume of prose and verse, was an officer of literary tastes, whose round English face did not indicate any especial degree of enterprise or resolution. He seems, however, to have had both; for, on a hint from the General, he had offered himself for the adventure, for which he was better fitted than most of his brother officers, inasmuch as he spoke French. He was dining, on the eve of his departure, in the tent of Bradstreet, when his host suddenly remarked, in the bluff way habitual to him, that he had a French fellow, a prisoner, whom he meant to hang; but that, if Morris would like him for an interpreter, he might have him. The prisoner in question was the Canadian Godefroy, who was presently led into the tent; and who, conscious of many misdemeanors, thought that his hour was come, and fell on his knees to beg his life. Bradstreet told him that he should be pardoned if he would promise to "go with this gentleman, and take good care of him," pointing to his guest. Godefroy promised; and, to the best of his power, he kept his word, for he imagined that Morris had saved his life.

Morris set out on the following afternoon with Godefroy, another Canadian, two servants, and a party of Indians, ascended the Maumee, and soon approached the camp of Pontiac; who, as already mentioned, had withdrawn to this river with his chosen warriors. The party disembarked from their canoes; and an Ottawa chief, who had joined them, lent them three horses. Morris and the Canadians mounted, and, preceded by their Indian attendants, displaying an English flag, advanced in state towards the camp, which was two leagues or more distant. As they drew near, they were met by a rabble of several hundred Indians, called by Morris "Pontiac's army." They surrounded him, beat his horse, and crowded between him and his followers, apparently trying to separate them. At the outskirts of the camp stood Pontiac himself, who met the ambassador with a scowling brow, and refused to offer his hand. Here, too, stood a man, in the uniform of a French officer, holding his gun with the butt resting on the ground, and assuming an air of great importance; while two Pawnee slaves stood close behind him. He proved to be a French drummer, calling himself St. Vincent, one of those renegades of civilization to be found in almost every Indian camp. He now took upon himself the office of a master of ceremonies; desired Morris to dismount, and seated himself at his side on a bear-skin. Godefroy took his place near them; and the throng of savages, circle within circle, stood crowded around. "Presently," says Morris, "came Pontiac, and squatted himself, after his fashion, opposite to me." He opened the interview by observing that the English were liars, and demanding of the ambassador if he had come to lie to them, like the rest. "This Indian," pursues Morris, "has a more extensive power than ever was known among that people, for every chief used to command his own tribe; but eighteen nations, by French intrigue, had been brought to unite and choose this man for their commander."

Pontiac now produced a letter directed to himself, and sent from New Orleans, though purporting to be written by the King of France. It contained, according to Morris, the grossest calumnies that the most ingenious malice could devise to incense the Indians against the English. The old falsehood was not forgotten: "Your French Father," said the writer, "is neither dead nor asleep; he is already on his way, with sixty great ships, to revenge himself on the English, and drive them out of America." Much excitement followed the reading of the letter, and Morris's situation became more than unpleasant; but St. Vincent befriended him, and hurried him off to his wigwam to keep him out of harm's way.

On the next day there was a grand council. Morris made a speech, in which he indiscreetly told the Indians that the King of France had given all the country to the King of England. Luckily, his auditors received the announcement with ridicule rather than anger. The chiefs, however, wished to kill him; but Pontiac interposed, on the ground that the life of an ambassador should be held sacred. "He made a speech," says Morris, "which does him honor, and shows that he was acquainted with the law of nations." He seemed in a mood more pacific than could have been expected, and said privately to Godefroy: "I will lead the nations to war no more. Let them be at peace if they choose; but I will never be a friend to the English. I shall be a wanderer in the woods; and, if they come there to seek me, I will shoot at them while I have an arrow left." Morris thinks that he said this in a fit of despair, and that, in fact, he was willing to come to terms.

The day following was an unlucky one. One of Morris's Indians, a Mohawk chief, ran off, having first stolen all he could lay hands on, and sold the ambassador's stack of rum, consisting of two barrels, to the Ottawas. A scene of frenzy ensued. A young Indian ran up to Morris, and stabbed at him savagely; but Godefroy caught the assassin's hand, and saved his patron's life. Morris escaped from the camp, and lay hidden in a cornfield till the howling and screeching subsided, and the Indians slept themselves sober. When he returned, an Indian, called the Little Chief, gave him a volume of Shakespeare,—the spoil of some slaughtered officer,—and then begged for gunpowder.

Having first gained Pontiac's consent, Morris now resumed his journey to the Illinois. The river was extremely low, and it was with much ado that they pushed their canoe against the shallow current, or dragged it over stones and sandbars. On the fifth day, they met an Indian mounted on a handsome white horse, said to have belonged to General Braddock, and to have been captured at the defeat of his army, nine years before. On the morning of the seventh day, they reached the neighborhood of Fort Miami. This post, captured during the preceding year, had since remained without a garrison; and its only tenants were the Canadians, who had built their houses within its palisades, and a few Indians, who thought fit to make it their temporary abode. The meadows about the fort were dotted with the lodges of the Kickapoos, a large band of whom had recently arrived; but the great Miami village was on the opposite side of the stream, screened from sight by the forest which intervened.

The party landed a little below the fort; and, while his followers were making their way through the border of woods that skirted the river, Morris remained in the canoe, solacing himself by reading Antony and Cleopatra in the volume he had so oddly obtained. It was fortunate that he did so; for his attendants had scarcely reached the open meadow, which lay behind the woods, when they were encountered by a mob of savages, armed with spears, hatchets, and bows and arrows, and bent on killing the Englishman. Being, for the moment, unable to find him, the chiefs had time to address the excited rabble, and persuade them to postpone their intended vengeance. The ambassador, buffeted, threatened, and insulted, was conducted to the fort, where he was ordered to remain; though, at the same time, the Canadian inhabitants were forbidden to admit him into their houses. Morris soon discovered that this unexpected rough treatment was owing to the influence of a deputation of Delaware and Shawanoe chiefs, who had recently arrived, bringing fourteen war-belts of wampum, and exciting the Miamis to renew their hostilities against the common enemy. Thus it was fully apparent that while the Delawares and Shawanoes were sending one deputation to treat of peace with Bradstreet on Lake Erie, they were sending another to rouse the tribes of the Illinois to war. From Fort Miami, the deputation had proceeded westward, spreading the contagion among all the tribes between the Mississippi and the Ohio; declaring that they would never make peace with the English, but would fight them as long as the sun should shine, and calling on their brethren of the Illinois to follow their example.

They had been aware of the approach of Morris, and had urged the Miamis to put him to death when he arrived. Accordingly, he had not been long at the fort when two warriors, with tomahawks in their hands, entered, seized him by the arms, and dragged him towards the river. Godefroy stood by, pale and motionless. "Eh bien, vous m'abandonnez donc!" said Morris.

"Non, mon capitaine," the Canadian answered, "je ne vous abandonnerai jamais;" and he followed, as the two savages dragged their captive into the water. Morris thought that they meant to drown and scalp him, but soon saw his mistake; for they led him through the stream, which was fordable, and thence towards the Miami village. As they drew near, they stopped, and began to strip him, but grew angry at the difficulty of the task; till, in rage and despair, he tore off his clothes himself. They then bound his arms behind him with his own sash, and drove him before them to the village, where they made him sit on a bench. A whooping, screeching mob of savages was instantly about him, and a hundred voices clamored together in dispute as to what should be done with him. Godefroy stood by him with a courageous fidelity that redeemed his past rascalities. He urged a nephew of Pontiac, who was present, to speak for the prisoner. The young Indian made a bold harangue to the crowd; and Godefroy added that, if Morris were killed, the English would take revenge on those who were in their power at Detroit. A Miami chief, called the Swan, now declared for the Englishman, untied his arms, and gave him a pipe to smoke; whereupon another chief, called the White Cat, snatched it from him, seized him, and bound him fast by the neck to a post. Naked, helpless, and despairing, he saw the crowd gathering around to torture him. "I had not the smallest hope of life," he says, "and I remember that I conceived myself as if going to plunge into a gulf, vast, immeasurable; and that, a few moments after, the thought of torture occasioned a sort of torpor and insensibility. I looked at Godefroy, and, seeing him exceedingly distressed, I said what I could to encourage him; but he desired me not to speak. I supposed it gave offence to the savages; and therefore was silent; when Pacanne, chief of the Miami nation, and just out of his minority, having mounted a horse and crossed the river, rode up to me. When I heard him calling to those about me, and felt his hand behind my neck, I thought he was going to strangle me, out of pity; but he untied me, saying, as it was afterwards interpreted to me: 'I give that man his life. If you want English meat, go to Detroit, or to the lake, and you'll find enough. What business have you with this man's flesh, who is come to speak with us?' I fixed my eyes steadfastly on this young man, and endeavored by looks to express my gratitude."

An Indian now offered him a pipe, and he was then pushed with abuse and blows out of the village. He succeeded in crossing the river and regaining the fort, after receiving a sharp cut of a switch from a mounted Indian whom he met on the way.

He found the Canadians in the fort disposed to befriend him. Godefroy and the metamorphosed drummer, St. Vincent, were always on the watch to warn him of danger; and one l'Esperance gave him an asylum in his garret. He seems to have found some consolation in the compassion of two handsome young squaws, sisters, he was told, of his deliverer, Pacanne; but the two warriors who had stripped and bound him were constantly lurking about the fort, watching an opportunity to kill him; and the Kickapoos, whose lodges were pitched on the meadow, sent him a message to the effect that, if the Miamis did not put him to death, they themselves would do so, whenever he should pass their camp. He was still on the threshold of his journey, and his final point of destination was several hundred miles distant; yet, with great resolution, he determined to persevere, and, if possible, fulfil his mission. His Indian and Canadian attendants used every means to dissuade him, and in the evening held a council with the Miami chiefs, the result of which was most discouraging. Morris received message after message, threatening his life, should he persist in his design; and word was brought him that several of the Shawanoe deputies were returning to the fort, expressly to kill him. Under these circumstances, it would have been madness to persevere; and, abandoning his mission, he set out for Detroit. The Indian attendants, whom he had brought from Sandusky, after behaving with the utmost insolence, abandoned him in the woods; their ringleader being a Christian Huron, of the Mission of Lorette, whom Morris pronounces the greatest rascal he ever knew. With Godefroy and two or three others who remained with him, he reached Detroit on the seventeenth of September, half dead with famine and fatigue. He had expected to find Bradstreet; but that agile commander had decamped, and returned to Sandusky. Morris, too ill and exhausted to follow, sent him his journal, together with a letter, in which he denounced the Delaware and Shawanoe ambassadors, whom he regarded, and no doubt with justice, as the occasion of his misfortunes. The following is his amiable conclusion:—

"The villains have nipped our fairest hopes in the bud. I tremble for you at Sandusky; though I was greatly pleased to find you have one of the vessels with you, and artillery. I wish the chiefs were assembled on board the vessel, and that she had a hole in her bottom. Treachery should be paid with treachery; and it is a more than ordinary pleasure to deceive those who would deceive us."

Bradstreet had retraced his course to Sandusky, to keep his engagement with the Delaware and Shawanoe deputies, and await the fulfilment of their worthless promise to surrender their prisoners, and conclude a definitive treaty of peace. His hopes were defeated. The appointed time expired, and not a chief was seen; though, a few days after, several warriors came to the camp, with a promise that, if Bradstreet would remain quiet, and refrain from attacking their villages, they would bring in the prisoners in the course of the following week. Bradstreet accepted their excuses; and, having removed his camp to the carrying-place of Sandusky, lay waiting in patient expectation. It was here that he received, for the first time, a communication from General Gage, respecting the preliminary treaty, concluded several weeks before. Gage condemned his conduct in severe terms, and ordered him to break the engagements he had made, and advance at once upon the enemy, choosing for his first objects of attack the Indians living upon the plains of the Scioto. The fury of Bradstreet was great on receiving this message; and it was not diminished when the journal of Captain Morris was placed in his hands, fully proving how signally he had been duped. He was in no temper to obey the orders of the commander-in-chief; and, to justify himself for his inaction, he alleged the impossibility of reaching the Scioto plains at that advanced season. Two routes thither were open to his choice, one by the River Sandusky, and the other by Cayahoga Creek. The water in the Sandusky was sunk low with the drought, and the carrying-place at the head of Cayahoga Creek was a few miles longer than had been represented; yet the army were ready for the attempt, and these difficulties could not have deterred a vigorous commander. Under cover of such excuses, Bradstreet remained idle at Sandusky for several days, while sickness and discontent were rife in his camp. The soldiers complained of his capricious, peremptory temper, his harshness to his troops, and the unaccountable tenderness with which he treated the Sandusky Indians, some of whom had not yet made their submission; while he enraged his Iroquois allies by his frequent rebukes and curses.

At length, declaring that provisions were failing and the season growing late, he resolved to return home; and broke up his camp with such precipitancy that two soldiers, who had gone out in the morning to catch fish for his table, were inhumanly left behind; the colonel remarking that they might stay and be damned. Soon after leaving Sandusky, he saw fit to encamp one evening on an open, exposed beach, on the south shore of Lake Erie, though there was in the neighborhood a large river, "wherein," say his critics, "a thousand boats could lie with safety." A storm came on: half his boats were dashed to pieces; and six pieces of cannon, with ammunition, provisions, arms, and baggage, were lost or abandoned. For three days the tempest raged unceasingly; and, when the angry lake began to resume its tranquillity, it was found that the remaining boats were insufficient to convey the troops. A body of Indians, together with a detachment of provincials, about a hundred and fifty in all, were therefore ordered to make their way to Niagara along the pathless borders of the lake. They accordingly set out, and, after many days of hardship, reached their destination; though such had been their sufferings, from fatigue, cold, and hunger; from wading swamps, swimming creeks and rivers, and pushing their way through tangled thickets, that many of the provincials perished miserably in the woods. On the fourth of November, seventeen days after their departure from Sandusky, the main body of the little army arrived in safety at Niagara; and the whole, re-embarking on Lake Ontario, proceeded towards Oswego. Fortune still seemed adverse; for a second tempest arose, and one of the schooners, crowded with troops, foundered in sight of Oswego, though most of the men were saved. The route to the settlements was now a short and easy one. On their arrival, the regulars went into quarters; while the troops levied for the campaign were sent home to their respective provinces.

This expedition, ill conducted as it was, produced some beneficial results. The Indians at Detroit had been brought to reason, and for the present, at least, would probably remain tranquil; while the re-establishment of the posts on the upper lakes must necessarily have great effect upon the natives of that region. At Sandusky, on the other hand, the work had been but half done. The tribes of that place felt no respect for the English; while those to the southward and westward had been left in a state of turbulence, which promised an abundant harvest of future mischief. In one particular, at least, Bradstreet had occasioned serious detriment to the English interest. The Iroquois allies, who had joined his army, were disgusted by his treatment of them, while they were roused to contempt by the imbecility of his conduct towards the enemy; and thus the efforts of Sir William Johnson to secure the attachment of these powerful tribes were in no small degree counteracted and neutralized.

While Bradstreet's troops were advancing upon the lakes, or lying idle in their camp at Sandusky, another expedition was in progress at the southward, with abler conduct and a more auspicious result.

BOUQUET FORCES THE DELAWARES

1764

The work of ravage had begun afresh upon the borders. The Indians had taken the precaution to remove all their settlements to the western side of the River Muskingum, trusting that the impervious forests, with their unnumbered streams, would prove a sufficient barrier against invasion. Having thus, as they thought, placed their women and children in safety, they had flung themselves upon the settlements with all the rage and ferocity of the previous season. So fierce and active were the war-parties on the borders, that the English governor of Pennsylvania had recourse to a measure which the frontier inhabitants had long demanded, and issued a proclamation, offering a high bounty for Indian scalps, whether of men or women; a barbarous expedient, fruitful of butcheries and murders, but incapable of producing any decisive result.

Early in the season, a soldier named David Owens, who, several years before, had deserted and joined the Indians, came to one of the outposts, accompanied by a young provincial recently taken prisoner on the Delaware, and bringing five scalps. While living among the Indians, Owens had formed a connection with one of their women, who had borne him several children. Growing tired, at length, of the forest life, he had become anxious to return to the settlements, but feared to do so without first having made some atonement for his former desertion. One night, he had been encamped on the Susquehanna, with four Shawanoe warriors, a boy of the same tribe, his own wife and two children, and another Indian woman. The young provincial, who came with him to the settlements, was also of the party. In the middle of the night, Owens arose, and looking about him saw, by the dull glow of the camp-fire, that all were buried in deep sleep.

Cautiously awakening the young provincial, he told him to leave the place, and lie quiet at a little distance, until he should call him. He next stealthily removed the weapons from beside the sleeping savages, and concealed them in the woods, reserving to himself two loaded rifles. Returning to the camp, he knelt on the ground between two of the yet unconscious warriors, and, pointing a rifle at the head of each, touched the triggers, and shot both dead at once. Startled by the reports, the survivors sprang to their feet in bewildered terror. The two remaining warriors bounded into the woods; but the women and children, benumbed with fright, had no power to escape, and one and all died shrieking under the hatchet of the miscreant. His devilish work complete, the wretch sat watching until daylight among the dead bodies of his children and comrades, undaunted by the awful gloom and solitude of the darkened forest. In the morning, he scalped his victims, with the exception of the two children, and, followed by the young white man, directed his steps towards the settlements, with the bloody trophies of his atrocity. His desertion was pardoned; he was employed as an interpreter, and ordered to accompany the troops on the intended expedition. His example is one of many in which the worst acts of Indian ferocity have been thrown into shade by the enormities of white barbarians.

Bouquet was now urging on his preparations for his march into the valley of the Ohio. We have seen how, in the preceding summer, he had been embarrassed by what he calls "the unnatural obstinacy of the government of Pennsylvania." "It disables us," he had written to the equally indignant Amherst, "from crushing the savages on this side of the lakes, and may draw us into a lingering war, which might have been terminated by another blow.... I see that the whole burden of this war will rest upon us; and while the few regular troops you have left can keep the enemy at a distance, the Provinces will let them fight it out without interfering."

Amherst, after vainly hoping that the Assembly of Pennsylvania would "exert themselves like men," had, equally in vain, sent Colonel James Robertson as a special messenger to the provincial commissioners. "I found all my pleading vain," the disappointed envoy had written, "and believe Cicero's would have been so. I never saw any men so determined in the right as these people are in this absurdly wrong resolve." The resolve in question related to the seven hundred men whom the Assembly had voted to raise for protecting the gathering of the harvest, and whom the commissioners stiffly refused to place at the disposition of the military authorities.

It is apparent in all this that, at an early period of the war, a change had come over the spirit of the commander-in-chief, whose prejudices and pride had revolted, at the outset, against the asking of provincial aid to "chastise the savages," but who had soon been brought to reason by his own helplessness and the exigencies of the situation. In like manner, a change, though at the eleventh hour, had now come over the spirit of the Pennsylvania Assembly. The invasion of the Paxton borderers, during the past winter, had scared the Quaker faction into their senses. Their old quarrel with the governor and the proprietaries, their scruples about war, and their affection for Indians, were all postponed to the necessity of the hour. The Assembly voted to raise three hundred men to guard the frontiers, and a thousand to join Bouquet. Their commissioners went farther; for they promised to send to England for fifty couples of bloodhounds, to hunt Indian scalping-parties.

In the preceding summer, half as many men would have sufficed; for, after the battle of Bushy Run, Bouquet wrote to Amherst from Fort Pitt, that, with a reinforcement of three hundred provincial rangers, he could destroy all the Delaware towns, "and clear the country of that vermin between this fort and Lake Erie;" but he added, with some bitterness, that the provinces would not even furnish escorts to convoys, so that his hands were completely tied.

It was past midsummer before the thousand Pennsylvanians were ready to move; so that the season for navigating the Ohio and its branches was lost. As for Virginia and Maryland, they would do absolutely nothing. On the fifth of August, Bouquet was at Carlisle, with his new levies and such regulars as he had, chiefly the veterans of Bushy Run. Before the tenth, two hundred of the Pennsylvanians had deserted, sheltered, as usual, by the country people. His force, even with full ranks, was too small; and he now took the responsibility of writing to Colonel Lewis, of the Virginia militia, to send him two hundred volunteers, to take the place of the deserters. A body of Virginians accordingly joined him at Fort Pitt, to his great satisfaction, for he set a high value on these backwoods riflemen; but the responsibility he had assumed proved afterwards a source of extreme annoyance to him.

The little army soon reached Fort Loudon, then in a decayed and ruinous condition, like all the wooden forts built during the French war. Here Bouquet received the strange communication from Bradstreet, informing him that he might return home with his troops, as a treaty had been concluded with the Delawares and Shawanoes. Bouquet's disgust found vent in a letter to the commander-in-chief: "I received this moment advice from Colonel Bradstreet.... The terms he gives them (the Indians) are such as fill me with astonishment.... Had Colonel Bradstreet been as well informed as I am of the horrid perfidies of the Delawares and Shawanese, whose parties as late as the 22d instant killed six men ... he never could have compromised the honor of the nation by such disgraceful conditions, and that at a time when two armies, after long struggles, are in full motion to penetrate into the heart of the enemy's country. Permit me likewise humbly to represent to your Excellency that I have not deserved the affront laid upon me by this treaty of peace, concluded by a younger officer, in the department where you have done me the honor to appoint me to command, without referring the deputies of the savages to me at Fort Pitt, but telling them that he shall send and prevent my proceeding against them. I can therefore take no notice of his peace, but (shall) proceed forthwith to the Ohio, where I shall wait till I receive your orders."

After waiting for more than a week for his wrath to cool, he wrote to Bradstreet in terms which, though restrained and temperate, plainly showed his indignation. He had now reached Fort Bedford, where more Pennsylvanians ran off, with their arms and horses, and where he vainly waited the arrival of a large reinforcement of friendly Indians, who had been promised by Sir William Johnson, but who never arrived. On reaching Fort Ligonier, he had the satisfaction of forwarding two letters, which the commander-in-chief had significantly sent through his hands, to Bradstreet, containing a peremptory disavowal of the treaty. Continuing to advance, he passed in safety the scene of his desperate fight of the last summer, and on the seventeenth of September arrived at Fort Pitt, with no other loss than that of a few men picked off from the flanks and rear by lurking Indian marksmen.

The day before his arrival, ten Delaware chiefs and warriors appeared on the farther bank of the river, pretending to be deputies sent by their nation to confer with the English commander. Three of them, after much hesitation, came over to the fort, where, being closely questioned, and found unable to give any good account of their mission, they were detained as spies; while their companions, greatly disconcerted, fled back to their villages. Bouquet, on his arrival, released one of the three captives, and sent him home with the following message to his people:—

"I have received an account, from Colonel Bradstreet, that your nations had begged for peace, which he had consented to grant, upon assurance that you had recalled all your warriors from our frontiers; and, in consequence of this, I would not have proceeded against your towns, if I had not heard that, in open violation of your engagements, you have since murdered several of our people.

"I was therefore determined to have attacked you, as a people whose promises can no more be relied on. But I will put it once more in your power to save yourselves and your families from total destruction, by giving us satisfaction for the hostilities committed against us. And, first, you are to leave the path open for my expresses from hence to Detroit; and as I am now to send two men with despatches to Colonel Bradstreet, who commands on the lakes, I desire to know whether you will send two of your people to bring them safe back with an answer. And if they receive any injury either in going or coming, or if the letters are taken from them, I will immediately put the Indians now in my power to death, and will show no mercy, for the future, to any of your nations that shall fall into my hands. I allow you ten days to have my letters delivered at Detroit, and ten days to bring me back an answer."

The liberated spy faithfully discharged his mission; and the firm, decisive tone of the message had a profound effect upon the hostile warriors; clearly indicating, as it did, with what manner of man they had to deal. Many, who were before clamorous for battle, were now ready to sue for peace, as the only means to avert their ruin.

Before the army was ready to march, two Iroquois warriors came to the fort, pretending friendship, but anxious, in reality, to retard the expedition until the approaching winter should make it impossible to proceed. They represented the numbers of the enemy, and the extreme difficulty of penetrating so rough a country; and affirmed that, if the troops remained quiet, the hostile tribes, who were already collecting their prisoners, would soon arrive to make their submission. Bouquet turned a deaf ear to their advice, and sent them to inform the Delawares and Shawanoes that he was on his way to chastise them for their perfidy and cruelty, unless they should save themselves by an ample and speedy atonement.

Early in October, the troops left Fort Pitt, and began their westward march into a wilderness which no army had ever before sought to penetrate. Encumbered with their camp equipage, with droves of cattle and sheep for subsistence, and a long train of pack-horses laden with provisions, their progress was tedious and difficult, and seven or eight miles were the ordinary measure of a day's march. The woodsmen of Virginia, veteran hunters and Indian-fighters, were thrown far out in front and on either flank, scouring the forest to detect any sign of a lurking ambuscade. The pioneers toiled in the van, hewing their way through woods and thickets; while the army dragged its weary length behind them through the forest, like a serpent creeping through tall grass. The surrounding country, whenever a casual opening in the matted foliage gave a glimpse of its features, disclosed scenery of wild, primeval beauty. Sometimes the army defiled along the margin of the Ohio, by its broad eddying current and the bright landscape of its shores. Sometimes they descended into the thickest gloom of the woods, damp, still, and cool as the recesses of a cavern, where the black soil oozed beneath the tread, where the rough columns of the forest seemed to exude a clammy sweat, and the slimy mosses were trickling with moisture; while the carcasses of prostrate trees, green with the decay of a century, sank into pulp at the lightest pressure of the foot. More frequently, the forest was of a fresher growth; and the restless leaves of young maples and basswood shook down spots of sunlight on the marching columns. Sometimes they waded the clear current of a stream, with its vistas of arching foliage and sparkling water. There were intervals, but these were rare, when, escaping for a moment from the labyrinth of woods, they emerged into the light of an open meadow, rich with herbage, and girdled by a zone of forest; gladdened by the notes of birds, and enlivened, it may be, by grazing herds of deer. These spots, welcome to the forest traveller as an oasis to a wanderer in the desert, form the precursors of the prairies; which, growing wider and more frequent as one advances westward, expand at last into the boundless plains beyond the Mississippi.

On the tenth day after leaving Fort Pitt, the army reached the River Muskingum, and approached the objects of their march, the haunts of the barbarian warriors, who had turned whole districts into desolation. Their progress had met no interruption. A few skulking Indians had hovered about them, but, alarmed by their numbers, feared to venture an attack. The Indian cabins which they passed on their way were deserted by their tenants, who had joined their western brethren. When the troops crossed the Muskingum, they saw, a little below the fording-place, the abandoned wigwams of the village of Tuscaroras, recently the abode of more than a hundred families, who had fled in terror at the approach of the invaders.

Bouquet was in the heart of the enemy's country. Their villages, except some remoter settlements of the Shawanoes, all lay within a few days' march; and no other choice was left them than to sue for peace, or risk the desperate chances of battle against a commander who, a year before, with a third of his present force, had routed them at the fight of Bushy Run. The vigorous and active among them might, it is true, escape by flight; but, in doing so, they must abandon to the victors their dwellings, and their secret hordes of corn. They were confounded at the multitude of the invaders, exaggerated, doubtless, in the reports which reached their villages, and amazed that an army should force its way so deep into the forest fastnesses, which they had thought impregnable. They knew, on the other hand, that Colonel Bradstreet was still at Sandusky, in a position to assail them in the rear. Thus pressed on both sides, they saw that they must submit, and bend their stubborn pride to beg for peace; not alone with words, which cost nothing, and would have been worth nothing, but by the delivery of prisoners, and the surrender of chiefs and warriors as pledges of good faith. Bouquet had sent two soldiers from Fort Pitt with letters to Colonel Bradstreet; but these men had been detained, under specious pretexts, by the Delawares. They now appeared at his camp, sent back by their captors, with a message to the effect that, within a few days, the chiefs would arrive and hold a conference with him.

Bouquet continued his march down the valley of the Muskingum, until he reached a spot where the broad meadows, which bordered the river, would supply abundant grazing for the cattle and horses; while the terraces above, shaded by forest-trees, offered a convenient site for an encampment. Here he began to erect a small palisade work, as a depot for stores and baggage. Before the task was complete, a deputation of chiefs arrived, bringing word that their warriors were encamped, in great numbers, about eight miles from the spot, and desiring Bouquet to appoint the time and place for a council. He ordered them to meet him, on the next day, at a point near the margin of the river, a little below the camp; and thither a party of men was at once despatched, to erect a sort of rustic arbor of saplings and the boughs of trees, large enough to shelter the English officers and the Indian chiefs. With a host of warriors in the neighborhood, who would gladly break in upon them, could they hope that the attack would succeed, it behooved the English to use every precaution. A double guard was placed, and a stringent discipline enforced.

In the morning, the little army moved in battle order to the place of council. Here the principal officers assumed their seats under the canopy of branches, while the glittering array of the troops was drawn out on the meadow in front, in such a manner as to produce the most imposing effect on the minds of the Indians, in whose eyes the sight of fifteen hundred men under arms was a spectacle equally new and astounding. The perfect order and silence of the far-extended lines; the ridges of bayonets flashing in the sun; the fluttering tartans of the Highland regulars; the bright red uniform of the Royal Americans; the darker garb and duller trappings of the Pennsylvania troops, and the bands of Virginia backwoodsmen, who, in fringed hunting-frocks and Indian moccasons, stood leaning carelessly on their rifles,—all these combined to form a scene of military pomp and power not soon to be forgotten.

At the appointed hour, the deputation appeared. The most prominent among them were Kiashuta, chief of the band of Senecas who had deserted their ancient homes to form a colony on the Ohio; Custaloga, chief of the Delawares; and the head chief of the Shawanoes, whose name sets orthography at defiance. As they approached, painted and plumed in all their savage pomp, they looked neither to the right hand nor to the left, not deigning, under the eyes of their enemy, to cast even a glance at the military display around them. They seated themselves, with stern, impassive looks, and an air of sullen dignity; while their sombre brows betrayed the hatred still rankling in their hearts. After a few minutes had been consumed in the indispensable ceremony of smoking, Turtle Heart, a chief of the Delawares, and orator of the deputation, rose, bearing in his hand a bag containing the belts of wampum. Addressing himself to the English commander, he spoke as follows, delivering a belt for every clause of his speech:—

"Brother, I speak in behalf of the three nations whose chiefs are here present. With this belt I open your ears and your hearts, that you may listen to my words.

"Brother, this war was neither your fault nor ours. It was the work of the nations who live to the westward, and of our wild young men, who would have killed us if we had resisted them. We now put away all evil from our hearts; and we hope that your mind and ours will once more be united together.

"Brother, it is the will of the Great Spirit that there should be peace between us. We, on our side, now take fast hold of the chain of friendship; but, as we cannot hold it alone, we desire that you will take hold also, and we must look up to the Great Spirit, that he may make us strong, and not permit this chain to fall from our hands.

"Brother, these words come from our hearts, and not from our lips. You desire that we should deliver up your flesh and blood now captive among us; and, to show you that we are sincere, we now return you as many of them as we have at present been able to bring. [Here he delivered eighteen white prisoners, who had been brought by the deputation to the council.] You shall receive the rest as soon as we have time to collect them."

In such figurative terms, not devoid of dignity, did the Indian orator sue for peace to his detested enemies. When he had concluded, the chiefs of every tribe rose in succession, to express concurrence in what he had said, each delivering a belt of wampum and a bundle of small sticks; the latter designed to indicate the number of English prisoners whom his followers retained, and whom he pledged himself to surrender. In an Indian council, when one of the speakers has advanced a matter of weight and urgency, the other party defers his reply to the following day, that due time may be allowed for deliberation. Accordingly, in the present instance, the council adjourned to the next morning, each party retiring to its respective camp. But, when day dawned, the weather had changed. The valley of the Muskingum was filled with driving mist and rain, and the meeting was in consequence postponed. On the third day, the landscape brightened afresh, the troops marched once more to the place of council, and the Indian chiefs convened to hear the reply of their triumphant foe. It was not of a kind to please them. The opening words gave an earnest of what was to come; for Bouquet discarded the usual address of an Indian harangue: fathers, brothers, or children,—terms which imply a relation of friendship, or a desire to conciliate,—and adopted a sterner and more distant form.

"Sachems, war-chiefs, and warriors, the excuses you have offered are frivolous and unavailing, and your conduct is without defence or apology. You could not have acted as you pretend to have done through fear of the western nations; for, had you stood faithful to us, you knew that we would have protected you against their anger; and as for your young men, it was your duty to punish them, if they did amiss. You have drawn down our just resentment by your violence and perfidy. Last summer, in cold blood, and in a time of profound peace, you robbed and murdered the traders, who had come among you at your own express desire. You attacked Fort Pitt, which was built by your consent; and you destroyed our outposts and garrisons, whenever treachery could place them in your power. You assailed our troops—the same who now stand before you—in the woods at Bushy Run; and, when we had routed and driven you off, you sent your scalping-parties to the frontier, and murdered many hundreds of our people. Last July, when the other nations came to ask for peace, at Niagara, you not only refused to attend, but sent an insolent message instead, in which you expressed a pretended contempt for the English; and, at the same time, told the surrounding nations that you would never lay down the hatchet. Afterwards, when Colonel Bradstreet came up Lake Erie, you sent a deputation of your chiefs, and concluded a treaty with him; but your engagements were no sooner made than broken; and, from that day to this, you have scalped and butchered us without ceasing. Nay, I am informed that, when you heard that this army was penetrating the woods, you mustered your warriors to attack us, and were only deterred from doing so when you found how greatly we outnumbered you. This is not the only instance of your bad faith; for, since the beginning of the last war, you have made repeated treaties with us, and promised to give up your prisoners; but you have never kept these engagements, nor any others. We shall endure this no longer; and I am now come among you to force you to make atonement for the injuries you have done us. I have brought with me the relatives of those you have murdered. They are eager for vengeance, and nothing restrains them from taking it but my assurance that this army shall not leave your country until you have given them an ample satisfaction.

"Your allies, the Ottawas, Ojibwas, and Wyandots, have begged for peace; the Six Nations have leagued themselves with us; the great lakes and rivers around you are all in our possession, and your friends the French are in subjection to us, and can do no more to aid you. You are all in our power, and, if we choose, we can exterminate you from the earth; but the English are a merciful and generous people, averse to shed the blood even of their greatest enemies; and if it were possible that you could convince us that you sincerely repent of your past perfidy, and that we could depend on your good behavior for the future, you might yet hope for mercy and peace. If I find that you faithfully execute the conditions which I shall prescribe, I will not treat you with the severity you deserve.

"I give you twelve days from this date to deliver into my hands all the prisoners in your possession, without exception: Englishmen, Frenchmen, women, and children; whether adopted into your tribes, married, or living among you under any denomination or pretence whatsoever. And you are to furnish these prisoners with clothing, provisions, and horses, to carry them to Fort Pitt. When you have fully complied with these conditions, you shall then know on what terms you may obtain the peace you sue for."

This speech, with the stern voice and countenance of the speaker, told with chilling effect upon the awe-stricken hearers. It quelled their native haughtiness, and sunk them to the depths of humiliation. Their speeches in reply were dull and insipid, void of that savage eloquence, which, springing from a wild spirit of independence, has so often distinguished the forest orators. Judging the temper of their enemies by their own insatiable thirst for vengeance, they hastened, with all the alacrity of terror, to fulfil the prescribed conditions, and avert the threatened ruin. They dispersed to their different villages, to collect and bring in the prisoners; while Bouquet, on his part, knowing that his best security for their good faith was to keep up the alarm which his decisive measures had created, determined to march yet nearer to their settlements. Still following the course of the Muskingum, he descended to a spot near its confluence with its main branch, which might be regarded as a central point with respect to the surrounding Indian villages. Here, with the exception of the distant Shawanoe settlements, they were all within reach of his hand, and he could readily chastise the first attempt at deceit or evasion. The principal chiefs of each tribe had been forced to accompany him as hostages.

For the space of a day, hundreds of axes were busy at their work. The trees were felled, the ground cleared, and, with marvellous rapidity, a town sprang up in the heart of the wilderness, martial in aspect and rigorous in discipline; with storehouses, hospitals, and works of defence, rude sylvan cabins mingled with white tents, and the forest rearing its sombre rampart around the whole. On one side of this singular encampment was a range of buildings, designed to receive the expected prisoners; and matrons, brought for this purpose with the army, were appointed to take charge of the women and children among them. At the opposite side, a canopy of branches, sustained on the upright trunks of young trees, formed a rude council-hall, in keeping with the savage assembly for whose reception it was designed.

And now, issuing from the forest, came warriors, conducting troops of prisoners, or leading captive children,—wild young barbarians, born perhaps among themselves, and scarcely to be distinguished from their own. Yet, seeing the sullen reluctance which the Indians soon betrayed in this ungrateful task, Bouquet thought it expedient to stimulate their efforts by sending detachments of soldiers to each of the villages, still retaining the chiefs in pledge for their safety. About this time, a Canadian officer, named Hertel, with a party of Caughnawaga Indians, arrived with a letter from Colonel Bradstreet, dated at Sandusky. The writer declared that he was unable to remain longer in the Indian country, and was on the point of retiring down Lake Erie with his army; a movement which, at the least, was of doubtful necessity, and which might have involved the most disastrous consequences. Had the tidings been received but a few days sooner, the whole effect of Bouquet's measures would probably have been destroyed, the Indians encouraged to resistance, and the war brought to the arbitration of a battle, which must needs have been a fierce and bloody one. But, happily for both parties, Bouquet now had his enemies firmly in his grasp, and the boldest warrior dared not violate the truce.

The messengers who brought the letter of Bradstreet brought also the tidings that peace was made with the northern Indians; but stated, at the same time, that these tribes had murdered many of their captives, and given up but few of the remainder, so that no small number were still within their power. The conduct of Bradstreet in this matter was the more disgraceful, since he had been encamped for weeks almost within gunshot of the Wyandot villages at Sandusky, where most of the prisoners were detained. Bouquet, on his part, though separated from this place by a journey of many days, resolved to take upon himself the duty which his brother officer had strangely neglected. He sent an embassy to Sandusky, demanding that the prisoners should be surrendered. This measure was in a great degree successful. He despatched messengers soon after to the principal Shawanoe village, on the Scioto, distant about eighty miles from his camp, to rouse the inhabitants to a greater activity than they seemed inclined to display. This was a fortunate step; for the Shawanoes of the Scioto, who had been guilty of atrocious cruelties during the war, had conceived the idea that they were excluded from the general amnesty, and marked out for destruction. This notion had been propagated, and perhaps suggested, by the French traders in their villages; and so thorough was the conviction of the Shawanoes, that they came to the desperate purpose of murdering their prisoners, and marching, with all the warriors they could muster, to attack the English. This plan was no sooner formed than the French traders opened their stores of bullets and gunpowder, and dealt them out freely to the Indians. Bouquet's messengers came in time to prevent the catastrophe, and relieve the terrors of the Shawanoes, by the assurance that peace would be granted to them on the same conditions as to the rest. Thus encouraged, they abandoned their design, and set out with lighter hearts for the English camp, bringing with them a portion of their prisoners. When about half-way on their journey, they were met by an Indian runner, who told them that a soldier had been killed in the woods, and their tribe charged with the crime. On hearing this, their fear revived, and with it their former purpose. Having collected their prisoners in a meadow, they surrounded the miserable wretches, armed with guns, war-clubs, and bows and arrows, and prepared to put them to death. But another runner arrived before the butchery began, and, assuring them that what they had heard was false, prevailed on them once more to proceed. They pursued their journey without farther interruption, and, coming in safety to the camp, delivered the prisoners whom they had brought.

These by no means included all of their captives, for nearly a hundred were left behind, because they belonged to warriors who had gone to the Illinois to procure arms and ammunition from the French; and there is no authority in an Indian community powerful enough to deprive the meanest warrior of his property, even in circumstances of the greatest public exigency. This was clearly understood by the English commander, and he therefore received the submission of the Shawanoes, at the same time compelling them to deliver hostages for the future surrender of the remaining prisoners.

Band after band of captives had been daily arriving, until upwards of two hundred were now collected in the camp; including, as far as could be ascertained, all who had been in the hands of the Indians, excepting those belonging to the absent warriors of the Shawanoes. Up to this time, Bouquet had maintained a stern and rigorous demeanor; repressing his natural clemency and humanity, refusing all friendly intercourse with the Indians, and telling them that he should treat them as enemies until they had fully complied with all the required conditions. In this, he displayed his knowledge of their character; for, like all warlike savages, they are extremely prone to interpret lenity and moderation into timidity and indecision; and he who, from good-nature or mistaken philanthropy, is betrayed into yielding a point which he has before insisted on, may have deep cause to rue it. As their own dealings with their enemies are not leavened with such humanizing ingredients, they can seldom comprehend them; and to win over an Indian foe by kindness should only be attempted by one who has already proved clearly that he is able and ready to subdue him by force.

But now, when every condition was satisfied, such inexorable rigor was no longer demanded; and, having convoked the chiefs in the sylvan council-house, Bouquet signified his willingness to receive their offers of peace.

"Brother," began the Indian orator, "with this belt of wampum I dispel the black cloud that has hung so long over our heads, that the sunshine of peace may once more descend to warm and gladden us. I wipe the tears from your eyes, and condole with you on the loss of your brethren who have perished in this war. I gather their bones together, and cover them deep in the earth, that the sight of them may no longer bring sorrow to your hearts; and I scatter dry leaves over the spot, that it may depart for ever from memory.

"The path of peace, which once ran between your dwellings and mine, has of late been choked with thorns and briers, so that no one could pass that way; and we have both almost forgotten that such a path had ever been. I now clear away all such obstructions, and make a broad, smooth road, so that you and I may freely visit each other, as our fathers used to do. I kindle a great council-fire, whose smoke shall rise to heaven, in view of all the nations; while you and I sit together and smoke the peace-pipe at its blaze."

In this strain, the orator of each tribe, in turn, expressed the purpose of his people to lay down their arms, and live for the future in friendship with the English. Every deputation received a separate audience, and the successive conferences were thus extended through several days. To each and all, Bouquet made a similar reply, in words to the following effect:—

"By your full compliance with the conditions which I imposed, you have satisfied me of your sincerity, and I now receive you once more as brethren. The King, my master, has commissioned me, not to make treaties for him, but to fight his battles; and though I now offer you peace, it is not in my power to settle its precise terms and conditions. For this, I refer you to Sir William Johnson, his Majesty's agent and superintendent for Indian affairs, who will settle with you the articles of peace, and determine every thing in relation to trade. Two things, however, I shall insist on. And, first, you are to give hostages, as security that you will preserve good faith, and send, without delay, a deputation of your chiefs to Sir William Johnson. In the next place, these chiefs are to be fully empowered to treat in behalf of your nation; and you will bind yourselves to adhere strictly to every thing they shall agree upon in your behalf."

These demands were readily complied with. Hostages were given, and chiefs appointed for the embassy; and now, for the first time, Bouquet, to the great relief of the Indians,—for they doubted his intentions,—extended to them the hand of friendship, which he had so long withheld. A prominent chief of the Delawares, too proud to sue for peace, had refused to attend the council; on which Bouquet ordered him to be deposed, and a successor, of a less obdurate spirit, installed in his place. The Shawanoes were the last of the tribes admitted to a hearing; and the demeanor of their orator clearly evinced the haughty reluctance with which he stooped to ask peace of his mortal enemies.

"When you came among us," such were his concluding words, "you came with a hatchet raised to strike us. We now take it from your hand, and throw it up to the Great Spirit, that he may do with it what shall seem good in his sight. We hope that you, who are warriors, will take hold of the chain of friendship which we now extend to you. We, who are also warriors, will take hold as you do; and we will think no more of war, in pity for our women, children, and old men."

On this occasion, the Shawanoe chiefs, expressing a hope for a renewal of the friendship which in former years had subsisted between their people and the English, displayed the dilapidated parchments of several treaties made between their ancestors and the descendants of William Penn,—documents, some of which had been preserved among them for more than half a century, with the scrupulous respect they are prone to exhibit for such ancestral records. They were told that, since they had not delivered all their prisoners, they could scarcely expect to meet the same indulgence which had been extended to their brethren; but that, nevertheless, in full belief of their sincerity, the English would grant them peace, on condition of their promising to surrender the remaining captives early in the following spring, and giving up six of their chiefs as hostages. These conditions were agreed to; and it may be added that, at the appointed time, all the prisoners who had been left in their hands, to the number of a hundred, were brought in to Fort Pitt, and delivered up to the commanding officer.

From the hard formalities and rigid self-control of an Indian council-house, where the struggles of fear, rage, and hatred were deep buried beneath a surface of iron immobility, we turn to scenes of a widely different nature; an exhibition of mingled and contrasted passions, more worthy the pen of the dramatist than that of the historian; who, restricted to the meagre outline of recorded authority, can reflect but a feeble image of the truth. In the ranks of the Pennsylvania troops, and among the Virginia riflemen, were the fathers, brothers, and husbands of those whose rescue from captivity was a chief object of the march. Ignorant what had befallen them, and doubtful whether they were yet among the living, these men had joined the army, in the feverish hope of winning them back to home and civilization. Perhaps those whom they sought had perished by the slow torments of the stake; perhaps by the more merciful hatchet; or perhaps they still dragged out a wretched life in the midst of a savage horde. There were instances in which whole families had been carried off at once. The old, the sick, or the despairing, had been tomahawked, as useless encumbrances; while the rest, pitilessly forced asunder, were scattered through every quarter of the wilderness. It was a strange and moving sight, when troop after troop of prisoners arrived in succession—the meeting of husbands with wives, and fathers with children, the reunion of broken families, long separated in a disastrous captivity; and, on the other hand, the agonies of those who learned tidings of death and horror, or groaned under the torture of protracted suspense. Women, frantic between hope and fear, were rushing hither and thither, in search of those whose tender limbs had, perhaps, long since fattened the cubs of the she-wolf; or were pausing, in an agony of doubt, before some sunburnt young savage, who, startled at the haggard apparition, shrank from his forgotten parent, and clung to the tawny breast of his adopted mother. Others were divided between delight and anguish: on the one hand, the joy of an unexpected recognition; and, on the other, the misery of realized fears, or the more intolerable pangs of doubts not yet resolved. Of all the spectators of this tragic drama, few were obdurate enough to stand unmoved. The roughest soldiers felt the contagious sympathy, and softened into unwonted tenderness.

Among the children brought in for surrender, there were some, who, captured several years before, as early, perhaps, as the French war, had lost every recollection of friends and home. Terrified by the novel sights around them, the flash and glitter of arms, and the strange complexion of the pale-faced warriors, they screamed and struggled lustily when consigned to the hands of their relatives. There were young women, too, who had become the partners of Indian husbands; and who now, with all their hybrid offspring, were led reluctantly into the presence of fathers or brothers whose images were almost blotted from their memory. They stood agitated and bewildered; the revival of old affections, and the rush of dormant memories, painfully contending with more recent attachments, and the shame of their real or fancied disgrace; while their Indian lords looked on, scarcely less moved than they, yet hardening themselves with savage stoicism, and standing in the midst of their enemies, imperturbable as statues of bronze. These women were compelled to return with their children to the settlements; yet they all did so with reluctance, and several afterwards made their escape, eagerly hastening back to their warrior husbands, and the toils and vicissitudes of an Indian wigwam.

Day after day brought renewals of these scenes, deepening in interest as they drew towards their close. A few individual incidents have been recorded. A young Virginian, robbed of his wife but a few months before, had volunteered in the expedition with the faint hope of recovering her; and, after long suspense, had recognized her among a troop of prisoners, bearing in her arms a child born during her captivity. But the joy of the meeting was bitterly alloyed by the loss of a former child, not two years old, captured with the mother, but soon taken from her, and carried, she could not tell whither. Days passed on; they could learn no tidings of its fate, and the mother, harrowed with terrible imaginations, was almost driven to despair; when, at length, she discovered her child in the arms of an Indian warrior, and snatched it with an irrepressible cry of transport.

When the army, on its homeward march, reached the town of Carlisle, those who had been unable to follow the expedition came thither in numbers, to inquire for the friends they had lost. Among the rest was an old woman, whose daughter had been carried off nine years before. In the crowd of female captives, she discovered one in whose wild and swarthy features she discerned the altered lineaments of her child; but the girl, who had almost forgotten her native tongue, returned no sign of recognition to her eager words, and the old woman bitterly complained that the daughter, whom she had so often sung to sleep on her knee, had forgotten her in her old age. Bouquet suggested an expedient which proves him a man of feeling and perception. "Sing the song that you used to sing to her when a child." The old woman obeyed; and a sudden start, a look of bewilderment, and a passionate flood of tears, removed every doubt, and restored the long-lost daughter to her mother's arms.

The tender affections by no means form a salient feature in the Indian character. They hold them in contempt, and scorn every manifestation of them; yet, on this occasion, they would not be repressed, and the human heart betrayed itself, though throbbing under a breastplate of ice. None of the ordinary signs of emotion, neither tears, words, nor looks, declared how greatly they were moved. It was by their kindness and solicitude, by their attention to the wants of the captives, by their offers of furs, garments, the choicest articles of food, and every thing which in their eyes seemed luxury, that they displayed their sorrow at parting from their adopted relatives and friends. Some among them went much farther, and asked permission to follow the army on its homeward march, that they might hunt for the captives, and supply them with better food than the military stores could furnish. A young Seneca warrior had become deeply enamoured of a Virginian girl. At great risk of his life, he accompanied the troops far within the limits of the settlements; and, at every night's encampment, approaching the quarters of the captives as closely as the sentinels would permit, he sat watching, with patient vigilance, to catch a glimpse of his lost mistress.

The Indian women, whom no idea of honor compels to wear an iron mask, were far from emulating the frigid demeanor of their lords. All day they ran wailing through the camp; and, when night came, the hills and woods resounded with their dreary lamentations.

The word prisoner, as applied to captives taken by the Indians, is a misnomer, and conveys a wholly false impression of their situation and treatment. When the vengeance of the conquerors is sated; when they have shot, stabbed, burned, or beaten to death, enough to satisfy the shades of their departed relatives, they usually treat those who survive their wrath with moderation and humanity; often adopting them to supply the place of lost brothers, husbands, or children, whose names are given to the successors thus substituted in their place. By a formal ceremony, the white blood is washed from their veins; and they are regarded thenceforth as members of the tribe, faring equally with the rest in prosperity or adversity, in famine or abundance. When children are adopted in this manner by Indian women, they nurture them with the same tenderness and indulgence which they extend, in a remarkable degree, to their own offspring; and such young women as will not marry an Indian husband are treated with a singular forbearance, in which superstition, natural temperament, and a sense of right and justice may all claim a share. The captive, unless he excites suspicion by his conduct, or exhibits peculiar contumacy, is left with no other restraint than his own free will. The warrior who captured him, or to whom he was assigned in the division of the spoil, sometimes claims, it is true, a certain right of property in him, to the exclusion of others; but this claim is soon forgotten, and is seldom exercised to the inconvenience of the captive, who has no other prison than the earth, the air, and the forest. Five hundred miles of wilderness, beset with difficulty and danger, are the sole bars to his escape, should he desire to effect it; but, strange as it may appear, this wish is apt to expire in his heart, and he often remains to the end of his life a contented denizen of the woods.

Among the captives brought in for delivery were some bound fast to prevent their escape; and many others, who, amid the general tumult of joy and sorrow, sat sullen and scowling, angry that they were forced to abandon the wild license of the forest for the irksome restraints of society. Thus to look back with a fond longing to inhospitable deserts, where men, beasts, and Nature herself, seem arrayed in arms, and where ease, security, and all that civilization reckons among the goods of life, are alike cut off, may appear to argue some strange perversity or moral malformation. Yet such has been the experience of many a sound and healthful mind. To him who has once tasted the reckless independence, the haughty self-reliance, the sense of irresponsible freedom, which the forest life engenders, civilization thenceforth seems flat and stale. Its pleasures are insipid, its pursuits wearisome, its conventionalities, duties, and mutual dependence alike tedious and disgusting. The entrapped wanderer grows fierce and restless, and pants for breathing-room. His path, it is true, was choked with difficulties, but his body and soul were hardened to meet them; it was beset with dangers, but these were the very spice of his life, gladdening his heart with exulting self-confidence, and sending the blood through his veins with a livelier current. The wilderness, rough, harsh, and inexorable, has charms more potent in their seductive influence than all the lures of luxury and sloth. And often he on whom it has cast its magic finds no heart to dissolve the spell, and remains a wanderer and an Ishmaelite to the hour of his death.

There is a chord, in the breasts of most men, prompt to answer loudly or faintly, as the case may be, to such rude appeals. But there is influence of another sort, strongest with minds of the finest texture, yet sometimes holding a controlling power over those who neither acknowledge nor suspect its workings. There are few so imbruted by vice, so perverted by art and luxury, as to dwell in the closest presence of Nature, deaf to her voice of melody and power, untouched by the ennobling influences which mould and penetrate the heart that has not hardened itself against them. Into the spirit of such an one the mountain wind breathes its own freshness, and the midsummer tempest, as it rends the forest, pours its own fierce energy. His thoughts flow with the placid stream of the broad, deep river, or dance in light with the sparkling current of the mountain brook. No passing mood or fancy of his mind but has its image and its echo in the wild world around him. There is softness in the mellow air, the warm sunshine, and the budding leaves of spring; and in the forest flower, which, more delicate than the pampered offspring of gardens, lifts its tender head through the refuse and decay of the wilderness. But it is the grand and heroic in the hearts of men which finds its worthiest symbol and noblest inspiration amid these desert realms,—in the mountain, rearing its savage head through clouds and sleet, or basking its majestic strength in the radiance of the sinking sun; in the interminable forest, the thunder booming over its lonely waste, the whirlwind tearing through its inmost depths, or the sun at length setting in gorgeous majesty beyond its waves of verdure. To the sick, the wearied, or the sated spirit, nature opens a theatre of boundless life, and holds forth a cup brimming with redundant pleasure. In the other joys of existence, fear is balanced against hope, and satiety against delight; but here one may fearlessly drink, gaining, with every draught, new vigor and a heightened zest, and finding no dregs of bitterness at the bottom.

Having accomplished its work, the army left the Muskingum, and, retracing its former course, arrived at Fort Pitt on the twenty-eighth of November. The recovered captives were sent to their respective homes in Pennsylvania or Virginia; and the provincial troops disbanded, not without warm praises for the hardihood and steadiness with which they had met the difficulties of the campaign. The happy issue of the expedition spread joy throughout the country. At the next session of the Pennsylvania Assembly, one of its first acts was to pass a vote of thanks to Colonel Bouquet, expressing in earnest terms its sense of his services and personal merits, and conveying its acknowledgments for the regard which he had constantly shown to the civil rights of the inhabitants. The Assembly of Virginia passed a similar vote; and both houses concurred in recommending Bouquet to the King for promotion.

Nevertheless, his position was far from being an easy or a pleasant one. It may be remembered that the desertion of his newly levied soldiers had forced him to ask Colonel Lewis to raise for him one or two companies of Virginian volunteers. Virginia, which had profited by the campaign, though contributing nothing to it, refused to pay these troops; and its agents tried to throw the burden upon Bouquet in person. The Assembly of Pennsylvania, with a justice and a generosity which went far to redeem the past, came to his relief and assumed the debt, though not till he had suffered the most serious annoyance. Certain recent military regulations contributed at the same time to increase his vexation and his difficulties. He had asked in vain, the year before, to be relieved from his command. He now asked again, and the request was granted; on which he wrote to Gage: "The disgust I have conceived from the ill-nature and ingratitude of those individuals (the Virginian officials) makes me accept with great satisfaction your obliging offer to discharge me of this department, in which I never desire to serve again, nor, indeed, to be commanding officer in any other, since the new regulations you were pleased to communicate to me; being sensible of my inability to carry on the service upon the terms prescribed."

He was preparing to return to Europe, when he received the announcement of his promotion to the rank of Brigadier General. He was taken completely by surprise; for he had supposed that the rigid prescriptions of the service had closed the path of advancement against him, as a foreigner. "I had, today," he wrote to Gage, "the honor of your Excellency's letter of the fifteenth instant. The unexpected honor, which his Majesty has condescended to confer upon me, fills my heart with the utmost gratitude. Permit me, sir, to express my sincere acknowledgments of my great obligation to you.... The flattering prospect of preferment, open to the other foreign officers by the removal of that dreadful barrier, gives me the highest satisfaction, being convinced that his Majesty has no subjects more devoted to his service."

Among the letters of congratulation which he received from officers serving under him is the following, from Captain George Etherington, of the first battalion of the Royal American regiment, who commanded at Michillimackinac when it was captured:—

"Lancaster, Pa., 19 April, 1765.

"Sir:

"Though I almost despair of this reaching you before you sail for Europe, yet I cannot deny myself the pleasure of giving you joy on your promotion, and can with truth tell you that it gives great joy to all the gentlemen of the battalion, for two reasons: first, on your account; and, secondly, on our own, as by that means we may hope for the pleasure of continuing under your command.

"You can hardly imagine how this place rings with the news of your promotion, for the townsmen and boors (i.e., German farmers) stop us in the streets to ask if it is true that the King has made Colonel Bouquet a general; and, when they are told it is true, they march off with great joy; so you see the old proverb wrong for once, which says, he that prospers is envied; for sure I am that all the people here are more pleased with the news of your promotion than they would be if the government would take off the stamp duty....

"Geo. Etherington.

"Brigadier General Henry Bouquet."

"And," concludes Dr. William Smith, the chronicler of the campaign, "as he is rendered as dear by his private virtues to those who have the honor of his more intimate acquaintance, as he is by his military services to the public, it is hoped he may long continue among us, where his experienced abilities will enable him, and his love of the English constitution entitle him, to fill any future trust to which his Majesty may be pleased to call him." This hope was not destined to fulfilment. Bouquet was assigned to the command of the southern military department; and, within three years after his return from the Muskingum, he was attacked with a fever at Pensacola, which closed the career of a gallant soldier and a generous man.

The Delawares and Shawanoes, mindful of their engagement and of the hostages which they had given to keep it, sent their deputies, within the appointed time, to Sir William Johnson, who concluded a treaty with them; stipulating, among the other terms, that they should grant free passage through their country to English troops and travellers; that they should make full restitution for the goods taken from the traders at the breaking out of the war; and that they should aid their triumphant enemies in the difficult task which yet remained to be accomplished,—that of taking possession of the Illinois, and occupying its posts and settlements with British troops.

THE ILLINOIS

1764

We turn to a region of which, as yet, we have caught but transient glimpses; a region which to our forefathers seemed remote and strange, as to us the mountain strongholds of the Apaches, or the wastes of farthest Oregon. The country of the Illinois was chiefly embraced within the boundaries of the state which now retains the name. Thitherward, from the east, the west, and the north, three mighty rivers rolled their tributary waters; while countless smaller streams—small only in comparison—traversed the land with a watery network, impregnating the warm soil with exuberant fecundity. From the eastward, the Ohio—La Belle Rivière—pursued its windings for more than a thousand miles. The Mississippi descended from the distant north; while from its fountains in the west, three thousand miles away, the Missouri poured its torrent towards the same common centre. Born among mountains, trackless even now, except by the adventurous footstep of the trapper,—nurtured amid the howling of beasts and the war-cries of savages, never silent in that wilderness,—it holds its angry course through sun-scorched deserts, among towers and palaces, the architecture of no human hand, among lodges of barbarian hordes, and herds of bison blackening the prairie to the horizon. Fierce, reckless, headstrong, exulting in its tumultuous force, it plays a thousand freaks of wanton power; bearing away forests from its shores, and planting them, with roots uppermost, in its quicksands; sweeping off islands, and rebuilding them; frothing and raging in foam and whirlpool, and, again, gliding with dwindled current along its sandy channel. At length, dark with uncurbed fury, it pours its muddy tide into the reluctant Mississippi. That majestic river, drawing life from the pure fountains of the north, wandering among emerald prairies and wood-crowned bluffs, loses all its earlier charm with this unhallowed union. At first, it shrinks as with repugnance; and along the same channel the two streams flow side by side, with unmingled waters. But the disturbing power prevails at length; and the united torrent bears onward in its might, boiling up from the bottom, whirling in many a vortex, flooding its shores with a malign deluge fraught with pestilence and fever, and burying forests in its depths, to insnare the heedless voyager. Mightiest among rivers, it is the connecting link of adverse climates and contrasted races; and, while at its northern source the fur-clad Indian shivers in the cold, where it mingles with the ocean, the growth of the tropics springs along its banks, and the panting negro cools his limbs in its refreshing waters.

To these great rivers and their tributary streams the country of the Illinois owed its wealth, its grassy prairies, and the stately woods that flourished on its deep, rich soil. This prolific land teemed with life. It was a hunter's paradise. Deer grazed on its meadows. The elk trooped in herds, like squadrons of cavalry. In the still morning, one might hear the clatter of their antlers for half a mile over the dewy prairie. Countless bison roamed the plains, filing in grave procession to drink at the rivers, plunging and snorting among the rapids and quicksands, rolling their huge bulk on the grass, rushing upon each other in hot encounter, like champions under shield. The wildcat glared from the thicket; the raccoon thrust his furry countenance from the hollow tree, and the opossum swung, head downwards, from the overhanging bough.

With the opening spring, when the forests are budding into leaf, and the prairies gemmed with flowers; when a warm, faint haze rests upon the landscape,—then heart and senses are inthralled with luxurious beauty. The shrubs and wild fruit-trees, flushed with pale red blossoms, and the small clustering flowers of grape-vines, which choke the gigantic trees with Laocoön writhings, fill the forest with their rich perfume. A few days later, and a cloud of verdure overshadows the land; while birds innumerable sing beneath its canopy, and brighten its shades with their glancing hues.

Yet this western paradise is not free from the primal curse. The beneficent sun, which kindles into life so many forms of loveliness and beauty, fails not to engender venom and death from the rank slime of pestilential swamp and marsh. In some stagnant pool, buried in the jungle-like depths of the forest, where the hot and lifeless water reeks with exhalations, the watersnake basks by the margin, or winds his checkered length of loathsome beauty across the sleepy surface. From beneath the rotten carcass of some fallen tree, the moccason thrusts out his broad flat head, ready to dart on the intruder. On the dry, sun-scorched prairie, the rattlesnake, a more generous enemy, reposes in his spiral coil. He scorns to shun the eye of day, as if conscious of the honor accorded to his name by the warlike race, who, jointly with him, claim lordship over the land. But some intrusive footstep awakes him from his slumbers. His neck is arched; the white fangs gleam in his distended jaws; his small eyes dart rays of unutterable fierceness; and his rattles, invisible with their quick vibration, ring the sharp warning which no man will dare to contemn.

The land thus prodigal of good and evil, so remote from the sea, so primitive in its aspect, might well be deemed an undiscovered region, ignorant of European arts; yet it may boast a colonization as old as that of many a spot to which are accorded the scanty honors of an American antiquity. The earliest settlement of Pennsylvania was made in 1681; the first occupation of the Illinois took place in the previous year. La Salle may be called the father of the colony. That remarkable man entered the country with a handful of followers, bent on his grand scheme of Mississippi discovery. A legion of enemies rose in his path; but neither delay, disappointment, sickness, famine, open force, nor secret conspiracy, could bend his soul of iron. Disasters accumulated upon him. He flung them off, and still pressed forward to his object. His victorious energy bore all before it; but the success on which he had staked his life served only to entail fresh calamity, and an untimely death; and his best reward is, that his name stands forth in history an imperishable monument of heroic constancy. When on his way to the Mississippi, in the year 1680, La Salle built a fort in the country of the Illinois; and, on his return from the mouth of the great river, some of his followers remained, and established themselves near the spot. Heroes of another stamp took up the work which the daring Norman had begun. Jesuit missionaries, among the best and purest of their order, burning with zeal for the salvation of souls, and the gaining of an immortal crown, here toiled and suffered, with a self-sacrificing devotion which extorts a tribute of admiration even from sectarian bigotry. While the colder apostles of Protestantism labored upon the outskirts of heathendom, these champions of the cross, the forlorn hope of the army of Rome, pierced to the heart of its dark and dreary domain, confronting death at every step, and well repaid for all, could they but sprinkle a few drops of water on the forehead of a dying child, or hang a gilded crucifix round the neck of some warrior, pleased with the glittering trinket. With the beginning of the eighteenth century, the black robe of the Jesuit was known in every village of the Illinois. Defying the wiles of Satan and the malice of his emissaries, the Indian sorcerers; exposed to the rage of the elements, and every casualty of forest life, they followed their wandering proselytes to war and to the chase; now wading through morasses, now dragging canoes over rapids and sandbars; now scorched with heat on the sweltering prairie, and now shivering houseless in the blasts of January. At Kaskaskia and Cahokia they established missions, and built frail churches from the bark of trees, fit emblems of their own transient and futile labors. Morning and evening, the savage worshippers sang praises to the Virgin, and knelt in supplication before the shrine of St. Joseph.

Soldiers and fur-traders followed where these pioneers of the church had led the way. Forts were built here and there throughout the country, and the cabins of settlers clustered about the mission-houses. The new colonists, emigrants from Canada or disbanded soldiers of French regiments, bore a close resemblance to the settlers of Detroit, or the primitive people of Acadia; whose simple life poetry has chosen as an appropriate theme, but who, nevertheless, are best contemplated from a distance. The Creole of the Illinois, contented, light-hearted, and thriftless, by no means fulfilled the injunction to increase and multiply; and the colony languished in spite of the fertile soil. The people labored long enough to gain a bare subsistence for each passing day, and spent the rest of their time in dancing and merry-making, smoking, gossiping, and hunting. Their native gayety was irrepressible, and they found means to stimulate it with wine made from the fruit of the wild grape-vines. Thus they passed their days, at peace with themselves, hand and glove with their Indian neighbors, and ignorant of all the world beside. Money was scarcely known among them. Skins and furs were the prevailing currency, and in every village a great portion of the land was held in common. The military commandant, whose station was at Fort Chartres, on the Mississippi, ruled the colony with a sway absolute as that of the Pacha of Egypt, and judged civil and criminal cases without right of appeal. Yet his power was exercised in a patriarchal spirit, and he usually commanded the respect and confidence of the people. Many years later, when, after the War of the Revolution, the Illinois came under the jurisdiction of the United States, the perplexed inhabitants, totally at a loss to understand the complicated machinery of republicanism, begged to be delivered from the intolerable burden of self-government, and to be once more subjected to a military commandant.

The Creole is as unchanging in his nature and habits as the Indian himself. Even at this day, one may see, along the banks of the Mississippi, the same low-browed cottages, with their broad eaves and picturesque verandas, which, a century ago, were clustered around the mission-house at Kaskaskia; and, entering, one finds the inmate the same lively, story-telling, and pipe-smoking being that his ancestor was before him. Yet, with all his genial traits, the rough world deals hardly with him. He lives a mere drone in the busy hive of an American population. The living tide encroaches on his rest, as the muddy torrent of the great river chafes away the farm and homestead of his fathers. Yet he contrives to be happy, though looking back regretfully to the better days of old.

At the date of this history, the population of the colony, exclusive of negroes, who, in that simple community, were treated rather as humble friends than as slaves, did not exceed two thousand souls, distributed in several small settlements. There were about eighty houses at Kaskaskia, forty or fifty at Cahokia, a few at Vincennes and Fort Chartres, and a few more scattered in small clusters upon the various streams. The agricultural portion of the colonists were, as we have described them, marked with many weaknesses, and many amiable virtues; but their morals were not improved by a large admixture of fur-traders,—reckless, harebrained adventurers, who, happily for the peace of their relatives, were absent on their wandering vocation during the greater part of the year.

Swarms of vagabond Indians infested the settlements; and, to people of any other character, they would have proved an intolerable annoyance. But the easy-tempered Creoles made friends and comrades of them; ate, drank, smoked, and often married with them. They were a debauched and drunken rabble, the remnants of that branch of the Algonquin stock known among the French as the Illinois, a people once numerous and powerful, but now miserably enfeebled, and corrupted by foreign wars, domestic dissensions, and their own licentious manners. They comprised the broken fragments of five tribes,—the Kaskaskias, Cahokias, Peorias, Mitchigamias, and Tamaronas. Some of their villages were in the close vicinity of the Creole settlements. On a hot summer morning, they might be seen lounging about the trading-house, basking in the sun, begging for a dram of whiskey, or chaffering with the hard-featured trader for beads, tobacco, gunpowder, and red paint.

About the Wabash and its branches, to the eastward of the Illinois, dwelt tribes of similar lineage, but more warlike in character, and less corrupt in manners. These were the Miamis, in their three divisions, their near kindred, the Piankishaws, and a portion of the Kickapoos. There was another settlement of the Miamis upon the River Maumee, still farther to the east; and it was here that Bradstreet's ambassador, Captain Morris, had met so rough a welcome. The strength of these combined tribes was very considerable; and, one and all, they looked with wrath and abhorrence on the threatened advent of the English.

PONTIAC RALLIES THE WESTERN TRIBES

1763 to 1765

When, by the treaty of Paris, in 1763, France ceded to England her territories east of the Mississippi, the Illinois was of course included in the cession. Scarcely were the articles signed, when France, as if eager to rob herself, at one stroke, of all her western domain, threw away upon Spain the vast and indefinite regions beyond the Mississippi, destined at a later day to return to her hands, and finally to swell the growing empire of the United States. This transfer to Spain was for some time kept secret; but orders were immediately sent to the officers commanding at the French posts within the territory ceded to England, to evacuate the country whenever British troops should appear to occupy it. These orders reached the Illinois towards the close of 1763. Some time, however, must necessarily elapse before the English could take possession; for the Indian war was then at its height, and the country was protected from access by a broad barrier of savage tribes, in the hottest ferment of hostility.

The colonists, hating the English with a more than national hatred, deeply imbittered by years of disastrous war, received the news of the treaty with disgust and execration. Many of them left the country, loath to dwell under the shadow of the British flag. Of these, some crossed the Mississippi to the little hamlet of St. Genevieve, on the western bank; others followed the commandant, Neyon de Villiers, to New Orleans; while others, taking with them all their possessions, even to the frames and clapboarding of their houses, passed the river a little above Cahokia, and established themselves at a beautiful spot on the opposite shore, where a settlement was just then on the point of commencement. Here a line of richly wooded bluffs rose with easy ascent from the margin of the water; while from their summits extended a wide plateau of fertile prairie, bordered by a framework of forest. In the shadow of the trees, which fringed the edge of the declivity, stood a newly-built storehouse, with a few slight cabins and works of defence, belonging to a company of fur-traders. At their head was Pierre Laclede, who had left New Orleans with his followers in August, 1763; and, after toiling for three months against the impetuous stream of the Mississippi, had reached the Illinois in November, and selected the spot alluded to as the site of his first establishment. To this he gave the name of St. Louis. Side by side with Laclede, in his adventurous enterprise, was a young man, slight in person, but endowed with a vigor and elasticity of frame which could resist heat or cold, fatigue, hunger, or the wasting hand of time. Not all the magic of a dream, nor the enchantments of an Arabian tale, could outmatch the waking realities which were to rise upon the vision of Pierre Chouteau. Where, in his youth, he had climbed the woody bluff, and looked abroad on prairies dotted with bison, he saw, with the dim eye of his old age, the land darkened for many a furlong with the clustered roofs of the western metropolis. For the silence of the wilderness, he heard the clang and turmoil of human labor, the din of congregated thousands; and where the great river rolled down through the forest, in lonely grandeur, he saw the waters lashed into foam beneath the prows of panting steamboats, flocking to the broad levee.

In the summer of 1764, the military commandant, Neyon, had abandoned the country in disgust, and gone down to New Orleans, followed by many of the inhabitants; a circumstance already mentioned. St. Ange de Bellerive remained behind to succeed him. St. Ange was a veteran Canadian officer, the same who, more than forty years before, had escorted Father Charlevoix through the country, and who is spoken of with high commendation by the Jesuit traveller and historian. He took command of about forty men, the remnant of the garrison of Fort Chartres; which, remote as it was, was then esteemed one of the best constructed military works in America. Its ramparts of stone, garnished with twenty cannon, scowled across the encroaching Mississippi, destined, before many years, to ingulf curtain and bastion in its ravenous abyss.

St. Ange's position was by no means an enviable one. He had a critical part to play. On the one hand, he had been advised of the cession to the English, and ordered to yield up the country whenever they should arrive to claim it. On the other, he was beset by embassies from Pontiac, from the Shawanoes, and from the Miamis, and plagued day and night by an importunate mob of Illinois Indians, demanding arms, ammunition, and assistance against the common enemy. Perhaps, in his secret heart, St. Ange would have rejoiced to see the scalps of all the Englishmen in the backwoods fluttering in the wind over the Illinois wigwams; but his situation forbade him to comply with the solicitations of his intrusive petitioners, and it is to be hoped that some sense of honor and humanity enforced the dictates of prudence. Accordingly, he cajoled them with flatteries and promises, and from time to time distributed a few presents to stay their importunity, still praying daily that the English might appear and relieve him from his uneasy dilemma.

While Laclede was founding St. Louis, while the discontented settlers of the Illinois were deserting their homes, and while St. Ange was laboring to pacify his Indian neighbors, all the tribes from the Maumee to the Mississippi were in a turmoil of excitement. Pontiac was among them, furious as a wild beast at bay. By the double campaign of 1764, his best hopes had been crushed to the earth; but he stood unshaken amidst the ruin, and still struggled with desperate energy to retrieve his broken cause. On the side of the northern lakes, the movements of Bradstreet had put down the insurrection of the tribes, and wrested back the military posts which cunning and treachery had placed within their grasp. In the south, Bouquet had forced to abject submission the warlike Delawares and Shawanoes, the warriors on whose courage and obstinacy Pontiac had grounded his strongest confidence. On every hand defeat and disaster were closing around him. One sanctuary alone remained, the country of the Illinois. Here the flag of France still floated on the banks of the Mississippi, and here no English foot had dared to penetrate. He resolved to invoke all his resources, and bend all his energies to defend this last citadel.

He was not left to contend unaided. The fur-trading French, living at the settlements on the Mississippi, scattered about the forts of Ouatanon, Vincennes, and Miami, or domesticated among the Indians of the Rivers Illinois and Wabash, dreaded the English as dangerous competitors in their vocation, and were eager to bar them from the country. They lavished abuse and calumny on the objects of their jealousy, and spared no falsehood which ingenious malice and self-interest could suggest. They gave out that the English were bent on the ruin of the tribes, and to that end were stirring them up to mutual hostility. They insisted that, though the armies of France had been delayed so long, they were nevertheless on their way, and that the bayonets of the white-coated warriors would soon glitter among the forests of the Mississippi. Forged letters were sent to Pontiac, signed by the King of France, exhorting him to stand his ground but a few weeks longer, and all would then be well. To give the better coloring to their falsehoods, some of these incendiaries assumed the uniform of French officers, and palmed themselves off upon their credulous auditors as ambassadors from the king. Many of the principal traders distributed among the warriors supplies of arms and ammunition, in some instances given gratuitously, and in others sold on credit, with the understanding that payment should be made from the plunder of the English.

Now that the insurrection in the east was quelled, and the Delawares and

Shawanoes were beaten into submission, it was thought that the English would lose no time in taking full possession of the country, which, by the peace of 1763, had been transferred into their hands. Two principal routes would give access to the Illinois. Troops might advance from the south up the great natural highway of the Mississippi, or they might descend from the east by way of Fort Pitt and the Ohio. In either case, to meet and repel them was the determined purpose of Pontiac.

In the spring, or early summer, he had come to the Illinois and visited the commandant, Neyon, who was then still at his post. Neyon's greeting was inauspicious. He told his visitor that he hoped he had returned at last to his senses. Pontiac laid before him a large belt of wampum. "My Father," he said, "I come to invite you and all your allies to go with me to war against the English." Neyon asked if he had not received his message of the last autumn, in which he told him that the French and English were thenceforth one people; but Pontiac persisted, and still urged him to take up the hatchet. Neyon at length grew angry, kicked away the wampum belt, and demanded if he could not hear what was said to him. Thus repulsed, Pontiac asked for a keg of rum. Which being given him, he caused to be carried to a neighboring Illinois village; and, with the help of this potent auxiliary, made the assembled warriors join him in the war-song.

It does not appear that, on this occasion, he had any farther success in firing the hearts of the Illinois. He presently returned to his camp on the Maumee, where, by a succession of ill-tidings, he learned the humiliation of his allies, and the triumph of his enemies. Towards the close of autumn, he again left the Maumee; and, followed by four hundred warriors, journeyed westward, to visit in succession the different tribes, and gain their co-operation in his plans of final defence. Crossing over to the Wabash, he passed from village to village, among the Kickapoos, the Piankishaws, and the three tribes of the Miamis, rousing them by his imperious eloquence, and breathing into them his own fierce spirit of resistance. Thence, by rapid marches through forests and over prairies, he reached the banks of the Mississippi, and summoned the four tribes of the Illinois to a general meeting. But these degenerate savages, beaten by the surrounding tribes for many a generation past, had lost their warlike spirit; and, though abundantly noisy and boastful, showed no zeal for fight, and entered with no zest into the schemes of the Ottawa war-chief. Pontiac had his own way of dealing with such spirits. "If you hesitate," he exclaimed, frowning on the cowering assembly, "I will consume your tribes as the fire consumes the dry grass on the prairie." The doubts of the Illinois vanished like the mist, and with marvellous alacrity they declared their concurrence in the views of the orator. Having secured these allies, such as they were, Pontiac departed, and hastened to Fort Chartres. St. Ange, so long tormented with embassy after embassy, and mob after mob, thought that the crowning evil was come at last, when he saw the arch-demon Pontiac enter at the gate, with four hundred warriors at his back. Arrived at the council-house, Pontiac addressed the commandant in a tone of great courtesy: "Father, we have long wished to see you, to shake hands with you, and, whilst smoking the calumet of peace, to recall the battles in which we fought together against the misguided Indians and the English dogs. I love the French, and I have come hither with my warriors to avenge their wrongs." Then followed a demand for arms, ammunition, and troops, to act in concert with the Indian warriors. St. Ange was forced to decline rendering the expected aid; but he sweetened his denial with soothing compliments, and added a few gifts, to remove any lingering bitterness. Pontiac would not be appeased. He angrily complained of such lukewarm friendship, where he had looked for ready sympathy and support. His warriors pitched their lodges about the fort, and threatening symptoms of an approaching rupture began to alarm the French.

In the mean time, Pontiac had caused his squaws to construct a belt of wampum of extraordinary size, six feet in length, and four inches wide. It was wrought from end to end with the symbols of the various tribes and villages, forty-seven in number, still leagued together in his alliance. He consigned it to an embassy of chosen warriors, directing them to carry it down the Mississippi, displaying it, in turn, at every Indian village along its banks; and exhorting the inhabitants, in his name, to watch the movements of the English, and repel any attempt they might make to ascend the river. This done, they were to repair to New Orleans, and demand from the governor, M. D'Abbadie, the aid which St. Ange had refused. The bark canoes of the embassy put out from the shore, and whirled down the current like floating leaves in autumn.

Soon after their departure, tidings came to Fort Chartres, which caused a joyous excitement among the Indians, and relieved the French garrison from any danger of an immediate rupture. In our own day, the vast distance between the great city of New Orleans and the populous state of Illinois has dwindled into insignificance beneath the magic of science; but at the date of this history, three or four months were often consumed in the upward passage, and the settlers of the lonely forest colony were sometimes cut off from all communication with the world for half a year together. The above-mentioned tidings, interesting as they were, had occupied no less time in their passage. Their import was as follows:—

Very early in the preceding spring, an English officer, Major Loftus, having arrived at New Orleans with four hundred regulars, had attempted to ascend the Mississippi, to take possession of Fort Chartres and its dependent posts. His troops were embarked in large and heavy boats. Their progress was slow; and they had reached a point not more than eighty leagues above New Orleans, when, one morning, their ears were greeted with the crack of rifles from the thickets of the western shore; and a soldier in the foremost boat fell, with a mortal wound. The troops, in dismay, sheered over towards the eastern shore; but, when fairly within gunshot, a score of rifles obscured the forest edge with smoke, and filled the nearest boat with dead and wounded men. On this, they steered for the middle of the river, where they remained for a time, exposed to a dropping fire from either bank, too distant to take effect.

The river was high, and the shores so flooded, that nothing but an Indian could hope to find foothold in the miry labyrinth. Loftus was terrified; the troops were discouraged, and a council of officers determined that to advance was impossible. Accordingly, with their best despatch, they steered back for New Orleans, where they arrived without farther accident; and where the French, in great glee at their discomfiture, spared no ridicule at their expense. They alleged, and with much appearance of truth, that the English had been repulsed by no more than thirty warriors. Loftus charged D'Abbadie with having occasioned his disaster by stirring up the Indians to attack him. The governor called Heaven to witness his innocence; and, in truth, there is not the smallest reason to believe him guilty of such villany. Loftus, who had not yet recovered from his fears, conceived an idea that the Indians below New Orleans were preparing an ambuscade to attack him on his way back to his station at Pensacola; and he petitioned D'Abbadie to interfere in his behalf. The latter, with an ill-dissembled sneer, offered to give him and his troops an escort of French soldiers to protect them. Loftus rejected the humiliating proposal, and declared that he only wished for a French interpreter, to confer with any Indians whom he might meet by the way. The interpreter was furnished; and Loftus returned in safety to Pensacola, his detachment not a little reduced by the few whom the Indians had shot, and by numbers who, disgusted by his overbearing treatment, had deserted to the French.

The futile attempt of Loftus to ascend the Mississippi was followed, a few months after, by another equally abortive. Captain Pittman came to New Orleans with the design of proceeding to the Illinois, but was deterred by the reports which reached him concerning the temper of the Indians. The latter, elated beyond measure by their success against Loftus, and excited, moreover, by the messages and war-belt of Pontiac, were in a state of angry commotion, which made the passage too hazardous to be attempted. Pittman bethought himself of assuming the disguise of a Frenchman, joining a party of Creole traders, and thus reaching his destination by stealth; but, weighing the risk of detection, he abandoned this design also, and returned to Mobile. Between the Illinois and the settlements around New Orleans, the Mississippi extended its enormous length through solitudes of marsh and forest, broken here and there by a squalid Indian village; or, at vast intervals, by one or two military posts, erected by the

French, and forming the resting-places of the voyager. After the failure of Pittman, more than a year elapsed before an English detachment could succeed in passing this great thoroughfare of the wilderness, and running the gauntlet of the savage tribes who guarded its shores. It was not till the second of December, 1765, that Major Farmar, at the head of a strong body of troops, arrived, after an uninterrupted voyage, at Fort Chartres, where the flag of his country had already supplanted the standard of France.

To return to our immediate theme. The ambassadors, whom Pontiac had sent from Fort Chartres in the autumn of 1764, faithfully acquitted themselves of their trust. They visited the Indian villages along the river banks, kindling the thirst for blood and massacre in the breasts of the inmates. They pushed their sanguinary mission even to the farthest tribes of Southern Louisiana, to whom the great name of Pontiac had long been known, and of late made familiar by repeated messages and embassies. This portion of their task accomplished, they repaired to New Orleans, and demanded an audience of the governor.

New Orleans was then a town of about seven thousand white inhabitants, guarded from the river floods by a levee extending for fifty miles along the banks. The small brick houses, one story in height, were arranged with geometrical symmetry, like the squares of a chess-board. Each house had its yard and garden, and the town was enlivened with the verdure of trees and grass. In front, a public square, or parade ground, opened upon the river, enclosed on three sides by the dilapidated church of St. Louis, a prison, a convent, government buildings, and a range of barracks. The place was surrounded by a defence of palisades strong enough to repel an attack of Indians, or insurgent slaves.

When Pontiac's ambassadors entered New Orleans, they found the town in a state of confusion. It had long been known that the regions east of the Mississippi had been surrendered to England; a cession from which, however, New Orleans and its suburbs had been excepted by a special provision. But it was only within a few weeks that the dismayed inhabitants had learned that their mother country had transferred her remaining American possessions to the crown of Spain, whose government and people they cordially detested. With every day they might expect the arrival of a Spanish governor and garrison. The French officials, whose hour was drawing to its close, were making the best of their short-lived authority by every species of corruption and peculation; and the inhabitants were awaiting, in anger and repugnance, the approaching change, which was to place over their heads masters whom they hated. The governor, D'Abbadie, an ardent soldier and a zealous patriot, was so deeply chagrined at what he conceived to be the disgrace of his country, that his feeble health gave way, and he betrayed all the symptoms of a rapid decline.

Haggard with illness, and bowed down with shame, the dying governor received the Indian envoys in the council-hall of the province, where he was never again to assume his seat of office. Besides the French officials in attendance, several English officers, who chanced to be in the town, had been invited to the meeting, with the view of soothing the jealousy with which they regarded all intercourse between the French and the Indians. A Shawanoe chief, the orator of the embassy, displayed the great war-belt, and opened the council. "These red dogs," he said, alluding to the color of the British uniform, "have crowded upon us more and more; and when we ask them by what right they come, they tell us that you, our French fathers, have given them our lands. We know that they lie. These lands are neither yours nor theirs, and no man shall give or sell them without our consent. Fathers, we have always been your faithful children; and we now have come to ask that you will give us guns, powder, and lead, to aid us in this war."

D'Abbadie replied in a feeble voice, endeavoring to allay their vindictive jealousy of the English, and promising to give them all that should be necessary to supply their immediate wants. The council then adjourned until the following day; but, in the mean time, the wasted strength of the governor gave way beneath a renewed attack of his disorder; and, before the appointed hour arrived, he had breathed his last, hurried to a premature death by the anguish of mortified pride and patriotism. M. Aubry, his successor, presided in his place, and received the savage embassy. The orator, after the solemn custom of his people, addressed him in a speech of condolence, expressing his deep regret for D'Abbadie's untimely fate. A chief of the Miamis then rose to speak, with a scowling brow, and words of bitterness and reproach. "Since we last sat on these seats, our ears have heard strange words. When the English told us that they had conquered you, we always thought that they lied; but now we have learned that they spoke the truth. We have learned that you, whom we have loved and served so well, have given the lands that we dwell upon to your enemies and ours. We have learned that the English have forbidden you to send traders to our villages to supply our wants; and that you, whom we thought so great and brave, have obeyed their commands like women, leaving us to starve and die in misery. We now tell you, once for all, that our lands are our own; and we tell you, moreover, that we can live without your aid, and hunt, and fish, and fight, as our fathers did before us. All that we ask of you is this: that you give us back the guns, the powder, the hatchets, and the knives which we have worn out in fighting your battles. As for you," he exclaimed, turning to the English officers, who were present as on the preceding day,—"as for you, our hearts burn with rage when we think of the ruin you have brought on us." Aubry returned but a weak answer to the cutting attack of the Indian speaker. He assured the ambassadors that the French still retained their former love for the Indians, that the English meant them no harm, and that, as all the world were now at peace, it behooved them also to take hold of the chain of friendship. A few presents were then distributed, but with no apparent effect. The features of the Indians still retained their sullen scowl; and on the morrow their canoes were ascending the Mississippi on their homeward voyage.

RUIN OF THE INDIAN CAUSE

1765

The repulse of Loftus, and rumors of the fierce temper of the Indians who guarded the Mississippi, convinced the commander-in-chief that to reach the Illinois by the southern route was an enterprise of no easy accomplishment. Yet, at the same time, he felt the strong necessity of a speedy military occupation of the country; since, while the fleur de lis floated over a single garrison in the ceded territory, it would be impossible to disabuse the Indians of the phantom hope of French assistance, to which they clung with infatuated tenacity. The embers of the Indian war would never be quenched until England had enforced all her claims over her defeated rival. Gage determined to despatch a force from the eastward, by way of Fort Pitt and the Ohio; a route now laid open by the late success of Bouquet, and the submission of the Delawares and Shawanoes.
To prepare a way for the passage of the troops, Sir William Johnson's deputy, George Croghan, was ordered to proceed in advance, to reason with the Indians as far as they were capable of reasoning; to soften their antipathy to the English, to expose the falsehoods of the French, and to distribute presents among the tribes by way of propitiation. The mission was a critical one; but, so far as regarded the Indians, Croghan was well fitted to discharge it. He had been for years a trader among the western tribes, over whom he had gained much influence by a certain vigor of character, joined to a wary and sagacious policy, concealed beneath a bluff demeanor. Lieutenant Fraser, a young officer of education and intelligence, was associated with him. He spoke French, and, in other respects also, supplied qualifications in which his rugged colleague was wanting. They set out for Fort Pitt in February, 1765; and after traversing inhospitable

mountains, and valleys clogged with snow, reached their destination at about the same time that Pontiac's ambassadors were entering New Orleans, to hold their council with the French.

A few days later, an incident occurred, which afterwards, through the carousals of many a winter evening, supplied an absorbing topic of anecdote and boast to the braggadocio heroes of the border. A train of pack-horses, bearing the gifts which Croghan was to bestow upon the Indians, followed him towards Fort Pitt, a few days' journey in the rear of his party. Under the same escort came several companies of traders, who, believing that the long suspended commerce with the Indians was about to be reopened, were hastening to Fort Pitt with a great quantity of goods, eager to throw them into the market the moment the prohibition should be removed. There is reason to believe that Croghan had an interest in these goods, and that, under pretence of giving presents, he meant to open a clandestine trade. The Paxton men, and their kindred spirits of the border, saw the proceeding with sinister eyes. In their view, the traders were about to make a barter of the blood of the people; to place in the hands of murdering savages the means of renewing the devastation to which the reeking frontier bore frightful witness. Once possessed with this idea, they troubled themselves with no more inquiries; and, having tried remonstrances in vain, they adopted a summary mode of doing themselves justice. At the head of the enterprise was a man whose name had been connected with more praiseworthy exploits, James Smith, already mentioned as leading a party of independent riflemen, for the defence of the borders, during the bloody autumn of 1763. He now mustered his old associates, made them resume their Indian disguise, and led them to their work with characteristic energy and address.

The government agents and traders were in the act of passing the verge of the frontiers. Their united trains amounted to seventy pack-horses, carrying goods to the value of more than four thousand pounds; while others, to the value of eleven thousand, were waiting transportation at Fort Loudon. Advancing deeper among the mountains, they began to descend the valley at the foot of Sidling Hill. The laden horses plodded knee-deep in snow. The mountains towered above the wayfarers in gray desolation; and the leafless forest, a mighty Æolian harp, howled dreary music to the wind of March. Suddenly, from behind snow-beplastered trunks and shaggy bushes of evergreen, uncouth apparitions started into view. Wild visages protruded, grotesquely horrible with vermilion and ochre, white lead and soot; stalwart limbs appeared, encased in buck-skin; and rusty rifles thrust out their long muzzles. In front, and flank, and all around them, white puffs of smoke and sharp reports assailed the bewildered senses of the travellers, who were yet more confounded by the hum of bullets shot by unerring fingers within an inch of their ears. "Gentlemen," demanded the traders, in deprecating accents, "what would you have us do?" "Unpack your horses," roared a voice from the woods, "pile your goods in the road, and be off." The traders knew those with whom they had to deal. Hastening to obey the mandate, they departed with their utmost speed, happy that their scalps were not numbered with the booty. The spoilers appropriated to themselves such of the plunder as pleased them, made a bonfire of the rest, and went on their way rejoicing. The discomfited traders repaired to Fort Loudon, and laid their complaints before Lieutenant Grant, the commandant; who, inflamed with wrath and zealous for the cause of justice, despatched a party of soldiers, seized several innocent persons, and lodged them in the guard-house. In high dudgeon at such an infraction of their liberties, the borderers sent messengers through the country, calling upon all good men to rise in arms. Three hundred obeyed the summons, and pitched their camp on a hill opposite Fort Loudon; a rare muster of desperadoes, yet observing a certain moderation in their wildest acts, and never at a loss for a plausible reason to justify any pranks which it might please them to exhibit. By some means, they contrived to waylay and capture a considerable number of the garrison, on which the commandant condescended to send them a flag of truce, and offer an exchange of prisoners. Their object thus accomplished, and their imprisoned comrades restored to them, the borderers dispersed for the present to their homes. Soon after, however, upon the occurrence of some fresh difficulty, the commandant, afraid or unable to apprehend the misdoers, endeavored to deprive them of the power of mischief by sending soldiers to their houses and carrying off their rifles. His triumph was short; for, as he rode out one afternoon, he fell into an ambuscade of countrymen, who, dispensing with all forms of respect, seized the incensed officer, and detained him in an uncomfortable captivity until the rifles were restored. From this time forward, ruptures were repeatedly occurring between the troops and the frontiersmen; and the Pennsylvania border retained its turbulent character until the outbreak of the Revolutionary War.

Whatever may have been Croghan's real attitude in this affair, the border robbers had wrought great injury to his mission; since the agency most potent to gain the affections of an Indian had been completely paralyzed in the destruction of the presents. Croghan found means, however, partially to repair his loss from the storehouse of Fort Pitt, where the rigor of the season and the great depth of the snow forced him to remain several weeks. This cause alone would have served to detain him; but he was yet farther retarded by the necessity of holding a meeting with the Delawares and Shawanoes, along whose southern borders he would be compelled to pass. An important object of the proposed meeting was to urge these tribes to fulfil the promise they had made, during the previous autumn, to Colonel Bouquet, to yield up their remaining prisoners, and send deputies to treat of peace with Sir William Johnson; engagements which, when Croghan arrived at the fort, were as yet unfulfilled, though, as already mentioned, they were soon after complied with.

Immediately on his arrival, he had despatched messengers inviting the chiefs to a council; a summons which they obeyed with their usual reluctance and delay, dropping in, band after band, with such tardiness that a month was consumed before a sufficient number were assembled. Croghan then addressed them, showing the advantages of peace, and the peril which they would bring on their own heads by a renewal of the war; and urging them to stand true to their engagements, and send their deputies to Johnson as soon as the melting of the snows should leave the forest pathways open. Several replies, all of a pacific nature, were made by the principal chiefs; but the most remarkable personage who appeared at the council was the Delaware prophet mentioned in an early portion of the narrative, as having been strongly instrumental in urging the tribes to war by means of pretended or imaginary revelations from the Great Spirit. He now delivered a speech by no means remarkable for eloquence, yet of most beneficial consequence; for he intimated that the Great Spirit had not only revoked his sanguinary mandates, but had commanded the Indians to lay down the hatchet, and smoke the pipe of peace. In spite of this auspicious declaration, and in spite of the chastisement and humiliation of the previous autumn, Croghan was privately informed that a large party among the Indians still remained balanced between their anger and their fears; eager to take up the hatchet, yet dreading the consequences which the act might bring. Under this cloudy aspect of affairs, he was doubly gratified when a party of Shawanoe warriors arrived, bringing with them the prisoners whom they had promised Colonel Bouquet to surrender; and this faithful adherence to their word, contrary alike to Croghan's expectations, and to the prophecies of those best versed in Indian character, made it apparent that, whatever might be the sentiments of the turbulent among them, the more influential portion were determined on a pacific attitude.

These councils, and the previous delays, consumed so much time, that Croghan became fearful that the tribes of the Illinois might, meanwhile, commit themselves by some rash outbreak, which would increase the difficulty of reconciliation. In view of this danger, his colleague, Lieutenant Fraser, volunteered to proceed in advance, leaving Croghan to follow when he had settled affairs at Fort Pitt. Fraser departed, accordingly, with a few attendants. The rigor of the season had now begun to relent, and the ice-locked Ohio was flinging off its wintry fetters. Embarked in a birch canoe, and aided by the current, Fraser floated prosperously downwards for a thousand miles, and landed safely in the country of the Illinois. Here he found the Indians in great destitution, and in a frame of mind which would have inclined them to peace but for the secret encouragement they received from the French. A change, however, soon took place. Boats arrived from New Orleans, loaded with a great quantity of goods, which the French, at that place, being about to abandon it, had sent in haste to the Illinois. The traders' shops at Kaskaskia were suddenly filled again. The Indians were delighted; and the French, with a view to a prompt market for their guns, hatchets, and gunpowder, redoubled their incitements to war. Fraser found himself in a hornet's nest. His life was in great danger; but Pontiac, who was then at Kaskaskia, several times interposed to save him. The French traders picked a quarrel with him, and instigated the Indians to kill him; for it was their interest that the war should go on. A party of them invited Pontiac to dinner; plied him with whiskey; and, having made him drunk, incited him to have Fraser and his servant seized. They were brought to the house where the debauch was going on; and here, among a crowd of drunken Indians, their lives hung by a hair. Fraser writes, "He (Pontiac) and his men fought all night about us. They said we would get off next day if they should not prevent our flight by killing us. This Pontiac would not do. All night they did nothing else but sing the death song; but my servant and I, with the help of an Indian who was sober, defended ourselves till morning, when they thought proper to let us escape. When Pontiac was sober, he made me an apology for his behavior; and told me it was owing to bad counsel he had got that he had taken me; but that I need not fear being taken in that manner for the future."

Fraser's situation was presently somewhat improved by a rumor that an English detachment was about to descend the Ohio. The French traders, before so busy with their falsehoods and calumnies, now held their peace, dreading the impending chastisement. They no longer gave arms and ammunition to the Indians; and when the latter questioned them concerning the fabrication of a French army advancing to the rescue, they treated the story as unfounded, or sought to evade the subject. St. Ange, too, and the other officers of the crown, confiding in the arrival of the English, assumed a more decisive tone; refusing to give the Indians presents, telling them that thenceforward they must trust to the English for supplies, reproving them for their designs against the latter, and advising them to remain at peace.

Nevertheless, Fraser's position was neither safe nor pleasant. He could hear nothing of Croghan, and he was almost alone, having sent away all his men; except his servant, to save them from being abused and beaten by the Indians. He had discretionary orders to go down to Mobile and report to the English commandant there; and of these he was but too glad to avail himself. He descended the Mississippi in disguise, and safely reached New Orleans.

Apparently, it was about this time that an incident took place, mentioned, with evident satisfaction, in a letter of the French commandant, Aubry. The

English officers in the south, unable to send troops up the Mississippi, had employed a Frenchman, whom they had secured in their interest, to ascend the river with a boat-load of goods, which he was directed to distribute among the Indians, to remove their prejudice against the English and pave the way to reconciliation. Intelligence of this movement reached the ears of Pontiac, who, though much pleased with the approaching supplies, had no mind that they should be devoted to serve the interests of his enemies. He descended to the river bank with a body of his warriors; and as La Garantais, the Frenchman, landed, he seized him and his men, flogged them severely, robbed them of their cargo, and distributed the goods with exemplary impartiality among his delighted followers.

Notwithstanding this good fortune, Pontiac daily saw his followers dropping off from their allegiance; for even the boldest had lost heart. Had any thing been wanting to convince him of the hopelessness of his cause, the report of his ambassadors returning from New Orleans would have banished every doubt. No record of his interview with them remains; but it is easy to conceive with what chagrin he must have learned that the officer of France first in rank in all America had refused to aid him, and urged the timid counsels of peace. The vanity of those expectations, which had been the mainspring of his enterprise, now rose clear and palpable before him; and, with rage and bitterness, he saw the rotten foundation of his hopes sinking into dust, and the whole structure of his plot crumbling in ruins about him.

All was lost. His allies were falling off, his followers deserting him. To hold out longer would be destruction, and to fly was scarcely an easier task. In the south lay the Cherokees, hereditary enemies of his people. In the west were the Osages and Missouries, treacherous and uncertain friends, and the fierce and jealous Dahcotah. In the east the forests would soon be filled with English traders, and beset with English troops; while in the north his own village of Detroit lay beneath the guns of the victorious garrison. He might, indeed, have found a partial refuge in the remoter wilderness of the upper lakes; but those dreary wastes would have doomed him to a life of unambitious exile. His resolution was taken. He determined to accept the peace which he knew would be proffered, to smoke the calumet with his triumphant enemies, and patiently await his hour of vengeance.

The conferences at Fort Pitt concluded, Croghan left that place on the fifteenth of May, and embarked on the Ohio, accompanied by several Delaware and Shawanoe deputies, whom he had persuaded those newly reconciled tribes to send with him, for the furtherance of his mission. At the mouth of the Scioto, he was met by a band of Shawanoe warriors, who, in compliance with a message previously sent to them, delivered into his hands seven intriguing Frenchmen, who for some time past had lived in their villages. Thence he pursued his voyage smoothly and prosperously, until, on the eighth of June, he reached a spot a little below the mouth of the Wabash. Here he landed with his party; when suddenly the hideous warwhoop, the explosion of musketry, and the whistling of arrows greeted him from the covert of the neighboring thickets. His men fell thick about him. Three Indians and two white men were shot dead on the spot; most of the remainder were wounded; and on the next instant the survivors found themselves prisoners in the hands of eighty yelling Kickapoos, who plundered them of all they had. No sooner, however, was their prey fairly within their clutches, than the cowardly assailants began to apologize for what they had done, saying it was all a mistake, and that the French had set them on by telling them that the Indians who accompanied Croghan were Cherokees, their mortal enemies; excuses utterly without foundation, for the Kickapoos had dogged the party for several days, and perfectly understood its character.

It is superfluous to inquire into the causes of this attack. No man practically familiar with Indian character need be told the impossibility of foreseeing to what strange acts the wayward impulses of this murder-loving race may prompt them. Unstable as water, capricious as the winds, they seem in some of their moods like ungoverned children fired with the instincts of devils. In the present case, they knew that they hated the English,—knew that they wanted scalps; and thinking nothing of the consequences, they seized the first opportunity to gratify their rabid longing. This done, they thought it best to avert any probable effects of their misconduct by such falsehoods as might suggest themselves to their invention.

Still apologizing for what they had done, but by no means suffering their prisoners to escape, they proceeded up the Wabash, to the little French fort and settlement of Vincennes, where, to his great joy, Croghan found among the assembled Indians some of his former friends and acquaintance. They received him kindly, and sharply rebuked the Kickapoos, who, on their part, seemed much ashamed and crestfallen. From Vincennes the English were conducted, in a sort of honorable captivity, up the river to Ouatanon, where they arrived on the twenty-third, fifteen days after the attack, and where Croghan was fortunate enough to find a great number of his former Indian friends, who received him, to appearance at least, with much cordiality. He took up his quarters in the fort, where there was at this time no garrison, a mob of French traders and Indians being the only tenants of the place. For several days, his time was engrossed with receiving deputation after deputation from the various tribes and sub-tribes of the neighborhood, smoking pipes of peace, making and hearing speeches, and shaking hands with greasy warriors, who, one and all, were strong in their professions of good will, promising not only to regard the English as their friends, but to aid them, if necessary, in taking possession of the Illinois.

While these amicable conferences were in progress, a miscreant Frenchman came from the Mississippi with a message from a chief of that region, urging the Indians of Ouatanon to burn the Englishman alive. Of this proposal the Indians signified their strong disapprobation, and assured the startled envoy that they would stand his friends,—professions the sincerity of which, happily for him, was confirmed by the strong guaranty of their fears.

The next arrival was that of Maisonville, a messenger from St. Ange, requesting Croghan to come to Fort Chartres, to adjust affairs in that quarter. The invitation was in accordance with Croghan's designs; and he left the fort on the following day, attended by Maisonville, and a concourse of the Ouatanon Indians, who, far from regarding him as their prisoner, were now studious to show him every mark of respect. He had advanced but a short distance into the forest when he met Pontiac himself, who was on his way to Ouatanon, followed by a numerous train of chiefs and warriors. He gave his hand to the English envoy, and both parties returned together to the fort. Its narrow precincts were now crowded with Indians, a perilous multitude, dark, malignant, inscrutable; and it behooved the Englishman to be wary, in his dealings with them, since a breath might kindle afresh the wildfire in their hearts.

At a meeting of the chiefs and warriors, Pontiac offered the calumet and belt of peace, and professed his concurrence with the chiefs of Ouatanon in the friendly sentiments which they expressed towards the English. The French, he added, had deceived him, telling him and his people that the English meant to enslave the Indians of the Illinois, and turn loose upon them their enemies the Cherokees. It was this which drove him to arms; and now that he knew the story to be false, he would no longer stand in the path of the English. Yet they must not imagine that, in taking possession of the French forts, they gained any right to the country; for the French had never bought the land, and lived upon it by sufferance only.

As this meeting with Pontiac and the Illinois chiefs made it needless for Croghan to advance farther on his western journey, he now bent his footsteps towards Detroit, and, followed by Pontiac and many of the principal chiefs, crossed over to Fort Miami, and thence descended the Maumee, holding conferences at the several villages which he passed on his way. On the seventeenth of August, he reached Detroit, where he found a great gathering of Indians, Ottawas, Pottawattamies, and Ojibwas; some encamped about the fort, and others along the banks of the River Rouge. They obeyed his summons to a meeting with alacrity, partly from a desire to win the good graces of a victorious enemy, and partly from the importunate craving for liquor and presents, which never slumbers in an Indian breast. Numerous meetings were held; and the old council-hall where Pontiac had essayed his scheme of abortive treachery was now crowded with repentant warriors, anxious, by every form of submission, to appease the conqueror.

Their ill success, their fears of chastisement, and the miseries they had endured from the long suspension of the fur-trade, had banished from their minds every thought of hostility. They were glad, they said, that the dark clouds were now dispersing, and the sunshine of peace once more returning; and since all the nations to the sunrising had taken their great father the King of England by the hand, they also wished to do the same. They now saw clearly that the French were indeed conquered; and thenceforth they would listen no more to the whistling of evil birds, but lay down the war-hatchet, and sit quiet on their mats. Among those who appeared to make or renew their submission was the Grand Sauteur, who had led the massacre at Michillimackinac, and who, a few years after, expiated his evil deeds by a bloody death. He now pretended great regret for what he had done. "We red people," he said, "are a very jealous and foolish people; but, father, there are some among the white men worse than we are, and they have told us lies, and deceived us. Therefore we hope you will take pity on our women and children, and grant us peace." A band of Pottawattamies from St. Joseph's were also present, and, after excusing themselves for their past conduct by the stale plea of the uncontrollable temper of their young men, their orator proceeded as follows:—

"We are no more than wild creatures to you, fathers, in understanding; therefore we request you to forgive the past follies of our young people, and receive us for your children. Since you have thrown down our former father on his back, we have been wandering in the dark, like blind people. Now you have dispersed all this darkness, which hung over the heads of the several tribes, and have accepted them for your children, we hope you will let us partake with them the light, that our women and children may enjoy peace. We beg you to forget all that is past. By this belt we remove all evil thoughts from your hearts.

"Fathers, when we formerly came to visit our fathers the French, they always sent us home joyful; and we hope you, fathers, will have pity on our women and young men, who are in great want of necessaries, and not let us go home to our towns ashamed."

On the twenty-seventh of August, Croghan held a meeting with the Ottawas, and the other tribes of Detroit and Sandusky; when, adopting their own figurative language, he addressed them in the following speech, in which, as often happened when white men borrowed the tongue of the forest orator, he lavished a more unsparing profusion of imagery than the Indians themselves:—

"Children, we are very glad to see so many of you here present at your ancient council-fire, which has been neglected for some time past; since then, high winds have blown, and raised heavy clouds over your country. I now, by this belt, rekindle your ancient fire, and throw dry wood upon it, that the blaze may ascend to heaven, so that all nations may see it, and

know that you live in peace and tranquillity with your fathers the English.
"By this belt I disperse all the black clouds from over your heads, that the sun may shine clear on your women and children, that those unborn may enjoy the blessings of this general peace, now so happily settled between your fathers the English and you, and all your younger brethren to the sunsetting.
"Children, by this belt I gather up all the bones of your deceased friends, and bury them deep in the ground, that the buds and sweet flowers of the earth may grow over them, that we may not see them any more.
"Children, with this belt I take the hatchet out of your hands, and pluck up a large tree, and bury it deep, so that it may never be found any more; and I plant the tree of peace, which all our children may sit under, and smoke in peace with their fathers.
"Children, we have made a road from the sunrising to the sunsetting. I desire that you will preserve that road good and pleasant to travel upon, that we may all share the blessings of this happy union."
On the following day, Pontiac spoke in behalf of the several nations assembled at the council.
"Father, we have all smoked out of this pipe of peace. It is your children's pipe; and as the war is all over, and the Great Spirit and Giver of Light, who has made the earth and every thing therein, has brought us all together this day for our mutual good, I declare to all nations that I have settled my peace with you before I came here, and now deliver my pipe to be sent to Sir William Johnson, that he may know I have made peace, and taken the King of England for my father, in presence of all the nations now assembled; and whenever any of those nations go to visit him, they may smoke out of it with him in peace. Fathers, we are obliged to you for lighting up our old council-fire for us, and desiring us to return to it; but we are now settled on the Miami River, not far from hence: whenever you want us, you will find us there."
"Our people," he added, "love liquor, and if we dwelt near you in our old village of Detroit, our warriors would be always drunk, and quarrels would arise between us and you." Drunkenness was, in truth, the bane of the whole unhappy race; but Pontiac, too thoroughly an Indian in his virtues and his vices to be free from its destructive taint, concluded his speech with the common termination of an Indian harangue, and desired that the rum barrel might be opened, and his thirsty warriors allowed to drink.
At the end of September, having brought these protracted conferences to a close, Croghan left Detroit, and departed for Niagara, whence, after a short delay, he passed eastward, to report the results of his mission to the commander-in-chief. But before leaving the Indian country, he exacted from Pontiac a promise that in the spring he would descend to Oswego, and, in behalf of the tribes lately banded in his league, conclude a treaty of

peace and amity with Sir William Johnson.

Croghan's efforts had been attended with signal success. The tribes of the west, of late bristling in defiance, and hot for fight, had craved forgiveness, and proffered the calumet. The war was over; the last flickerings of that wide conflagration had died away; but the embers still glowed beneath the ashes, and fuel and a breath alone were wanting to rekindle those desolating fires.

In the mean time, a hundred Highlanders of the 42d Regiment, those veterans whose battle-cry had echoed over the bloodiest fields of America, had left Fort Pitt under command of Captain Sterling, and, descending the Ohio, arrived at Fort Chartres just as the snows of early winter began to whiten the naked forests. The flag of France descended from the rampart; and with the stern courtesies of war, St. Ange yielded up his post, the citadel of the Illinois, to its new masters. In that act was consummated the double triumph of British power in America. England had crushed her hereditary foe; and France, in her fall, had left to irretrievable ruin the savage tribes to whom her policy and self-interest had lent a transient support.

DEATH OF PONTIAC

1766 to 1769

The Winter passed quietly away. Already the Indians began to feel the blessings of returning peace in the partial reopening of the fur-trade; and the famine and nakedness, the misery and death, which through the previous season had been rife in their encampments, were exchanged for comparative comfort and abundance. With many precautions, and in meagre allowances, the traders had been permitted to throw their goods into the Indian markets; and the starving hunters were no longer left, as many of them had been, to gain precarious sustenance by the bow, the arrow, and the lance—the half-forgotten weapons of their fathers. Some troubles arose along the frontiers of Pennsylvania and Virginia. The reckless borderers, in contempt of common humanity and prudence, murdered several straggling Indians, and enraged others by abuse and insult; but these outrages could not obliterate the remembrance of recent chastisement, and, for the present at least, the injured warriors forbore to draw down the fresh vengeance of their destroyers.

Spring returned, and Pontiac remembered the promise he had made to visit Sir William Johnson at Oswego. He left his encampment on the Maumee, accompanied by his chiefs, and by an Englishman named Crawford, a man of vigor and resolution, who had been appointed, by the superintendent, to the troublesome office of attending the Indian deputation, and supplying their wants.

We may well imagine with what bitterness of mood the defeated war-chief urged his canoe along the margin of Lake Erie, and gazed upon the horizon-bounded waters, and the lofty shores, green with primeval verdure. Little could he have dreamed, and little could the wisest of that day have imagined, that, within the space of a single human life, that lonely lake would be studded with the sails of commerce; that cities and villages would rise upon the ruins of the forest; and that the poor mementoes of his lost race—the wampum beads, the rusty tomahawk, and the arrowhead of stone, turned up by the ploughshare—would become the wonder of schoolboys, and the prized relics of the antiquary's cabinet. Yet it needed no prophetic eye to foresee that, sooner or later, the doom must come. The star of his people's destiny was fading from the sky; and, to a mind like his, the black and withering future must have stood revealed in all its desolation. The birchen flotilla gained the outlet of Lake Erie, and, shooting downwards with the stream, landed beneath the palisades of Fort Schlosser. The chiefs passed the portage, and, once more embarking, pushed out upon Lake Ontario. Soon their goal was reached, and the cannon boomed hollow salutation from the batteries of Oswego.

Here they found Sir William Johnson waiting to receive them, attended by the chief sachems of the Iroquois, whom he had invited to the spot, that their presence might give additional weight and solemnity to the meeting. As there was no building large enough to receive so numerous a concourse, a canopy of green boughs was erected to shade the assembly from the sun; and thither, on the twenty-third of July, repaired the chiefs and warriors of the several nations. Here stood the tall figure of Sir William Johnson, surrounded by civil and military officers, clerks, and interpreters; while before him reclined the painted sachems of the Iroquois, and the great Ottawa war-chief, with his dejected followers.

Johnson opened the meeting with the usual formalities, presenting his auditors with a belt of wampum to wipe the tears from their eyes, with another to cover the bones of their relatives, another to open their ears that they might hear, and another to clear their throats that they might speak with ease. Then, amid solemn silence, Pontiac's great peace-pipe was lighted and passed round the assembly, each man present inhaling a whiff of the sacred smoke. These tedious forms, together with a few speeches of compliment, consumed the whole morning; for this savage people, on whose supposed simplicity poets and rhetoricians have lavished their praises, may challenge the world to outmatch their bigoted adherence to usage and ceremonial.

On the following day, the council began in earnest, and Sir William Johnson addressed Pontiac and his attendant chiefs.

"Children, I bid you heartily welcome to this place; and I trust that the Great Spirit will permit us often to meet together in friendship, for I have now opened the door and cleared the road, that all nations may come hither from the sunsetting. This belt of wampum confirms my words.

"Children, it gave me much pleasure to find that you who are present behaved so well last year, and treated in so friendly a manner Mr. Croghan, one of my deputies; and that you expressed such concern for the bad behavior of those, who, in order to obstruct the good work of peace, assaulted and wounded him, and killed some of his party, both whites and Indians; a thing before unknown, and contrary to the laws and customs of all nations. This would have drawn down our strongest resentment upon those who were guilty of so heinous a crime, were it not for the great lenity and kindness of your English father, who does not delight in punishing those who repent sincerely of their faults.

"Children, I have now, with the approbation of General Gage (your father's chief warrior in this country), invited you here in order to confirm and strengthen your proceedings with Mr. Croghan last year. I hope that you will remember all that then passed, and I desire that you will often repeat it to your young people, and keep it fresh in your minds.

"Children, you begin already to see the fruits of peace, from the number of traders and plenty of goods at all the garrisoned posts; and our enjoying the peaceable possession of the Illinois will be found of great advantage to the Indians in that country. You likewise see that proper officers, men of honor and probity, are appointed to reside at the posts, to prevent abuses in trade, to hear your complaints, and to lay before me such of them as they cannot redress. Interpreters are likewise sent for the assistance of each of them; and smiths are sent to the posts to repair your arms and implements. All this, which is attended with a great expense, is now done by the great King, your father, as a proof of his regard; so that, casting from you all jealousy and apprehension, you should now strive with each other who should show the most gratitude to this best of princes. I do now, therefore, confirm the assurances which I give you of his Majesty's good will, and do insist on your casting away all evil thoughts, and shutting your ears against all flying idle reports of bad people."

The rest of Johnson's speech was occupied in explaining to his hearers the new arrangements for the regulation of the fur-trade; in exhorting them to forbear from retaliating the injuries they might receive from reckless white men, who would meet with due punishment from their own countrymen; and in urging them to deliver up to justice those of their people who might be guilty of crimes against the English. "Children," he concluded, "I now, by this belt, turn your eyes to the sunrising, where you will always find me your sincere friend. From me you will always hear what is true and good; and I charge you never more to listen to those evil birds, who come, with lying tongues, to lead you astray, and to make you break the solemn engagements which you have entered into, in presence of the Great Spirit, with the King your father and the English people. Be strong, then, and keep fast hold of the chain of friendship, that your children, following your example, may live happy and prosperous lives."

Pontiac made a brief reply, and promised to return on the morrow an answer in full. The meeting then broke up.

The council of the next day was opened by the Wyandot chief, Teata, in a short and formal address; at the conclusion of which Pontiac himself arose, and addressed the superintendent in words, of which the following is a translation:

"Father, we thank the Great Spirit for giving us so fine a day to meet upon such great affairs. I speak in the name of all the nations to the westward, of whom I am the master. It is the will of the Great Spirit that we should meet here to-day; and before him I now take you by the hand. I call him to witness that I speak from my heart; for since I took Colonel Croghan by the hand last year, I have never let go my hold, for I see that the Great Spirit will have us friends.

"Father, when our great father of France was in this country, I held him fast by the hand. Now that he is gone, I take you, my English father, by the hand, in the name of all the nations, and promise to keep this covenant as long as I shall live."

Here he delivered a large belt of wampum.

"Father, when you address me, it is the same as if you addressed all the nations of the west. Father, this belt is to cover and strengthen our chain of friendship, and to show you that, if any nation shall lift the hatchet against our English brethren, we shall be the first to feel it and resent it."

Pontiac next took up in succession the various points touched upon in the speech of the superintendent, expressing in all things a full compliance with his wishes. The succeeding days of the conference were occupied with matters of detail relating chiefly to the fur-trade, all of which were adjusted to the apparent satisfaction of the Indians, who, on their part, made reiterated professions of friendship. Pontiac promised to recall the war-belts which had been sent to the north and west, though, as he alleged, many of them had proceeded from the Senecas, and not from him; adding that, when all were gathered together, they would be more than a man could carry. The Iroquois sachems then addressed the western nations, exhorting them to stand true to their engagements, and hold fast the chain of friendship; and the councils closed on the thirty-first, with a bountiful distribution of presents to Pontiac and his followers.

Thus ended this memorable meeting, in which Pontiac sealed his submission to the English, and renounced for ever the bold design by which he had trusted to avert or retard the ruin of his race. His hope of seeing the empire of France restored in America was scattered to the winds, and with it vanished every rational scheme of resistance to English encroachment. Nothing now remained but to stand an idle spectator, while, in the north and in the south, the tide of British power rolled westward in resistless might; while the fragments of the rival empire, which he would fain have set up as a barrier against the flood, lay scattered a miserable wreck; and while the remnant of his people melted away or fled for refuge to remoter deserts. For them the prospects of the future were as clear as they were calamitous. Destruction or civilization—between these lay their choice; and few who knew them could doubt which alternative they would embrace.

Pontiac, his canoe laden with the gifts of his enemy, steered homeward for the Maumee; and in this vicinity he spent the following winter, pitching his lodge in the forest with his wives and children, and hunting like an ordinary warrior. With the succeeding spring, 1767, fresh murmurings of discontent arose among the Indian tribes, from the lakes to the Potomac, the first precursors of the disorders which, a few years later, ripened into a brief but bloody war along the borders of Virginia. These threatening symptoms might easily be traced to their source. The incorrigible frontiersmen had again let loose their murdering propensities; and a multitude of squatters had built their cabins on Indian lands beyond the limits of Pennsylvania, adding insult to aggression, and sparing neither oaths, curses, nor any form of abuse and maltreatment against the rightful owners of the soil. The new regulations of the fur-trade could not prevent disorders among the reckless men engaged in it. This was particularly the case in the region of the Illinois, where the evil was aggravated by the renewed intrigues of the French, and especially of those who had fled from the English side of the Mississippi, and made their abode around the new settlement of St. Louis. It is difficult to say how far Pontiac was involved in this agitation. It is certain that some of the English traders regarded him with jealousy and fear, as prime mover of the whole, and eagerly watched an opportunity to destroy him.

The discontent among the tribes did not diminish with the lapse of time; yet for many months we can discern no trace of Pontiac. Records and traditions are silent concerning him. It is not until April, 1769, that he appears once more distinctly on the scene. At about that time he came to the Illinois, with what design does not appear, though his movements excited much uneasiness among the few English in that quarter. Soon after his arrival, he repaired to St. Louis, to visit his former acquaintance, St. Ange, who was then in command at that post, having offered his services to the Spaniards after the cession of Louisiana. After leaving the fort, Pontiac proceeded to the house of which young Pierre Chouteau was an inmate; and to the last days of his protracted life, the latter could vividly recall the circumstances of the interview. The savage chief was arrayed in the full uniform of a French officer, which had been presented to him as a special mark of respect and favor by the Marquis of Montcalm, towards the close of the French war, and which Pontiac never had the bad taste to wear, except on occasions when he wished to appear with unusual dignity. St. Ange, Chouteau, and the other principal inhabitants of the infant settlement, whom he visited in turn, all received him cordially, and did their best to entertain him and his attendant chiefs. He remained at St. Louis for two or three days, when, hearing that a large number of Indians were assembled at Cahokia, on the opposite side of the river, and that some drinking bout or other social gathering was in progress, he told St. Ange that he would cross over to see what was going forward. St. Ange tried to dissuade him, and urged the risk to which he would expose himself; but Pontiac persisted, boasting that he was a match for the English, and had no fear for his life. He entered a canoe with some of his followers, and Chouteau never saw him again.

He who, at the present day, crosses from the city of St. Louis to the opposite shore of the Mississippi, and passes southward through a forest festooned with grape-vines, and fragrant with the scent of flowers, will soon emerge upon the ancient hamlet of Cahokia. To one fresh from the busy suburbs of the American city, the small French houses, scattered in picturesque disorder, the light-hearted, thriftless look of their inmates, and the woods which form the background of the picture, seem like the remnants of an earlier and simpler world. Strange changes have passed around that spot. Forests have fallen, cities have sprung up, and the lonely wilderness is thronged with human life. Nature herself has taken part in the general transformation; and the Mississippi has made a fearful inroad, robbing from the luckless Creoles a mile of rich meadow and woodland. Yet, in the midst of all, this relic of the lost empire of France has preserved its essential features through the lapse of a century, and offers at this day an aspect not widely different from that which met the eye of Pontiac, when he and his chiefs landed on its shore.

The place was full of Illinois Indians; such a scene as in our own time may often be met with in some squalid settlement of the border, where the vagabond guests, bedizened with dirty finery, tie their small horses in rows along the fences, and stroll idly among the houses, or lounge about the dramshops. A chief so renowned as Pontiac could not remain long among the friendly Creoles of Cahokia without being summoned to a feast; and at such primitive entertainment the whiskey-bottle would not fail to play its part. This was in truth the case. Pontiac drank deeply, and, when the carousal was over, strode down the village street to the adjacent woods, where he was heard to sing the medicine songs, in whose magic power he trusted as the warrant of success in all his undertakings.

An English trader, named Williamson, was then in the village. He had looked on the movements of Pontiac with a jealousy probably not diminished by the visit of the chief to the French at St. Louis; and he now resolved not to lose so favorable an opportunity to despatch him. With this view, he gained the ear of a strolling Indian, belonging to the Kaskaskia tribe of the Illinois, bribed him with a barrel of liquor, and promised him a farther reward if he would kill the chief. The bargain was quickly made.

When Pontiac entered the forest, the assassin stole close upon his track; and, watching his moment, glided behind him, and buried a tomahawk in his brain.

The dead body was soon discovered, and startled cries and wild howlings announced the event. The word was caught up from mouth to mouth, and the place resounded with infernal yells. The warriors snatched their weapons. The Illinois took part with their guilty countryman; and the few followers of Pontiac, driven from the village, fled to spread the tidings and call the nations to revenge. Meanwhile the murdered chief lay on the spot where he had fallen, until St. Ange, mindful of former friendship, sent to claim the body, and buried it with warlike honors, near his fort of St. Louis.

Thus basely perished this champion of a ruined race. But could his shade have revisited the scene of murder, his savage spirit would have exulted in the vengeance which overwhelmed the abettors of the crime. Whole tribes were rooted out to expiate it. Chiefs and sachems, whose veins had thrilled with his eloquence; young warriors, whose aspiring hearts had caught the inspiration of his greatness, mustered to revenge his fate; and, from the north and the east, their united bands descended on the villages of the Illinois. Tradition has but faintly preserved the memory of the event; and its only annalists, men who held the intestine feuds of the savage tribes in no more account than the quarrels of panthers or wildcats, have left but a meagre record. Yet enough remains to tell us that over the grave of Pontiac more blood was poured out in atonement, than flowed from the veins of the slaughtered heroes on the corpse of Patroclus; and the remnant of the Illinois who survived the carnage remained for ever after sunk in utter insignificance.

Neither mound nor tablet marked the burial-place of Pontiac. For a mausoleum, a city has risen above the forest hero; and the race whom he hated with such burning rancor trample with unceasing footsteps over his forgotten grave.

APPENDIX A

THE IROQUOIS.—EXTENT OF THEIR CONQUESTS.—POLICY PURSUED TOWARDS THEM BY
THE FRENCH AND THE ENGLISH.—MEASURES OF SIR WILLIAM JOHNSON.

1. Territory of the Iroquois. (Vol. I. p. 19.)
Extract from a Letter—Sir W. Johnson to the Board of Trade, November 13, 1763:—
My Lords:
In obedience to your Lordships' commands of the 5th of August last, I am now to lay before you the claims of the Nations mentioned in the State of the Confederacies. The Five Nations have in the last century subdued the Shawanese, Delawares, Twighties, and Western Indians, so far as Lakes Michigan and Superior, received them into an alliance, allowed them the possession of the lands they occupied, and have ever since been in peace with the greatest part of them; and such was the prowess of the Five Nations' Confederacy, that had they been properly supported by us, they would have long since put a period to the Colony of Canada, which alone they were near effecting in the year 1688. Since that time, they have admitted the Tuscaroras from the Southward, beyond Oneida, and they have ever since formed a part of that Confederacy.
As original proprietors, this Confederacy claim the country of their residence, south of Lake Ontario to the great Ridge of the Blue Mountains, with all the Western Part of the Province of New York towards Hudson River, west of the Catskill, thence to Lake Champlain, and from Regioghne, a Rock at the East side of said Lake, to Oswegatche or La Gallette, on the River St. Lawrence, (having long since ceded their claim north of said line

in favor of the Canada Indians, as Hunting-ground,) thence up the River St. Lawrence, and along the South side of Lake Ontario to Niagara.

In right of conquest, they claim all the country (comprehending the Ohio) along the great Ridge of Blue Mountains at the back of Virginia, thence to the head of Kentucky River, and down the same to the Ohio above the Rifts, thence Northerly to the South end of Lake Michigan, then along the Eastern shore of said lake to Michillimackinac, thence Easterly across the North end of Lake Huron to the great Ottawa River, (including the Chippewa or Mississagey County,) and down the said River to the Island of Montreal. However, these more distant claims being possessed by many powerful nations, the Inhabitants have long begun to render themselves independent, by the assistance of the French, and the great decrease of the Six Nations; but their claim to the Ohio, and thence to the Lakes, is not in the least disputed by the Shawanese, Delawares, andc., who never transacted any sales of land or other matters without their consent, and who sent Deputies to the grand Council at Onondaga on all important occasions.

2. French and English Policy towards the Iroquois.—Measures of Sir William Johnson. (Vol. I. pp. 74-78.)

Extract from a Letter—Sir W. Johnson to the Board of Trade, May 24, 1765:—

The Indians of the Six Nations, after the arrival of the English, having conceived a desire for many articles they introduced among them, and thereby finding them of use to their necessities, or rather superfluities, cultivated an acquaintance with them, and lived in tolerable friendship with their Province for some time, to which they were rather inclined, for they were strangers to bribery, and at enmity with the French, who had espoused the cause of their enemies, supplied them with arms, and openly acted against them. This enmity increased in proportion as the desire of the French for subduing those people, who were a bar to their first projected schemes. However, we find the Indians, as far back as the very confused manuscript records in my possession, repeatedly upbraiding this province for their negligence, their avarice, and their want of assisting them at a time when it was certainly in their power to destroy the infant colony of Canada, although supported by many nations; and this is likewise confessed by the writings of the managers of these times. The French, after repeated losses discovering that the Six Nations were not to be subdued, but that they could without much difficulty effect their purpose (which I have good authority to show were ... standing) by favors and kindness, on a sudden, changed their conduct in the reign of Queen Anne, having first brought over many of their people to settle in Canada; and ever since, by the most endearing kindnesses and by a vast profusion of favors, have secured them to their interest; and, whilst they aggravated our frauds and designs, they covered those committed by themselves under a load of gifts, which obliterated the malpractices of ... among them, and enabled them to establish themselves wherever they pleased, without fomenting the Indians' jealousy. The able agents were made use of, and their unanimous indefatigable zeal for securing the Indian interest, were so much superior to any thing we had ever attempted, and to the futile transactions of the ... and trading Commissioners of Albany, that the latter became universally despised by the Indians, who daily withdrew from our interest, and conceived the most disadvantageous sentiments of our integrity and abilities. In this state of Indian affairs I was called to the management of these people, as my situation and opinion that it might become one day of service to the public, had induced me to cultivate a particular intimacy with these people, to accommodate myself to their manners, and even to their dress on many occasions. How I discharged this trust will best appear from the transactions of the war commenced in 1744, in which I was busily concerned. The steps I had then taken alarmed the jealousy of the French; rewards were offered for me, and I narrowly escaped assassination on more than one occasion. The French increased their munificence to the Indians, whose example not being at all followed at New York, I resigned the management of affairs on the ensuing peace, as I did not choose to continue in the name of an office which I was not empowered to discharge as its nature required. The Albany Commissioners (the men concerned in the clandestine trade to Canada, and frequently upbraided for it by the Indians) did then reassume their seats at that Board, and by their conduct so exasperated the Indians that several chiefs went to New York, 1753, when, after a severe speech to the Governor, Council, and Assembly, they broke the covenant chain of friendship, and withdrew in a rage. The consequences of which were then so much dreaded, that I was, by Governor, Council, and House of Assembly, the two latter then my enemies, earnestly entreated to effect a reconciliation with the Indians, as the only person equal to that task, as will appear by the Minutes of Council and resolves of the House. A commission being made out for me, I proceeded to Onondaga, and brought about the much wished for reconciliation, but declined having any further to say of Indian affairs, although the Indians afterwards refused to meet the Governor and Commissioners till I was sent for. At the arrival of General Braddock, I received his Commission with reluctance, at the same time assuring him that affairs had been so ill conducted, and the Indians so estranged from our interest, that I could not take upon me to hope for success. However, indefatigable labor, and (I hope I may say without vanity) personal interest, enabled me to exceed my own expectations; and my conduct since, if fully and truly known, would, I believe, testify that I have not been an unprofitable servant. 'Twas then that the Indians began to give public sign of their avaricious dispositions. The French had long taught them it; and the desire of some persons to carry a greater number of Indians into the field in 1755 than those who accompanied me, induced them to employ any agent at a high salary, who had the least interest with the Indians; and to grant the latter Captains' and Lieutenants' Commissions, (of which I have a number now by me,) with sterling pay, to induce them to desert me, but to little purpose, for tho' many of them received the Commissions, accompanied with large sums of money, they did not comply with the end proposed, but served with me; and this had not only served them with severe complaints against the English, as they were not afterwards all paid what had been promised, but has established a spirit of pride and avarice, which I have found it ever since impossible to subdue; whilst our extensive connections since the reduction of Canada, with so many powerful nations so long accustomed to partake largely of French bounty, has of course increased the expense, and rendered it in no small degree necessary for the preservation of our frontiers, outposts, and trade....

Extract from a Letter—Cadwallader Colden to the Earl of Halifax, December 22, 1763:—

Before I proceed further, I think it proper to inform your Lordship of the different state of the Policy of the Five Nations in different periods of time. Before the peace of Utrecht, the Five Nations were at war with the French in Canada, and with all the Indian Nations who were in friendship with the French. This put the Five Nations under a necessity of depending on this province for a supply of every thing by which they could carry on the war or defend themselves, and their behavior towards us was accordingly.

After the peace of Utrecht, the French changed their measures. They took every method in their power to gain the friendship of the Five Nations, and succeeded so far with the Senecas, who are by far the most numerous, and at the greatest distance from us, that they were entirely brought over to the French interest. The French obtained the consent of the Senecas to the building of the Fort at Niagara, situated in their country.

When the French had too evidently, before the last war, got the ascendant among all the Indian Nations, we endeavored to make the Indians jealous of the French power, that they were thereby in danger of becoming slaves to the French, unless they were protected by the English....

APPENDIX B

CAUSES OF THE INDIAN WAR.

Extract from a Letter—Sir W. Johnson to the Board of Trade, November 13, 1763. (Chap. VII. Vol. I. p. 131.)

... The French, in order to reconcile them [the Indians] to their encroachments, loaded them with favors, and employed the most intelligent Agents of good influence, as well as artful Jesuits among the several Western and other Nations, who, by degrees, prevailed on them to admit of Forts, under the Notion of Trading houses, in their Country; and knowing that these posts could never be maintained contrary to the inclinations of the Indians, they supplied them thereat with ammunition and other necessaries in abundance, as also called them to frequent congresses, and dismissed them with handsome presents, by which they enjoyed an extensive commerce, obtained the assistance of these Indians, and possessed their frontiers in safety; and as without these measures the Indians would never have suffered them in their Country, so they expect that whatever European power possesses the same, they shall in some measure reap the like advantages. Now, as these advantages ceased on the Posts being possessed by the English, and especially as it was not thought prudent to indulge them with ammunition, they immediately concluded that we had designs against their liberties, which opinion had been first instilled into them by the French, and since promoted by Traders of that nation and others who retired among them on the surrender of Canada and are still there, as well as by Belts of Wampum and other exhortations, which I am confidently assured have been sent among them from the Illinois, Louisiana, and even Canada, for that purpose. The Shawanese and Delawares about the Ohio, who were never warmly attached to us since our neglects to defend them against the encroachments of the French, and refusing to erect a post at the Ohio, or assist them and the Six Nations with men or ammunition, when they requested both of us, as well as irritated at the loss of several of their people killed upon the communication of Fort Pitt, in the years 1759 and 1761, were easily induced to join with the Western Nations, and the Senecas, dissatisfied at many of our posts, jealous of our designs, and displeased at our neglect and contempt of them, soon followed their example.

These are the causes the Indians themselves assign, and which certainly occasioned the rupture between us, the consequence of which, in my opinion, will be that the Indians (who do not regard the distance) will be supplied with necessaries by the Wabache and several Rivers, which empty into the Mississippi, which it is by no means in our power to prevent, and in return the French will draw the valuable furs down that river to the advantage of their Colony and the destruction of our Trade; this will always induce the French to foment differences between us and the Indians, and the prospects many of them entertain, that they may hereafter become possessed of Canada, will incline them still more to cultivate a good understanding with the Indians, which, if ever attempted by the French, would, I am very apprehensive, be attended with a general defection of them from our interest, unless we are at great pains and expense to regain their friendship, and thereby satisfy them that we have no designs to their prejudice....

The grand matter of concern to all the Six Nations (Mohawks excepted) is the occupying a chain of small Posts on the communication thro' their country to Lake Ontario, not to mention Fort Stanwix, exclusive of which there were erected in 1759 Fort Schuyler on the Mohawk River, and the Royal Blockhouse at the East end of Oneida Lake, in the Country of the Oneidas Fort Brewerton and a Post at Oswego Falls in the Onondagas Country; in order to obtain permission for erecting these posts, they were promised they should be demolished at the end of the war. General Shirley also made them a like promise for the posts he erected; and as about these posts are their fishing and hunting places, where they complain, that they are often obstructed by the troops and insulted, they request that they may not be kept up, the war with the French being now over.

In 1760, Sir Jeffrey Amherst sent a speech to the Indians in writing, which was to be communicated to the Nations about Fort Pitt, andc., by General Monkton, then commanding there, signifying his intentions to satisfy and content all Indians for the ground occupied by the posts, as also for any land about them, which might be found necessary for the use of the garrisons; but the same has not been performed, neither are the Indians in the several countries at all pleased at our occupying them, which they look upon as the first steps to enslave them and invade their properties.

And I beg leave to represent to your Lordships, that one very material advantage resulting from a continuance of good treatment and some favors to the Indians, will be the security and toleration thereby given to the Troops for cultivating lands about the garrisons, which the reduction of their Rations renders absolutely necessary....

Ponteach: or the Savages of America. A Tragedy. London. Printed for the Author; and Sold by J. Millan, opposite the Admiralty, Whitehall. MDCCLXVI.

The author of this tragedy was evidently a person well acquainted with Indian affairs and Indian character. Various allusions contained in it, as well as several peculiar forms of expression, indicate that Major Rogers had a share in its composition. The first act exhibits in detail the causes which led to the Indian war. The rest of the play is of a different character. The plot is sufficiently extravagant, and has little or no historical foundation. Chekitan, the son of Ponteach, is in love with Monelia, the daughter of Hendrick, Emperor of the Mohawks. Monelia is murdered by Chekitan's brother Philip, partly out of revenge and jealousy, and partly in furtherance of a scheme of policy. Chekitan kills Philip, and then dies by his own hand; and Ponteach, whose warriors meanwhile have been defeated by the English, overwhelmed by this accumulation of public and private calamities, retires to the forests of the west to escape the memory of his griefs. The style of the drama is superior to the plot, and the writer displays at times no small insight into the workings of human nature.

The account of Indian wrongs and sufferings given in the first act accords so nearly with that conveyed in contemporary letters and documents, that two scenes from this part of the play are here given, with a few omissions, which good taste demands.

ACT I.

Scene I.—An Indian Trading House.

Enter M'Dole and Murphey, Two Indian Traders, and their Servants.

M'Dole. So, Murphey, you are come to try your Fortune
Among the Savages in this wild Desart?

Murphey. Ay, any thing to get an honest Living,
Which, faith, I find it hard enough to do;
Times are so dull, and Traders are so plenty,
That Gains are small, and Profits come but slow.

M'Dole. Are you experienced in this kind of Trade?
Know you the Principles by which it prospers,
And how to make it lucrative and safe?
If not, you're like a Ship without a Rudder,
That drives at random, and must surely sink.

Murphey. I'm unacquainted with your Indian Commerce
And gladly would I learn the arts from you,
Who're old, and practis'd in them many Years.

M'Dole. That is the curst Misfortune of our Traders;
A thousand Fools attempt to live this Way,
Who might as well turn Ministers of State.
But, as you are a Friend, I will inform you
Of all the secret Arts by which we thrive,
Which if all practis'd, we might all grow rich,
Nor circumvent each other in our Gains.
What have you got to part with to the Indians?

Murphey. I've Rum and Blankets, Wampum, Powder, Bells,
And such like Trifles as they're wont to prize.

M'Dole. 'Tis very well: your Articles are good:
But now the Thing's to make a Profit from them,
Worth all your Toil and Pains of coming hither.
Our fundamental Maxim then is this,

That it's no Crime to cheat and gull an Indian.

Murphey. How! Not a Sin to cheat an Indian, say you?
Are they not Men? hav'nt they a Right to Justice
As well as we, though savage in their Manners?

M'Dole. Ah! If you boggle here, I say no more;
This is the very Quintessence of Trade,
And ev'ry Hope of Gain depends upon it;
None who neglect it ever did grow rich,
Or ever will, or can by Indian Commerce.
By this old Ogden built his stately House,
Purchased Estates, and grew a little King.
He, like an honest Man, bought all by weight,
And made the ign'rant Savages believe
That his Right Foot exactly weighed a Pound.
By this for many years he bought their Furs,
And died in Quiet like an honest Dealer.

Murphey. Well, I'll not stick at what is necessary;
But his Devise is now grown old and stale,
Nor could I manage such a barefac'd Fraud.

M'Dole. A thousand Opportunities present
To take Advantage of their Ignorance;
But the great Engine I employ is Rum,
More pow'rful made by certain strength'ning Drugs.
This I distribute with a lib'ral Hand,
Urge them to drink till they grow mad and valiant;
Which makes them think me generous and just,
And gives full Scope to practise all my Art.
I then begin my Trade with water'd Rum;
The cooling Draught well suits their scorching Throats.
Their Fur and Peltry come in quick Return:
My Scales are honest, but so well contriv'd,
That one small Slip will turn Three Pounds to One;
Which they, poor silly Souls! ignorant of Weights
And Rules of Balancing, do not perceive.
But here they come; you'll see how I proceed.
Jack, is the Rum prepar'd as I commanded?

Jack. Yes, Sir, all's ready when you please to call.

M'Dole. Bring here the Scales and Weights immediately;
You see the Trick is easy and conceal'd.

[Showing how to slip the Scale.
Murphey. By Jupiter, it's artfully contriv'd;
And was I King, I swear I'd knight th' Inventor.
Tom, mind the Part that you will have to act.

Tom. Ah, never fear; I'll do as well as Jack.
But then, you know, an honest Servant's Pain Deserves Reward.

Murphey. O! I'll take care of that.

[Enter a Number of Indians with Packs of Fur.
1st Indian. So, what you trade with Indians here to-day?

M'Dole. Yes, if my Goods will suit, and we agree.

2d Indian. 'Tis Rum we want; we're tired, hot, and thirsty.

3d Indian. You, Mr. Englishman, have you got Rum?

M'Dole. Jack, bring a Bottle, pour them each a Gill.
You know which Cask contains the Rum. The Rum?

1st Indian. It's good strong Rum; I feel it very soon.

M'Dole. Give me a Glass. Here's Honesty in Trade;
We English always drink before we deal.

2d Indian. Good way enough; it makes one sharp and cunning.

M'Dole. Hand round another Gill. You're very welcome.

3d Indian. Some say you Englishmen are sometimes Rogues;
You make poor Indians drunk, and then you cheat.

1st Indian. No, English good. The Frenchmen give no Rum.

2d Indian. I think it's best to trade with Englishmen.

M'Dole. What is your Price for Beaver Skins per Pound?

1st Indian. How much you ask per Quart for this strong Rum?

M'Dole. Five Pounds of Beaver for One Quart of Rum.

1st Indian. Five Pounds? Too much. Which is't you call Five Pound?

M'Dole. This little Weight. I cannot give you more.

1st Indian. Well, take 'em; weigh 'em. Don't you cheat us now.

M'Dole. No; He that cheats an Indian should be hanged.

[Weighing the Packs.
There's Thirty Pounds precisely of the Whole;
Five times Six is Thirty. Six Quarts of Rum.
Jack, measure it to them; you know the Cask.
This Rum is sold. You draw it off the best.

[Exeunt Indians to receive their Rum.
Murphey. By Jove, you've gained more in a single Hour
Than ever I have done in Half a Year:
Curse on my Honesty! I might have been
A little King, and lived without Concern,
Had I but known the proper Arts to thrive.

M'Dole. Ay, there's the Way, my honest Friend, to live.

[Clapping his shoulder.
There's Ninety Weight of Sterling Beaver for you,
Worth all the Rum and Trinkets in my Store;
And, would my Conscience let me do the Thing,
I might enhance my Price, and lessen theirs,
And raise my Profits to a higher Pitch.

Murphey. I can't but thank you for your kind Instructions,
As from them I expect to reap Advantage.
But should the Dogs detect me in the Fraud,
They are malicious, and would have Revenge.

M'Dole. Can't you avoid them? Let their Vengeance light
On others Heads, no matter whose, if you
Are but Secure, and have the Gain in Hand;

For they're indiff'rent where they take Revenge,
Whether on him that cheated, or his Friend,
Or on a Stranger whom they never saw,
Perhaps an honest Peasant, who ne'er dreamt
Of Fraud or Villainy in all his Life;
Such let them murder, if they will, a Score,
The Guilt is theirs, while we secure the Gain,
Nor shall we feel the bleeding Victim's Pain.

[Exeunt.
Scene II.—A Desart.
Enter Orsbourn and Honnyman, Two English Hunters.
Orsbourn. Long have we toil'd, and rang'd the woods in vain;
No Game, nor Track, nor Sign of any Kind
Is to be seen; I swear I am discourag'd
And weary'd out with this long fruitless Hunt.
No Life on Earth besides is half so hard,
So full of Disappointments, as a Hunter's:
Each Morn he wakes he views the destin'd Prey,
And counts the Profits of th' ensuing Day;
Each Ev'ning at his curs'd ill Fortune pines,
And till next Day his Hope of Gain resigns.
By Jove, I'll from these Desarts hasten home,
And swear that never more I'll touch a Gun.

Honnyman. These hateful Indians kidnap all the Game.
Curse their black Heads! they fright the Deer and Bear,
And ev'ry Animal that haunts the Wood,
Or by their Witchcraft conjure them away.
No Englishman can get a single Shot,
While they go loaded home with Skins and Furs.
'Twere to be wish'd not one of them survived,
Thus to infest the World, and plague Mankind.
Curs'd Heathen Infidels! mere savage Beasts!
They don't deserve to breathe in Christian Air,
And should be hunted down like other Brutes.

Orsbourn. I only wish the Laws permitted us
To hunt the savage Herd where-e'er they're found;
I'd never leave the Trade of Hunting then,
While one remain'd to tread and range the Wood.

Honnyman. Curse on the Law, I say, that makes it Death

To kill an Indian, more than to kill a Snake.
What if 'tis Peace? these Dogs deserve no Mercy;
They kill'd my Father and my eldest Brother,
Since which I hate their very Looks and Name.

Orsbourn. And I, since they betray'd and kill'd my Uncle;
Tho' these are not the same, 'twould ease my Heart
To cleave their painted Heads, and spill their Blood.
I do abhor, detest, and hate them all,
And now cou'd eat an Indian's Heart with Pleasure.

Honnyman. I'd join you, and soop his savage Brains for Sauce;
I lose all Patience when I think of them,
And, if you will, we'll quickly have amends
For our long Travel and successless Hunt,
And the sweet Pleasure of Revenge to boot.

Orsbourn. What will you do? Present, and pop one down?

Honnyman. Yes, faith, the first we meet well fraught with Furs;
Or if there's Two, and we can make sure Work,
By Jove, we'll ease the Rascals of their Packs,
And send them empty home to their own Country.
But then observe, that what we do is secret,
Or the Hangman will come in for Snacks.

Orsbourn. Trust me for that; I'll join with all my Heart;
Nor with a nicer Aim, or steadier Hand
Would shoot a Tyger than I would an Indian.
There is a Couple stalking now this way
With lusty Packs; Heav'n favor our Design.
Are you well charged?

Honnyman. I am. Take you the nearest,
And mind to fire exactly when I do.

Orsbourn. A charming Chance!

Honnyman. Hush, let them still come nearer.

[They shoot, and run to rifle the Indians.
They're down, old Boy, a Brace of noble Bucks!

Orsbourn. Well tallow'd faith, and noble Hides upon 'em.

[Taking up a Pack.
We might have hunted all the Season thro'
For Half this Game, and thought ourselves well paid.

Honnyman. By Jove, we might, and been at great Expense
For Lead and Powder; here's a single Shot.

Orsbourn. I swear, I have got as much as I can carry.

Honnyman. And faith, I'm not behind; this Pack is heavy.
But stop; we must conceal the tawny Dogs,
Or their bloodthirsty Countrymen will find them,
And then we're bit. There'll be the Devil to pay;
They'll murder us, and cheat the Hangman too.

Orsbourn. Right. We'll prevent all Mischief of this Kind.
Where shall we hide their Savage Carcases?

Honnyman. There they will lie conceal'd and snug enough.

[They cover them.
But stay—perhaps ere long there'll be a War,
And then their Scalps will sell for ready Cash,
Two Hundred Crowns at least, and that's worth saving.

Orsbourn. Well! that is true; no sooner said than done—

[Drawing his Knife.
I'll strip this Fellow's painted greasy Skull.

[Strips off the Scalp.
Honnyman. Now let them sleep to Night without their Caps,

[Takes the other Scalp.
And pleasant Dreams attend their long Repose.

Orsbourn. Their Guns and Hatchets now are lawful Prize,
For they'll not need them on their present Journey.

Honnyman. The Devil hates Arms, and dreads the Smell
of Powder;

He'll not allow such Instruments about him;
They're free from training now, they're in his Clutches.

Orsbourn. But, Honnyman, d'ye think this is not Murder?
I vow I'm shocked a little to see them scalp'd,
And fear their Ghosts will haunt us in the Dark.

Honnyman. It's no more Murder than to crack a Louse,
That is, if you've the Wit to keep it private.
And as to Haunting, Indians have no Ghosts,
But as they live like Beasts, like Beasts they die.
I've killed a Dozen in this selfsame Way,
And never yet was troubled with their Spirits.

Orsbourn. Then I'm content; my Scruples are removed.
And what I've done, my Conscience justifies.
But we must have these Guns and Hatchets alter'd,
Or they'll detect th' Affair, and hang us both.

Honnyman. That's quickly done—Let us with Speed return,
And think no more of being hang'd or haunted;
But turn our Fur to Gold, our Gold to Wine,
Thus gaily spend what we've so slily won,
And Bless the first Inventor of a Gun.

[Exeunt.
The remaining scenes of this act exhibit the rudeness and insolence of British officers and soldiers in their dealings with the Indians, and the corruption of British government agents. Pontiac himself is introduced and represented as indignantly complaining of the reception which he and his warriors meet with. These scenes are overcharged with blasphemy and ribaldry, and it is needless to preserve them here. The rest of the play is written in better taste, and contains several vigorous passages.

APPENDIX C

DETROIT AND MICHILLIMACKINAC.

1. The Siege of Detroit. (Chap. IX.-XV.)
The authorities consulted respecting the siege of Detroit consist of numerous manuscript letters of officers in the fort, including the official correspondence of the commanding officer; of several journals and fragments of journals; of extracts from contemporary newspapers; and of traditions and recollections received from Indians or aged Canadians of Detroit.

The Pontiac Manuscript.
This curious diary was preserved in a Canadian family at Detroit, and afterwards deposited with the Historical Society of Michigan. It is conjectured to have been the work of a French priest. The original is written in bad French, and several important parts are defaced or torn away. As a literary composition, it is quite worthless, being very diffuse and encumbered with dull and trivial details; yet this very minuteness affords strong internal evidence of its authenticity. Its general exactness with respect to facts is fully proved by comparing it with contemporary documents. I am indebted to General Cass for the copy in my possession, as well as for other papers respecting the war in the neighborhood of Detroit.

The manuscript appears to have been elaborately written out from a rough journal kept during the progress of the events which it describes. It commences somewhat ambitiously, as follows:—

"Pondiac, great chief of all the Ottawas, Chippewas, and Pottawattamies, and of all the nations of the lakes and rivers of the North, a man proud, vindictive, warlike, and easily offended, under pretence of some insult which he thought he had received from Maj. Gladwin, Commander of the Fort, conceived that, being great chief of all the Northern nations, only himself and those of his nations were entitled to inhabit this portion of the earth, where for sixty and odd years the French had domiciliated for the purpose of trading, and where the English had governed during three years by right of the conquest of Canada. The Chief and all his nation, whose bravery consists in treachery, resolved within himself the entire destruction of the English nation, and perhaps the Canadians. In order to succeed in his undertaking, which he had not mentioned to any of his nation the Ottawas, he engaged their aid by a speech, and they, naturally inclined to evil, did not hesitate to obey him. But, as they found themselves too weak to undertake the enterprise alone, their chief endeavored to draw to his party the Chippewa nation by means of a council. This nation was governed by a chief named Ninevois. This man, who acknowledged Pondiac as his chief, whose mind was weak, and whose disposition cruel, listened to his advances, and joined him with all his band. These two nations consisted together of about four hundred men. This number did not appear to him sufficient. It became necessary to bring into their interests the Hurons. This nation, divided into two bands, was governed by two different chiefs of dissimilar character, and nevertheless both led by their spiritual father, a Jesuit. The two chiefs of this last nation were named, one Takee, of a temper similar to Pondiac's, and the other Teata, a man of cautious disposition and of perfect prudence. This last was not easily won, and having no disposition to do evil, he refused to listen to the deputies sent by Pondiac, and sent them back. They therefore addressed themselves to the first-mentioned of this nation, by whom they were listened to, and from whom they received the war-belt, with promise to join themselves to Pondiac and Ninevois, the Ottawas and Chippewas chiefs. It was settled by means of wampum belts, (a manner of making themselves understood amongst distant savages,) that they should hold a council on the 27th of April, when should be decided the day and hour of the attack, and the precautions necessary to take in order that their perfidy should not be discovered. The manner of counting used by the Indians is by the moon; and it was resolved in the way I have mentioned, that this council should be held on the 15th day of the moon, which corresponded with Wednesday the 27th of the month of April."

The writer next describes the council at the River Ecorces, and recounts at full length the story of the Delaware Indian who visited the Great Spirit. "The Chiefs," he says, "listened to Pondiac as to an oracle, and told him they were ready to do any thing he should require."

He relates with great minuteness how Pontiac, with his chosen warriors, came to the fort on the 1st of May, to dance the calumet dance, and observe the strength and disposition of the garrison, and describes the council subsequently held at the Pottawattamie village, in order to adjust the plan of attack.

"The day fixed upon having arrived, all the Ottawas, Pondiac at their head, and the bad band of the Hurons, Takee at their head, met at the Pottawattamie village, where the premeditated council was to be held. Care was taken to send all the women out of the village, that they might not discover what was decided upon. Pondiac then ordered sentinels to be placed around the village, to prevent any interruption to their council. These precautions taken, each seated himself in the circle, according to his rank, and Pondiac, as great chief of the league, thus addressed them:—

"It is important, my brothers, that we should exterminate from our land this nation, whose only object is our death. You must be all sensible, as well as myself, that we can no longer supply our wants in the way we were accustomed to do with our Fathers the French. They sell us their goods at double the price that the French made us pay, and yet their merchandise is good for nothing; for no sooner have we bought a blanket or other thing to cover us than it is necessary to procure others against the time of departing for our wintering ground. Neither will they let us have them on credit, as our brothers the French used to do. When I visit the English chief, and inform him of the death of any of our comrades, instead of lamenting, as our brothers the French used to do, they make game of us. If I ask him for any thing for our sick, he refuses, and tells us he does not want us, from which it is apparent he seeks our death. We must therefore, in return, destroy them without delay; there is nothing to prevent us: there are but few of them, and we shall easily overcome them,—why should we not attack them? Are we not men? Have I not shown you the belts I received from our Great Father the King of France? He tells us to strike,—why should we not listen to his words? What do you fear? The time has arrived. Do you fear that our brothers the French, who are now among us, will hinder us? They are not acquainted with our designs, and if they did know them, could they prevent them? You know, as well as myself, that when the English came upon our lands, to drive from them our father Bellestre, they took from the French all the guns that they have, so that they have now no guns to defend themselves with. Therefore now is the time: let us strike. Should there be any French to take their part, let us strike them as we do the English. Remember what the Giver of Life desired our brother the Delaware to do: this regards us as much as it does them. I have sent belts and speeches to our friends the Chippeways of Saginaw, and our brothers the Ottawas of Michillimakinac, and to those of the Rivière à la Tranche, (Thames River,) inviting them to join us, and they will not delay. In the mean time, let us strike. There is no longer any time to lose, and when the English shall be defeated, we will stop the way, so that no more shall return upon our lands.

"This discourse, which Pondiac delivered in a tone of much energy, had upon the whole council all the effect which he could have expected, and they all, with common accord, swore the entire destruction of the English nation.

"At the breaking up of the council, it was decided that Pondiac, with sixty chosen men, should go to the Fort to ask for a grand council from the English commander, and that they should have arms concealed under their blankets. That the remainder of the village should follow them armed with tomahawks, daggers, and knives, concealed under their blankets, and should enter the Fort, and walk about in such a manner as not to excite suspicion, whilst the others held council with the Commander. The Ottawa women were also to be furnished with short guns and other offensive weapons concealed under their blankets. They were to go into the back streets in the Fort. They were then to wait for the signal agreed upon, which was the cry of death, which the Grand Chief was to give, on which they should altogether strike upon the English, taking care not to hurt any of the French inhabiting the Fort."

The author of the diary, unlike other contemporary writers, states that the plot was disclosed to Gladwyn by a man of the Ottawa tribe, and not by an Ojibwa girl. He says, however, that on the day after the failure of the design Pontiac sent to the Pottawattamie village in order to seize an Ojibwa girl whom he suspected of having betrayed him.

"Pondiac ordered four Indians to take her and bring her before him; these men, naturally inclined to disorder, were not long in obeying their chief; they crossed the river immediately in front of their village, and passed into the Fort naked, having nothing but their breech-clouts on and their knives in their hands, and crying all the way that their plan had been defeated, which induced the French people of the Fort, who knew nothing of the designs of the Indians, to suspect that some bad design was going forward, either against themselves or the English. They arrived at the Pottawattamie village, and in fact found the woman, who was far from thinking of them; nevertheless they seized her, and obliged her to march before them, uttering cries of joy in the manner they do when they hold a victim in their clutches on whom they are going to exercise their cruelty: they made her enter the Fort, and took her before the Commandant, as if to confront her with him, and asked him if it was not from her he had learnt their design; but they were no better satisfied than if they had kept themselves quiet. They obtained from that Officer bread and beer for themselves, and for her. They then led her to their chief in the village."

The diary leaves us in the dark as to the treatment which the girl received; but there is a tradition among the Canadians that Pontiac, with his own hand, gave her a severe beating with a species of racket, such as the Indians use in their ball-play. An old Indian told Henry Conner, formerly United

States interpreter at Detroit, that she survived her punishment, and lived for many years; but at length, contracting intemperate habits, she fell, when intoxicated, into a kettle of boiling maple-sap, and was so severely scalded that she died in consequence.

The outbreak of hostilities, the attack on the fort, and the detention of Campbell and McDougal are related at great length, and with all the minuteness of an eye-witness. The substance of the narrative is incorporated in the body of the work. The diary is very long, detailing the incidents of every passing day, from the 7th of May to the 31st of July. Here it breaks off abruptly in the middle of a sentence, the remaining part having been lost or torn away. The following extracts, taken at random, will serve to indicate the general style and character of the journal:—

"Saturday, June 4th. About 4 P. M. cries of death were heard from the Indians. The cause was not known, but it was supposed they had obtained some prize on the Lake.

"Sunday, June 5th. The Indians fired a few shots upon the Fort to-day. About 2 P. M. cries of death were again heard on the opposite side of the River. A number of Indians were descried, part on foot and part mounted. Others were taking up two trading boats, which they had taken on the lake. The vessel fired several shots at them, hoping they would abandon their prey, but they reached Pondiac's camp uninjured....

"About 7 P. M. news came that a number of Indians had gone down as far as Turkey Island, opposite the small vessel which was anchored there, but that, on seeing them, she had dropped down into the open Lake, to wait for a fair wind to come up the river.

"Monday, June 20th. The Indians fired some shots upon the fort. About 4 P. M. news was brought that Presquisle and Beef River Forts, which had been established by the French, and were now occupied by the English, had been destroyed by the Indians....

"Wednesday, June 22d. The Indians, whose whole attention was directed to the vessel, did not trouble the Fort. In the course of the day, the news of the taking of Presquisle was confirmed, as a great number of the Indians were seen coming along the shore with prisoners. The Commandant was among the number, and with him one woman: both were presented to the Hurons. In the afternoon, the Commandant received news of the lading of the vessel, and the number of men on board. The Indians again visited the French for provisions.

"Thursday, June 23d. Very early in the morning, a great number of Indians were seen passing behind the Fort: they joined those below, and all repaired to Turkey Island. The river at this place is very narrow. The Indians commenced making intrenchments of trees, andc., on the beach, where the vessel was to pass, whose arrival they awaited. About ten of the preceding night, the wind coming aft, the vessel weighed anchor, and came up the river. When opposite the Island the wind fell, and they were obliged to throw the anchor; as they knew they could not reach the Fort without being attacked by the Indians, they kept a strict watch. In order to deceive the Indians, the captain had hid in the hold sixty of his men, suspecting that the Indians, seeing only about a dozen men on deck, would try to take the vessel, which occurred as he expected. About 9 at night they got in their canoes, and made for the vessel, intending to board her. They were seen far off by one of the sentinels. The captain immediately ordered up all his men in the greatest silence, and placed them along the sides of the vessel, with their guns in their hands, loaded, with orders to wait the signal for firing, which was the rap of a hammer on the mast. The Indians were allowed to approach within less than gunshot, when the signal was given, and a discharge of cannon and small arms made upon them. They retreated to their intrenchment with the loss of fourteen killed and fourteen wounded; from which they fired during the night, and wounded two men. In the morning the vessel dropped down to the Lake for a more favorable wind.

"Friday, June 24th. The Indians were occupied with the vessel. Two Indians back of the Fort were pursued by twenty men, and escaped.

"Saturday, June 25th. Nothing occurred this day.

"Sunday, June 26th. Nothing of consequence.

"Monday, June 27th. Mr. Gamelin, who was in the practice of visiting Messrs. Campbell and McDougall, brought a letter to the Commandant from Mr. Campbell, dictated by Pondiac, in which he requested the Commandant to surrender the Fort, as in a few days he expected Kee-no-chameck, great chief of the Chippewas, with eight hundred men of his nation; that he (Pondiac) would not then be able to command them, and as soon as they arrived, they would scalp all the English in the Fort. The Commandant only answered that he cared as little for him as he did for them....

"This evening, the Commandant was informed that the Ottawas and Chippewas had undertaken another raft, which might be more worthy of attention than the former ones: it was reported to be of pine boards, and intended to be long enough to go across the river. By setting fire to every part of it, it could not help, by its length, coming in contact with the vessel, which by this means they expected would certainly take fire. Some firing took place between the vessel and Indians, but without effect.

"Tuesday, July 19th. The Indians attempted to fire on the Fort, but being discovered, they were soon made to retreat by a few shot.

"Wednesday, July 20th. Confirmation came to the Fort of the report of the 18th, and that the Indians had been four days at work at their raft, and that it would take eight more to finish it. The Commandant ordered that two boats should be lined or clapboarded with oak plank, two inches thick, and the same defence to be raised above the gunnels of the boats of two feet high. A swivel was put on each of them, and placed in such a way that they could be pointed in three different directions.

"Thursday, July 21st. The Indians were too busily occupied to pay any attention to the Fort; so earnest were they in the work of the raft that they hardly allowed themselves time to eat. The Commandant farther availed himself of the time allowed him before the premeditated attack to put every thing in proper order to repulse it. He ordered that two strong graplins should be provided for each of the barges, a strong iron chain of fifteen feet was to be attached to the boat, and conducting a strong cable under water, fastened to the graplins, and the boats were intended to be so disposed as to cover the vessel, by mooring them, by the help of the above preparations, above her. The inhabitants of the S. W. ridge, or hill, again got a false alarm. It was said the Indians intended attacking them during the night: they kept on their guard till morning.

"Friday, July 22d. An Abenakee Indian arrived this day, saying that he came direct from Montreal, and gave out that a large fleet of French was on its way to Canada, full of troops, to dispossess the English of the country. However fallacious such a story might appear, it had the effect of rousing Pondiac from his inaction, and the Indians set about their raft with more energy than ever. They had left off working at it since yesterday"....

It is needless to continue these extracts farther. Those already given will convey a sufficient idea of the character of the diary.

REMINISCENSES OF AGED CANADIANS.

About the year 1824, General Cass, with the design of writing a narrative of the siege of Detroit by Pontiac, caused inquiry to be made among the aged Canadian inhabitants, many of whom could distinctly remember the events of 1763. The accounts received from them were committed to paper, and were placed by General Cass, with great liberality, in the writer's hands. They afford an interesting mass of evidence, as worthy of confidence as evidence of the kind can be. With but one exception,—the account of Maxwell,—they do not clash with the testimony of contemporary documents. Much caution has, however, been observed in their use; and no essential statement has been made on their unsupported authority. The most prominent of these accounts are those of Peltier, St. Aubin, Gouin, Meloche, Parent, and Maxwell.

Peltier's Account.

M. Peltier was seventeen years old at the time of Pontiac's war. His narrative, though one of the longest of the collection, is imperfect, since, during a great part of the siege, he was absent from Detroit in search of runaway horses, belonging to his father. His recollection of the earlier part of the affair is, however, clear and minute. He relates, with apparent credulity, the story of the hand of the murdered Fisher protruding from the earth, as if in supplication for the neglected rites of burial. He remembers that, soon after the failure of Pontiac's attempt to surprise the garrison, he punished, by a severe flogging, a woman named Catharine, accused of having betrayed the plot. He was at Detroit during the several attacks on the armed vessels, and the attempts to set them on fire by means of blazing rafts.

St. Aubin's Account.

St. Aubin was fifteen years old at the time of the siege. It was his mother who crossed over to Pontiac's village shortly before the attempt on the garrison, and discovered the Indians in the act of sawing off the muzzles of their guns, as related in the narrative. He remembers Pontiac at his headquarters, at the house of Meloche; where his commissaries served out provision to the Indians. He himself was among those who conveyed cattle across the river to the English, at a time when they were threatened with starvation. One of his most vivid recollections is that of seeing the head of Captain Dalzell stuck on the picket of a garden fence, on the day after the battle of Bloody Bridge. His narrative is one of the most copious and authentic of the series.

Gouin's Account.

M. Gouin was but eleven years old at the time of the war. His father was a prominent trader, and had great influence over the Indians. On several occasions, he acted as mediator between them and the English; and when Major Campbell was bent on visiting the camp of Pontiac, the elder Gouin strenuously endeavored to prevent the attempt. Pontiac often came to him for advice. His son bears emphatic testimony to the extraordinary control which the chief exercised over his followers, and to the address which he displayed in the management of his commissary department. This account contains many particulars not elsewhere mentioned, though bearing all the appearance of truth. It appears to have been composed partly from the recollections of the younger Gouin, and partly from information derived from his father.

Meloche's Account.

Mad. Meloche lived, when a child, on the borders of the Detroit, between the river and the camp of Pontiac. On one occasion, when the English were cannonading the camp from their armed schooner in the river, a shot struck her father's house, throwing down a part of the walls. After the death of Major Campbell, she picked up a pocket-book belonging to him, which the Indians had left on the ground. It was full of papers, and she carried it to the English in the fort.

Parent's Account.

M. Parent was twenty-two years old when the war broke out. His recollections of the siege are, however, less exact than those of some of the former witnesses, though his narrative preserves several interesting incidents.

Maxwell's Account.

Maxwell was an English provincial, and pretended to have been a soldier under Gladwyn. His story belies the statement. It has all the air of a narrative made up from hearsay, and largely embellished from imagination. It has been made use of only in a few instances, where it is amply supported by less questionable evidence. This account seems to have been committed to paper by Maxwell himself, as the style is very rude and illiterate.

The remaining manuscripts consulted with reference to the siege of Detroit have been obtained from the State Paper Office of London, and from a few private autograph collections. Some additional information has been derived from the columns of the New York Mercury, and the Pennsylvania Gazette for 1763, where various letters written by officers at Detroit are published.

2. The Massacre of Michillimackinac.
(Chap. XVII.)

The following letter may be regarded with interest, as having been written by the commander of the unfortunate garrison a few days after the massacre. A copy of the original was procured from the State Paper Office of London.

Michillimackinac, 12 June, 1763.

Sir:

Notwithstanding that I wrote you in my last, that all the savages were arrived, and that every thing seemed in perfect tranquillity, yet, on the 2d instant, the Chippewas, who live in a plain near this fort, assembled to play ball, as they had done almost every day since their arrival. They played from morning till noon; then throwing their ball close to the gate, and observing Lieut. Lesley and me a few paces out of it, they came behind us, seized and carried us into the woods.

In the mean time the rest rushed into the Fort, where they found their squaws, whom they had previously planted there, with their hatchets hid under their blankets, which they took, and in an instant killed Lieut. Jamet and fifteen rank and file, and a trader named Tracy. They wounded two, and took the rest of the garrison prisoners, five [seven, Henry] of whom they have since killed.

They made prisoners all the English Traders, and robbed them of every thing they had; but they offered no violence to the persons or property of any of the Frenchmen.

When that massacre was over, Messrs. Langlade and Farli, the Interpreter, came down to the place where Lieut. Lesley and me were prisoners; and on their giving themselves as security to return us when demanded, they obtained leave for us to go to the Fort, under a guard of savages, which gave time, by the assistance of the gentlemen above-mentioned, to send for the Outaways, who came down on the first notice, and were very much displeased at what the Chippeways had done.

Since the arrival of the Outaways they have done every thing in their power to serve us, and with what prisoners the Chippeways had given them, and what they have bought, I have now with me Lieut. Lesley and eleven privates; and the other four of the Garrison, who are yet living, remain in the hands of the Chippeways.

The Chippeways, who are superior in number to the Ottaways, have declared in Council to them that if they do not remove us out of the Fort, they will cut off all communication to this Post, by which means all the Convoys of Merchants from Montreal, La Baye, St. Joseph, and the upper posts, would perish. But if the news of your posts being attacked (which they say was the reason why they took up the hatchet) be false, and you can send up a strong reinforcement, with provisions, andc., accompanied by some of your savages, I believe the post might be re-established again.

Since this affair happened, two canoes arrived from Montreal, which put in my power to make a present to the Ottaway nation, who very well deserve any thing that can be done for them.

I have been very much obliged to Messrs. Langlade and Farli, the Interpreter, as likewise to the Jesuit, for the many good offices they have done us on this occasion. The Priest seems inclinable to go down to your post for a day or two, which I am very glad of, as he is a very good man, and had a great deal to say with the savages, hereabout, who will believe every thing he tells them on his return, which I hope will be soon. The Outaways say they will take Lieut. Lesley, me, and the Eleven men which I mentioned before were in their hands, up to their village, and there keep us, till they hear what is doing at your Post. They have sent this canot for that purpose.

I refer you to the Priest for the particulars of this melancholy affair, and am, Dear Sir,

Yours very sincerely,

  [Signed] Geo. Etherington.

To Major Gladwyn.

P. S. The Indians that are to carry the Priest to Detroit will not undertake to land him at the Fort, but at some of the Indian villages near it; so you must not take it amiss that he does not pay you the first visit. And once more I beg that nothing may stop your sending of him back, the next day after his arrival, if possible, as we shall be at a great loss for the want of him, and I make no doubt that you will do all in your power to make peace, as you see the situation we are in, and send up provision as soon as possible, and Ammunition, as what we had was pillaged by the savages.

Adieu.

Geo. Etherington.

APPENDIX D

THE WAR ON THE BORDERS.
The Battle of Bushy Run. (Chap. XX.)
The despatches written by Colonel Bouquet, immediately after the two battles near Bushy Run, contain so full and clear an account of those engagements, that the collateral authorities consulted have served rather to decorate and enliven the narrative than to add to it any important facts. The first of these letters was written by Bouquet under the apprehension that he should not survive the expected conflict of the next day. Both were forwarded to the commander-in-chief by the same express, within a few days after the victory. The letters as here given were copied from the originals in the London offices.
Camp at Edge Hill, 26 Miles from
Fort Pitt, 5th August, 1763.
Sir:
The Second Instant the Troops and Convoy Arrived at Ligonier, whence I could obtain no Intelligence of the Enemy; The Expresses Sent since the beginning of July, having been Either killed, or Obliged to Return, all the Passes being Occupied by the Enemy: In this uncertainty I Determined to Leave all the Waggons with the Powder, and a Quantity of Stores and Provisions, at Ligonier; And on the 4th proceeded with the Troops, and about 350 Horses Loaded with Flour.
I Intended to have Halted to Day at Bushy Run, (a Mile beyond this Camp,) and after having Refreshed the Men and Horses, to have Marched in the Night over Turtle Creek, a very Dangerous Defile of Several Miles, Commanded by High and Craggy Hills: But at one o'clock this Afternoon, after a march of 17 Miles, the Savages suddenly Attacked our Advanced Guard, which was immediately Supported by the two Light Infantry

Companies of the 42d Regiment, Who Drove the Enemy from their Ambuscade, and pursued them a good Way. The Savages Returned to the Attack, and the Fire being Obstinate on our Front, and Extending along our Flanks, We made a General Charge, with the whole Line, to Dislodge the Savages from the Heights, in which attempt We succeeded without Obtaining by it any Decisive Advantage; for as soon as they were driven from One Post, they Appeared on Another, 'till, by continual Reinforcements, they were at last able to Surround Us, and attacked the Convoy left in our Rear; This Obliged us to March Back to protect it; The Action then became General, and though we were attacked on Every Side, and the Savages Exerted themselves with Uncommon Resolution, they were constantly Repulsed with Loss.—We also Suffered Considerably: Capt. Lieut. Graham, and Lieut. James McIntosh of the 42d, are Killed, and Capt. Graham Wounded.

Of the Royal Amer'n Regt., Lieut. Dow, who acted as A. D. Q. M. G. is shot through the Body.

Of the 77th, Lieut. Donald Campbell, and Mr. Peebles, a Volunteer, are Wounded.

Our Loss in Men, Including Rangers, and Drivers, Exceeds Sixty, Killed or Wounded.

The Action has Lasted from One O'Clock 'till Night, And We Expect to Begin again at Day Break. Whatever Our Fate may be, I thought it necessary to Give Your Excellency this Early Information, that You may, at all Events, take such Measures as You will think proper with the Provinces, for their own Safety, and the Effectual Relief of Fort Pitt, as in Case of Another Engagement I Fear Insurmountable Difficulties in protecting and Transporting our Provisions, being already so much Weakened by the Losses of this Day, in Men and Horses; besides the Additional Necessity of Carrying the Wounded, Whose Situation is truly Deplorable.

I Cannot Sufficiently Acknowledge the Constant Assistance I have Received from Major Campbell, during this long Action; Nor Express my Admiration of the Cool and Steady Behavior of the Troops, Who Did not Fire a Shot, without Orders, and Drove the Enemy from their Posts with Fixed Bayonets.—The Conduct of the Officers is much above my Praises.

I Have the

Honor to be, with great Respect,

Sir,

Henry Bouquet.

His Excellency Sir Jeffrey Amherst.

Camp at Bushy Run, 6th August, 1763.

Sir:

I Had the Honor to Inform Your Excellency in my letter of Yesterday of our first Engagement with the Savages.

We Took Post last Night on the Hill, where Our Convoy Halted, when the Front was Attacked, (a commodious piece of Ground, and Just Spacious Enough for our Purpose.) There We Encircled the Whole, and Covered our Wounded with the Flour Bags.

In the Morning the Savages Surrounded our Camp, at the Distance of about 500 Yards, and by Shouting and Yelping, quite Round that Extensive Circumference, thought to have Terrified Us, with their Numbers. They Attacked Us Early, and, under Favour of an Incessant Fire, made Several Bold Efforts to Penetrate our Camp; And tho' they Failed in the Attempt, our Situation was not the Less Perplexing, having Experienced that Brisk Attacks had Little Effect upon an Enemy, who always gave Way when Pressed, and Appeared again Immediately; Our Troops were besides Extremely Fatigued with the Long March, and as long Action of the Preceding Day, and Distressed to the Last Degree, by a Total Want of Water, much more Intolerable than the Enemy's Fire.

Tied to our Convoy We could not Lose Sight of it, without Exposing it, and our Wounded, to Fall a prey to the Savages, who Pressed upon Us on Every Side; and to Move it was Impracticable, having lost many horses, and most of the Drivers, Stupified by Fear, hid themselves in the Bushes, or were Incapable of Hearing or Obeying Orders.

The Savages growing Every Moment more Audacious, it was thought proper still to increase their Confidence; by that means, if possible, to Entice them to Come Close upon Us, or to Stand their Ground when Attacked. With this View two Companies of Light Infantry were Ordered within the Circle, and the Troops on their Right and Left opened their Files, and Filled up the Space that it might seem they were intended to Cover the Retreat; The Third Light Infantry Company, and the Grenadiers of the 42d, were Ordered to Support the two First Companys. This Manœuvre Succeeded to Our Wish, for the Few Troops who Took possession of the Ground lately Occupied by the two Light Infantry Companys being Brought in Nearer to the Centre of the Circle, the Barbarians, mistaking these Motions for a Retreat, Hurried Headlong on, and Advancing upon Us, with the most Daring Intrepidity, Galled us Excessively with their Heavy Fire; But at the very moment that, Certain of Success, they thought themselves Masters of the Camp, Major Campbell, at the Head of the two First Companys, Sallied out from a part of the Hill they Could not Observe, and Fell upon their Right Flank; They Resolutely Returned the Fire, but could not Stand the Irresistible Shock of our Men, Who, Rushing in among them, Killed many of them, and Put the Rest to Flight. The Orders sent to the Other Two Companys were Delivered so timely by Captain Basset, and Executed with such Celerity and Spirit, that the Routed Savages, who happened to Run that Moment before their Front, Received their Full Fire, when Uncovered by the Trees: The Four Companys Did not give them time to Load a Second time, nor Even to Look behind them, but Pursued them 'till they were Totally Dispersed. The Left of the Savages, which had not been Attacked, were kept in Awe by the Remains of our Troops, Posted on the Brow of the Hill, for that Purpose; Nor Durst they Attempt to Support, or Assist their Right, but being Witness to their Defeat, followed their Example and Fled. Our Brave Men Disdained so much to Touch the Dead Body of a Vanquished Enemy, that Scarce a Scalp was taken, Except by the Rangers, and Pack Horse Drivers.

The Woods being now Cleared and the Pursuit over, the Four Companys took possession of a Hill in our Front; and as soon as Litters could be made for the Wounded, and the Flour and Every thing Destroyed, which, for want of Horses, could not be Carried, We Marched without Molestation to this Camp. After the Severe Correction We had given the Savages a few hours before, it was Natural to Suppose We should Enjoy some Rest; but We had hardly Fixed our Camp, when they fired upon Us again: This was very Provoking! However, the Light Infantry Dispersed them, before they could Receive Orders for that purpose.—I Hope We shall be no more Disturbed, for, if We have another Action, We shall hardly be able to Carry our Wounded.

The Behavior of the Troops, on this Occasion, Speaks for itself so Strongly, that for me to Attempt their Eulogium, would but Detract from their merit.
Sir,
Henry Bouquet.
P. S. I Have the Honor to Enclose the Return of the Killed, Wounded, and Missing in the two Engagements.
H. B.
His Excellency Sir Jeffrey Amherst.

APPENDIX E

THE PAXTON RIOTS.
1. Evidence Against the Indians of Conestoga.
(Chap. XXIV.)

Abraham Newcomer, a Mennonist, by trade a Gunsmith, upon his affirmation, declared that several times, within these few years, Bill Soc and Indian John, two of the Conestogue Indians, threatened to scalp him for refusing to mend their tomahawks, and swore they would as soon scalp him as they would a dog. A few days before Bill Soc was killed, he brought a tomahawk to be steeled. Bill said, "If you will not, I'll have it mended to your sorrow," from which expression I apprehended danger.

Mrs. Thompson, of the borough of Lancaster, personally appeared before the Chief Burgess, and upon her solemn oath, on the Holy Evangelists, said that in the summer of 1761, Bill Soc came to her apartment, and threatened her life, saying, "I kill you, all Lancaster can't catch me," which filled me with terror; and this lady further said, Bill Soc added, "Lancaster is mine, and I will have it yet."

Colonel John Hambright, gentleman, an eminent Brewer of the Borough of Lancaster, personally appeared before Robert Thompson, Esq., a justice for the county of Lancaster, and made oath on the Holy Evangelists, that, in August, 1757, he, an officer, was sent for provision from Fort Augusta to Fort Hunter, that on his way he rested at M'Kee's old place; a Sentinel was stationed behind a tree, to prevent surprise. The Sentry gave notice Indians were near; the deponent crawled up the bank and discovered two Indians; one was Bill Soc, lately killed at Lancaster. He called Bill Soc to come to him, but the Indians ran off. When the deponent came to Fort Hunter, he learnt that an old man had been killed the day before; Bill Soc and his

companion were believed to be the perpetrators of the murder. He, the deponent, had frequently seen Bill Soc and some of the Conestogue Indians at Fort Augusta, trading with the Indians, but, after the murder of the old man, Bill Soc did not appear at that Garrison.
John Hambright.
Sworn and Subscribed the 28th of Feb., 1764, before me,
Robert Thompson, Justice.
Charles Cunningham, of the county of Lancaster, personally appeared before me, Thomas Foster, Esq., one of the Magistrates for said county, and being qualified according to law, doth depose and say, that he, the deponent, heard Joshua James, an Indian, say, that he never killed a white man in his life, but six dutchmen that he killed in the Minisinks.
Charles Cunningham.
Sworn To, and Subscribed before Thomas Foster, Justice.
Alexander Stephen, of the county of Lancaster, personally appeared before Thomas Foster, Esq., one of the Magistrates, and being duly qualified according to law, doth say, that Connayak Sally, an Indian woman, told him that the Conestogue Indians had killed Jegrea, an Indian, because he would not join the Conestogue Indians in destroying the English. James Cotter told the deponent that he was one of the three that killed old William Hamilton, on Sherman's Creek, and also another man, with seven of his family. James Cotter demanded of the deponent a canoe, which the murderers had left, as Cotter told him when the murder was committed.
Alexander Stephen.
Thomas Foster, Justice.

Note.—Jegrea was a Warrior Chief, friendly to the Whites, and he threatened the Conestogue Indians with his vengeance, if they harmed the English. Cotter was one of the Indians, killed in Lancaster county, in 1763.

Anne Mary Le Roy, of Lancaster, appeared before the Chief Burgess, and being sworn on the Holy Evangelists of Almighty God, did depose and say, that in the year 1755, when her Father, John Jacob Le Roy, and many others, were murdered by the Indians, at Mahoney, she, her brother, and some others were made prisoners, and taken to Kittanning; that stranger Indians visited them; the French told them they were Conestogue Indians, and that Isaac was the only Indian true to their interest; and that the Conestogue Indians, with the exception of Isaac, were ready to lift the hatchet when ordered by the French. She asked Bill Soc's mother whether she had ever been at Kittanning? she said "no, but her son, Bill Soc, had been there often; that he was good for nothing."
Mary Le Roy.

2. Proceedings of the Rioters. (Chap. XXIV., XXV.)
Deposition of Felix Donolly, keeper of Lancaster Jail.
This deposition is imperfect, a part of the manuscript having been defaced or torn away. The original, in the handwriting of Edward Shippen, the chief magistrate of Lancaster, was a few years since in the possession of Redmond Conyngham, Esq.

The breaking open the door alarmed me; armed men broke in; they demanded the strange Indian to be given up; they ran by me; the Indians guessed their intention; they seized billets of wood from the pile; but the three most active were shot; others came to their assistance; I was stupefied; before I could shake off my surprise, the Indians were killed and their murderers away.

Q. You say, "Indians armed themselves with wood;" did those Indians attack the rioters?
A. They did. If they had not been shot, they would have killed the men who entered, for they were the strongest.
Q. Could the murder have been prevented by you?
A. No: I nor no person here could have prevented it.
Q. What number were the rioters?
A. I should say fifty.
Q. Did you know any of them?
A. No; they were strangers.
Q. Do you now know who was in command?
A. I have been told, Lazarus Stewart of Donegal.
Q. If the Indians had not attempted resistance, would the men have fled? (fired?)
A. I couldn't tell; I do not know.
Q. Do you think or believe that the rioters came with the intent to murder?
A. I heard them say, when they broke in, they wanted a strange Indian.
Q. Was their object to murder him?
A. From what I have heard since, I think they meant to carry him off; that is my belief.
Q. What was their purpose?
A. I do not know.
Q. Were the Indians killed all friends of this province?
A. I have been told they were not. I cannot tell of myself; I do not know.

Donolly was suspected of a secret inclination in favor of the rioters. In private conversation he endeavored to place their conduct in as favorable a light as possible, and indeed such an intention is apparent in the above deposition.
Letter from Edward Shippen to Governor Hamilton.

Lancaster, ———, 1764.

Honoured Sir:

I furnish you with a full detail of all the particulars that could be gathered of the unhappy transactions of the fourteenth and twenty-seventh of December last, as painful for you to read as me to write. The Depositions can only state the fact that the Indians were killed. Be assured the Borough Authorities, when they placed the Indians in the Workhouse, thought it a place of security. I am sorry the Indians were not removed to Philadelphia, as recommended by us. It is too late to remedy. It is much to be regretted that there are evil-minded persons among us, who are trying to corrupt the minds of the people by idle tales and horrible butcheries—are injuring the character of many of our most respectable people. That printers should have lent their aid astonishes me when they are employed by the Assembly to print their laws. I can see no good in meeting their falsehoods by counter statements.

The Rev. Mr. Elder and Mr. Harris are determined to rely upon the reputation they have so well established.

For myself, I can only say that, possessing your confidence, and that of the Proprietaries, with a quiet conscience, I regard not the malignant pens of secret assailants—men who had not the courage to affix their names. Is it not strange that a too ready belief was at first given to the slanderous epistles? Resting on the favor I have enjoyed of the Government; on the confidence reposed in me, by you and the Proprietaries; by the esteem of my fellow-men in Lancaster, I silently remain passive.

Yours affectionately,

Edward Shippen.

Extract from a letter of the Rev. Mr. Elder to Governor Penn, December 27, 1763.

The storm which had been so long gathering, has at length exploded. Had Government removed the Indians from Conestoga, which had frequently been urged, without success, this painful catastrophe might have been avoided. What could I do with men heated to madness? All that I could do, was done; I expostulated; but life and reason were set at defiance. And yet the men, in private life, are virtuous and respectable; not cruel, but mild and merciful.

The time will arrive when each palliating circumstance will be calmly weighed. This deed, magnified into the blackest of crimes, shall be considered one of those youthful ebullitions of wrath caused by momentary excitement, to which human infirmity is subjected.

Extract from "The Paxtoniade," a poem in imitation of Hudibras, published at Philadelphia, 1764, by a partisan of the Quaker faction:—

O'Hara mounted on his Steed,
(Descendant of that self-same Ass,

That bore his Grandsire Hudibras,)
And from that same exalted Station,
Pronounced an hortory Oration:
For he was cunning as a fox,
Had read o'er Calvin and Dan Nox;
A man of most profound Discerning,
Well versed in P———n Learning.
So after hemming thrice to clear
His Throat, and banish thoughts of fear,
And of the mob obtaining Silence,
He thus went on—"Dear Sirs, a while since
Ye know as how the Indian Rabble,
With practices unwarrantable,
Did come upon our quiet Borders,
And there commit most desperate murders;
Did tomahawk, butcher, wound and cripple,
With cruel Rage, the Lord's own People;
Did war most implacable wage
With God's own chosen heritage;
Did from our Brethren take their lives,
And kill our Children, kine and wives.
Now, Sirs, I ween it is but right,
That we upon these Canaanites,
Without delay, should Vengeance take,
Both for our own, and the K——k's sake;
Should totally destroy the heathen,
And never till we've killed 'em leave 'em;—
Destroy them quite frae out the Land;
And for it we have God's Command.
We should do him a muckle Pleasure,
As ye in your Books may read at leisure."
He paused, as Orators are used,
And from his pocket quick produced
A friendly Vase well stor'd and fill'd
With good old whiskey twice distill'd,
And having refresh'd his inward man,
Went on with his harangue again.
"Is't not, my Brethren, a pretty Story
That we who are the Land's chief Glory,
Who are i' the number of God's elected,
Should slighted thus be and neglected?
That we, who're the only Gospel Church,
Should thus be left here in the lurch;

Whilst our most antichristian foes,
Whose trade is war and hardy blows,
(At least while some of the same Colour,
With those who've caused us all this Dolor,)
In matchcoats warm and blankets drest,
Are by the Q———rs much caress'd,
And live in peace by good warm fires,
And have the extent of their desires?
Shall we put by such treatment base?
By Nox, we wont!"—And broke his Vase.
"Seeing then we've such good cause to hate 'em,
What I intend's to extirpate 'em;
To suffer them no more to thrive,
And leave nor Root nor Branch alive;
But would we madly leave our wives
And Children, and expose our lives
In search of these wh' infest our borders,
And perpetrate such cruel murders;
It is most likely, by King Harry,
That we should in the end miscarry.
I deem therefore the wisest course is,
That those who've beasts should mount their horses,
And those who've none should march on foot,
With as much quickness as will suit,
To where those heathen, nothing fearful,
That we will on their front and rear fall,
Enjoy Sweet Otium in their Cotts,
And dwell securely in their Hutts.
And as they've nothing to defend them,
We'll quickly to their own place send them!"

The following letter from Rev. John Elder to Colonel Shippen will serve to exhibit the state of feeling among the frontier inhabitants.
Paxton, Feb. 1, 1764.
Dear Sir:
Since I sealed the Governor's Letter, which you'll please to deliver to him, I suspect, from the frequent meetings I hear the people have had in divers parts of the Frontier Counties, that an Expedition is immediately designed against the Indians at Philadelphia. It's well known that I have always used my utmost endeavors to discourage these proceedings; but to little purpose: the minds of the Inhabitants are so exasperated against a particular set of men, deeply concerned in the government, for the singular regards they have always shown to savages, and the heavy burden by their means laid on

the province in maintaining an expensive Trade and holding Treaties from time to time with the savages, without any prospect of advantage either to his Majesty or to the province, how beneficial soever it may have been to individuals, that it's in vain, nay even unsafe for any one to oppose their measures; for were Col. Shippen here, tho' a gentleman highly esteemed by the Frontier inhabitants, he would soon find it useless, if not dangerous, to act in opposition to an enraged multitude. At first there were but, as I think, few concerned in these riots, and nothing intended by some but to ease the province of part of its burden, and by others, who had suffered greatly in the late war, the gratifying a spirit of Revenge, yet the manner of the Quakers resenting these things has been, I think, very injurious and impolitick. The Presbyterians, who are the most numerous, I imagine, of any denomination in the province, are enraged at their being charged in bulk with these facts, under the name of Scotch-Irish, and other ill-natured titles, and that the killing the Conestogoe Indians is compared to the Irish Massacres, and reckoned the most barbarous of either, so that things are grown to that pitch now that the country seems determined that no Indian Treaties shall be held, or savages maintained at the expense of the province, unless his Majesty's pleasure on these heads is well known; for I understood to my great satisfaction that amid our great confusions, there are none, even of the most warm and furious tempers, but what are warmly attached to his Majesty, and would cheerfully risk their lives to promote his service. What the numbers are of those going on the above-mentioned Expedition, I can't possibly learn, as I'm informed they are collecting in all parts of the province; however, this much may be depended on, that they have the good wishes of the country in general, and that there are few but what are now either one way or other embarked in the affair, tho' some particular persons, I'm informed, are grossly misrepresented in Philadelphia; even my neighbor, Mr. Harris, it's said, is looked on there as the chief promoter of these riots, yet it's entirely false; he had aided as much in opposition to these measures as he could with any safety in his situation. Reports, however groundless, are spread by designing men on purpose to inflame matters, and enrage the parties against each other, and various methods used to accomplish their pernicious ends. As I am deeply concerned for the welfare of my country, I would do every thing in my power to promote its interests. I thought proper to give you these few hints; you'll please to make what use you think proper of them. I would heartily wish that some effectual measures might be taken to heal these growing evils, and this I judge may be yet done, and Col. Armstrong, who is now in town, may be usefully employed for this purpose.

Sir,

I am, etc.,

John Elder.

Extracts from a Quaker letter on the Paxton riots.

This letter is written with so much fidelity, and in so impartial a spirit, that it must always remain one of the best authorities in reference to these singular events. Although in general very accurate, its testimony has in a few instances been set aside in favor of the more direct evidence of eye-witnesses. It was published by Hazard in the twelfth volume of his Pennsylvania Register. I have, however, examined the original, which is still preserved by a family in Philadelphia. The extracts here given form but a small part of the entire letter.

Before I proceed further it may not be amiss to inform thee that a great number of the inhabitants here approved of killing the Indians, and declared that they would not offer to oppose the Paxtoneers, unless they attacked the citizens, that is to say, themselves—for, if any judgment was to be formed from countenances and behavior, those who depended upon them for defence and protection, would have found their confidence shockingly misplaced.

The number of persons in arms that morning was about six hundred, and as it was expected the insurgents would attempt to cross at the middle or upper ferry, orders were sent to bring the boats to this side, and to take away the ropes. Couriers were now seen continually coming in, their horses all of a foam, and people running with the greatest eagerness to ask them where the enemy were, and what were their numbers. The answers to these questions were various: sometimes they were at a distance, then near at hand—sometimes they were a thousand strong, then five hundred, then fifteen hundred; in short, all was doubt and uncertainty.

About eleven o'clock it was recollected the boat at the Sweed's ford was not secured, which, in the present case, was of the utmost consequence, for, as there was a considerable freshet in the Schuylkill, the securing that boat would oblige them to march some distance up the river, and thereby retard the execution of their scheme at least a day or two longer. Several persons therefore set off immediately to get it performed; but they had not been gone long, before there was a general uproar—They are coming! they are coming! Where? where? Down Second street! down Second street! Such of the company as had grounded their firelocks, flew to arms, and began to prime; the artillery-men threw themselves into order, and the people ran to get out of the way, for a troop of armed men, on horseback, appeared in reality coming down the street, and one of the artillery-men was just going to apply the fatal match, when a person, perceiving the mistake, clapped his hat upon the touch-hole of the piece he was going to fire. Dreadful would have been the consequence, had the cannon discharged; for the men that appeared proved to be a company of German butchers and porters, under the command of Captain Hoffman. They had just collected themselves, and being unsuspicious of danger, had neglected to give notice of their coming;—a false alarm was now called out, and all became quiet again in a few minutes....

The weather being now very wet, Capt. Francis, Capt. Wood, and Capt. Mifflin, drew up their men under the market-house, which, not affording shelter for any more, they occupied Friends' meeting-house, and Capt. Joseph Wharton marched his company up stairs, into the monthly meeting room, as I have been told—the rest were stationed below. It happened to be the day appointed for holding of Youths' meeting, but never did the Quaker youth assemble in such a military manner—never was the sound of the drum heard before within those walls, nor ever till now was the Banner of War displayed in that rostrum, from whence the art has been so zealously declaimed against. Strange reverse of times, James—. Nothing of any consequence passed during the remainder of the day, except that Captain Coultas came into town at the head of a troop, which he had just raised in his own neighborhood. The Captain was one of those who had been marked out as victims by these devout conquerors, and word was sent to him from Lancaster to make his peace with Heaven, for that he had but about ten days to live.

In the evening our Negotiators came in from Germantown. They had conferred with the Chiefs of this illustrious—, and have prevailed with them to suspend all hostility till such time as they should receive an answer to their petition or manifesto, which had been sent down the day before....

The weather now clearing, the City forces drew up near the Court House where a speech was made to them, informing them that matters had been misrepresented,—that the Paxtoneers were a set of very worthy men (or something to that purpose) who labored under great distress,—that Messrs. Smith, andc., were come (by their own authority) as representatives, from several counties, to lay their complaints before the Legislature, and that the reason for their arming themselves was for fear of being molested or abused. By whom? Why, by the peaceable citizens of Philadelphia! Ha! ha! ha! Who can help laughing? The harangue concluded with thanks for the trouble and expense they had been at (about nothing), and each retired to their several homes. The next day, when all was quiet, and nobody dreamed of any further disturbance, we were alarmed again. The report now was, that the Paxtoneers had broke the Treaty, and were just entering the city. It is incredible to think with what alacrity the people flew to arms; in one quarter of an hour near a thousand of them were assembled, with a determination to bring the affair to a conclusion immediately, and not to suffer themselves to be harassed as they had been several days past. If the whole body of the enemy had come in, as was expected, the engagement would have been a bloody one, for the citizens were exasperated almost to madness; but happily those that appeared did not exceed thirty, (the rest having gone homewards), and as they behaved with decency, they were suffered to pass without opposition. Thus the storm blew over, and the Inhabitants dispersed themselves....

The Pennsylvania Gazette, usually a faithful chronicler of the events of the day, preserves a discreet silence on the subject of the Paxton riots, and contains no other notice of them than the following condensed statement:—

On Saturday last, the City was alarmed with the News of Great Numbers of armed Men, from the Frontiers, being on the several Roads, and moving towards Philadelphia. As their designs were unknown, and there were various Reports concerning them, it was thought prudent to put the City in some Posture of Defence against any Outrages that might possibly be intended. The Inhabitants being accordingly called upon by the Governor, great numbers of them entered into an Association, and took Arms for the Support of Government, and Maintenance of good Order.

Six Companies of Foot, one of Artillery, and two Troops of Horse, were formed, and paraded, to which, it is said, some Thousands, who did not appear, were prepared to join themselves, in case any attempt should be made against the Town. The Barracks also, where the Indians are lodged, under Protection of the regular Troops, were put into a good Posture of Defence; several Works being thrown up about them, and eight Pieces of Cannon planted there.

The Insurgents, it seems, intended to rendezvous at Germantown; but the Precautions taken at the several Ferries over Schuylkill impeded their Junction; and those who assembled there, being made acquainted with the Force raised to oppose them, listened to the reasonable Discourses and Advice of some prudent Persons, who voluntarily went out to meet and admonish them; and of some Gentlemen sent by the Governor, to know the Reasons of their Insurrection; and promised to return peaceably to their Habitations, leaving only two of their Number to present a Petition to the Governor and Assembly; on which the Companies raised in Town were thanked by the Governor on Tuesday Evening, and dismissed, and the City restored to its former Quiet.

But on Wednesday Morning there was a fresh Alarm, occasioned by a false Report, that Four Hundred of the same People were on their March to Attack the Town. Immediately, on Beat of Drum, a much greater number of the Inhabitants, with the utmost Alacrity, put themselves under Arms; but as the Truth was soon known, they were again thanked by the Governor, and dismissed; the Country People being really dispersed, and gone home according to their Promise.—Pennsylvania Gazette, No. 1833.

The following extract from a letter of Rev. John Ewing to Joseph Reed affords a striking example of the excitement among the Presbyterians. (See Life and Correspondence of Joseph Reed, I. 34.)

Feb. —, 1764.

As to public affairs, our Province is greatly involved in intestine feuds, at a time, when we should rather unite, one and all, to manage the affairs of our several Governments, with prudence and discretion. A few designing men, having engrossed too much power into their hands, are pushing matters beyond all bounds. There are twenty-two Quakers in our Assembly, at present, who, although they won't absolutely refuse to grant money for the King's use, yet never fail to contrive matters in such a manner as to afford little or no assistance to the poor, distressed Frontiers; while our public money is lavishly squandered away in supporting a number of savages, who have been murdering and scalping us for many years past. This has so enraged some desperate young men, who had lost their nearest relations, by these very Indians, to cut off about twenty Indians that lived near Lancaster, who had, during the war, carried on a constant intercourse with our other enemies; and they came down to Germantown to inquire why Indians, known to be enemies, were supported, even in luxury, with the best that our markets afforded, at the public expense, while they were left in the utmost distress on the Frontiers, in want of the necessaries of life. Ample promises were made to them that their grievances should be redressed, upon which they immediately dispersed and went home. These persons have been unjustly represented as endeavoring to overturn Government, when nothing was more distant from their minds. However this matter may be looked upon in Britain, where you know very little of the matter, you may be assured that ninety-nine in an hundred of the Province are firmly persuaded, that they are maintaining our enemies, while our friends back are suffering the greatest extremities, neglected; and that few, but Quakers, think that the Lancaster Indians have suffered any thing but their just deserts. 'Tis not a little surprising to us here, that orders should be sent from the Crown, to apprehend and bring to justice those persons who have cut off that nest of enemies that lived near Lancaster. They never were subjects to his Majesty; were a free, independent state, retaining all the powers of a free state; sat in all our Treaties with the Indians, as one of the tribes belonging to the Six Nations, in alliance with us; they entertained the French and Indian spies—gave intelligence to them of the defenceless state of our Province—furnished them with Gazette every week, or fortnight—gave them intelligence of all the dispositions of the Province army against them—were frequently with the French and Indians at their forts and towns—supplied them with warlike stores—joined with the strange Indians in their war-dances, and in the parties that made incursions on our Frontiers—were ready to take up the hatchet against the English openly, when the French requested it—actually murdered and scalped some of the Frontier inhabitants—insolently boasted of the murders they had committed, when they saw our blood was cooled, after the last Treaty at Lancaster—confessed that they had been at war with us, and would soon be

at war with us again (which accordingly happened), and even went so far as to put one of their own warriors, Jegarie, to death, because he refused to go to war with them against the English. All these things were known through the Frontier inhabitants, and are since proved upon oath. This occasioned them to be cut off by about forty or fifty persons, collected from all the Frontier counties, though they are called by the name of the little Township of Paxton, where, possibly, the smallest part of them resided. And what surprises us more than all the accounts we have from England, is, that our Assembly, in a petition they have drawn up, to the King, for a change of Government, should represent this Province in a state of uproar and riot, and when not a man in it has once resisted a single officer of the Government, nor a single act of violence committed, unless you call the Lancaster affair such, although it was no more than going to war with that tribe, as they had done before with others, without a formal proclamation of war by the Government. I have not time, as you may guess by this scrawl, to write more at this time, but only that I am yours, andc.
John Ewing.
3. Memorials of the Paxton Men. (Chap. XXV)

5. To the Honorable John Penn, Esq., Governor of the Province of Pennsylvania, and of the Counties of New-Castle, Kent, and Sussex, upon Delaware; and to the Representatives of the Freemen of the said Province, in General Assembly met.
We, Matthew Smith and James Gibson, in Behalf of ourselves and his Majesty's faithful and loyal Subjects, the Inhabitants of the Frontier Counties of Lancaster, York, Cumberland, Berks, and Northampton, humbly beg Leave to remonstrate and lay before you the following Grievances, which we submit to your Wisdom for Redress.
First. We apprehend that, as Freemen and English Subjects, we have an indisputable Title to the same Privileges and immunities with his Majesty's other Subjects, who reside in the interior Counties of Philadelphia, Chester, and Bucks, and therefore ought not to be excluded from an equal Share with them in the very important Privilege of Legislation;—nevertheless, contrary to the Proprietor's Charter, and the acknowledged Principles of common Justice and Equity, our five Counties are restrained from electing more than ten Representatives, viz., four for Lancaster, two for York, two for Cumberland, one for Berks, and one for Northampton, while the three Counties and City of Philadelphia, Chester, and Bucks elect Twenty-six. This we humbly conceive is oppressive, unequal and unjust, the Cause of many of our Grievances, and an Infringement of our natural Privileges of Freedom and Equality; wherefore we humbly pray that we may be no longer deprived of an equal Number with the three aforesaid Counties to represent us in Assembly.

Secondly. We understand that a Bill is now before the House of Assembly, wherein it is provided, that such Persons as shall be charged with killing any Indians in Lancaster County, shall not be tried in the County where the Fact was committed, but in the Counties of Philadelphia, Chester, or Bucks. This is manifestly to deprive British Subjects of their known Privileges, to cast an eternal Reproach upon whole Counties, as if they were unfit to serve their Country in the Quality of Jury-men, and to contradict the well known Laws of the British Nation, in a Point whereon Life, Liberty, and Security essentially depend; namely, that of being tried by their Equals, in the Neighbourhood where their own, their Accusers, and the Witnesses Character and Credit, with the Circumstances of the Fact, are best known, and instead thereof putting their Lives in the Hands of Strangers, who may as justly be suspected of Partiality to, as the Frontier Counties can be of Prejudices against, Indians; and this too, in favour of Indians only, against his Majesty's faithful and loyal Subjects: Besides, it is well known, that the Design of it is to comprehend a Fact committed before such a Law was thought of. And if such Practices were tolerated, no Man could be secure in his most invaluable Interest.—We are also informed, to our great Surprise, that this Bill has actually received the Assent of a Majority of the House; which we are persuaded could not have been the Case, had our Frontier Counties been equally represented in Assembly.—However, we hope that the Legislature of this Province will never enact a Law of so dangerous a Tendency, or take away from his Majesty's good Subjects a Privilege so long esteemed sacred by Englishmen.

Thirdly. During the late and present Indian War, the Frontiers of this Province have been repeatedly attacked and ravaged by skulking Parties of the Indians, who have, with the most Savage Cruelty, murdered Men, Women, and Children, without Distinction, and have reduced near a Thousand Families to the most extreme Distress.—It grieves us to the very Heart to see such of our Frontier Inhabitants as have escaped Savage Fury, with the Loss of their Parents, their Children, their Wives or Relatives, left Destitute by the Public, and exposed to the most cruel Poverty and Wretchedness, while upwards of an Hundred and Twenty of these Savages, who are, with great Reason, suspected of being guilty of these horrid Barbarities, under the Mask of Friendship, have procured themselves to be taken under the Protection of the Government, with a View to elude the Fury of the brave Relatives of the Murdered, and are now maintained at the public Expense.—Some of these Indians, now in the Barracks of Philadelphia, are confessedly a Part of the Wyalusing Indians, which Tribe is now at War with us; and the others are the Moravian Indians, who, living with us, under the Cloak of Friendship, carried on a Correspondence with our known Enemies on the Great Island.—We cannot but observe, with Sorrow and Indignation, that some Persons in this Province are at Pains to extenuate the barbarous Cruelties practised by these Savages on our murdered Brethren and Relatives, which are shocking to human Nature, and must pierce every Heart, but that of the hardened Perpetrators or their Abettors. Nor is it less distressing to hear Others pleading, that although the Wyalusing Tribe is at War with us, yet that Part of it which is under the Protection of the Government, may be friendly to the English, and innocent:—In what Nation under the Sun was it ever the Custom, that when a neighbouring Nation took up Arms, not an Individual should be touched, but only the Persons that offered Hostilities?—Who ever proclaimed War with a Part of a Nation and not with the whole?—Had these Indians disapproved of the Perfidy of their Tribe, and been willing to cultivate and preserve Friendship with us, why did they not give Notice of the War before it happened, as it is known to be the Result of long Deliberations, and a preconcerted Combination among them?—Why did they not leave their Tribe immediately, and come among us, before there was Ground to suspect them, or War was actually waged with their Tribe?—No, they stayed amongst them, were privy to their Murders and Ravages, until we had destroyed their provisions, and when they could no longer subsist at Home, they come not as Deserters, but as Friends, to be maintained through the Winter, that they may be able to scalp and butcher us in the Spring.

And as to the Moravian Indians, there are strong Grounds at least to suspect their Friendship, as it is known that they carried on a Correspondence with our Enemies on the Great Island.—We killed three Indians going from Bethlehem to the Great Island with Blankets, Ammunition, and Provisions, which is an undeniable Proof that the Moravian Indians were in Confederacy with our open Enemies. And we cannot but be filled with Indignation to hear this Action of ours painted in the most odious and detestable Colours, as if we had inhumanly murdered our Guides, who preserved us from perishing in the Woods; when we only killed three of our known Enemies, who attempted to shoot us when we surprised them.—And, besides all this, we understand that one of these very Indians is proved, by the Oath of Stinton's Widow, to be the very Person that murdered her Husband.—How then comes it to pass, that he alone, of all the Moravian Indians, should join the Enemy to murder that family?—Or can it be supposed that any Enemy Indians, contrary to their known Custom of making War, should penetrate into the Heart of a settled Country, to burn, plunder, and murder the Inhabitants, and not molest any Houses in their Return, or ever be seen or heard of?—Or how can we account for it, that no Ravages have been committed in Northampton County since the Removal of the Moravian Indians, when the Great Cove has been struck since?—These Things put it beyond Doubt with us that the Indians now at Philadelphia are his Majesty's perfidious Enemies, and therefore, to protect and maintain them at the public Expence, while our suffering Brethren on the Frontiers are almost destitute of the Necessaries of Life, and are neglected by the Public, is sufficient to make us mad with Rage, and tempt us to do what nothing but the most violent Necessity can vindicate.—We humbly and earnestly pray therefore, that those Enemies of his Majesty may be removed as soon as possible out of the Province.

Fourthly. We humbly conceive that it is contrary to the Maxims of good Policy and extremely dangerous to our Frontiers, to suffer any Indians, of what Tribe soever, to live within the inhabited Parts of this Province, while we are engaged in an Indian War, as Experience has taught us that they are all perfidious, and their Claim to Freedom and Independency, puts it in their Power to act as Spies, to entertain and give Intelligence to our Enemies, and to furnish them with Provisions and warlike Stores.—To this fatal Intercourse between our pretended Friends and open Enemies, we must ascribe the greatest Part of the Ravages and Murders that have been committed in the Course of this and the last Indian War.—We therefore pray that this Grievance be taken under Consideration, and remedied.

Fifthly. We cannot help lamenting that no Provision has been hitherto made, that such of our Frontier Inhabitants as have been wounded in Defence of the Province, their Lives and Liberties may be taken Care of, and cured of their Wounds, at the public Expence.—We therefore pray that this Grievance may be redressed.

Sixthly. In the late Indian War this Province, with others of his Majesty's Colonies, gave Rewards for Indian Scalps, to encourage the seeking them in their own Country, as the most likely Means of destroying or reducing them to Reason; but no such Encouragement has been given in this War, which has damped the Spirits of many brave Men, who are willing to venture their Lives in Parties against the Enemy.—We therefore pray that public Rewards may be proposed for Indian Scalps, which may be adequate to the Dangers attending Enterprises of this Nature.

Seventhly. We daily lament that Numbers of our nearest and dearest Relatives are still in Captivity among the savage Heathen, to be trained up in all their Ignorance and Barbarity, or to be tortured to Death with all the Contrivances of Indian Cruelty, for attempting to make their Escape from Bondage. We see they pay no Regard to the many solemn Promises which they have made to restore our Friends who are in Bondage amongst them.—We therefore earnestly pray that no Trade may hereafter be permitted to be carried on with them until our Brethren and Relatives are brought Home to us.

Eighthly. We complain that a certain Society of People in this Province in the late Indian War, and at several Treaties held by the King's Representatives, openly loaded the Indians with Presents; and that F. P., a Leader of the said Society, in Defiance of all Government, not only abetted our Indian Enemies, but kept up a private Intelligence with them, and publickly received from them a Belt of Wampum, as if he had been our Governor, or authorized by the King to treat with his Enemies.—By this means the Indians have been taught to despise us as a weak and disunited People, and from this fatal Source have arose many of our Calamities under which we groan.—We humbly pray, therefore, that this Grievance may be redressed, and that no private Subject be hereafter permitted to treat with, or carry on a Correspondence with our Enemies.

Ninthly. We cannot but observe with Sorrow, that Fort Augusta, which has been very expensive to this Province, has afforded us but little Assistance during this or the last War. The Men that were stationed at that Place neither helped our distressed Inhabitants to save their Crops, nor did they attack our Enemies in their Towns, or patrol on our Frontiers.—We humbly request that proper Measures may be taken to make that Garrison more serviceable to us in our Distress, if it can be done.

N. B. We are far from intending any Reflection against the Commanding Officer stationed at Augusta, as we presume his Conduct was always directed by those from whom he received his Orders.

Signed on Behalf of ourselves, and by Appointment of a great Number of the Frontier Inhabitants,

Matthew Smith.

James Gibson.

The Declaration of the injured Frontier Inhabitants, together with a brief Sketch of Grievances the good Inhabitants of the Province labor under.

Inasmuch as the Killing those Indians at Conestogoe Manor and Lancaster has been, and may be, the Subject of much Conversation, and by invidious Representations of it, which some, we doubt not, will industriously spread, many, unacquainted with the true State of Affairs, may be led to pass a severe Censure on the Authors of those Facts, and any others of the like Nature which may hereafter happen, than we are persuaded they would, if Matters were duly understood and deliberated; we think it therefore proper thus openly to declare ourselves, and render some brief Hints of the Reasons of our Conduct, which we must, and frankly do, confess nothing but Necessity itself could induce us to, or justify us in, as it bears an Appearance of flying in the Face of Authority, and is attended with much Labour, Fatigue and Expence.

Ourselves then, to a Man, we profess to be loyal Subjects to the best of Kings, our rightful Sovereign George the Third, firmly attached to his Royal Person, Interest and Government, and of Consequence equally opposite to the Enemies of his Throne and Dignity, whether openly avowed, or more dangerously concealed under a Mask of falsely pretended Friendship, and chearfully willing to offer our Substance and Lives in his Cause.

These Indians, known to be firmly connected in Friendship with our openly avowed embittered Enemies, and some of whom have, by several Oaths, been proved to be Murderers, and who, by their better Acquaintance with the Situation and State of our Frontier, were more capable of doing us Mischief, we saw, with Indignation, cherished and caressed as dearest Friends;—But this, alas! is but a Part, a small Part, of that excessive Regard manifested to Indians, beyond his Majesty's loyal Subjects, whereof we complain, and which, together with various other Grievances, have not only inflamed with Resentment the Breasts of a Number, and urged them to the disagreeable Evidence of it, they have been constrained to give, but have heavily displeased, by far, the greatest Part of the good Inhabitants of this Province.

Should we here reflect to former Treaties, the exorbitant Presents, and great Servility therein paid to Indians, have long been oppressive Grievances we have groaned under; and when at the last Indian Treaty held at Lancaster, not only was the Blood of our many murdered Brethren tamely covered, but our poor unhappy captivated Friends abandoned to Slavery among the Savages, by concluding a Friendship with the Indians, and allowing them a plenteous trade of all kinds of Commodities, without those being restored, or any properly spirited Requisition made of them:—How general Dissatisfaction those Measures gave, the Murmurs of all good people (loud as they dare to utter them) to this Day declare. And had here infatuated Steps of Conduct, and a manifest Partiality in Favour of Indians, made a final Pause, happy had it been:—We perhaps had grieved in Silence for our abandoned enslaved Brethren among the Heathen, but Matters of a later Date are still more flagrant Reasons of Complaint.—When last Summer his Majesty's Forces, under the Command of Colonel Bouquet, marched through this Province, and a Demand was made by his Excellency, General Amherst, of Assistance, to escort Provisions, andc., to relieve that important Post, Fort Pitt, yet not one Man was granted, although never any Thing appeared more reasonable or necessary, as the Interest of the Province lay so much at Stake, and the Standing of the Frontier Settlements, in any Manner, evidently depended, under God, on the almost despaired of Success of his Majesty's little Army, whose Valour the whole Frontiers with Gratitude acknowledge, as the happy Means of having saved from Ruin great Part of the Province:—But when a Number of Indians, falsely pretended Friends and having among them some proved on Oath to have been guilty of Murder, since this War begun; when they, together with others, known to be his Majesty's Enemies, and who had been in the Battle against Colonel Bouquet, reduced to Distress by the Destruction of their Corn at the Great Island, and up the East Branch of Susquehanna, pretend themselves Friends, and desire a Subsistence, they are openly caressed, and the Public, that could not be indulged the Liberty of contributing to his Majesty's Assistance, obliged, as Tributaries to Savages, to Support these

Villains, these Enemies to our King and our Country; nor only so, but the Hands that were closely shut, nor would grant his Majesty's General a single Farthing against a savage Foe, have been liberally opened, and the public Money basely prostituted, to hire, at an exorbitant Rate, a mercenary Guard to protect his Majesty's worst of Enemies, those falsely pretended Indian Friends, while, at the same Time, Hundreds of poor, distressed Families of his Majesty's Subjects, obliged to abandon their Possessions, and fly for their Lives at least, are left, except a small Relief at first, in the most distressing Circumstances to starve neglected, save what the friendly Hand of private Donations has contributed to their Support, wherein they who are most profuse towards Savages have carefully avoided having any Part.— When last Summer the Troops raised for Defence of the Province were limited to certain Bounds, nor suffered to attempt annoying our Enemies in their Habitations, and a Number of brave Volunteers, equipped at their own Expence, marched in September up the Susquehanna, met and defeated their Enemy, with the Loss of some of their Number, and having others dangerously wounded, not the least Thanks or Acknowledgment was made them from the Legislature for the confessed Service they had done, nor any the least Notice or Care taken of their Wounded; whereas, when a Seneca Indian, who, by the Information of many, as well as by his own Confession, had been, through the last War, our inveterate Enemy, had got a Cut in his Head last summer in a Quarrel he had with his own Cousin, and it was reported in Philadelphia that his Wound was dangerous, a Doctor was immediately employed, and sent to Fort Augusta to take Care of him, and cure him, if possible.—To these may be added, that though it was impossible to obtain through the Summer, or even yet, any Premium for Indian Scalps, or Encouragement to excite Volunteers to go forth against them, yet when a few of them, known to be the Fast Friends of our Enemies, and some of them Murderers themselves, when these have been struck by a distressed, bereft, injured Frontier, a liberal Reward is offered for apprehending the Perpetrators of that horrible Crime of killing his Majesty's cloaked Enemies, and their Conduct painted in the most atrocious Colors; while the horrid Ravages, cruel Murders, and most shocking Barbarities, committed by Indians on his Majesty's Subjects, are covered over, and excused, under the charitable Term of this being their Method of making War.

But to recount the many repeated Grievances whereof we might justly complain, and Instances of a most violent Attachment to Indians, were tedious beyond the Patience of a Job to endure; nor can better be expected; nor need we be surprised at Indians Insolence and Villainy, when it is considered, and which can be proved from the public Records of a certain County, that some Time before Conrad Weiser died, some Indians belonging to the Great Island or Wyalousing, assured him that Israel

Pemberton, (an ancient Leader of that Faction which, for so long a Time, have found Means to enslave the Province to Indians,) together with others of the Friends, had given them a Rod to scourge the white People that were settled on the purchased Lands; for that Onas had cheated them out of a great Deal of Land, or had not given near sufficient Price for what he had bought; and that the Traders ought also to be scourged, for that they defrauded the Indians, by selling Goods to them at too dear a Rate; and that this Relation is Matter of Fact, can easily be proved in the County of Berks.—Such is our unhappy Situation, under the Villainy, Infatuation and Influence of a certain Faction, that have got the political Reins in their Hands, and tamely tyrannize over the other good Subjects of the Province!—And can it be thought strange, that a Scene of such Treatment as this, and the now adding, in this critical Juncture, to all our former Distresses, that disagreeable Burden of supporting, in the very Heart of the Province, at so great an Expence, between One and Two hundred Indians, to the great Disquietude of the Majority of the good Inhabitants of this Province, should awaken the Resentment of a People grossly abused, unrighteously burdened, and made Dupes and Slaves to Indians?—And must not all well-disposed People entertain a charitable Sentiment of those who, at their own great Expence and Trouble, have attempted, or shall attempt, rescuing a laboring Land from a Weight so oppressive, unreasonable, and unjust?—It is this we design, it is this we are resolved to prosecute, though it is with great Reluctance we are obliged to adopt a Measure not so agreeable as could be desired, and to which Extremity alone compels.—God save the King.

APPENDIX F

CAMPAIGN OF 1764.
1. Bouquet's Expedition.
Letter—General Gage to Lord Halifax, December 13, 1764. (Chap. XXVII.)

The Perfidy of the Shawanese and Delawares, and their having broken the ties, which even the Savage Nations hold sacred amongst each other, required vigorous measures to reduce them. We had experienced their treachery so often, that I determined to make no peace with them, but in the Heart of their Country, and upon such terms as should make it as secure as it was possible. This conduct has produced all the good effects which could be wished or expected from it. Those Indians have been humbled and reduced to accept of Peace upon the terms prescribed to them, in such a manner as will give reputation to His Majesty's Arms amongst the several Nations. The Regular and Provincial Troops under Colonel Bouquet, having been joined by a good body of Volunteers from Virginia, and others from Maryland and Pennsylvania, marched from Fort Pitt the Beginning of October, and got to Tuscaroras about the fifteenth. The March of the Troops into their Country threw the Savages into the greatest Consternation, as they had hoped their Woods would protect them, and had boasted of the Security of their Situation from our Attacks. The Indians hovered round the Troops during their March, but despairing of success in an Action, had recourse to Negotiations. They were told that they might have Peace, but every Prisoner in their possession must first be delivered up. They brought in near twenty, and promised to deliver the Rest; but as their promises were not regarded, they engaged to deliver the whole on the 1st of November, at the Forks of the Muskingham, about one hundred and fifty miles from Fort Pitt, the Centre of the Delaware Towns, and near to the most considerable settlement of the Shawanese. Colonel Bouquet kept them in sight, and moved his Camp to that Place. He soon obliged the Delawares and some broken tribes of Mohikons, Wiandots, and Mingoes, to bring in all their Prisoners, even to the Children born of White Women, and to tie those who were grown as Savage as themselves and unwilling to leave them, and bring them bound to the Camp. They were then told that they must appoint deputies to go to Sir William Johnson to receive such terms as should be imposed upon them, which the Nations should agree to ratify; and, for the security of their performance of this, and that no farther Hostilities should be committed, a number of their Chiefs must remain in our hands. The above Nations subscribed to these terms; but the Shawanese were more obstinate, and were particularly averse to the giving of Hostages. But finding their obstinacy had no effect, and would only tend to their destruction, the Troops having penetrated into the Heart of their Country, they at length became sensible that there was no safety but in Submission, and were obliged to stoop to the same Conditions as the other nations. They immediately gave up forty Prisoners, and promised the Rest should be sent to Fort Pitt in the Spring. This last not being admitted, the immediate Restitution of all the Prisoners being the sine qua non of peace, it was agreed, that parties should be sent from the Army into their towns, to collect the Prisoners, and conduct them to Fort Pitt. They delivered six of their principal Chiefs as hostages into our Hands, and appointed their deputies to go to Sir William Johnson, in the same manner as the Rest. The Number of Prisoners already delivered exceeds two hundred, and it was expected that our Parties would bring in near one hundred more from the Shawanese Towns. These Conditions seem sufficient Proofs of the Sincerity and Humiliation of those Nations, and in justice to Colonel Bouquet, I must testify the Obligations I have to him, and that nothing but the firm and steady conduct, which he observed in all his Transactions with those treacherous savages, would ever have brought them to a serious Peace.

I must flatter myself, that the Country is restored to its former Tranquillity, and that a general, and, it is hoped, lasting Peace is concluded with all the Indian Nations who have taken up Arms against his Majesty.
I remain,
etc.,
Thomas Gage.
In Assembly, January 15, 1765, A. M.
To the Honourable Henry Bouquet, Esq., Commander in Chief of His Majesty's Forces in the Southern Department of America.
The Address of the Representatives of the Freemen of the Province of Pennsylvania, in General Assembly met

Sir:

The Representatives of the Freemen of the Province of Pennsylvania, in General Assembly met, being informed that you intend shortly to embark for England, and moved with a due Sense of the important Services you have rendered to his Majesty, his Northern Colonies in general, and to this Province in particular, during our late Wars with the French, and barbarous Indians, in the remarkable Victory over the savage Enemy, united to oppose you, near Bushy Run, in August, 1763, when on your March for the Relief of Pittsburg, owing, under God, to your Intrepidity and superior Skill in Command, together with the Bravery of your Officers and little Army; as also in your late March to the Country of the savage Nations, with the Troops under your Direction; thereby striking Terror through the numerous Indian Tribes around you; laying a Foundation for a lasting as well as honorable Peace, and rescuing, from savage Captivity, upwards of Two Hundred of our Christian Brethren, Prisoners among them. These eminent Services, and your constant Attention to the Civil Rights of his Majesty's Subjects in this Province, demand, Sir, the grateful Tribute of Thanks from all good Men; and therefore we, the Representatives of the Freemen of Pennsylvania, unanimously for ourselves, and in Behalf of all the People of this Province, do return you our most sincere and hearty Thanks for these your great Services, wishing you a safe and pleasant Voyage to England, with a kind and gracious Reception from his Majesty.
Signed, by Order of the House,
  Joseph Fox, Speaker.

2. Condition and Temper of the Western Indians.
Extract from a letter of Sir William Johnson to the Board of Trade, 1764, December 26:—

Your Lordships will please to observe that for many months before the march of Colonel Bradstreet's army, several of the Western Nations had expressed a desire for peace, and had ceased to commit hostilities, that even Pontiac inclined that way, but did not choose to venture his person by coming into any of the posts. This was the state of affairs when I treated with the Indians at Niagara, in which number were fifteen hundred of the Western Nations, a number infinitely more considerable than those who were twice treated with at Detroit, many of whom are the same people, particularly the Hurons and Chippewas. In the mean time it now appears, from the very best authorities, and can be proved by the oath of several respectable persons, prisoners at the Illinois and amongst the Indians, as also from the accounts of the Indians themselves, that not only many French traders, but also French officers came amongst the Indians, as they said, fully authorized to assure them that the French King was determined to support them to the utmost, and not only invited them to the Illinois, where they were plentifully supplied with ammunition and other necessaries, but also sent several canoes at different times up the Illinois river, to the Miamis, and others, as well as up the Ohio to the Shawanese and Delawares, as by Major Smallman's account, and several others, (then prisoners), transmitted me by Colonel Bouquet, and one of my officers who accompanied him, will appear. That in an especial manner the French promoted the interest of Pontiac, whose influence is now become so considerable, as General Gage observes in a late letter to me, that it extends even to the Mouth of the Mississippi, and has been the principal occasion of our not as yet gaining the Illinois, which the French as well as Indians are interested in preventing. This Pontiac is not included in the late Treaty at Detroit, and is at the head of a great number of Indians privately supported by the French, an officer of whom was about three months ago at the Miamis Castle, at the Scioto Plains, Muskingum, and several other places. The Western Indians, who it seems ridicule the whole expedition, will be influenced to such a pitch, by the interested French on the one side, and the influence of Pontiac on the other, that we have great reason to apprehend a renewal of hostilities, or at least that they and the Twightees (Miamis) will strenuously oppose our possessing the Illinois, which can never be accomplished without their consent. And indeed it is not to be wondered that they should be concerned at our occupying that country, when we consider that the French (be their motive what it will) loaded them with favors, and continue to do so, accompanied with all outward marks of esteem, and an address peculiarly adapted to their manners, which infallibly gains upon all Indians, who judge by extremes only, and with all their acquaintance with us upon the frontiers, have never found any thing like it, but on the contrary, harsh treatment, angry words, and in short any thing which can be thought of to inspire them with a dislike to our manners and a jealousy of our views. I have seen so much of these matters, and I am so well convinced of the utter aversion that our people have for them in general, and of the imprudence with which they constantly express it, that I absolutely despair of our seeing tranquillity established, until your Lordships' plan is fully settled, so as I may have proper persons to reside at the Posts, whose business it shall be to remove their prejudices, and whose interest it becomes to obtain their esteem and friendship.

The importance of speedily possessing the Illinois, and thereby securing a considerable branch of trade, as well as cutting off the channel by which our enemies have been and will always be supplied, is a matter I have very much at heart, and what I think may be effected this winter by land by Mr. Croghan, in case matters can be so far settled with the Twightees, Shawanoes, and Pontiac, as to engage the latter, with some chiefs of the before-mentioned nations, to accompany him with a garrison. The expense attending this will be large, but the end to be obtained is too considerable to be neglected. I have accordingly recommended it to the consideration of General Gage, and shall, on the arrival of the Shawanoes, Delawares, andc., here, do all in my power to pave the way for effecting it. I shall also make such a peace with them, as will be most for the credit and advantage of the crown, and the security of the trade and frontiers, and tie them down to such conditions as Indians will most probably observe.

Printed in Great Britain
by Amazon